Romancing My Love

The Bradens

Love in Bloom Series

Melissa Foster

ISBN-13: 978-1-941480-04-5
ISBN-10: 1941480047

Cover Design: Natasha Brown

WORLD LITERARY PRESS
PRINTED IN THE UNITED STATES OF AMERICA

A Note to Readers

If this is your first Braden book, then you have a whole family of loyal, sexy, and wickedly naughty Bradens to catch up on. Hal and Adriana Braden have six children (featured in the first six Braden books). This book features one of Hal Braden's nephews, Pierce Braden. Pierce has five siblings as well, and he is the son of Hal's sister, Catherine. When I finished writing the first six Braden books, the demand for more lovable Bradens was overwhelming. I hope you enjoy the Braden cousins as much as I've enjoyed writing about them. But don't expect Catherine's children to be the same as Hal's. They're a little edgier, but just as warm and wonderful. In *Romancing My Love*, you will meet Pierce Braden and Rebecca Rivera. Rebecca's trying to pull her life back together after the devastating loss of her mother. She's fierce, protective of reputation, and has an enormous heart, but she's nothing like the women Pierce is used to. Hang on to your seat, because they're about to take you on a wild ride.

Romancing My Love is the ninth book in The Bradens and the seventeenth book in the Love in Bloom series. While it may be read as a stand-alone novel, for even more enjoyment you may want to read the rest of the Love in Bloom novels (Snow Sisters, The Bradens, The Remingtons & Seaside Summers).

Melissa Foster

For anyone who feels like it's you against the world
All it takes is a single moment for your life to change
You just have to be open to it

PRAISE FOR MELISSA FOSTER

"Contemporary romance at its hottest. Each Braden sibling left me craving the next. Sensual, sexy, and satisfying, the Braden series is a captivating blend of the dance between lust, love, and life."
—*Bestselling author Keri Nola, LMHC*
(on The Bradens)

"[LOVERS AT HEART] Foster's tale of stubborn yet persistent love takes us on a heartbreaking and soul-searing journey."
—*Reader's Favorite*

"Smart, uplifting, and beautifully layered.
I couldn't put it down!"
—*National bestselling author Jane Porter*
(on SISTERS IN LOVE)

"Steamy love scenes, emotionally charged drama, and a family-driven story make this the perfect story for any romance reader."
—*Midwest Book Review (on SISTERS IN BLOOM)*

"HAVE NO SHAME is a powerful testimony to love and the progressive, logical evolution of social consciousness, with an outcome that readers will find engrossing, unexpected, and ultimately eye-opening."
—*Midwest Book Review*

"TRACES OF KARA is psychological suspense at its best, weaving a tight-knit plot, unrelenting action, and tense moments that don't let up and ending in a fiery, unpredictable revelation."
—*Midwest Book Review*

"[MEGAN'S WAY] A wonderful, warm, and thought-provoking story...a deep and moving book that speaks to men as well as women, and I urge you all to put it on your reading list."
—*Mensa Bulletin*

"[CHASING AMANDA] Secrets make this tale outstanding."
—*Hagerstown* magazine

"COME BACK TO ME is a hauntingly beautiful love story set against the backdrop of betrayal in a broken world."
—*Bestselling author Sue Harrison*

Chapter One

PIERCE BRADEN NEEDED to relax. He'd had a damn hard day. He'd sat through too many meetings, strategizing over the potential acquisition of the Grand Casino, a local property that he'd been eyeing for three years. Not to mention that he'd forgotten to turn on his phone that morning and missed calls from both his mother and one of his brothers, and when he'd called them back, they'd given him crap about it. The last thing he needed was to be fawned over by his employees, but when you owned most of the happening digs around Reno, and several more around the world, there weren't many places he could go unnoticed. King's Bar was a dive on the outskirts of town, and he hoped, a place he could just fucking relax.

He was crossing the dance floor to the bar when the scent of Curious—a perfume he hadn't smelled in a decade—wafted past, trailing a hot, curvy ass, which was attached to a woman blazing a path toward the door. He didn't blame her. The place reeked of alcohol and testosterone.

Some drunk guy stopped her, and Pierce watched as she turned on the guy. Holy shit. She was a hell of a lot more than a great ass. She was scorching hot, with dark—and at the moment, angry—eyes, heavy breasts, and a sweet little waist.

Another greasy-haired, sweaty guy grabbed her, and Pierce circled back, fire rushing through his veins. He couldn't watch drunken assholes manhandle a woman. He took a step toward helping her as the guy leaned in close, his lips about to assail hers.

Through gritted teeth, she said in a low growl, "Let go of me."

Before Pierce could push through the gathering crowd, the woman kneed the asshole in the groin, and when he doubled over with a loud groan, she grabbed his massive shoulders and slammed his face into her knee. His friend stepped in behind him, and the woman clocked the guy who was doubled over with a right cross to his chin, sending him sprawling backward against his friend. They both stumbled into a group of people. Pierce set a threatening, narrow-eyed stare on the asshole, then grabbed the woman's arm and dragged her toward the door before the guy decided to retaliate or the manager kicked her out. She flailed and fought against his grip. Her body was trembling, and when the cool night air hit her, she blinked several times, as if she were trying to regain control. After what he'd just witnessed, he knew she could protect herself, but it was the momentary flash of vulnerability in her eyes that kept his hand on her

2

arm.

"Let me go," she demanded. "God, what is it about men grabbing me tonight?"

"I'm sorry. I was just trying to help by getting you out of there before the manager called the cops." Pierce released her arm.

"Oh, he would have loved that. The jerk." She shook her head.

"You're shivering. Here, take my shirt." He took off his Armani dress shirt and draped it over her bare shoulders, covering her tank top and leaving him in his undershirt.

She shrugged off the shirt and stepped back. "I'm fine."

Pierce caught the shirt in one hand as it sailed toward the ground. "Okay. I just thought you might be cold. Can I get you a cab?"

She looked up and down the street, giving Pierce a moment to assess the feisty brunette. Her hair had been pinned up when he first noticed her inside the bar, and during the fight the messy bun had slipped to the nape of her neck. She had sharp features—a pointy chin, high cheekbones, thin lips, and a nose that perked up at the end. They might have looked harsh, or on the opposite end of the spectrum, perhaps elfin, on any other woman, but her dark eyes were big and round, softening all those sharp edges into a mask of angry seduction.

"Cab? No, thanks." She drew in a deep breath and put her hands on her hips.

He wanted to put his hands on her hips.

Pierce was thirty-six years old and had more

money than he could ever spend and more women than nights to pleasure them. He was the supreme bachelor. He'd give his own life to protect his family, but when it came to women outside of his family, they had always been expendable.

Ever since two of his younger brothers, Wes and Luke, had fallen in love, and he'd watched their lives transform into blissful coupledom with women they adored, he'd begun to wonder if he was missing out. Now, this delicious, angry, slightly vulnerable woman was sparking a familiar spike in adrenaline, tugging at the protective urges that were reserved for his family, and he couldn't let her just walk away. She seemed anything but expendable.

She walked away while he stood there in a fog of confusion over the instant desire to protect her when she obviously didn't need him. He caught up to her a few steps later.

"Okay, no cabs. My car's in the garage around the corner. I could drive you home."

She continued walking at a fast pace. "Thanks. I really appreciate it, but I can walk." Her tone was still incensed. She shoved her hands in the pockets of her jeans, and her slim shoulders rounded forward against the chilly night air. It was just after eleven, still early by Reno standards.

Why on earth he couldn't walk away when she clearly wanted him to was a mystery to him. She was gorgeous, but hot women were a dime a dozen in Pierce's circles. He wasn't used to being turned down, even for just a drink or a ride, and could barely believe she had done so. Pierce was a man who was used to getting what he wanted, and she was too fine to give up that easily. He could think of no reason for her to turn him down, except...He wondered if she thought he frequented that dive of a bar and was judging him by those surroundings. *What the hell was she doing there, anyway?*

"I don't usually hang out there," he explained.

She stopped walking and finally turned to face him. He didn't even know her name, but when he saw that the anger in her eyes had been replaced by a well of sadness, he wanted to fold her into his arms until the sadness that turned the edges of her lips down disappeared. He thought of his younger sister, Emily. If Emily looked as sad as this woman, he hoped someone would be there to make her feel safe without any ulterior motive.

"Look, you seem like a nice enough guy, but I'm not a damsel in distress, okay? Some jerks took the brunt of a really bad night." She shrugged as if it were commonplace for her to deck a guy in a bar. "I'm fine. They didn't even call the cops, so he must be fine. Go do your thing and I'll go do mine, okay?" Her words were strong, but her voice wasn't quite as determined, and her eyes—those big, beautiful, sad eyes—gave her heartache away.

"How about I make sure you get home okay?" Pierce offered.

"You don't have to." She began walking again.

"I know. But if you go around decking every guy who bugs you, your arms are bound to get tired." They turned down another street. "You'll need backup."

She smiled, and the tension around her eyes and

her sweet lips eased. He felt her resolve softening. She rubbed the goose bumps that pebbled her arms. "I have pretty strong arms."

"No doubt, but it's chilly out. How about if I buy you a cup of coffee?"

She stopped walking again and tilted her head. In the fluorescent lights of the main drag, her eyes changed again. Pierce had never met such a chameleon. She no longer looked angry or devastatingly sad; she looked feminine and a little fragile. But he already knew better than to say that to her.

"Look…"

"Pierce," he said.

"Pierce? Is that your real name or some kind of casino or stage name?" She crossed her arms and jutted one curvy hip out to the side.

He ran his hand through his thick dark hair. "Apparently, my mother thought I needed a casino name." *Most women dig my name.*

She smiled again, and it shot a strange sensation to the center of his chest. "Well, *Pierce*, I really appreciate your efforts to help me. I'm sorry if I seem ungrateful. It's just been an *interesting* night. But really, I'm not looking for a guy to buy me a drink, or to hook up, or any of that." She dragged her eyes down his body. At six three and two hundred and ten pounds of solid muscle, Pierce knew he was irresistible to women, and now that she'd finally looked at him, he readied himself for her acceptance of his offer.

"Besides, my mother warned me about men who look like you." She drew in a deep breath and blew it

6

out slowly. "So, I thank you, and I bid you a good night."

Are you fucking kidding me? Your mother warned you? He forced his ego aside for a second before he said something he shouldn't and focused on her choice of words, which were equally as surprising.

"Bid me? Now who belongs in a casino?"

"Good one." She walked backward, lengthening the distance between them.

"Just tell me your name," he called.

She narrowed her eyes, and her mouth quirked up at the edge, taking her from sexy to goddamn cute and making her even more intriguing.

"Ronda Rousy," she answered, then spun on her heels and disappeared around the corner.

Ronda Rousy, my ass. Ronda Rousy was one of the best mixed martial arts fighters, and attractive as hell. *You're one hundred times as pretty and one hundred times as clever.*

He headed back toward his car, wondering how in the hell he'd concentrate on anything else with "Ronda's" sassy personality and her red-hot image seared into his mind.

REBECCA WALKED BACK toward the parking garage where she'd left her car, thinking about Pierce and forcing the memories of the terrible night away before she collapsed to her knees in a puddle of tears—or boiled in fury and punched someone else. *God, I punched a guy—and Pierce saw it all.* When he'd dragged her from the bar, she couldn't hear past the blood rushing through her ears, but she'd sensed people moving away, and she'd seen fear and surprise on their faces; then everything blurred together as Pierce dragged her quaking and shivering self out of the bar and into the night.

He'd been as determined to change her mind about the drive home as she was to stand firm. She'd almost caved under the weight of his beguiling dark eyes. That tight undershirt left every drool-worthy muscle on display. Not to mention that all six feet something of pure male sexuality beckoned to her private parts, which she thought she'd turned off years ago.

Pierce. What type of name was that, anyway? *Pierce.* She rolled it over in her mind, imagined saying it in a dark bedroom atop satin sheets, with his thighs pressed to hers.

Don't even go there, Rebecca.

She hadn't had a social life of any sort in three years. It was kind of hard to focus on anything other than the business classes she took and caring for her ailing mother, especially toward the end of her mother's life. Not for the first time in the last six weeks, her eyes teared up. It wasn't because of the fight she'd had with her boss, or the fact that she told him he could shove the damn job up his scrawny ass. No. That was nothing new in Rebecca's life, either. She was thinking of the last moments with her mother, before she closed her eyes for the final time and the last puff of air left her lungs. Before Rebecca was left alone in this crazy world.

Magda Rivera had always been the picture of health, at least from the outside. But that had been an illusion. Cancer was an unfair assailant that snuck in when they weren't looking and stole pieces of her mother, consuming her until her very last breath. Now her mother's ashes lay in an urn in the safe of her previous landlord's office. Mr. Fralin had been nice enough to hold the urn for her until she found a permanent place to live.

She took the elevator in the Astral resort parking garage to the fifth floor, where she'd left her car. She loathed this part of the evening. The parking garage was at least ten degrees colder than the street, and even though Rebecca had been coming *home* to it for three days now, she knew it would never lose the icy chill of concrete. She surveyed her surroundings as she crossed the dimly lit parking garage and noticed a man getting out of his car at the far end of the lot. She slipped into the driver's seat of her 1999 Toyota Corolla and waited for him to enter the elevator before putting up the sunshades on the windows and reclining her seat. She'd only been staying in her car for three days, since she'd had to give up her apartment for lack of rent money, but three days of worrying about being caught in her car felt like three years. She had excuses at the ready, just in case security banged on her window in the middle of the night. *I didn't want to drive after drinking too much* was her favorite excuse. Who could argue with that in the garage of a casino?

As soon as she had enough money saved, she'd find a room to rent. She missed the privacy of her tiny efficiency. Before her mother's illness, when Rebecca had rented her own apartment and had a normal life for a twentysomething woman, she'd made it a practice never to take men back to her apartment. Her home was her private oasis, and she liked to keep it that way. She thought about how nice it would be to go home at the end of the day and kick her feet up on her own couch, in her own living room. Now that she'd quit her job, finding a room to rent would be pushed back for God only knew how long. She could have kicked herself for quitting. Why hadn't she just shut her mouth and let Martin the asshole yell at her for the millionth time? Her mother's voice floated through her mind. *Because,* mi dulce niña, *you matter.* She closed her eyes and rested her head back, wondering what her mother would think of her *sweet girl* living in her car.

Rebecca didn't rue her circumstances. Mr. Fralin had been kind enough to allow her and her mother to stay in their apartment rent free during the final two months of her mother's life. Rebecca had been at her side every minute until the end, making it impossible for her to hold a job, and her mother had earned so little money when she was healthy that even her disability didn't cover their bills. Not to mention that her mother hadn't realized she was responsible for paying taxes on the disability income because her employer had paid for the insurance premiums. Rebecca was still working to pay off the debt her mother had accrued during her illness—it was the least she could do for the woman who gave up so much of her own life for her. Luckily, Mr. Fralin was a generous man, and he'd allowed Rebecca to remain in the apartment for almost six weeks after her mother had died, while Rebecca tried to pull herself together. Mr. Fralin did all he could, but he needed the rent money, and once again, Rebecca did what she had to in order to survive. Not wanting to be any more of a burden on Mr. Fralin, she found the pride she'd set aside to ensure her mother's comfort, and she'd moved out of the apartment and into her car.

While Rebecca didn't rue her dire circumstances, she did have a bone to pick with God, or whomever, or whatever, powers that be had stolen her mother away like a thief in the night.

Chapter Two

REBECCA WALKED INTO Fitness Heaven with her gym bag over her shoulder at six thirty the next morning. She'd joined the gym three months ago on a month-to-month basis when the water in her apartment had decided to take a vacation. She figured a shower was worth the $19.99 membership fee. While she was there, she did a quick workout, which, it turned out, was just about the best stress reliever a girl could hope for. Giving up a few groceries had been worth it. And now, since the month was already paid for, she had a place to exercise while she caught up on the morning news, had a cup of free coffee, and took a warm shower with clean, fresh towels. If only her bedroom didn't have four wheels and a gas tank, she'd be all set.

"Hey, Bec. How are ya today?" Andy Brandt was a personal trainer, built like a marine, with a military-style haircut and a face that could stop most girls' hearts. He was the one person Rebecca looked forward to talking to each morning.

"Oh, same, same. I quit my job last night." She slowed on her way to the ladies' locker room.

"Finally. I told you that guy's a prick."

Tell me about it. "I really thought I could grin and bear it, you know? But last night I was talking to this woman. She must have been sixty or older, a really sweet lady. Her husband left her for a twenty-five-year-old. Why do men always do that?"

"They don't. Assholes do," Andy answered.

"True. Anyway, he gave me shit about talking to her, right there in front of the customers. Hello? I'm a bartender! Listening is, like, a job *requirement.*"

"There's a reason he's in that part of town. I'm really sorry that you had to quit." Andy leaned over the counter and whispered, "You sure you don't want to borrow a few bucks? Just to get out of your car?"

She had told Andy about living in her car in a moment of weakness, and now she hated that he knew about it. "Don't, okay? I'll get through this."

"Oh, I have no doubt. I was just offering."

She softened, despite her embarrassment. The compassion in his eyes looked strikingly similar to the look in Pierce's eyes last night. *God, Pierce has soulful eyes.* "I know. Thanks, Andy. I'll catch you after my workout."

Rebecca made her way to the back of the gym and put her clothes in a locker, then went through her normal routine. She worked through forty minutes of cardio—today she rode the recumbent bicycle so she could scroll through her phone looking at the want ads around town—and twenty minutes of weights. She pushed herself harder each time her mind traveled back to Pierce, replaying last night over and over— offering her his shirt like a knight in shining armor, then the way he'd gone from looking at her like he wanted to take her to bed to looking at her like he wanted to offer her comfort. Part of her had wanted so badly to snuggle against his broad chest and soak in his strength, but she'd done the right thing. She pushed the thoughts away on her way back to the locker room. No sense dwelling on what couldn't be.

After her shower, she dressed in her favorite interview outfit—a sleek black pencil skirt, smart white blouse, and comfortable, but not dowdy, secondhand heels—and carried her bag back out to the front to grab a cup of coffee on her way out the door.

Andy whistled as she was filling up her to-go cup with coffee.

"Damn, girl. You're going to knock someone's socks off in that outfit."

She held up her to-go cup. "That's the hope. I'm interviewing everywhere I can today."

"I wish we had something here to offer you." His eyes widened. "Hey, my girlfriend, Chiara, works over at the Astral resort. She's in HR. I bet she can hook you up. Want me to give her a call?"

"I don't know..." Rebecca was used to handling things on her own, and she hated to take handouts of any kind.

"Why not? The Astral is a great place. Chiara loves working there." Andy assessed her as she mulled over the offer.

I could use a stable position, and he wouldn't be getting me the job, just the potential of an interview. It still felt like a handout.

"You've got that look, Rebecca."

She darted her eyes away. Andy knew her too well.

"Look, it's a phone call. I know you have a hard time accepting help, but come on. This is a phone call, not a million bucks."

She rolled her eyes. "I'm sorry. You're right. Thank you. That would be great. But please make sure she doesn't feel obligated or anything."

"Of course. Let me call her quickly." He walked away with his cell phone to his ear and came back a few minutes later. "Here you go." He handed her a piece of paper with Chiara's name and phone number. "She said to go over if you have time toward the end of the day and she'll see what she can find."

"Really? Oh, Andy. You're a lifesaver. Thank you." She reached across the counter and hugged him, feeling silly for her initial hesitation.

"I told her you were taking business courses." He shrugged. "Who knows if she'll have anything, but in this town, it's about who you know. I hope she can hook you up."

"A job in a *real* business would be like a dream come true, but at this point I'd take just about anything." Before her mother became ill, Rebecca had graduated with a two-year degree from the local community college, and with grants and her near-perfect grade point average, she'd been awarded a nearly full ride to the University of Nevada in Reno.

She'd been forced to drop out of school and give up her scholarship to care for her mother, and now she had only two more courses to complete before she graduated. She loved the academic world and found everything she'd learned about business fascinating.

Maybe her mother was right. Maybe it really was her turn to live.

IT WAS ALMOST seven o'clock in the evening by the time Rebecca crossed the marble lobby floors of the Astral after her meeting with Chiara Twain, Andy's girlfriend and the human resources administrator for the Astral casino, restaurant, and resort. She'd arrived at five thirty after filling out applications at every place along the main drag that was hiring. She'd waited twenty minutes to see Chiara, but it had been worth it. They'd hit it off right away. Chiara took her through one of the restaurants and bars and spoke to her about jobs in both areas, as well as potential growth opportunities in other areas of the casino and administrative offices. The restaurant was decked out like a Western ranch, with photographs of the most beautiful horses she'd ever seen, with lush manes and tails and long feathery hair around their hooves. Chiara explained that the owner of the resort was very family oriented and that he'd outfitted each of the three restaurants in ways that reminded him of his family. The pictures on the walls were of his brother's gypsy horses, which she explained were like Clydesdales, only with fuller manes, tails, and feathering. Chiara confided in Rebecca about how the owner was great to work for. Rebecca loved hearing that a business owner would honor his family in such a way. She had a good feeling about her meeting with Chiara. She said she'd contact her in a few days, and when Rebecca mentioned she was looking for an apartment or a room to rent in the area, Chiara said that they had an employee bulletin board and there was always someone looking for a roommate.

All sorts of hope swelled inside Rebecca—hope for a new job, a place to live, and maybe, just maybe, she'd eventually let herself think about having a real life. It had been years since she'd had time to think about herself, much less a relationship, and ever since last night, she couldn't get Pierce out of her mind.

"Rebecca!" Chiara hurried across the lobby with papers in her hand. "Sorry to catch you on your way out, but we forgot to give you back your driver's license after we copied it for the application."

"Thank you. I would have been searching everywhere for it." She took the driver's license and slipped it into the pocket of her skirt. She didn't like carrying a purse and did so infrequently. It was harder to steal from a person's pocket than a purse, and Reno was full of pickpockets. When she'd worked at the bar, a purse was an easy target for theft. Depending on where she was going, Rebecca kept her driver's license, money, and other important items in her pocket, or if she wasn't in a situation where she needed to whip them out, she carried them in her bra or sometimes in the bottom of her sock. She wasn't taking any chances of them being stolen.

"Rebecca."

Rebecca turned at the sound of the male voice that

had been seared into her brain since last night. It sent her stomach aflutter. When her eyes met Pierce's, the air left her lungs. He wore a dark suit that probably cost more than a year's rent, and he was even more handsome in the light of day. And—*oh my*—he was heading her way.

"Hi," she managed, wondering how he knew her name. She caught sight of Chiara standing at the elevators and realized he must have heard Chiara call her name across the lobby.

"So, it's not Ronda, then?" His eyes held a tease.

She forced her legs to move before the blush she felt creeping up her chest from the Ronda Rousy reference seared her skin and turned her legs to Jell-O.

"Rebecca Rivera, actually." She headed for the rotating doors, and he followed her out, walking so close she could smell his musky scent. Inside the glass enclosure of the doors, she breathed him in, and good Lord, heat rolled off the man. He was like a sexual magnet. It was all she could do to keep a straight face. She didn't think men like him existed outside of Hollywood.

"That's a much prettier name," he said as they reached the sidewalk. "Are you just getting off work?"

Shit. Shit. Shit. "No. I was applying for a job." She looked around as if she had someplace to go. Why couldn't she have someplace to go? His voice was sending tingles to places that weren't used to tingling.

"Really? Is the Astral hiring MMA fighters?" He arched a brow, which eased her nerves a little, so she went with the ruse.

"They usually don't, but, well, you know. I'm

special like that." *Oh God, really?* It had been so long since a man flirted with her that she had no idea how to react. Her tingling parts must have taken over her brain.

"Yes, you are." He held her gaze just long enough to send a shiver down her spine. "I'm just getting off work. Would you like to grab a drink?"

"Sure. Why not?" *What? You live in your car. Do. Not. Go Out. With. Him.* Her mother's voice pushed the thoughts away. *It's your turn, my sweet girl.* She'd spent the last few years putting aside what *she* wanted. It was a drink, not a date, and, boy, did she want to go.

SURE, WHY NOT? That was far from the typical responses Pierce received. Rebecca's shoulders lifted and she crinkled her nose in an adorable way that made him want to hug her—and was in sharp contrast to not only the offhand way she answered but also to the angry, determined woman he'd seen last night. He wondered if he was being pranked, and half expected his brother Jake to appear and make a joke about Rebecca's less-than-enthusiastic response. This was just the type of joke his competitive brother would play on him. Jake would take great pleasure in seeing Pierce befuddled by a woman. He glanced around just to be sure Jake hadn't flown in from Los Angeles for a surprise visit.

Nope. This was all Rebecca, which threw him for an even bigger loop. Pierce watched Anderson Claymore, the valet, talking with a young man in a dark suit. Anderson finished his conversation and joined them.

"Good afternoon, Mr. Braden. I'll bring your car around." Anderson was in his midfifties and had worked for Pierce for four years. He was respectful, and he had a good sense of humor and a solid sense of loyalty.

"Thank you, Anderson."

A few minutes later his charcoal-gray Jaguar arrived. Rebecca's eyes bounced from his expensive car to the high-fashioned casino patrons in a way that made Pierce wonder if she felt out of place, which was nonsense. She wore a primly buttoned white blouse and a tight black skirt that stopped just above her knees. She looked feminine and even more beautiful than she had last night. With a face and a body like hers, she could wear a paper bag and she'd be more beautiful than the cars and the patrons combined.

Pierce caught Anderson's eye and guided Rebecca around him, as if the Jaguar wasn't his. "Actually, Anderson, I think we'll walk." The last thing he wanted to do was to make her more uncomfortable, or give her a reason to change her mind.

"Yes, sir. I'll cancel your car."

"Thank you." Pierce slid Anderson a nod, indicating that he'd give him a little something extra later. He didn't want to whip out a fifty in front of Rebecca. She was nervous enough already. Out of habit, he placed his hand on her lower back and immediately felt her body tense. He removed his hand and hoped a cozy environment would ease her nerves. "There's a nice pub around the corner."

"Will he mind that you did that?" She glanced over

her shoulder at Anderson.

"Anderson? No, not at all." Most women would be so focused on going out with him that they'd ignore Anderson altogether and relish in his extravagant cars. Pierce wasn't anyone's fool. He knew that many women he went out with were in it for the visibility of being seen on the arm of a handsome millionaire, which suited him just fine, because all he usually wanted was a good time. It did bother him when women ignored Anderson or doormen, hostesses, or waitresses, and seeing Rebecca's reaction made her even more attractive.

They walked around the corner to a quiet pub that faced a park. Rebecca pulled open the door before Pierce could reach for it, and as he reached above her to hold the door, she'd already walked in.

"This is cute. I've never been here before." She smiled at the blond hostess. "Hi. A table for two, please?"

The hostess, Eva, smiled, then furrowed her brow at Pierce. He'd been in the pub many times, usually with a woman draped all over him. Eva clearly noticed how different Rebecca was. "Good evening, ma'am. Mr. Braden. It's nice to see you."

"You, too, Eva." Having been raised to be a proper gentleman, Pierce acted as such in public. The way Rebecca opened the door and requested the table took him as much by surprise as he could see that it did Eva. He smiled and raised a shoulder.

They followed her to a table, and Pierce pulled out a chair for Rebecca, but by the time he looked up, she was already sitting down across from where he held the chair. He cocked his head in question, but she didn't seem to notice that either as she glanced around the pub. He wasn't sure if she was making a statement or completely oblivious to his efforts. Either way, he was damn curious about this beautiful woman who wasn't giving him one inch to impress her.

He handed her a drink menu. "What's your pleasure?"

Normally, he'd have taken her in his Jag to a four-star restaurant, ordered a nice bottle of wine, and pretty much followed his usual routine, ending the night with her beneath him in a bedroom at the resort. But there wasn't anything typical about Rebecca, and he had no desire to try anything *routine* with her.

"I'll just have a glass of wine." She set the menu down.

Ah, she'd given him an inch to choose white or red wine.

"Wine it is." He flagged the waiter.

"Good evening, Mr. Braden." The waiter smiled at Rebecca. "What can I get for you?"

Pierce opened his mouth to respond, but Rebecca beat him to it.

"I'll have white wine, please," Rebecca answered.

He should have expected her to order for herself, but she'd thrown him off his game. He smiled at Brian, the waiter, then cleared his throat to regain his momentum. "We'll have a bottle of F.X. Pichler M Smaragd Grüner Veltliner, please."

"Yes, sir." Michael disappeared into the back. Pierce knew that Brian would descend the steps to the wine cellar below the pub and find that particular bottle of wine in the rear, right corner, where they kept a stock of his favorite wines.

Rebecca didn't bat an eye. He could have ordered ice water and she would probably have the same laid-back look in her eyes. She'd gone from nervous to comfortable in a few short blocks—and he'd gone from mildly confused to intensely intrigued.

"Do you work at the casino?"

You might say that. "Yes, in the executive offices."

"Oh, nice." She crossed her legs beneath the table and he felt the tip of her shoe touch his leg. Her eyes widened. "I'm sorry. I didn't mean to kick you."

"It's okay. It's better than a knee to the groin."

Rebecca covered her face with a hand and laughed. "I'm not going to live that down, am I?"

The waiter brought their wine to the table and poured them each a glass. "Can I get you anything else?"

"Rebecca? Would you like dinner?" he asked.

"Oh…" She lowered her eyes to her wineglass. "No, thank you. This is more than enough." She lifted her glass and took a sip.

"Thank you, Brian," Pierce said to the waiter. "I think we're okay for now."

"This is delicious," Rebecca said.

"I'm glad you like it." He held up his glass. "To you. May you get the job you want, and I hope it's more than you ever dreamed of." They clinked glasses.

"I hope so. There were a few positions they were considering me for, and Chiara, the person I met with, was really great. She said the managers are all really nice, so that'd be a refreshing change."

"Is your current boss unpleasant?"

She took another drink of wine. "Ex-boss. Anyone's better than him."

"What happened with your last boss?" The employer in him waved a red flag. He wondered if he should pay a visit to Chiara and get the scoop on Rebecca's previous employer.

She sighed and leaned forward. The edge of her foot rubbed against his leg again, but if she noticed, she didn't react. Pierce, however, was hyperaware of the foot sliding down his calf.

"He was sort of the reason I was in such a bad mood last night. He yelled all the time, so I finally quit." She leaned back and her foot slid up and then down his calf again.

He forced himself to focus on what she'd said and not the sparks her foot was causing. "What did you do for him?"

As she spoke, she pulled clips from her hair. "Bartending, at King's Bar." Her hair tumbled down over her shoulders—tousled in a *just had a good romp* fashion—to the middle of her breasts.

Holy hell, she was breathtaking. He shifted his eyes away to keep her from reading his thoughts.

"It wasn't like it was rocket science," she explained. "Just something to hold me over until I could find something in my field."

Pierce was still picturing her hair spread across his pillow. "What's...what's your field?"

"I've been going to school for business. Anyway, I could do no right by him. He didn't like us talking to the customers, and, well, I think people come into bars to unload, you know?" She unbuttoned the top two buttons of her blouse, taking her from prim and proper to holy mother of all things sexy.

She had to know what she was doing to him, but her eyes were still serious and not at all overtly sexual. How the hell she was doing that, he had no clue. Most women spent years trying to achieve what she obviously came by naturally.

"Oh, that's better. Much less stuffy. You should take your coat and tie off. Relax."

Christ. She didn't seem to have any clue that what she said was usually a show of hand on a date, an indication that she was an ace in the hole.

She didn't give him time to respond. "Some of the customers had heavy stuff going on in their lives. Divorces, diseases, down on their luck. Talking seemed to help them get into a better frame of mind."

"So you were *too* empathetic? Did it hold you up from helping other customers?" Pierce rubbed the muscles at the back of his neck that had begun to knot. He didn't like the idea of anyone yelling at Rebecca, and yelling at her for talking to customers was, at the very least, unreasonable and, more likely, simply an asshole move.

"Goodness, no. I can multitask. He was just a jerk. A jerk that I have the pleasure of going back to see in order to collect my last paycheck."

Not alone, you're not. She was confident and obviously capable of handling picking up a paycheck by herself, but even if she *could* do it, it didn't mean she had to, and the more he got to know her, the more Pierce didn't want her subjected to a man like her previous boss.

They finished the bottle of wine, and Pierce asked her again if she'd like to order dinner.

"Oh no, thank you. You've done enough already. This was really nice."

"It's still early. Are you up for a walk in the park?" He didn't want the evening to end, and though it was totally out of his realm of understanding, it wasn't only because he wanted to sleep with her. He wanted to get to know her better. She was real, and it was refreshing to talk to someone who wasn't trying to impress him.

She held his gaze just long enough for the space between them to sizzle, before dropping her eyes. "Sure."

He paid for the wine, and this time when they reached the door, he made sure he reached it first and held it open for her.

"Thank you," she said.

"My pleasure." He settled his hand on the curve of her back and felt her tense beneath his touch again. She was giving off so many mixed signals that he couldn't read her.

They waited by the curb to cross the road toward the park. An old man stood with a cane, squinting in the direction of the crosswalk sign. When the light changed, indicating they could cross the street, he remained still. Pierce was about to ask him if he needed assistance when Rebecca tapped his shoulder.

"One second," she whispered to Pierce. She moved beside the old man. "Sir? Are you crossing? The light has changed."

The old man looked at her with a confused gaze,

and suddenly his eyes widened. "Yes, thank you."

Rebecca walked with him, protectively holding one of his arms while they crossed the road. When they got to the other side, the man thanked her, and she rejoined Pierce without a word.

"That was nice of you."

"What?"

He shook his head. "Helping that man."

"Oh. Anyone would do it. If I didn't, you would have."

Would they? He wasn't so sure.

"Tell me something about yourself," he said as they followed the footpath into the dimly lit park. "Not about work or school, but..." He shrugged and let her fill in the gap.

She leaned toward him. "Tell me about *you*, Pierce Braden."

He laughed. "You don't like to give up control, do you?"

"It's not a very comfortable thing for me. Do you like to give up control?" She blinked up at him with a lascivious look in her eyes, and Pierce fought the urge to reach out and touch her cheek.

"Not easily." He lowered his voice. "And certainly not in public."

She held his steady gaze. "Well, then, I guess we have something in common."

He'd like to see just how much more they had in common. They walked in silence for a few minutes as they passed beneath old-fashioned streetlights that illuminated the path.

"What did you do before bartending?" They

crossed a narrow bridge, and Pierce stopped in the middle and took off his suit coat. He placed it over the railing and looked out over the water.

"Whatever I could." Rebecca stood beside him and her gaze turned thoughtful. "Caretaking, mostly." She ran her thumb over a slim silver ring with a channel of blue stones running down the center that she wore on her index finger.

"Caretaking?"

Her smiled faded and her lips pressed tightly together. Rebecca's chest expanded as she drew in a deep breath, and as if the breath was exactly what she needed to tear herself from whatever she'd been thinking, she blew that breath out and turned toward him with a semi smile. Her hair fell over one eye. Pierce reached up and tucked it behind her ear, and her smile widened.

He wondered what would make such a strong woman look so vulnerable in seconds, and why she would reveal that she'd been a caretaker if she didn't want to talk about it. What type of internal reserves did Rebecca possess in order to push aside whatever she was hiding and flash a smile that made Pierce once again want to take her in his arms and make the pain go away?

"Are you okay?" His voice sounded oddly quiet.

She dropped her eyes to the ring again and waved a hand in dismissal. "Oh, yeah. I'm fine." She turned away from him, and though he couldn't see her face, he sensed her gathering her wits about her like a bird gathers pieces of its nest.

He folded his jacket over his arm and, wanting to

comfort her, reached for her hand. "Let's walk."

When she took his hand, he was both relieved and surprised.

"So, to answer your question—"

"It's okay, Rebecca. You don't have to tell me anything you'd rather not." She didn't respond, but again, he sensed her fighting some sort of internal battle. Her hand was soft and her grip relaxed, but as they strolled around the lake, her hand tensed several times, then relaxed again. He noticed that each time her hand tensed, a flash of worry passed over her face.

"You're a pretty nice guy," she finally said.

Her observation made him smile. "I'm not sure everyone would agree with you."

She shifted her eyes to his with a coy smile. "Because you're a womanizer or because you're a shrewd businessman?"

He drew back and couldn't hide his wide-eyed surprise at her brazen question. If she were anyone else, he might dispute the first accusation. Despite her earlier innuendos that he was sure she was oblivious to, he had the impression that she was streetwise and savvy. He had a feeling she'd see right through his cover.

No one saw through Pierce but his family.

"Probably a little of both, I'd imagine." He watched her smile grow.

"Honesty. That's refreshing." She slowed by a grassy knoll beneath the umbrella of a tall tree. "Do you mind if we sit for a few minutes? I like it out here."

Before sitting, she leaned on his shoulder and slipped off her heels; then she sat in the grass with her knees to one side, leaning her weight on one hand in the grass. Pierce sat beside her. He leaned back on his palms—his hands close to hers—and crossed his feet at the ankle.

"I think the last time I sat in the grass was after wrestling my brothers."

"When you were a kid?"

"No." He laughed. "We pretty much wrestle whenever we see each other."

"Really? How fun. How many siblings do you have?" An easy smile lifted her lips, and she sighed, seeming more at ease than she'd been earlier, which added to her complexity.

"Four brothers and one sister, and yeah, we do have fun." He thought back to the last time they were all together, at his brother Luke's house when Jake came for a visit. Jake had jumped Pierce the minute he'd seen him, and their other brothers had been quick to join in on the fun. They'd rumbled on Luke's lawn like teenagers until they were covered in grass stains and laughing like fools. They were always laughing like fools when they got together. *Good times.*

"Wow. I don't have any siblings. I can only imagine how fun that must have been. Where did you grow up?" She ran her finger along the seam of her skirt.

"In good old Trusty, Colorado, a typical small town, where everyone knows everyone else's business. The local diner should be called gossip central. We lived in a slightly bigger town for a few years, Weston, Colorado. I still have family there. How about you? Where did you grow up?" He didn't want to think about Weston, the town in which he was born.

He had fond memories of spending time with his uncle Hal Braden, and his six cousins when he lived in Weston, but the memories he had of his father were not all peaches and cream.

"I grew up here. Talk about polar opposites." Rebecca smiled up at him. "I would have given anything to live where people watched over me."

"Oh, it gets old; trust me. When you're a teenager, it's a nuisance that everyone knows your business, and as an adult...well, it's always a bit of a nuisance to know that anything you say or do might be the daily dish the next day. But it's a friendly town, and there is a certain comfort that takes away the annoyance of the gossip. Most of my family still lives in Trusty. How about your parents? Are you close with them?"

She rubbed her thumb over that ring again. "I was super close to my mom." Her voice cracked. "But I don't know my father."

Pierce inched his fingers over and settled them on top of hers in the grass. She lifted her eyes to his. The air between them heated, but not with the burn of desire, with something more ethereal, something Pierce had never before experienced. It pulled at his chest and made the pit of his stomach clench tight. His protective urges returned, and he didn't try to figure them out. He simply reached up and cupped her cheek, his thumb brushing the column of her neck. Her skin was soft and warm, and he felt her swallow against his thumb. He didn't move to kiss her, though he wanted to more than he wanted his next breath. He just held her cheek, as if to say he was sorry she never knew her father and to let her know she wasn't alone. When he opened his mouth to say just that, he was surprised by what came out.

"My father left a few days after I turned six." Pierce withdrew his hand and looked away, trying to figure out why he was talking about his father, Buddy Walsh, whom he never spoke of. Not with his siblings, not with his mother, and certainly not with a woman he'd known only a few hours.

She leaned closer to him. "That must have been so hard. Do you ever see him?"

Pierce shook his head. "No, and I don't have any interest in seeing him. He was a bast—" He drew in a deep breath. "He wasn't a very nice man." Buddy was a bastard and a thief, but Pierce wasn't a man who publicly disparaged others. His mother, Catherine, had seen to that. Love came first in their house, but wrapped in that love, he and his siblings learned respect, manners, and valuable work ethics. His mother had set her feelings about their father aside, which as an adult, Pierce now knew must have taken tremendous willpower, especially since Buddy had run off with another woman.

"That's what gets me about life. The people we love are taken away forever, and the ones we could live without still get to walk on this beautiful earth."

Her words sent a chill down his spine. He was beginning to put the pieces of Rebecca's life into place, and Pierce hoped his interpretation of what she was saying was wrong. "You mentioned caretaking." He moved the fingers that had been covering hers in the grass to cover her whole hand. "Your mom?"

She looked down at their hands and drew in an

33

uneven breath. "Yeah. My mom."

"I'm sorry, Rebecca." He lifted her chin with his index finger so he could see her eyes. He wanted her to know that his words weren't empty, as they might have been to any other woman. When their eyes connected, the tether between them was as strong as a cable.

"I am really, truly sorry, Rebecca. I can't pretend to know exactly what you're feeling, but I'm close to my mom, and I can only imagine how devastating it would be to lose her."

She drew her shoulders back, and he could practically see her stepping into the safety of the invisible iron cloak she hid behind. No wonder he saw flashes of vulnerability. That cloak must get too heavy to bear the burden full-time.

"Thanks, but I'm okay. It was hard, but you know, pull yourself up by your bootstraps and all that." She cleared her throat and looked away.

"Yeah, I know all about bootstraps. Either they're made of leather and easy to pull, or they're made of lead and they drag you down."

A genuine smile crossed her lips, and the balls of her cheeks rose. "I do miss her, Pierce. I'm not trying to deny that. She was my best friend, and I know that doesn't say much about me, but..." She shrugged. "She really was."

"I think that speaks volumes about both of you."

She rolled her eyes. "Yeah, a twenty-seven-year old with no life." Her face grew serious again. "That's not really true. I had a life. It was different from most people's lives, but it was a good life."

He could barely keep up with the undercurrent of emotional torment she experienced, and damn did he want to.

"We were close. My mom wasn't just a really good mother, but she was a good person, and we had fun together before she got sick. We used to take walks a lot, and when I was little, she'd wake me in the middle of the night to watch a movie together, or we'd stay up past bedtime cooking or baking."

"It sounds like she loved you very much."

"Oh yes. Without a doubt. Sometimes I feel guilty about that. She never dated, and she never even went out with friends. She gave up her entire life for me, at least until I got my own apartment near the university. But then I moved back in three years ago when she was diagnosed with lung cancer. I treasure the time I had with her. It's like she knew she was going to...you know...be taken away early. And one day I'll pay her back for all she did. She always wanted to go back to Punta Allen, where she spent time as a little girl. I'm going to save enough money to bring her ashes back and spread them there." She looked out over the park and sighed.

"Was your mom from Mexico?" Pierce owned a resort in Tulum, which was very close to Punta Allen, a small fishing village with fewer than five hundred residents.

"No. My grandmother was, though. She gave birth to my mother here in the United States, and she and my mother visited Punta Allen several times when my mother was young. She never went as an adult, but she talked about it all the time."

It made him sad to think that her mother died without realizing her dream, and he was impressed with Rebecca's determination to bring her mother's ashes to Punta Allen.

"I don't mean to bum you out. I'm sorry," she said. "I never talk about her, and listen to me. Did you slip truth serum into that wine?"

Pierce sat up and took her hand in his. "You aren't bumming me out. Truth serum would explain why I talked about my father, too. I never talk about him, either."

"Well, let's see. Two control freaks, each revealing their secrets to the other." Their eyes met, and her voice quieted. "Sounds like we're either going to—"

He slid his hand to the back of her neck, silencing her with his impulsive move as they stared into each other's eyes.

She whispered, "End up in a horror flick where you belt out a sinister laugh or—"

Pierce moved closer, her lips parted, a breath away from his. There was so much he wanted to say, to ask, like how the hell she touched the most intimate, hidden places in his heart in just a few hours, but he couldn't find his voice. He was too busy restraining himself from taking her in an impassioned kiss. His lips grazed over hers on the way to her cheek, where he pressed a soft kiss.

When he drew back, her eyes fluttered open.

"No sinister laugh," he whispered.

She fisted her hands in his shirt and sealed her lips over his. Her kiss was everything he thought it would be and more. She met each lap of his tongue with her own. Good Lord, she tasted of sweet wine and strength, despite all she'd been through, and he wanted more of her. *So much more.* Pierce was no stranger to hiding from emotions in the safety of a woman's arms, but his heart and mind were struggling against his desires, joining forces for the first time in his life and forcing him to tear his lips from hers, refusing to allow him to hide from the emotions swelling within him.

What the hell?

He wanted more of Rebecca; he wanted to touch her full breasts, to run his tongue along her lower lip, and to taste every inch of her sweet skin. He didn't want to draw back and take her hand in his again, and yet that's exactly what he did.

She licked her lips and he nearly went back for more.

"Sorry. I'm sorry." She tried to pull her hand from his, but he held on tight.

"Rebecca, I'm the one who should apologize. I'm sorry." Jesus, he was so *not* sorry, but goddamn conflicted.

"No. You kissed my cheek, and I..." She covered her face with her hand. "I'm really not like that. I haven't been with a guy in years. I'm just..." She drew in a deep breath.

"Years?" *Did she mean weeks, maybe?*

"My life hasn't really been conducive to a romantic relationship. Hell, Pierce." She yanked her hand from his. "I have no excuse. I can't even say I'm an emotional wreck, because I'm not. Yes, I lost my mom six weeks ago, but after three years, we both knew it was coming. I just...I don't know. You were looking insanely handsome and listening to every word I said like you really wanted to hear them, and...Ugh. I should go."

"Insanely handsome?" he joked, in an effort to lighten the mood.

She shook her head. "Like you don't know that? Please don't play coy with me. I don't have a high threshold for bullshit."

"Okay, fine. I'm as insanely handsome as you are wickedly, exotically, lovely. How about we both write it off to a nice kiss?" The last thing he wanted to do was irritate her. She was just beginning to open up to him, and he hoped she'd continue.

She rolled her eyes. "You don't have to go over the top. Bullshit limits, remember?"

"Okay, scratch the *nice* kiss, and make it *scorching-hot* kiss."

She laughed. "That's better."

"Come on." Pierce pulled her to her feet. "Let's walk off our desires before you take advantage of me again."

Without her heels, she couldn't have been more than five four or five five. He held her hips—Jesus, they felt good. He'd been dying to touch them since they'd met. Most curvy women worried about their body image, but she didn't primp or suck in her stomach the way he'd noticed other women did. She didn't fiddle with her blouse or do any of the other things that signaled insecurity. Rebecca seemed to pay no mind to her curves, and that confidence made her sexy as hell. He was tempted to lower his mouth to the crook of her neck, enjoy one little taste to make her insides crave him. Instead, he folded her into his arms. Her body stiffened, and he held her tighter. His mind flew back thirty years, to the days after his father left. In an effort to comfort his younger brothers, Ross, Jake, and Wes, he'd held them close, and they'd fought against his embrace as Rebecca was doing now, but somehow, Pierce had known even then that they needed to know they were loved despite being abandoned by their asshole father. His mother was still pregnant with Luke at the time, and Emily had been only about a year old, too young to understand the magnitude of what was going on. They'd had only one another in the days after their father left. He couldn't count the times he'd woken up and found his brothers sleeping on his bedroom floor, as if they wanted to make sure he wasn't leaving, too. There was safety in numbers.

Rebecca didn't seem to have anyone, and the thought that she'd gone through losing her mother alone made him warm to her even more than it had when he'd seen the hint of vulnerability the night they'd met. She was tough as nails, but now he was beginning to understand where her underlying vulnerability came from.

After another full minute, maybe two, he felt the tension in Rebecca's arms ease, and he felt her hands touch his back. Despite the way she'd gone rigid in his arms, it felt natural to press a kiss to the top of her head. When his lips touched her hair, he hoped like hell she didn't bolt.

Chapter Three

AT FIRST REBECCA wanted to push away from Pierce's embrace. It was too intimate; she'd already let him in too much. But he held her so tightly, and he felt so safe and smelled so good, that she allowed herself a minute of enjoying the feel of being wrapped in his arms. *Okay, just two.*

When they'd met the other night, she thought that with his good looks and his pressuring her to have a drink with him, he was going to be self-centered and easy to walk away from. Boy, had she been wrong. She'd never met a man who listened so intently or could restrain his desires so well. She felt his arousal against her, but he didn't push her for more—and when they'd kissed...God, when they'd kissed, he was the one who'd pulled away.

Pierce smiled, and it pulled her from her thoughts. "You must be starved. I'll cook you dinner. I'm a wicked good cook, believe it or not," Pierce said.

Her body went rigid again. Cook her dinner? At his

place? *No. No, no, no.* She'd already been unable to keep from slapping her lips on to his and nearly swallowing him whole. She honestly hadn't kissed a man in years. Not since her mother's diagnosis turned terminal. She stepped back and drank him in one last time. He wore his thick, shiny dark hair brushed back, away from his face, but when she was groping him, a few strands had fallen forward, giving him a younger, less edgy look. How could a man look one minute like he walked out of *GQ* and, with a few wayward strands of hair, then look like he belonged on the front of a rugged outdoorsy magazine?

That was totally unfair.

And totally made her knees weak.

The idea of going back to her car sucked, but as much as landing in his bed, beneath his magnificent body, with those bedroom eyes looking down at her and his powerful thighs pressed against hers—*Stop it! No.*

"Well?" he asked, and she realized she was spacing out. He picked up her heels from the grass and went down on one knee. She pressed her fingers to his shoulders as he placed a hand on her calf, sending a shiver up her thighs. He slid her foot into her shoe, and then he gently set that foot down and ran his hand back down her calf as he lifted her other foot. How was he turning her inside out by simply putting on her heels? His other hand grazed the back of her knee. Rebecca imagined him doing all sorts of dirty things while kneeling before her. She had no idea that putting on heels could feel so erotic, and she couldn't help but wonder...If he could make this feel so good, what would it feel like to be beneath all that power, that confidence, that sexual prowess?

"Um...I..." She couldn't think clearly with him touching her like that. "Actually, I have to be..." *Oh God.* He slid his hand down her calf and then rose to his full height again. "Up early tomorrow to go to the gym, so I'd better take a rain check." *Gym? Idiot. Fool. I bet you could give me a great workout.*

Stop it!

"A rain check?" He arched a brow.

Great. Now I've invited myself on another date with him. Okay, time to leave. "Listen, I've got to go." *Before I kiss you again.* "I'm sorry. I had a great time."

He took her hand in his. "I'll walk you back to your car. Is it parked at the Astral?"

You mean my temporary residence? Oh yeah, it's there. "Yes, in the garage."

They walked back around the lake, and Rebecca struggled to ignore the way her body was reacting to him. Her stomach was fluttering like a schoolgirl, she was breathing like she was still kissing him, and between her legs certain parts that had been hibernating for three years were suddenly begging to have another bear in the den.

A Pierce bear.

Good Lord, woman.

She felt her cheeks flush and was glad it was dark so Pierce couldn't see them pink up.

"What was it like caring for your mom? Was she at home with you?"

"Yeah. She was. She refused to go to the hospital at the end. She was always worried about—" *Finances, and leaving me with too much debt.* "She didn't like to be away from home. And we couldn't really afford to have full-time home health aides, so I took her to her treatments and appointments. That's why I went from job to job. It turns out that most employers don't like when you can't show up for work because your mother had a really bad night, or she needed to go to an unexpected medical appointment. That's why it's taken me so long to finish my degree, but I don't mind. It was really only the last two and a half years or so that things got really bad. But even near the end she'd say things like, *Mi dulce niña, this is nothing. A blip on your radar screen of life,* or, *When I get to heaven, I'm going to pull all the right strings so your life is amazing. Just you wait and see.*" Rebecca shook her head. "It's funny. Sometimes I still spin around when something happens, and I want to share it with her. Then I remember she's gone, and..." She stopped herself from saying more. She couldn't believe she'd revealed so much already, but Pierce was so easy to talk to, so attentive and interested. She felt comfortable with him, but she didn't need to break down in tears. She'd done that so often in the last six weeks that tonight had been a much-needed—deserved?—change.

They were nearing the casino parking lot and Rebecca slowed her pace, not wanting the night to end. Even if she'd still been living in her apartment, she wouldn't have wanted it to end. She liked talking about her mother, but she never allowed herself to do it.

"You know, this is going to sound strange, but I don't think that the people we love, the ones we're really connected to in a spiritual sense, ever really leave us. I think they're physically gone, but I can't believe we aren't still somehow connected."

She looked up at this man who was slowly rocking her world off balance and wondered how he could know what she felt, and was too afraid to fully believe?

"I feel her around me all the time," she admitted.

He nodded, as if he understood. "My aunt Adriana died more than thirty years ago, and her husband, my uncle Hal, the one who lives in Weston, swears she's still around."

"I know it sounds crazy, but I do believe that some loves are so strong that nothing could ever sever the connection. So who knows? Their lives might have been so deeply rooted to each other that she is still around him." There was much more to Pierce than met the eye. He was certainly more than a businessman looking for a good time. He was too interested, too open, to be just that.

"It doesn't sound crazy to me at all, and my uncle would attest to just how sane that belief is." Pierce looked up at the garage. "What floor is your car on?"

"The fifth." She wanted to keep talking, and she liked that he held her hand. When they stepped into the elevator, he pulled her in front of him and placed his hands on her hips again, and she liked that a hell of a lot more than hand-holding.

"Go out with me tomorrow night, Rebecca." It wasn't a question, and it wasn't a command. He obviously knew how to take control without overstepping the invisible gray line that could make him come across as arrogant.

Everything about him had her body humming with anticipation. "I have to pick up my paycheck tomorrow night, but I'd like to go out afterward."

The elevator stopped on the fifth floor, and she wanted to reach over and push the Stop button so she could stay right there against him for a few minutes longer. *Hours. A few hours. Or maybe for the night.*

He didn't move when the elevator doors opened, and when he spoke, his voice was serious. "What time are you picking it up?"

"I think he said he'll be in around six."

"I'll pick you up at five forty-five and we can go together." The elevator doors closed and began a slow descent toward the first floor again. The edge of his lips perked up and his eyes darkened.

"Okay," she said in one long breath.

The elevator stopped on the first floor, and another couple joined them in the elevator. Rebecca tried to move to Pierce's side, but he held her in place. He leaned forward and whispered, "Stay with me."

His voice sent a shiver down her back, rooting her to the floor. He was a man with a dangerous edge. A man who was used to getting what he wanted. She could tell he had the power to slice a woman open with his voice and take every sweet piece of her he desired. His eyes were as dangerous as a wolf. His swollen desire against her hips said python *and* wolf. Hadn't he said as much when he hadn't disputed being a womanizer? Why, then, was she sensing that beneath that practiced, expert facade, lay a purebred, fluffy, loyal Labrador heart?

When they reached her car, Pierce leaned his hip

casually against it and dragged his eyes down her body, causing another full-body shudder. Damn it to hell, and sleeping in her car, she couldn't even pleasure herself to take the edge off of her newly awakened desires.

"Where could you possibly keep your keys?" he asked.

She turned her back, reached into her bra, and withdrew a single key. "Voila."

His eyes darkened. "Makes me wonder where you keep your cell phone."

"Secrets are a girl's best friend." She put the key in the lock and he moved behind her. Sensing his heat before his hands touched her hips, she closed her eyes. He brushed her hair from one shoulder, and his hot breath whispered across her skin.

"Where should I pick you up tomorrow?"

Shit. What was she doing? *Oh, pick me up right here. In fact, just climb in my car now. I'll have my way with you in the backseat and we'll pretend we're fifteen years old. Then I can realize you're my biggest mistake—biggest, most delicious mistake—right before you realize the same thing.*

She turned to face him and—*Oh God*—that was worse. He was looking at her like he really liked her, not like she was a piece of ass, as she was trying to convince herself.

"Why don't we meet here, in the lobby? You work here, and I have to be in the area anyway." *Since I live here.*

"I don't mind picking you up at your place." He touched her cheek. "I know you're used to doing

47

everything yourself, but it's okay to let your date do a few things, like pick you up."

Not for me it's not. "I know, but I have things to do, and my place is kind of a wreck right now." That part was true. One glance inside her car and he'd see her stuff piled up on the floor in the backseat. God forbid he opened the trunk. Her whole life was in there. She'd sold her landlord the few pieces of furniture she and her mother had owned in order to pay the last of their utility bills.

He furrowed his brow. "Okay. You're not married, are you? Because I don't date married women."

She laughed. "Definitely not married, and since it's been a few years since I even kissed a man, I think if I were married, he'd have grounds for divorce."

His smile gave away his relief. "Five forty-five, then? In the lobby." He pressed his big hands to her cheeks, tilted her face up, and gazed into her eyes.

She'd never bought into the moment in movies when a woman gazed into a man's eyes and fell into his arms, willing to do whatever he wanted, but there she was. And God help her, she'd go and do anything he wanted her to. It should be illegal to look at a woman like that. She craved his lips, his touch, his...

He kissed her forehead. "Thank you for a lovely night." He pulled open the driver's side door and waved a hand for her to climb in.

Please let my legs work. Please, please.

She felt his hand on her back as she climbed into the driver's seat and snagged a piece of paper. She scribbled down her number and handed it to him.

"Sleep well, Rebecca Rivera." He leaned in and

kissed her cheek.

She doubted she'd be doing any sleeping tonight. She had a big day tomorrow of getting her life a little more in order, and the way her heart was racing as she watched Pierce walk away, she wondered if she'd be able to function at all.

Chapter Four

PIERCE WOKE UP groggy eyed and pissed off. It took him a minute to figure out where he was. He owned several private residences in addition to casinos and other resort properties. Though he usually liked the convenience and luxury of staying at the resorts, there were times when he wanted to escape the scrutiny of the staff, or just plain wanted to have some time alone. Last night was one of those times. By the time he'd left Rebecca, he was not only turned on, but his brain was taking all sorts of winding turns into his past, and those turns eventually led him back to the present. He'd driven out to his estate and spent the night thinking about Rebecca and wrestling with the unfamiliar feelings she'd stirred within him.

What was it about her that made him talk about his father? Christ Almighty, Buddy wasn't a guy Pierce wanted to give any of his emotional or mental time to, and there he was, telling her about when Buddy had left. As if Buddy mattered, when in reality, Buddy leaving had been the best goddamn thing that could have ever happened to their family. The guy was a low-down thief, the way he came back twice asking their mother for money. And she'd given it to him at first. The Braden family wealth had been handed down for generations. He and his siblings had significant trust funds, though they'd each made their own careers separate from those funds. The measly twenty-five grand Buddy had demanded from his mother was a pittance, but it was the demand of money in exchange for his children that had Pierce breathing fire. Pierce didn't know the whole story, but his uncle Hal had intervened and finally put a stop to Buddy's coercion for good. The truth was, he didn't care how his protective uncle had done it; he was just damn glad he had, because Buddy was more than a thief. He was a cheat to boot.

That skeleton in his closet was what had him running faster than normal on his morning run, as he circled back down the private road that led to his modest, stone home. He couldn't outrun his past, no matter how hard he pushed, and thinking about his past threw him into a tunnel of introspection. Pierce wasn't a one-woman man, never had been. And although he'd had moments of wondering what he was missing out on as he watched Luke and Wes fall madly in love with Daisy Honey and Callie Barnes, until last night, he'd almost been proud of that fact that he was, for lack of a better term, a *player*. There wasn't a woman alive who he believed could make him think twice about giving up the freedom to enjoy the company of whomever he pleased. Relationships took time and attention, but more than that, they took heart. A person had to care to be in a relationship, and sure, he'd cared about women in the past. He just hadn't cared enough to want to put that kind of effort into them. He wasn't a low-down, dirty bastard. But last night all of that surety came tumbling back at him, and he began to pick it apart.

There was something in Rebecca's eyes that took what he'd thought he was proud of and twisted it into a knot of clarity. She'd woken up that sleeping heart of his, and he'd spent the rest of the night mulling over the *real* reasons he enjoyed his bachelor lifestyle. He might have only been six when Buddy left, but his six-year-old mind was sharp, and he had a painfully accurate memory. He'd watched his mother's heart break, and even though his father hadn't been the best father on earth, and even though he'd hurt their family and abandoned them all, Pierce's heart had been broken, too. Hell, he'd not only seen his mother's heart get crushed; he felt the earth shift beneath them when his father left.

Pierce knew all about calculating risks and valuing effort. Love was a gamble, and he knew the payoff could be astronomical, or it could be devastating. That was a risk he wasn't willing to take. And if he didn't take the risk of falling in love, there was no risk of being hurt.

By the time he reached his house, he was out of breath and dripping with sweat. And he had no better answers to what it was about Rebecca that made him question what he'd always believed.

After a grueling weight workout in his fully

equipped home gym, he headed to the casino. At seven thirty he was driving through the parking garage, slowing as he reached the fifth floor, and remembering the hunger of Rebecca's kiss and the way she'd clutched at his shirt. He'd behaved himself last night, and he knew damn well that keeping things casual tonight was going to be hard as hell. Who was he kidding? He was getting hard just thinking about kissing her again.

Inside the Astral, Pierce passed the elegant, handcrafted furniture in the lobby and paused at the reception desk to greet Patricia, an attractive brunette who ran the front desk.

"Good morning, Patricia. How's Larissa?" He made a point of getting to know his staff. He didn't like the idea of being known as *that Braden guy who owns the place.* Pierce liked to be more hands-on, and he knew Patricia had been out last week for two days because her five-year-old daughter had been sick.

"Good morning, Mr. Braden. She's much better, sir. Thank you for asking." Patricia smiled as he passed on the way to the executive elevator.

"I'm glad to hear it."

He rode the elevator to the tenth floor, where Kendra Peterson, his executive assistant, stood by the reception desk in her superbly fitted Chanel suit. She held a day planner in one hand and had a pen tucked above her ear.

"Good morning, Pierce. You just missed a call from Treat. He said he tried your cell but was unable to reach you."

Pierce pulled his cell from his pocket. "I forgot to

turn the ringer on again. I'll call him now. Thank you."

Kendra shook her head, and her dark eyes filled with a look he'd seen too often in his mother's eyes.

"You really need a woman in your life, Pierce. Women remember to take care of things like that." Kendra was in her midfifties, as tall as Iman, with skin as smooth and rich as melted chocolate. She'd been married for twenty-five years. Her efficiency was unmatched, and her pushiness in the relationship department was relentless. Pierce's mother, and his older, engaged or married cousins, had also joined in on the push-the-relationship wagon recently. Luckily, Pierce was adept at ignoring their efforts.

"Thanks, Kendra, but I think I can handle it." He held up his phone and showed her the volume bar spreading across the screen.

She shook her head in that way that said, *You don't get it.*

After spending just a few hours with Rebecca, she had him viewing his thoughts on all things women related differently. He wondered if maybe all women weren't just looking for an easy step to wealth. Pierce knew he was an easy ladder to climb, which was one of the many reasons why he kept a wall between his heart and what lay between his legs.

He dialed his cousin Treat's number on the way into his office. Treat was a few years older than Pierce and was also in the resort business. Like Pierce, he was a keen negotiator with a nose for bullshit. Treat, his wife, Max, and their daughter, Adriana, lived in Weston on the property adjacent to Hal Braden's ranch. Treat was the oldest of Hal's six children.

"Pierce, I just called you five minutes ago."

It was good to hear Treat's familiar deep voice. People who knew them often wondered if they were competitive, since they were both in the resort business. Pierce's standard answer was, *Not with each other*, while Treat's standard answer was a hearty laugh. They, like all Bradens, were fiercely loyal to their families, and when properties came up for sale, they often consulted each other first, to ensure they weren't bidding against family.

"I forgot to turn the ringer on. Sorry about that. How's Adriana?"

"Cuter than hell. I swear, even at almost two, she can get anything she wants with a smile." Treat laughed. "How are things with you? Are you making any headway with the Grand Casino?"

"We're scheduled to begin due diligence next week. The guy's shady, at best. I can feel it in my bones." Pierce and Treat had spent their early years as close as brothers, but after Pierce's father left, his mother had moved their family to Trusty, where she and most of Pierce's siblings still lived. He and Treat remained close despite the distance, and made a point of visiting each other as often as they were able.

"Well, you know how to handle shady," Treat said.

"With laser-beam focus. I've got it covered." Pierce checked his watch. He had a meeting at eight fifteen with the financial team handling the due diligence for the potential acquisition.

"I heard that Luke's engaged. Did you hear that Josh is finalizing his wedding plans?" Josh was one of Treat's younger brothers, a world-renowned fashion designer. He was marrying his childhood crush and business partner, Riley Banks.

"Man, Treat. Everyone's heading down the aisle. Did Josh set a date yet?"

"No, not yet. But they're working on it. You know, Pierce, you're getting older; you might consider settling down yourself sometime soon. I highly recommend it." Like Pierce, Treat had been a workaholic and a bit of a player himself before meeting Max, but as with Wes and Luke, the right woman had come along and he couldn't live without her.

"You're like a drug pusher, but with commitment." Pierce laughed, but he was replaying the conversation with Kendra in his mind. He wondered if she and Treat could sense something different in him since he'd met Rebecca. He certainly felt different, and he was thinking differently. He supposed it was possible they'd pick up on something.

"What can I say? Marrying Max was the smartest thing I've ever done. Speaking of my gorgeous wife, she has a meeting with a sponsor for the film festival next week out your way. I thought I'd join her and we could get together for dinner."

"Sure. Tell me when and I'll clear my schedule. Are you bringing Adriana?"

"Jade's watching her. I think she's getting itchy for marriage and a baby." Jade Johnson was Treat's younger brother Rex's fiancée.

"Adriana's so damn cute, she could make *me* want a baby. I'd imagine Rex will be an easy sell. He'd do anything for Jade. They'll be the next ones down the aisle. That's my bet."

"Maybe I should bring Adriana so you start thinking about it."

"I'll tell you what, Treat. Why don't you start working on Ross?" Ross was a year younger than Pierce and was a veterinarian in Trusty, Colorado. His veterinary practice was so busy that he rarely had time to date. "He lives in the next town over from you. He's an easy target. Hell, I'm sure you know a hundred women to set him up with."

Treat laughed again. "You know he's on Jade and Max's list of Men to Introduce to Single Women, right? If Jake lived in Colorado, he'd be on there, too."

"I don't think either of them has a hard time finding women." The Bradens had a running joke among themselves about *the Braden curse*. They were all tall, dark, and handsome, and the women were crazy beautiful, smart, and strong willed. They would be an intimidating group if they weren't also down-to-earth and generous to a fault. While none of the Bradens had trouble getting dates, settling down hadn't come easily or quickly for any of them. Treat and his five siblings had been well into their thirties before settling down, and while Emily, Ross, Jake, and Pierce were in their thirties and still single, two of their siblings had already dropped off the market.

"Yeah, Max gets a kick out of seeing Jake in the rag mags with actresses on his arm. Reminds me of how Hugh was before he married Brianna." Hugh, Treat's youngest brother, was a professional race-car driver, and before marrying Brianna and becoming stepfather to her daughter, he'd also been a major player.

"Hugh took me by surprise. I never thought he'd settle down."

"See? If Hugh can settle down, I have hope that you will one day, too. Don't you ever look at my dad and wonder what you're missing?" Treat asked with a serious tone. Treat's mother, Adriana, had died when he was eleven, and his father, Hal, still exuded love for her with every breath he took.

"Only every time I see him, Treat. If ever there was a man who deserved more than life handed him, it is Uncle Hal." His throat thickened just thinking about the sadness in Hal's eyes when he spoke of missing his wife.

They made plans for dinner the following week, and after they ended the call, Pierce's mind shifted from his cousins to Rebecca and the look in her eyes when she spoke of missing her mother. Pierce texted Rebecca before going into his meeting.

Hey, gorgeous. Can't wait to see you. P. He read the text a few times and decided it sounded cheesy. He deleted it and typed another one. *Who's meeting me tonight? Ronda or Rebecca? P.*

AFTER HITTING THE gym and thanking Andy profusely for connecting her with Chiara, Rebecca filled out a handful of retail applications, then headed across town to meet with Mr. Fralin, her previous landlord. She read the text from Pierce for the tenth time since it came in that morning. She'd been trying to think of a sassy response, but ever since they kissed—*correction*—ever since *she* kissed *him*, her thoughts had been one tangled mess. She wasn't in a position to date. She was in a position to find a job and to collect her last paycheck so she could start looking for a room to rent.

She stared at the phone and decided not to respond until she had more time to think. She was pretty sure, *Both. Ronda can hold you down while I kiss you*, wasn't the most responsible answer she could give, even if it was what she wanted to say and do. *Sorry, Mom. I know you must think I've turned into a slut, but he's like a decadent dessert at a fine restaurant, incredibly tempting and probably worth every bit of guilt that is sure to follow.* She sighed at the thought of not kissing Pierce again, then smiled, thinking of how her mother might *really* respond. Her mother believed in love, even if her love life had never panned out. She would never think Rebecca had turned into a slut. *Mi dulce niña, don't be silly. Enjoy the man. You deserve him.*

Okay, maybe the thoughts about not being silly were her mother's, and the part about *enjoying* him was all Rebecca. But who was keeping track?

Thinking like that just might get me into trouble.

She shoved the phone in the glove compartment and headed into the apartment building.

Village View Apartments weren't located in the nicest part of town, and the banged-up, rusted cars in the parking lot were a testament to the inexpensive rent. But those things had nothing to do with what made a home for Rebecca and her mother. Their home wasn't defined by its location or the material items within. Home was wherever they were, as long as they were together. Where they could relax and let their hair down. For Rebecca, hearing her mother's easy, contagious laugh and the clank of dishes at odd hours when her mother got up with a dire need for sweets were some of the pleasures she associated with their home, along with smelling her mother's perfume as she tucked Rebecca into bed when she was younger. After her mother became ill, the scent of disease and the sight of prescription bottles and salves became a hallmark of home.

They'd lived in the same apartment complex since she was five years old. It still felt like she was coming home. She opened the door to the building, remembering how easily they'd given up their two-bedroom apartment when her mother had gone on disability. And later, when her mother's illness took a turn for the worse and Rebecca hadn't been the most reliable employee because of caring for her mother, they'd had to cut expenses even further and moved from the one-bedroom to an efficiency. Rebecca had never minded sleeping on the couch. She'd have slept on the floor if it came to it, as long as her mother had a warm bed and a comfortable place to spend her last days.

She inhaled deeply before entering the office. It occurred to her that breathing deeply, gathering courage and strength, had become such a way of life to her that she barely noticed the habitual breaths she took throughout the day.

Mr. Fralin was a short man with hair the color of Pepsi and eyes as vivid as the sea. Even in his midsixties he still had the body of a prepubescent boy, soft, with little facial hair to speak of, save for the dark peppering on the peak of his pointy chin. He stood from behind his desk and held a hand out, palm up.

"Rebecca. How are you, dear?"

Rebecca took his hand and her heart warmed. He'd been so good to them, and she was so thankful, that the empathy in his eyes caused her throat to thicken. She swallowed, trying to keep a lump of emotions from clogging her throat.

"I'm good. Thank you for asking."

"Please, sit down." He motioned to the chair across from the desk, and then he sat down beside her. He crossed one leg over the other and folded his hands in his lap. "Tell me, Rebecca. What can I do for you?"

That was just like him, always willing to help. "Mr. Fralin, you've done so much for me already. I wanted to come by and thank you again and let you know that as soon as I have permanent employment, I plan on paying you back for the last few months' rent."

"Nonsense—"

"No. I insist. Allowing us to stay here when we couldn't afford it during the last two months of my mom's life and then allowing me to stay for almost six weeks after that was beyond generous. I'm not sure I can pay much until I'm back on my feet, but I would imagine that I'd be able to afford twenty dollars a week. I know it will take a long time to pay off three and a half months' rent at that rate, and if I can pay more, I will."

"That is unnecessary, Rebecca. Your mother was a good woman, and it was my pleasure to help you both. I only wish that I could have allowed you to stay longer."

"That's very generous of you to say, but you went above and beyond what anyone else would ever do, and we appreciated it greatly. I appreciate it. You allowed me to stay here for almost six weeks after my mother passed, Mr. Fralin, and you have her urn in your safe. You've done more for me than I could have ever hoped for." It had been Rebecca and her mother against the world for so long, trying to survive from day to day and to make ends meet, that she was trying her damnedest not to remain in that needy of a position. She was determined not to depend on anyone for a place to live or to put food on the table.

"Have you found another place to stay?"

"I'm just waiting for the approval to come through." The little white lie was not just to save her pride, but she didn't want him worrying about her, either. "I'm between jobs right now, but I hope to have a new position soon, and when I do, I'll be in touch."

He walked her to the door and held his hand out again. Rebecca placed her hand in his.

"Rebecca," he began. "Your mother would be very proud of you."

Rebecca wasn't taking care of their debts to make her mother proud. She knew her mother was proud of her regardless of the debt she'd incurred. She was making amends for her own peace of mind. Rebecca wanted—*needed*—to know that she could not only stand on her own two feet, but leave a good reputation in her wake. Her mother's death didn't define her, and she was determined that the circumstances they'd endured wouldn't determine her future. She wasn't, and she had no desire to be, the type of woman people pitied, or the type of woman whose poor station in life was written off as, *Well, her mother died, you know, so cut her some slack.*

She wasn't going to maintain a poor station in life, either. She just needed to find her niche. Everyone had one, and she wasn't giving up on finding hers at twenty-seven.

Back in her car, she pulled out her cell phone and was surprised to see a message from a number she didn't recognize. She listened to the message and screamed, then covered her mouth and looked around the parking lot. She listened again just to be sure she had heard it correctly.

"Hi, Rebecca. This is Chiara. Good news. We'd like to hire you for a waitressing position in the restaurant that I took you through. I know waitressing wasn't your job of choice, but it's a start, and since I know you are looking to start right away, if you're interested in the position and are free this afternoon, stop by and we can complete the remaining paperwork."

Rebecca rested her head back. *I can do this. I can SO do this!*

Waitressing. It *was* a start, and it was a job with a stable company and, she hoped, growth potential. With hope in her heart, she called Chiara and confirmed that she'd come by later that afternoon. She closed her eyes and breathed deeply, trying to quell the flutter of excitement that had her wishing she could tell her mother about her job. *You already know, don't you?* She didn't expect a sign or a whiff of her mother's scent to know in her heart that her mother was pulling all the right strings.

Not only was she going to find her niche, but why shouldn't she enjoy the company of a man who set fire in her belly and made her heart come alive? She read his text again and responded with renewed hope.

I'm not into sharing, so if Ronda shows up, I might have to kick her butt, too.

Chapter Five

REBECCA STOOD IN the lobby of the Astral resort beside a wide golden column. It was Friday evening and the lobby was much busier than it had been the evening before. The casino entrance was down a corridor to her left, and indiscernible, excited noises filtered down the hall. Women passed in droves, with spiky heels, perfectly coiffed hair, and makeup that looked professionally done. They were draped on the arms of handsome men wearing expensive suits and shoes that glistened from the overhead lights. Slicked-back hair and manicured eyebrows were apparently commonplace among the male casino patrons. There was a time when Rebecca would have felt out of place surrounded by such rich beauty, but after the first minute or two, she was able to see past the rush of insecure thoughts. She pulled back her shoulders and adjusted her mind-set—another skill she'd honed during the years of caring for her mother. Her adjusted perspective offered a different view of those glamour people. Now she saw insecure people flaunting their means too loudly, and when she turned those new lenses introspectively, she saw a confident woman who was on her way to sure footing. And it felt damn good.

The twisting and turning in her stomach had nothing to do with being in the presence of the rich and maybe even some of the famous. Her nerves were knotting in anticipation of seeing Pierce and in excitement over her new job. She'd met with Chiara, and she'd met her new boss, Marlow Villada, and a few of the other people she'd be working with. Rebecca was no newbie to waitressing, but waitressing at the Astral was completely different from waitressing at IHOP and Ben's Breakfast Bar. She was starting the job on Monday, and she needed to memorize the menu before then. It would take dedication and focus, but it was worth it. She'd already done the math in her head, and she'd be earning almost twice what she'd earned in the past, which meant that finding a reasonable place to live and paying back Mr. Fralin wasn't out of the question. She'd thought she might try to rent from Mr. Fralin again, but after returning to the complex, she realized that it would be too painful to live there knowing that her mother would never walk through the door again. Rebecca was moving forward.

She felt his hand on her shoulder and smelled his masculine, musky scent before she heard Pierce's voice.

"Sweet Rebecca."

She turned so fast she nearly smacked into him. "Hi. Sorry." *Oh God*. He looked like he'd stepped out of one of those glossy magazines again. He carried his suit coat and tie over one arm, and the top buttons of his white dress shirt were undone, revealing a glimpse of the athletic body that lay beneath.

He leaned in close and kissed her cheek. "Did I keep you waiting?"

"No, not at all."

He smiled and it cut right through her. He had the greatest smile, a magical combination of friendly welcome and sweet seduction. He placed his hand on her lower back, as he'd done the evening before, and this time her body didn't tense with nervous energy. She'd been thinking about his touch all day. This time she felt drenched in pleasure, and she longed for more.

As they walked outside, he leaned in close again. "You look lovely."

She felt her cheeks flush. She loved how he moved close each time he spoke to her. It made his words feel that much more intimate. "Thank you." Rebecca didn't have many fancy clothes, but she was glad she'd changed after filling out the paperwork. She had a few short dresses that she knew were at least slightly fashionable, even if not high-end. Consignment shops were great for finding deals on nice clothing. Tonight she wore a heather-gray, off-the-shoulder dress with three-quarter-length sleeves. It was blousy up top and gathered at her waist. It was a little short, stopping just above midthigh, and with her heels, it looked more expensive than it was.

"If that makes you blush, then I'm glad I didn't say what I really felt."

Oh, please, make me blush.

"Pierce." A tall, blond-haired man reached for Pierce's hand. "Man, it's good to see you."

In a split second Pierce's flirtatious eyes turned serious. He shook the man's hand, his other hand never leaving her back.

"Larry, it's a pleasure." He turned toward Rebecca. "This is my lovely date, Rebecca. Rebecca, this is my good friend Larry Hooper."

Rebecca loved that he didn't hesitate to introduce her as his lovely date, but it felt practiced, and that stole a tiny piece of her joy.

"It's nice to meet you, Larry," she said.

"Enjoy your evening, Larry. We have plans, so we'd better go before we're late."

She felt Pierce guiding her toward the valet. Anderson opened the door to a midnight-blue Jaguar. She'd wondered the other day if the gray Jaguar had been his, but he'd rushed her away from the valet so quickly she hadn't been able to figure it out. Now she wondered if he owned *two* Jags.

"Thank you," she said as she slid onto the fine leather seat, squelching the first few seconds of feeling like she was way out of her league. Which she was, but her mother had taught her at a young age that *leagues* were only a frame of mind. *Take away the cars and money and they're just people, like you and me, niña.*

Her stomach fluttered at the prospect of being in such close proximity to Pierce. In an effort to quell her nerves, before Anderson closed the car door, and in earshot of Pierce, she joked, "If I go missing, please remember that he's the last person I was seen with."

Anderson nodded. "As you wish, ma'am." He slid

Pierce a knowing smile and closed the door.

Pierce climbed into the driver's seat. "That was quite a statement. Do I look like a killer?"

"A lady-killer, maybe." She nervously ran her finger along the center console.

He reached across the console and held her hand. "Does that mean you don't trust me?"

"If I didn't trust you, I'd never get in your car. I just don't have you all figured out yet."

"Well, a man can't give away his hand in a few short hours, can he? You've got all night to figure me out, or at least I hope you do."

Oh, good Lord. So do I.

"First things first. King's Bar to get your paycheck?"

"Oh my gosh. I have had such a busy day that I totally forgot." She couldn't believe he remembered. "Thank you for remembering, but if you'd rather not, I can get it another day."

"I'd rather." He lifted her hand to his lips and kissed it.

The kiss should have made her more nervous, but it had the opposite effect. It felt natural and right, which was pretty damn scary. How could riding in a Jaguar with a handsome guy feel right to a woman who was currently *living* in her car?

A few minutes later, Pierce pulled up in front of King's Bar. The Jaguar looked out of place on the dark street.

"I'll just be a minute." Rebecca reached for the door.

Pierce cut the engine. "I'm going with you." He

stepped from the car and came around to her side.

"You really don't have to." She didn't want him to see what a condescending ass Martin could be, or how she might have to handle him. She wasn't afraid to speak her mind, and though Pierce had seen her deck a guy, he hadn't seen her get up in a man's face and tell him exactly what she thought of him. That was not the woman she wanted him to think she was. She'd only done what she'd had to do. All she wanted was a normal life. Was that too much to hope for? After tonight, she hoped to move forward, presenting a calmer image.

"I want to." He reached for her hand again.

Rebecca looked at their hands. "Pierce, I really don't need a babysitter. I know it's chivalrous of you to want to be there, but..."

He drew his brows together and stepped closer. "Rebecca, I'm not being chivalrous, although I do enjoy hearing the word connected to me." He smiled and it made her smile, too. "If this guy was nasty enough to cause you to quit, then he's probably not going to be very nice when you ask for your paycheck. I just don't want it to be any more uncomfortable than it needs to be."

"I know, and thank you for that, but I'm a big girl. I can handle this on my own. Really." She watched his jaw clench as he turned away and ran his hand through his hair.

"How about I wait just inside the door?"

"How about you just wait here?" She didn't mean to sound so final, but she hadn't ever needed a man to handle her affairs, and she wasn't going to start now just because an incredibly gorgeous, kind, and generous, muscular man who smelled like heaven wanted her to. To soften the blow of her rebuttal—and because she was dying to—she touched his cheek.

"Thank you for wanting to help, Pierce. Just give me five minutes, okay? If I'm not out in five, you can barge through the door and do whatever you have in mind."

"Are you sure you don't know my sister?" He laughed. "She's just as stubborn as you."

"I'm pretty sure we'd get along great, then. Thank you for wanting to help, Pierce." She pulled the door open and headed inside, trying to ignore the tug of how good it felt to have someone offer to help her for a change. She wouldn't let herself revel in those good feelings for long, though. She needed to look her most confident and serious when she approached Martin, not glinty eyed and swooning.

Martin looked up from behind the bar as she approached. His beady eyes caught hers. Rebecca drew in a deep breath and met his snakelike stare.

"I'm here for my paycheck."

"Well, well, if it isn't chatty Cathy." Martin laughed, and two men who were drinking at the bar looked her up and down.

"Martin, I'm not here to play games. Just give me my check and I'll get out of your bar and never look back." She held his annoyingly amused gaze as he casually dried a glass and set it on a shelf behind him.

He slung the towel over his shoulder and leaned his hands on the bar, motioning for her to come closer. "You decked a guy in here the other night and then took off. I could have gotten sued."

She rolled her eyes. "You didn't. The check, Martin. Focus on what's important."

He dropped his eyes to her breasts. "How about you come in the back room and we'll talk about it?"

How did I ever work for you? She'd been so desperate for employment that she'd ignored Andy's warnings about working for Martin. Never again, she vowed. From here forward, she wasn't going to settle—in any aspect of her life.

"How about you get your scrawny ass into the back office and get my check before I go back, get the check myself, and leave you in worse shape than the guy from the other night?" She stomped toward the back office.

He beat her to the office door and stepped in front of it, arms crossed, snake eyes returned. "Give me two good reasons why I should give you this check. You quit."

"I quit because you're a pig who treats people like shit. That's reason number one. Reason number two is that I earned it, and I'll throw a third in there just for the heck of it. If you don't give me my check, you can kiss your family jewels goodbye."

He scoffed.

"*Ugh.* You're an idiot." She reached for the doorknob and he grabbed her wrist. "You have three seconds to let go of me."

"Right." He narrowed his eyes.

"She was being generous. I'll give you one."

Rebecca spun around at the sound of Pierce's deep, serious voice. His feet were set hip distance apart, arms crossed, and even in his dress slacks and dress shirt, he went from smoking hot to menacing in a fraction of a second.

He stepped forward and said in the most calm, chilling voice Rebecca had ever heard, "You will release her wrist and give her the money that is owed to her or your next move will be made from the floor."

Martin dropped Rebecca's wrist and she plowed into the office, grabbed her check from the paycheck box on his desk, and stormed from the bar, leaving Pierce and Martin behind. Her heart beat triple time as she paced the sidewalk, embarrassed and so damned pissed off that she could barely see straight.

Pierce walked out a few minutes later and she felt his hand settle into its usual place on her back. She spun around, all the pieces of her perfect day crashed and shattered. Shards of the last ten minutes came at her from all angles. It was all she could do to stand there and look at him.

"I asked you to stay outside." She didn't mean to yell.

"I did. You said five minutes. I waited six." His eyes ran over her face, and she turned away to keep from yelling again. "Rebecca, I'm sorry if I overstepped my bounds, but I'm not the kind of guy who can sit back and do nothing when I think some asshole is going to treat you badly."

She turned to face him again, teeth clenched, arms crossed over her chest. "I could have handled him."

"I'm sure you could have."

"Then why did you come in after me, Pierce? I don't need saving." Her body was trembling. *Damn it.*

Tears of anger threatened to spill. *Don't cry. Do not fucking cry.*

"I'm sorry. Rebecca, I didn't think you needed saving. I'm..." He narrowed his eyes. "Babe, you're shaking. Did he hurt you?" He placed a hand gently on her arm, and she shrugged away again.

"I'm not your babe, and no, he didn't hurt me. I'm shaking because I'm angry." *Goddamn it. Way to ruin a good night.* She drew in a deep breath as Pierce took a step back.

"I'm a guy, Rebecca. It's not my nature to be told to just let someone treat a woman badly." He ran his hand through his hair as he'd done earlier. "I was trying to help. That's all."

"I know you were. I just...I could have handled him. Now *he* thinks I couldn't have." That was the worst part. She was ten times stronger of a person than Martin and about a zillion times more respectful and appropriate. She hated looking weak in front of him, or that he thought she needed a fricking bodyguard.

Pierce held his hands up. "You're right. I'm sorry."

"*Ugh.* You don't have to be sorry. What you did was nice. Thank you. I just...I don't need a savior." Rebecca wiped her eyes and shook out her hands, as if that might loosen the constriction in her chest.

Pierce lowered his voice and closed the distance between them. "You're right. I guess I'm used to a lot of things that are different from what you're used to, and I'm not used to women—other than my sister and maybe my cousin Savannah—who can take on guys like that. It was my issue, not yours, and I'll be sure to try to check my urge to help at the door from now on."

She crossed and uncrossed her arms, feeling like an utter fool. He was being nice and she was acting like a bitch.

"God, Pierce. I'm sorry." She sighed loudly. "You can take me back to my car. I...You don't need someone like me in your life. Look at you. You've got your life together, and I'm just starting to piece mine back together. I overreacted and, honestly, I have no business going up against a guy like Martin even if I am capable of it. The guy's an ass. I wish I was in a position to have just left without my check, but I'm not. I probably never will be, and that's okay, but I don't want to be the type of woman who makes you wonder what the hell she's going to do next. I'm really not a rampant crazy woman who hits men or tells them off."

"I don't think of you in that way." His voice was so sincere it softened her anger.

She looked up at the sky and closed her eyes for a second while she mentally pulled herself back together.

"I don't think of myself in that way either," she admitted. "Really. I'm not that person. I mean, I am if I *have* to be, and unfortunately, you've witnessed two terrible situations in as many days, but really, I'm just a girl who lost her mother and wants to get on with her life. I want to finish school, land a job I love, and I don't know, have some modicum of a life far away from places like this."

"How about if we start with the fact that I'm a man who just wants to have dinner with you. Whether or not you went up against Martin and despite the fact that I acted out of turn."

She had to smile at the absurdness of it all. "Gosh, Pierce. Are you really this nice of a guy, or is this all some farce?" She walked back toward the car.

Pierce grabbed her hand and stopped her cold with his serious stare. "I assure you, I am not just this nice of a guy. I can also assure you that this isn't a farce. I have my faults, and you've just seen one of them."

He opened the car door and she climbed in. "That was a fault?"

He went around to the driver's side and settled into the driver's seat. "Yeah, it is a fault. I should have listened to you. Remember, we talked about how neither of us likes to give up control?"

Rebecca covered her face with a groan. "Oh God. We're going to butt heads a lot, aren't we?"

He drove away, leaving the city lights behind. "I don't have a clue. Everything about you throws me for a loop." He took her hand in his again. "And for whatever reason, I like it."

Chapter Six

BY THE TIME they reached Pierce's driveway, Rebecca's nerves had calmed, and with the help of Pierce's jokes, she'd shed the embarrassment of going to pieces in front of him. They drove through a stone and iron gate, beneath an umbrella of trees, and followed the in-ground lights up the long driveway. Acres of grass fell away to either side of the driveway as the house came into view.

"It's really serene out here." Given Pierce's clothing and that he worked in the executive offices of the casino, Rebecca had expected that he would have a fancy house and car. She was totally taken off guard when he parked at the end of the circular drive, in front of the cutest stone house she'd ever seen.

"Your house is adorable." She took in the large picture windows, the gable over a deep front porch, and twin peaks that rose from either side of the roof.

"Adorable." Pierce let out a little laugh. "I think my sister was going for elegant without being flashy when she designed it for me."

"Your sister designed this?" She opened her car door.

"Yeah. She's an architect, and she's really well known in the passive house industry. This was one of her first, and I love it."

"What's a passive house? Are there aggressive houses, too?" She arched a brow with the question.

Pierce smiled. "Maybe there should be." She loved that he fell right into teasing her back. "Passive houses use a higher standard for energy efficiency and leave a much smaller ecological footprint. Changing the world one house at a time and all that."

Pierce arrived at her side of the car after she'd already stepped out. He retrieved her purse, then reached for her hand. "Do you ever let men open doors for you?"

She bit her lower lip. "I'm sorry. I don't do that on purpose." They walked through the heavy wooden doors into a beautiful, high-ceilinged foyer that led to an open living space with glass along the far wall and a fireplace tucked into the corner of the room. Rebecca had expected marble floors and chandeliers, not warm, dark wood floors and a room full of family photographs. To their left was an arched opening into a library with two full walls of books and a blue sofa that arced in a half circle. The front windows ran almost ceiling to floor, and on the far wall was a gorgeous fireplace with a slate hearth and a decorative wood mantel.

"Your house is beautiful, and I'm sorry about the car door. I guess I've spent so many years being the one to hold doors open and taking care of my mom that the dating world is still a little foreign to me." She couldn't help but wonder how often he brought women home. Every night? Weekly? A man like him had to have a plethora of women at his beck and call.

"Well, I was brought up to open doors and pull out chairs for women, so is it something you can get used to, or should I retrain my brain?" Still holding her hand, Pierce led her through an archway to their right to a beautiful wooden bar. He set her purse down. She was trying to get used to carrying one again. If she was going to break out of the working in bars and IHOP scenes, she couldn't very well carry her key and driver's license in her heels.

Pierce placed his hands on her hips.

She loved the feel of them, steady and sure. Around Pierce she didn't feel like her ass was wide or her body was out of proportion. He looked at her like she was beautiful, and when he touched her, everything inside her sizzled and came alive.

"Would you like a glass of wine?"

His voice brought her mind back to reality, and reality was even hotter. He stood so close, his lips a breath away. She could pucker hers and they'd probably touch. *Let yourself enjoy him, even if it's only for a night*, the woman in her pleaded. Three years without a man was a very long time, and his touch felt so good. She reminded herself that she was living in her car, that this date couldn't lead anywhere serious. And she needed a one-night stand like she needed to lose another job. The sensible side of her brain took over. *This is a dinner date, and that's what it is going to remain.*

"Sure," she managed. He moved around the bar and she wanted him back, touching her again, looking at her like she was beautiful, and sexy, and—

"How was your day?" he asked, as if they'd been dating forever. Or maybe every guy asked simple questions like that; she couldn't remember.

"Really great, other than the whole Martin fiasco. I got a job at the casino. It's just a waitress job, but I start Monday, and there's growth potential, so you never know."

He joined her again and handed her a glass of wine. "That's great. Have you waitressed before?"

"Oh, goodness, yes." She swatted the air, as if she were an expert. "I mean, not at anyplace as nice as the casino, but how hard can it be? I do need to memorize the menu, but I'm a quick study. I have it in my purse."

"Ah, it wouldn't fit in your bra?" The side of his mouth quirked up with the tease.

"Actually..." She pulled the top of her dress out from her chest and looked down. "I'm not wearing one tonight, so..."

His eyes darkened, narrowed. "I'm going to pretend I don't know that; otherwise I'll have a hard time concentrating on cooking dinner."

Nice to know I have that effect on you.

He took her hand again, and it was starting to feel familiar, the way his big hand engulfed hers. Strong and Protective. "Come on, braless wonder. I hope you like steak."

She laughed. "There isn't much I don't like." Pierce was easy to be with. She loved the way he joked, and the way he looked at her made her feel special, though she knew she had to be careful there. Before her mother became ill, when Rebecca had been in the dating realm, it had been her experience that most men were after something sexual without the desire for anything more, and as much as she wanted an end to her three years of abstinence, she wasn't interested in being a notch on anyone's belt. Not even Pierce's.

They went into a beautiful kitchen with stainless-steel appliances and warm, wooden cabinets. "Is this how you woo all your women?" She had to ask, and it wasn't her nature to be coy about such things.

The surprise in his eyes and his gaping jaw told her that maybe she'd been a little too brusque.

"I'm sorry. I'm not judging you. I just do better when I know where I stand. You know, going in with my eyes open." She tucked her hair behind her ear and watched as he opened the fridge and withdrew a glass dish of marinating steak.

He set it on the counter without answering, then returned to her side.

"No holding doors and questions that could make the most confident man falter. I like you, Rebecca Rivera." He took her hand in his and rubbed his thumb over the ring on her index finger.

Her mother's ring. When he met her gaze again, the honesty in his eyes was unyielding. The warmth in his touch reassuring.

"I'm not going to lie to you. I have used my wealth to impress women in the past. Fancy cars tend to have that effect. But as far as this house goes, this is my private residence. I usually bring women I date to a room at the resort."

"Why?"

He stepped closer and settled his free hand on her hip again. "I'm going to answer honestly and you may not like it, but I'm not a liar, so what you see is what you get." He lowered his chin and looked deeply into her eyes. "Are you sure you want to know?"

Gulp. No. "Yes."

"Because my private residence is just that. Private. The women I usually date are..." He shrugged. "Not the type of women you bring home."

She drew in a deep breath. She did understand that. Before her mother had become ill, she'd dated guys she wouldn't bring home, either.

"I've done that myself. So, why am I here?"

"You've done that yourself?" He tilted his head.

Ah, so what's good for the goose isn't good for the gander? Better to find out now, because Rebecca was nothing if not confident in what she'd done in her life and her reasons for doing them. Not that she owed anyone an explanation.

She shrugged, an action he could understand, given he'd just done so himself. She sipped her wine, enjoying the torturous wait she was rolling out for him.

"I'm not a saint either." She nibbled on her lower lip and let that sink in. "Let's just say that we all have needs."

"I thought you said it had been years since you'd been with a man." He arched a brow. A challenge.

She took another sip of wine and licked her lips slowly, evocatively, and felt his grip on her hip tighten.

"It has been. But I did have a life before that. I'm twenty-seven years old, Pierce, not seventeen. My home is my private, intimate space. It's where I let my hair down, where I can throw on sweatpants and eat a pint of ice cream without judgment. And the last few years, it was the place my mother and I shared. I've never met a man who was good enough to bring home." As she recounted her feelings, she missed having a home. She suppressed the longing and focused on him looking at her with a quizzical expression. She wanted to know what he was thinking. His eyes narrowed, and when she lifted her glass for another sip of wine, he stilled it with his hand.

"I like you, Rebecca. You're a no-bullshit woman."

"Well, I like you, too, Pierce." She eyed the wineglass, then drew her eyes back to his. "But you still haven't told me why I'm here."

An easy smile spread across his lips. "I have no idea. You tell me."

Oh boy. "My best guess..."

He released her hand and she lifted the glass to her lips, then licked the sweet alcohol from them, realizing too late that while she was licking the last drop, Pierce read it as an invitation. He moved in closer and pressed his lips to hers. His kiss was deadly. Sinful. A fury of heat that swirled through every part of her body, and by the time he drew away, she could barely breathe.

"Your best guess?" he whispered.

She set the glass on the counter and tried to think past the fresh gust of desire that was whipping through her like a hurricane.

"My best guess is that I'm here because you think you'll get a night of hot sex and maybe you don't want the people at the resort to know you're seeing me because I was a prospective employee—and now I *am* an employee—and you work there." *Holy cow.* Where had that come from? She hadn't even put the whole job-dating thing together before that minute. *No, no, no. Please don't let that be why he brought me home.*

He ran his index finger down her cheek and then touched the ends of her hair. "You are sadly mistaken, Rebecca. If I were worried about being seen with you, I would never have agreed to meet you in the lobby." His voice turned serious. "And if I thought dinner might lead to a night of hot sex and nothing more, you would most certainly *not* be in my house."

"Oh." It was a hollow reply, but the only one she could muster.

"Is that what you were thinking when you said you'd meet me in the lobby? That I wasn't good enough for you to take home? That I was going to be a night of amazing sex and nothing more?" He touched her bare shoulder, stealing her ability to think clearly. "It's okay if you were. I just want to know where I stand. You know...go in with my eyes open."

"No." *I was thinking that I didn't have a home where you could pick me up, and now I just can't think at all.*

"Well, that's good to hear." He took a step back, but Rebecca still felt the heat of him compressing her chest. "If you want the truth, I liked you. You didn't strike me as a *get-her-plastered-and-take-her-to-bed* type of date. Hell, I don't know what you struck me as.

You confused me. You clocked a guy in a bar, you blew me off, and then you opened up to me and I got a glimpse of who you were. And as crazy as it sounds, I was attracted to you in a way that I've never been attracted to a woman before. Ever."

She finished her wine in one gulp. "I...liked you, too."

"Liked, or like?"

"Like, definitely like." She reached for his hand, and when she touched his warm skin, it startled her. What was she thinking? Her brain told her arm to come back to her side, but it didn't listen. Thank God it didn't listen.

"Talking to you last night was nice. It was something that I wanted to do more of, and I figured if we went out to a fancy restaurant, we'd be sidetracked by the glitz of it, and I really just wanted to get to know you."

Slowly, her ability to breathe returned. He didn't sound like he was spewing lines, like the introduction he'd given to his friend outside of the Astral. This felt true and genuine. "I want to get to know you, too."

He squeezed her hand and then gathered the steaks, took a plate of shrimp on skewers from the refrigerator, and handed Rebecca the bottle of wine. "Come on; let's talk out by the grill."

One flick of a switch illuminated a stone patio, and white lights lit up the surrounding trees, giving the evening a romantic feel. Another switch brought music to speakers mounted on the back wall of the house. Pierce fired up the grill, put the steaks on, and then refilled their wineglasses. A few minutes later a warm breeze picked up the scent of seasoned steaks and carried it into the night.

"You don't really think I want to hide you from anyone, do you?" Pierce flipped the steaks and set a skewer of shrimp on the grill beside it.

"I don't know. Maybe?"

"Wow, brutal honesty again." He shook his head, but he smiled, and she knew he wasn't offended.

"I don't believe it now. But is there a problem with dating someone from work? They didn't cover that in the interview." She liked watching him at the grill. She liked the way he stole glances at her, and when he rolled up his shirtsleeves, exposing muscular forearms, she couldn't help but reach out and trace a muscle from elbow to wrist. She felt his eyes on her while hers were trained on his arm.

"Sorry," she whispered, and lifted her finger from his warm skin.

"Don't be. I don't think we have to worry about anyone saying anything if we continue to date."

If we continue to date.

"Which I hope we do," he added.

Oh, thank God. "Okay. I don't want to get either of us in trouble."

Pierce finished cooking, and after they set the table, he went inside and brought out two candles in beautiful wooden candleholders.

"Want to do the honors?" He handed her a lighter and Rebecca lit them. When she reached for a chair, he gently touched her arm. "I would be honored if you'd allow me to do that."

She felt her cheeks flush. "Thank you. I'm kind of

hardheaded, so I'm afraid I'll need reminders."

He pushed her chair in and crouched beside her. "Rebecca, I really don't want you to think that I would keep the fact that I'm seeing you a secret from anyone. You're beautiful, and to be honest, even if you weren't, I'd still be proud to be seen with you. I was just being selfish. I wanted you all to myself."

She softened a little more to him. If he was just throwing out lines, they were the perfect ones, but again she sensed that everything out of Pierce's mouth reflected his real feelings. She wasn't sure how to respond. *Thank you? Oh good? That's a relief?* She went with honesty. It was, after all, what came easiest to her.

"Thank you, but you don't have to keep explaining. I'm glad I'm here, and it's nice that you didn't think I was just a hot piece of ass."

He kissed her hand. "Oh, don't get me wrong. You are a hot piece of ass, but you're not *just* a hot piece of ass." He rose to his feet, and she smacked his butt.

"You're not so bad yourself."

Dinner was delicious and conversation came easily. After they ate, they carried the dishes inside and Rebecca moved toward the sink to help clean up.

"Leave them," he said against her cheek. "I'll get them later. I want to spend time with you."

Pierce wrapped his arms around her from behind and kissed the base of her neck. She closed her eyes and reminded herself that, despite the way her private parts were tingling, achingly aware of Pierce's scent, the strength of his arms around her, and—*oh Lord*— the feel of all those sexy muscles pressed against her back, this was a *dinner* date.

PIERCE COULDN'T REMEMBER the last time he didn't have an endgame, but with Rebecca, it shouldn't surprise him that he didn't. *Nothing* should surprise him where Rebecca was concerned, because damn near everything she did sent his head spinning. When he'd seen the way her boss was treating her, he'd wanted to grab him by the neck and slam the cockiness out of him, but Pierce knew that confidence could be just as threatening, and even more demeaning, than fisticuffs. Of course, he didn't expect the reaction he'd gotten from Rebecca, although he'd understood her point. He, too, hated anyone to think they got the better of him.

He watched her now, standing before his sofa table, looking over the pictures of his family. She looked so relaxed, soft, and feminine. He wondered about her even more now. Was it her mother's illness and taking care of her that made her so self-sufficient and capable? Was it that reality that made her believe she needed to be competent enough at all things to take on the world? He realized that maybe getting to know Rebecca *was* his endgame.

Rebecca turned one of the photographs toward him. "Your family?" she asked.

"Yeah. Those are my younger brothers and sister." He pointed to each as he spoke. "This is Ross. He's a vet in Trusty, where I grew up. Jake's the one with lighter hair. He's a stuntman in LA." Pierce laughed. "I remember when we took that picture. That's Luke, my youngest brother. See how he's looking at Wes?" He pointed to Wes. "Right after we took the picture, Jake threw Wes down on the ground in a fake pile driver move. Wes's expression was priceless." He pointed to his sister. "That's Emily. She rolls her eyes at us a lot."

"She's the one who designed your house?" She glanced up at him, and her eyes caught the soft light.

He leaned in close, wanting to kiss her. To run his tongue along the swell of her upper lip. Her eyes darkened, and it took all of his willpower to remind himself to take it slow. He didn't want Rebecca to feel as though she was just like the other women he'd dated, when she was anything but.

"Yes, she did." He moved his lips a little farther away from temptation.

"She's really pretty."

"Really bossy, too."

She set the frame down. "I like her already."

"Oh, she'd get a kick out of you." He shook his head at the thought of Rebecca and Emily joining forces. "You two could put the five of us in our places."

Pierce filled their wineglasses to keep his hands busy, but he wanted to be closer to her, and he didn't want her staring at pictures of his handsome brothers.

"Sit with me." He led her to the couch in the living room.

Rebecca didn't seem to give his expensive, handmade furniture a thought as she slipped off her heels and tucked her legs beneath her, which made her even more appealing to Pierce. She was so different from the money-hungry women he usually dated. She was comfortable in her own skin and was not trying to impress him. Her knees pressed against his leg, and that sexy little dress of hers inched higher, revealing the curve of her thigh. She had one arm stretched along the back of the couch, and Pierce laid his arm over hers. He'd already slipped off his shoes, and he realized that the stress he'd felt earlier was gone. She'd made him forget about his impending acquisition and the stresses of his workday. He couldn't remember the last time he'd spent an evening without those things looming over him.

He brushed her hair from her shoulder, and it was so soft and silky that he held on to a lock and ran it over his fingers.

"I'm really glad you're here." He didn't have to work at conversation. The truth came easily.

"Me too. I thought you'd take me straight back to my car after the incident with Martin." She held his gaze, and he could tell she was no longer embarrassed by what had happened.

"Not a chance. I'd like to know more about you. If it's not too personal, I'd love to know what your life was like before your mom got sick."

"Gosh, it seems like a lifetime ago. I had a pretty normal life, I guess. I got my own apartment after I graduated from community college. I've always worked a lot, but I had time for friends back then, so I had more of a social life. Not much of one, but some. I did all the normal twenty-year-old stuff. I worked, of course, and went out to bars, danced, drank, studied when I started taking classes at the university. My mom and I got together for lunch or dinner once a week." She smiled and met his eyes. "Life was good, you know? Normal."

"Was it *easy?*" He brushed her shoulder with his fingertips.

"You know, once you have the kind of perspective that I have, you realize that all the bitching and moaning you've done in the past, over boyfriends, or homework, or five extra pounds, it's all such garbage." She ran her finger along the seam of his sleeve across the back of the couch. "If you'd have asked me when I was twenty if life was easy, I probably would have complained about working and going to school. Isn't that ridiculous?"

"No. I think every age has its difficulties."

"True. It would have been valid then. But now I know what difficult really means. When my mom was first diagnosed with lung cancer, it wasn't real to us. We thought she'd beat it. There was no doubt in my mind. She'd never smoked; she didn't work around asbestos. The whole thing seemed unimaginable. But a year later, when they found a brain tumor, things became real." She paused, and Pierce inched a little closer, bringing her knees onto his lap so he could wrap his arm further around her shoulders and back.

"That's when I moved in with her. And from then on my life became a circle of medical appointments, scans, and medications. You do what you have to for family, you know?"

"Yes, that I do know, and I'm so sorry, Rebecca, for all you've gone through." Pierce thought about his own life, taking care of his siblings after his father left and watching over them as they grew up. Protecting Emily from guys who were no good for her. He understood family love and loyalty well, and listening to all that

Rebecca had gone through made him realize how much of life he, and most of the people he knew, took for granted.

"I've only told one friend about all of this. I don't want to unload on you. I'm sorry." She inched back, and Pierce touched her shoulder and her legs at the same time, hoping to keep her close.

"Please don't move away. If you'd like to talk about it, I'd like to listen. I want to know more about you, all of you."

He heard her breath catch, and she pressed her lips together. "I'm not a—"

"This isn't pity, or my effort to save you, Rebecca. I like you. I want to know about you because I like who you are."

"Oh." She glanced down at his hand touching her thigh. "Okay. Well...that's when things got hard. Time-consuming. Pretty heartrending. It was hard to hold a job, and we had Mom's medical bills, so I went into survival mode. I worked when I could, moved us to an efficiency apartment, and just made the best of every day so that my mom wouldn't feel guilty about being sick."

She inhaled a shaky breath. "It's still pretty new, you know? Six weeks is enough time to realize she's not coming back, but not quite enough time to stop feeling pitied when you tell someone."

"I don't pity you. I feel sad that you've gone through losing someone so close to you, but it's not pity." He touched her cheek. "And now? You said you're picking up the pieces of your life."

Her face brightened, and when she spoke, every

word carried hope. "I am. I've got a strong business sense, and I only have a couple classes left before I graduate. I don't know if that will help in finding a job, but it can't hurt. At some point I'll move from waitressing and bartending to the business field, I hope. But for now, I'm good with people. Well, other than yelling at Martin and decking that doofus in the bar."

"I can tell that you're good with people. Besides, Chiara wouldn't have hired you if you weren't. Every job at the resort revolves around people."

"Oh my gosh. I almost forgot. I should probably go. I have to memorize the menu, and I only have a few days to learn it."

"I'll help you." The offer surprised him as much as it surprised Rebecca. Pierce had never held a waiter job, and truth be known, he had no idea how difficult it might be. In fact, he had no idea that the waitstaff had to memorize the menu. He left those details up to the restaurant managers to handle. But he wasn't ready for this date to end, and if that meant helping her study, he'd damn well do it.

"You don't want to spend Friday night learning a menu when you can be out carousing."

"Carousing? Didn't you hear anything I said to you?"

"Sure, but what did that have to do with not carousing?"

He slid his hand up her thigh to her hip and scooted closer. Up close, he noticed the quickening of the pulse at the base of her neck. "I like you. I want to get to know you, Rebecca. I guess I haven't said it enough. I've been saying it in my head, though."

Her soft, full lips parted, and he leaned forward and kissed her.

"Sorry. I've been dying to do that all night."

Her cheeks heated. "Me too."

"Now maybe I can think a little clearer." He kissed her again, longer, more sensually, basking in the taste of her and the feel of her sweet mouth against his.

He drew back, hoping the distance would ease the desire pulsing through his body. He wanted to touch and taste every inch of her, to claim her as his own, marking her with his mouth, his hands....At the same time, a different torrent of desire coursed through him—he wanted to protect and care for her. He knew it was fast, and yet he could no sooner stop the feelings from swelling inside him than he could stop making business deals for a living.

She touched her kiss-swollen lips, as if she wanted the feel of him to linger. Pierce was compelled to explain his feelings in a way he never had before.

"I'm thirty-six, Rebecca. I've done a lot of *carousing*, and I know it's a little crazy, but I've never met anyone like you. I don't have an interest in going out tonight. I want more time with you, not less."

"But studying a menu? Talk about boring." She pulled her knees closer to her chest, and the skirt of her dress bunched around her upper thighs.

"Well, if you do that, it won't be boring—but we also won't get much studying done." He forced himself to stand and untucked his shirt to hide how that flash of skin had aroused him. "I'll get your purse."

When he returned, she was sitting on the edge of

the couch, nervously wringing her hands. "Are you sure, Pierce? Because I feel kind of guilty. I mean, you must have better things to do than hang out with me while I study for a waitress job."

"I can't think of anything I'd rather do." He handed her the purse.

She shrugged and withdrew the menu from her purse. "Okay, well, I'll try to learn fast." She scanned the menu as she drank her wine. She glanced at him. "Do you want to go watch television or read or something?"

He realized he was standing beside the couch staring at her. It was hard not to when she looked hot, sexy, and smart all at once.

"Actually, I have a file I need to review for an acquisition. I'll be back in a second." He went down the hall to his home office and printed the file he needed, and when he returned, Rebecca was sitting across the couch with her knees pulled up and a pencil tucked behind her ear.

"You look so sexy, Bec. Maybe I should just spend my time studying you."

She laughed and slid him a coy look. "Bec? I love that. You'll get sick of looking at me after a few minutes, so go for it."

He sat on the couch by her feet, and she buried her toes under his thigh. Damn, he liked that as much as he liked the way *Bec* felt coming from his lips. She studied the menu, making notes along the margins, while he tried like hell to concentrate on the file in his lap and not to notice the way her dress had gathered at the base of her ass or how cute she looked when she crinkled her nose and closed her eyes as she studied. She didn't say a word, but just having her there with him felt good. Every so often, she'd wiggle her toes beneath his thigh, and without any thoughts, he massaged her calf. Working beside Rebecca was nice, and something he'd never done with a woman he was interested in. A comfortable silence settled in around them, and eventually he fell into focusing on his papers.

"Okay, ready to test me?" She leaned forward and touched his shoulder.

"Already?" He glanced at the clock and was surprised that more than an hour had passed.

She handed him the menu and wrapped her arms around her knees. "Go ahead. Ask me anything."

"Okay. Let's see." He scanned the menu, which wasn't the menu that was given to customers. It was a menu that included a brief description of major ingredients for each dish, along with information about how they were prepared. There was no way she'd memorized it that quickly. There must have been fifty or more items on the menu.

"Come on," she urged. "Just pick one. I don't think I'll remember them all, but I'm close."

"Okay, the first one. Chicken cordon bleu."

"Oh my gosh, that's so easy." She rattled off the meal description and preparation perfectly.

"Nice."

She threw her arms up into the air. "Score! Ha-ha! Told you!"

Her excitement was infectious. "Pasta primavera."

She rolled her eyes and once again aced it. She

knew every step of every dish he named.

"Are you a closet cook?" Pierce asked.

"No. I just organized it in my head. You know, poultry, red meat, fish; then I knock down to spices, sauces, creams. It's just like organizing a pantry, but it's in my brain."

He slid his finger down the column of her neck and along the ridge of her shoulder, touching the places that begged to be kissed. "I like that beautiful brain of yours."

Their eyes caught, and he gently moved her legs across his lap, buried his hand beneath her hair, and brought his lips to hers. He kissed her slowly, deeply, savoring every second, every delicious stroke of her tongue. She touched his cheek, and he swallowed a groan at the simple touch.

"Wow." It came out like a breeze. "All I needed was a smart brain and it earned me a kiss like that? You should see what I can do with spreadsheets."

"Oh, baby, talk dirty to me."

He took her in another kiss, disappearing into the scent of her, her sweet, delicious tenderness. She ran her fingers through his hair, kissing him hard and ravenous, then soft and subtle, notching up the heat stroke by mind-numbing stroke. When she slid onto his lap and wrapped her arms around his neck, all those confusing signals she'd been sending him for the past twenty-four hours became clearer. He let her control the kiss so as not to misconstrue her intentions. She ran her tongue along his lower lip, then lingered on the curve of his upper lip, drawing his eyes open. Her eyes were dark, seductive, teasing, and controlling all at once, as she trapped his lower lip between her teeth and drew back, then ran her finger over the slickness she'd left behind.

Holy. Hell.

"Rebecca." Sweet Jesus, she *was* as controlling as him. He arched his hips against her bottom. "Feel what you're doing to me?"

She lowered her cheek to his and whispered, "Oh, yes, I feel it."

He gripped her impossibly small waist as she licked his earlobe, then took it between her teeth. He groaned, despite himself, and forced himself to make sure she wasn't just playing with him. This didn't feel like playing.

He cupped her face and looked deeply into her eyes. "Talk to me, Bec." He'd already claimed the nickname as his own. "I want nothing more than to flip you onto your back and make love to you until everything you've memorized is forgotten, replaced with thoughts of us and memories of earth-shaking orgasms that leave you craving me every second of the day."

Every breath pulsed with anticipation as contemplation skirted across her face.

"Oh God, yes," she said quickly.

He wrapped one powerful arm around her, and in the next breath she was beneath him, the soft cushions of her breasts pressing against his chest, her hips writhing against his, as he claimed his control with another deep kiss. Soulful sounds of surrender seeped from her lungs into his.

Pierce's teeth grazed her lips. "I could kiss you all

night long."

Rebecca pulled his mouth back to hers, and Pierce felt the two of them spiraling together as they groped and pawed for more. He kissed her graceful neck, her shoulders, and ran his hands up her ribs. One gentle tug of her strapless dress freed her breasts. Two perfect mounds that he had to have.

"Sweet Jesus, Bec. You're too magnificent for words. Beautiful is too small a word; lovely is too soft. You're..." He raked his tongue over her nipple, feeling her body shudder beneath him. "Sinfully exquisite."

He filled his palm with one breast, brushing his thumb over her nipple again and again as he licked and sucked and took his fill of the other. Rebecca's breaths came fast and hitched as she fumbled with his shirt buttons. Pierce made quick work of divesting himself of his shirt, then drew her dress over her head and tossed it aside. She lay beneath him in a lacy white thong he wanted to tear off with his teeth, her body was more glorious than he could have imagined. She traced the dragon tattoo that snaked over his shoulder and around the top of his biceps and reached for him. He took hold of her rounded hip.

"I just want to feel you, to look at you." *To pay homage to your incredible body.*

"Three years is a long time," she whispered. "I feel like I can't breathe I'm so nervous."

Her honesty touched him, and he gave it right back to her. "I'm nervous, too. We don't have to go all the way." What was he saying? He was not the type of man who delayed gratification, but for Rebecca, he would. Hell, he was hard as a rock, ready to take her to places she'd never experienced before, but one look in her trusting eyes and he was struck right in the center of his chest. *Trust.* That's what had been missing before.

She didn't respond when he said they didn't have to go all the way, and she clung to his bare back like she was afraid he might disappear.

"Do you trust me, Rebecca?" He slid his hand down her thigh, stifling the desire to follow it with his mouth.

"I don't trust easily, but I do trust you."

Everything he'd been feeling came rushing forward with her admission. He kissed her again as she clung to him, her hands traveling up and down the muscles of his back, drawing out his need for her with every arch of her hips. He repressed the urge to move faster and kissed the corner of her lips.

"I love your lips." He kissed the ridge of her jaw. "And your neck." He kissed his way down between her full, mountainous breasts, pushed them together, and took both nipples into his mouth.

"Pierce, oh God, that feels good."

He laved them with his tongue, moving lower, gripping her rib cage and holding her tight. He wanted her to feel safe, in control. For her, he'd give her the control she so desperately needed.

"Tell me what you want, Becca. I won't do anything you don't want me to."

"Kiss me," she said in one long breath.

As he lowered his lips to hers, she whispered, "Not my lips."

Holy fuck, there was no misconstruing that

command. Pierce felt her breathing quicken as he kissed each of her ribs, caressing her hips as he moved lower, kissing, licking, tasting his way to those beautiful full curves. He ran his finger beneath the lacy thread of her thong and drew it down to her thigh on one side, then licked a path from the crease of her thigh back up that luscious hip.

"More," she pleaded.

He moved the other side of her thong down, revealing a soft tuft of curls. He forced himself to go slowly, licking the same path up the other crease of her hip, then kissed his way down to her thighs.

"Rebecca," he whispered. This was no endgame. This was totally new to him, totally different. His touch was softer, his words were honest, and everything he did was pulled directly from his heart.

"Touch me," she directed. "Pierce, I trust you. Touch me."

He drew off her panties and tossed them to the floor, leaving her naked, vulnerable, open. So very open. And he knew how hard that must be for her, so he loved her with the care that she deserved. He kissed around her damp curls, leaving her most intimate areas untouched. He licked the crease beside her sex, up one side, down the other, then took that sensitive skin in his teeth, drawing a gasp of need from Rebecca. She fisted her hands in his hair, causing him to throb with need.

She pushed his shoulders, urging him for more.

With a feathery touch, he dipped a fingertip into her wetness and felt her shudder beneath him again. He stroked her lightly as she rocked her hips.

"Please, Pierce," she begged.

He placed his thumbs on either side of her sex, holding her tight with his large hands as she trembled, wanting, arching for more. Her scent was intoxicating. He stroked her with his thumbs, painfully slowly, until she was drenched and eager, and then he dragged his tongue along her overly sensitive folds. She tasted so goddamn sweet, he had to go back for more.

"Oh...God."

She writhed against his mouth, spreading her legs further, opening up to him as he slid his fingers into her velvety center and drawing his tongue to the bundle of nerves that was swollen with need. He stroked and licked, sucked and nipped, as she gasped one breath after another.

"Oh God...Oh...God." She panted. "It's been...so long. I must have been—*Oh God*—waiting for you. You're so worth the wait."

She flexed her thighs, and he knew she was on the edge. He quickened his pace, driving his fingers deeper, flicking her clit with his tongue until her whole body tensed. She bucked against him, squeezing his fingers tight, in pulse after magnificent pulse. She clawed at his shoulders, and when he lifted his head, she pushed it back for more. Damn, she was amazing, and Pierce was more than happy to comply. He took her right back up to the edge and quickly learned the secrets of bringing her the ecstasy she craved. Her entire body shuddered and shook with one intense orgasm after another, and as the last of them released her from its grasp, she reached for him with a trembling arm, breathing heavily, eyes closed, and a gratified smile on her lips.

"Lie with me." She rolled onto her side, and he moved into the space behind her and spooned his body around hers.

Rebecca snuggled in against him, her bare back against his chest. A contented sigh slipped from her lips. Pierce closed his eyes, listening to the cadence of her breathing as she eased into sleep. He wasn't thinking about his ache to be inside her, or the fact that he was still hard. It was the feelings she stirred within him that had him moving carefully, so as not to wake her as he covered her with the throw blanket from the back of the couch. He closed his eyes, and for the first time in ages, he fell asleep beside a woman whom he wanted to wake up next to.

Chapter Seven

REBECCA WAS DRIFTING in the clouds. Everything felt sumptuous and sensual. The air smelled warm and familiar, and as she lay in the hazy state of not quite awake and not quite asleep, the discomfort she'd felt the last few mornings when she'd awoken in her car was missing. She reached for her blanket, unwilling to open her eyes and face the reality of the cold parking garage.

Coffee.

She smelled *coffee*, not grease and gasoline and cool concrete.

She rubbed her fingers along the silky material of the blanket that wasn't her cotton comforter.

Oh. Shit.

She clenched her eyes shut as the night came back in full color—and sound. *Oh God! Sound!* She reached beneath the blanket. *Naked. Oh. My. God.*

She had to open her eyes. She did. She knew she did, but just for a minute she wanted to remember what it felt like to be in Pierce's arms, on his lap, to have his—*Oh God*—mouth, fingers, tongue, inside her. Something deep inside her tightened and heated, pleading for more of him. She felt herself smile, then remembered she was naked and on his couch. She opened one eye and surveyed the living room. She sensed him before her eyes met his. How could she not have felt him?

Pierce sat at the end of the couch, his legs tucked behind her, with a thick file on his lap and a pen in his hand.

"Morning, beautiful." He was wearing the same dress pants from last night, shirtless, with all those planes of glorious muscle making her want him all over again.

"I'm so sorry. I didn't mean to fall asleep." She sat up and drew the blanket around her.

"Why are you sorry? I loved waking up with you in my arms."

She clutched the blanket against her. "I'm naked as a jaybird and you're..."

He looked down at his trousers. "Not?"

"Not."

"Well, I can always fix that." He wiggled his eyebrows and flashed an easy, sexy grin.

She splayed her hand over her face. "I left you high and dry." She peeked at him through her fingers. "That was rude. I'm so sorry."

"No, you're not." He set his file down and scooped her into his lap.

"Hey." She pushed away halfheartedly. The truth was, she remembered every single touch, every kiss, every blessed orgasm, and he was right; she craved more.

"You weren't kidding about control, little missy."

She didn't say a word. What could she say? *Yeah, I like to be in control? I know, and guys usually hate it? Thanks for playing along?*

He pressed his lips to hers. "It's okay. I liked it."

His breath was minty fresh, and she realized hers must be horrible morning-after breath. She clamped her mouth shut.

He tucked a lock of hair behind her ear. "I wouldn't kiss you if I minded morning breath."

He sealed his lips to her again, and her mind drifted again into some faraway place that felt wonderful and safe. She wrapped her arms around his neck, and oh yeah, this was what she remembered. Kissing Pierce was like being consumed by tenderness in one breath, and in the next, being taken and ravished. She felt the blanket fall from her shoulders, felt her nipples harden as they grazed his chest.

No, no, no. She had to gain control. Oh, but he felt so good. Just one hug; that's all she wanted. She deepened the kiss and pressed her chest to his. The skin-to-skin contact excited her even more. When their lips finally parted, her eyes were at half-mast, her breathing shallow, and her mind—forget her mind. It was lost.

Pierce gently gathered the blanket around her and handed her the edges.

"Come on, before I end up buried deep inside you and we spend the whole day in bed."

Holy smokes. Yes. Please.

No! She had things to do, didn't she? Study the menu? Look for a place to live? Go to the gym. Shower, for God's sake. She must stink. Although the way Pierce was nuzzling against her neck told her that she must not smell too bad.

"Shower?" he asked.

Shower? She shook away her jumbled thoughts and realized he was asking her if she wanted to take a shower. With him or alone? With him. *God, yes, with you, please.* What was happening to her? She'd never showered with a man before, and she was ready to jump in with Mr. Sweet 'n' Sexy.

"Oh, um. If you take me back to my car, I can shower at the gy—" She caught herself, and realized the gym was a reasonable answer. "I usually go to the gym in the mornings, so I can just wash up and then shower after I'm done there."

"You go to the gym in the morning? Great. I have a full gym downstairs."

Of course you do. "I usually go for a run while I'm there."

"Perfect." He kissed her chin. "I run, too. Let's go for a run together, then work out, shower, and spend the day getting to know each other better. Unless you have other plans."

"I would love that, but my gym bag is in my car back at the hotel."

He helped her to the floor, then secured the blanket around her again and picked up her folded dress, panties, and bra from the coffee table. How had she missed those? *Folded?*

"Let's wash up, eat some breakfast, and then we'll

get your bag. We can go by your place and pick up clothes if you want. Then we can come back here and work out." He took her hand and led her down a hallway.

My place? She could see his reaction. *Welcome to my car. I have two bedrooms, the front and the rear. Shoot me now. Please.*

"I don't know. I have to get that check to the bank." She thought about the things she needed to do. Definitely study the menu, but while she needed to find a place to live, she should at least wait until she started work to ensure she'd really have a paycheck coming in. She didn't want to jinx anything at this point. Absolutely nothing sounded better than spending the day with Pierce, but she wasn't used to spending so much time with anyone other than her mother, much less a man. A man whom she was quickly coming to like way too much too fast.

He folded her in his arms and touched his forehead to hers. Oh no, she really loved that. A lot. When he closed his eyes, her resolve softened. He was so tender and was such a good listener—and lover. Oh yes, an amazing lover. When he opened his eyes, they were serious again.

"Rebecca, did I totally misread you? Was last night supposed to be a one-night stand?" He drew back from her.

She clung to his waist, holding his body close to hers. She opened her mouth, but words didn't come. She swallowed, trying to figure out how to say what she needed to—*wanted* to. They'd been so open with each other last night, and it had felt natural. He was looking at her with his caring, dark eyes, filled with desire, and something warmer, deeper. Something so real and big it made her entire body fill with a sense of him.

"No, it wasn't supposed to be a one-night stand. Maybe it was supposed to be just a date, but..." She didn't understand why she felt the need to share what she felt after hiding behind thick, impenetrable walls for so many years. How had he torn them down without even trying? "But it felt like a lot more than a date. God, Pierce, I fell asleep in your arms. Naked. I don't *do* that."

"And?"

He was giving control over to her again, just as he had last night. How did he know what she needed? How did he know what fed her trust?

"And I liked it. A lot. But it's also scary for me. I'm not a wake-up-naked kind of girl." She turned away. "Especially in a house like this, with a guy like you." Then she remembered. She turned back and looked him in the eye. "You're a player, Pierce. You told me so, and I don't mean that judgmentally. I was kind of the same way a few years ago, but I'm just finding my footing again, and I can't afford to open my heart for a guy who's going to hurt me." A shiver of worry snaked up her spine right before her mother's words snuck in—*You matter, mi dulce niña*—easing her worries and giving her the approval she didn't realize she needed.

His brow furrowed, and he reached for her again. His eyes softened, reeling her right in. She actually felt her body melting to his touch, to all of him. She wasn't a melter, and she was powerless to fight the feeling that she was exactly where she belonged. And it scared her a little more.

"You're right. I've always been *that* guy." He kissed her forehead and this time she closed her eyes. If this was goodbye, she wanted to memorize the feel of his lips before she went back to her lonely, Pierceless car.

"I can't explain it, and as I said last night. I want to date you, Becca. I want to see where we go."

"But—"

"Please let me finish." His voice was a gentle caress, soothing her worries. "I can't make promises or declare my love for you, but I'm a man of my word. If I tell you that I want to date you, I'm not going to date other women, and, Rebecca, let me be very clear. I *want* to date you. I want to see where whatever this is between us takes us."

OhGodohGod.

"I don't want to scare you off, but I have to tell you that when you fell asleep in my arms, it was the first time I'd wanted to fall asleep with a woman in years, and when I woke up with you cuddled against me, I didn't want to move." He searched her eyes, and he must have read her mind, because what he said next softened the lingering sharpness of her worries.

"I don't want to save you, Rebecca. But I get the feeling that we were supposed to come together, and I think maybe you were supposed to save me."

Chapter Eight

THEY WERE DRIVING back to the Astral to get Rebecca's gym bag from her car. He'd seen her struggling with the decision, but he knew she felt the same attraction winding its way around them and binding them together as he did. She'd finally agreed to spend the day with him.

"Why don't we swing by your place and pick up whatever you need?" It was a breezy morning, and all she had was the dress she'd worn last night. He wanted her to have whatever clothing or personal items she needed—and he didn't want her to have any excuses to leave. Call it control, or call it the newness of their relationship. Whatever it was he was feeling, it was bigger than anything he'd ever felt before and he wasn't about to ignore it.

Rebecca looked up from the menu she was studying. "It's okay. I always keep extra clothes in my car."

"Should that worry me?" He arched a brow.

She playfully smacked his arm. "Not for those reasons, you gross hog. Just in case I spill something on my clothes."

"Okay, but I don't mind if you want to. I'd like to see where you live."

"Trust me, you're not missing anything." They pulled into the parking garage. "I'm on the fourth floor, aisle C."

He pulled up behind her car and opened his door. She grabbed his arm. "I've got it. I'll only be a second."

"Nonsense. I'm a guy. I open doors *and* car trunks." He stepped from the car, and Rebecca hurried toward her trunk.

"It's embarrassing how messy my trunk is. I'd really feel better if you didn't see it. Please? It's like seeing a messy room."

"It's a trunk, Bec." He reached for her keys, and she lifted her hand out of his reach.

"Okay, fine." She put the key in her trunk and then drew in a deep breath. "You know what? I need my purse. I want to throw a few things in it. Would you mind grabbing it for me?"

"Not at all." He went around to the passenger seat. "Finally, you let me do something for you." He ducked into the car, and when he came back around with her purse, she had already retrieved her clothes and gym bag from the trunk.

"All set?" She snagged her purse and tossed her keys in.

"I thought you wanted to put something in your purse." He eyed her trunk.

"Yeah, well, I decided not to. Come on. I should

really get to the bank."

Pierce had a sinking feeling in his stomach that there was something she wasn't telling him.

They went to the bank to deposit Rebecca's check and then went back to Pierce's house to go for a run. He could barely believe he was with a woman who actually enjoyed running as much as he did. He had to slow his pace, but not by much. Rebecca was surprisingly athletic. They ran three and a half miles, and when they got back to his place, they paced the driveway while they cooled down.

"I've never run with a guy before," Rebecca admitted. She looked hot in her running bra and spandex shorts. Her body was lean and fit, but still held womanly curves, so different from most of the pin-thin women in his circles. He felt like a kid lusting after a crush, the way his eyes were drawn to her.

"Can't say I've ever gone for a run with a woman before, either. It was fun."

"It was fun, although I'm sure I slowed you down. Thank you for that." She walked over to him and touched his waist. "I thought I knew all about fast-talking guys like you. I warned myself that night I met you not to get too close to a guy like you."

He smiled at the memory of her piss-ass angry as she stormed out of the bar. "You warned yourself about a guy like me?"

"Pretty much. A girl's got to protect herself, but then I realized you're anything but a fast talker. You slowed down for me in more ways than just during your run."

"You're worth it. But, Becca, should I worry about

a woman like you? Is there something you're not telling me? Because guys can get hurt, too." He was falling hard for her, and the thought of her hiding something that could threaten their relationship had been on his mind since they'd gone to retrieve her bag from her car.

"What do you mean?"

He shrugged. "You tell me." He felt a twinge of guilt over not telling her that he owned the resort, and he pushed it away. He'd tell her soon.

"I'm not sure I understand." She reached for his hand. "I told you what my past was like. I didn't hide anything."

"Just assure me you're not really married, or running from something dangerous." He tightened his grip on her hand so she couldn't escape the question. He had to know, and it didn't matter how much he liked her. Better to know now than to find out after his heart had taken the plunge into never-never land.

"What would ever give you that crazy idea? I've never been married, and I'm not running from anything." She pulled the elastic band from her hair and shook her hair free, looking sexy as hell as she slipped the elastic band around her wrist and closed the distance between them. Her hands were warm on his bare skin, and the way she looked at him, like she really liked him, softened his worry. "Did I miss something?"

"No, I'm sorry. I just..." He leaned down and kissed her rather than explaining, and when she pressed her body to his, he was instantly aroused.

"Mm," she mumbled against his lips. "This is what

a run does to you?"

"This is what *you* do to me."

AFTER THEY WORKED out, Pierce left Rebecca to shower alone—partially to give her privacy and partially to keep from rushing her into going any further, even though the whole time she was in the bathroom he could think of nothing else than lathering her up and how her soapy body would feel against him. To take his mind off of Rebecca, he pulled out his phone and checked his voicemail. He had two calls from his brother Wes.

"Dude, do you *ever* turn on your phone? Call me." He deleted the message and listened to the next one. "Holy Christ, Pierce. What are you doing out there in Reno? How do you get anything done? Pick up your damn phone."

Pierce dialed Wes's number, and it went straight to voicemail.

"Hey, buddy. Sorry I missed your calls. Forgot to turn my phone on. Catch up when you can." Pierce ended the call and eyed the bedroom, then turned away as he began to imagine Rebecca's naked body again.

After they showered and had breakfast, they took in an early-afternoon movie, and in the evening they ate dinner on the patio again. Pierce could get used to this. In fact, as they cuddled together and watched the sun set, he *was* getting used to it. Rebecca was tucked beneath his arm, like the space was made just for her. One of her hands rested on his abs, and every so often she'd touch his skin beneath his T-shirt. He was aroused, but more than that, he realized that he was happy. Truly happy and content, just sitting right there with her. As the day progressed, Rebecca's edginess had ceased. The transformation was like watching a person with emphysema breathe through new lungs. He felt himself changing, too. They'd talked all day about their lives, his siblings, and a myriad of other topics, but she hadn't asked about what exactly he did for a living. As much as he loved that she didn't seem to care, he wanted to tell her before she started work on Monday. There was no way that he was going to be able to hide the fact that he was dating her, and he knew it was only a matter of time before someone mentioned him by name. He worried that if she found out from someone else, it might change things between them, and even though the relationship was new, he wasn't about to risk it.

"What do you usually do on Saturday nights?" Rebecca asked.

"Work, mostly. I haven't spent a Saturday like this in a very long time." He pulled her closer and kissed the top of her head. "How about you?"

"Work, usually. It's weird not to have a job to go to today, but I'm really looking forward to starting work on Monday. I know that probably sounds silly, since you work in the executive offices, but to me, the job holds the opportunity for a future." She looked up at him and slid her hand under his shirt again.

Work in the executive offices. Hearing the words made him feel like a liar, and he didn't like that feeling at all, especially where it concerned Rebecca. "It's not silly at all. Becca, I want to tell you something."

"Wait." She pressed her face to his chest and settled her hand over his heart. "You're a little nervous, which is different from how your heart felt when you were turned on. Should I worry?"

"You can tell that from touching my chest?" He couldn't see her face, but he sensed her smile.

"No. It's a cheek-hand combo thing. I learned it when my mom was sick. It's just intuition or something, I think. I could always tell when my mom was scared. She'd never tell me. Even right before she died, I asked her if she was afraid to die, and she looked me in the eye. I remember her eyes were so puffy from the medications and treatments that they were almost closed, and she was so tired, it was hard for her. She said, *No, mi dulce niña. Nothing scares me anymore. I know you'll be okay.*"

He rested his forehead on hers. "She was worried about you more than herself." He gathered her in his arms and held her tight. "I wish I could bring her back for you." He had an overwhelming feeling of not only wanting to protect her, but wanting to bring her happiness.

"You can't think like that. That's why people don't move on, and I can't afford to get stuck in the *if onlys.*" Her voice was so serious that he pulled back and looked into her eyes again to try to decipher why she was so upset. "I'm not coldhearted. I miss my mom like crazy." She pressed her palms to his chest again. "I can't live in the past, Pierce. I'm moving forward with my mom in my heart, but not longing for something that can never happen. She's not coming back, but her memory will drive me forward." Her brows were knitted together. As if she'd had to shift from the place her mind was in to something else a million times over recent days—which she probably did. She breathed deeply, and the worry lines on her forehead disappeared. "What did you want to tell me?"

He had so many emotions rushing through him that he didn't want to try to pick them apart. He just wanted to be closer to her—to climb into her skin and keep anything bad or upsetting away from her. When their lips met, he lost all hope of doing anything else. His insides were clawing for more, demanding more of her, and she was kissing him back like she couldn't breathe without him, stimulating every erotic nerve he had, bringing his body to life with an insatiable appetite for her. He gathered her in his arms and carried her inside, down the hall, and to his bedroom. He'd pictured her in his bed a million times since he'd met her, and now that she was in his arms, kissing him, moaning hungrily and relinquishing herself to him, she was bringing words like *love* and *forever* to mind.

He stood in the dimly lit room holding her in his arms, kissing her like they only had this moment. And she was hot. So damn hot his mind nearly got lost in her and forgot to tell his legs to move. He lowered her feet to the floor, and she whimpered against his lips.

"I like being in your arms. I've never been in someone's arms before."

He lifted her again. "Jesus, Becca. I'm falling for you, and I barely know you."

She pressed her hands to his cheeks and kissed him eagerly, lovingly. Adoringly. Like he'd never been kissed before. Her hands slid to the back of his neck, and she ran her fingers through his hair, driving him crazier, sending fresh shocks of lust through his body like wildfire. She arched her neck, and his mouth met her heated skin. He dragged his teeth over the arc of her shoulder, and she guided his mouth lower and released her hands long enough to draw her shirt over her head and drop it to the floor.

"Becca, I've got to put you down. I need to touch you, to feel you beneath me, to feel your legs around me. I need to disappear inside of you." *I need to love you.*

She grabbed his cheeks again and took him in a deep, greedy kiss, heightening his need.

"Is that a yes? Because I don't want to get kneed in the groin."

She laughed. "Yes. Yes, Pierce. Hurry."

"Oh, baby, I might be anxious to get inside you, but I'm not going to rush making love to you." He lowered her to her feet, and she wiggled out of her jeans and panties, stealing the thrill of him doing it. He took her by the shoulders and stared into her eyes. "I don't know what you're used to, but one day you're going to let me be the man I am and rip those damn clothes off of you, hold your frigging doors open, and open your goddamn trunk."

Her eyes widened; then she frantically pushed his shirt up, and he ripped it over his head while she fumbled with the button on his jeans. He kicked them off and Rebecca's eyes dropped.

"Holy smokes." Her lips spread in a wide smile.

She pressed her hands to his chest and raised her

brows, before slithering down his body and taking him into her mouth. He stilled at the feel of her lips pressed around his arousal and her tongue circling the tip. He tangled his hands in her hair, helping her efforts as she drew him in and out of her mouth, stroking and sucking him hungrily, taking him right up to the goddamn edge of release. He tugged her head back, and she licked her lips, leaving them wet and inviting.

"You're a dirty girl." He lifted her easily and laid her on the bed.

"You have no idea," she said with a wicked look in her eyes. "Get over here."

"Demanding, aren't we?"

He grabbed a condom from his dresser drawer and tore it open with his teeth. Rebecca pushed his hand away and rose to take him in her mouth again. *Holy fuck.* He gritted his teeth against the best damn feeling he'd ever felt, and when she tickled his balls, she owned him. Completely, utterly owned him. He gripped her wrist and pulled it away from his body. She smiled up at him—*smiled*—her luscious mouth open wide as she flicked the head of his thick length with her tongue. Jesus, he was never going to last with her doing that shit. He yanked her head back, and kneeling over her, he crashed his mouth over hers in a collision of tongues and teeth. He tore away long enough to roll on the condom.

"Are you sure, babe?" He was breathing so hard he could barely spit the words out. "No misunderstandings. It's still okay if you want to back out."

She narrowed her eyes and guided him between

her legs. "Take me, Pierce. Now."

Done.

He drove into her deep and fast, until he was buried to the hilt, and he forced himself to lie still, to enjoy her—but it didn't last. He had to move, to feel and taste her. Everything in the dimly lit room fell away; there was only him and Rebecca and this heated, intimate moment when his heart dripped with emotions. And the look in her eyes as she reached up and touched his cheek, like she felt it too, like she was the absent piece of his heart he never knew was missing. It was a feeling he would never forget.

"Don't move," she whispered.

"Am I hurting you?"

Her lips curved up. "No, Pierce. You're completing me."

Chapter Nine

"I THINK I'M addicted to you." Pierce wrapped his arms around Rebecca from behind. He nuzzled against her neck, and when she reached behind her and ran her fingers through his hair, he nipped at her earlobe. "Careful, or you'll be late for your first day of work."

They'd spent much of Sunday making love and experiencing the pleasures of each other's bodies, parting only out of need for nourishment or to reluctantly spend an hour here or there seeing to their responsibilities. Rebecca studied for her new position, while Pierce prepared for his upcoming acquisition, and when the alarm went off Monday morning, they'd reached for each other again.

She turned in to him and cupped him through his trousers. "Mm. If I let go, will you remember to turn your phone on so Wes doesn't get mad at you again?"

He'd missed another call from Wes, and Rebecca had heard Wes giving him shit about it. It was such a usual occurrence that Pierce had already forgotten the incident. He held her sensual gaze and tried to act cool. "How do you know it's not on?"

She arched a brow.

"Fine." He took out his phone and turned it on, privately loving that she remembered, surely saving him from missing calls that he'd have to pay for later.

Rebecca hadn't asked about Pierce's work, or the documents he'd been poring over. And even though he loved knowing that she liked him for *him*, not for what he owned or what he represented, he wanted to tell her that he didn't just work in the executive offices. If there was one thing Pierce was sure of, it was that honesty mattered. His mother had drilled that into his mind from a young age. Pierce wasn't used to *wanting* to expose his life, or his wealth, to anyone, but this weekend, whether they were laughing over breakfast, teasing throughout the day, or sharing their most intimate secrets, he felt the earth shifting, and he felt himself evolving with every passing hour. He wanted to nurture that change, and he wanted to nurture their relationship.

"Becca." He brought his lips to hers and kissed her softly. "Bec, I don't want any secrets between us." She was dressed for work in a black pencil skirt and white button-down blouse. She looked professional and so sexy that Pierce felt a flash of jealousy when he watched her dress. Now he felt her body tense within his arms.

"I need to tell you something, and I hope it won't change anything between us."

She drew back with a furrowed brow, and he brought her close again. "Stay close to me, so I can feel your heartbeat against mine." Ever since she'd said that she could read his feelings by his heartbeat, he'd been reaching out more, trying to become just as in tune to her as she was to him—and holy Christ was she in tune with him.

He tucked her hair behind her ear, hoping that she wouldn't suddenly turn into one of those money-hungry women he loathed. "I don't just work in the executive offices of the Astral. I own it."

She smiled. "Own what?"

"The Astral Resort—and about thirty-two other properties around the world. Thirty-three if all goes well with an upcoming meeting."

He felt her heartbeat quicken. But her eyes didn't widen, and she didn't smile or look impressed. Her lack of response made Pierce's stomach sink.

"You *own* them? Like, your name is on the deed, own them?"

He nodded, focusing on keeping her close.

She dropped her eyes to his chest, and when she looked up at him again, she looked confused. "I don't understand."

"I own the properties. I—"

"No, not that. I'm not stupid. I understand that you own them, but why would that change things between us?" Now her eyes widened, and when she took a step back, he gathered her close again.

"You mean you don't want people to know you're dating a waitress?"

"No. No, Bec. That's not what I mean at all."

"I'm confused. So what if you own a million properties? How does that change things between us?

I'm a waitress. You're a business owner." She shrugged. "Big deal." She said it easily, as if she'd said, *I'm a girl, and you're a boy*, and her smile was so sweet and genuine that he almost fell over. "That's what we do, Pierce. It doesn't define us or change us as people."

"Are you for real?" The whisper in his voice surprised him.

"Do you mean because I'm not jumping up and down because you own the resort?"

He kissed her softly. "Yes, that's exactly what I mean."

"Pierce, we're dating, not getting married. I don't need your money. I've never needed anyone's money in my life. I'm a little bothered that you'd even think it would change things between us. But honestly, it's a relief, too, because I thought you were trying to tell me that you didn't want people to know you were dating a waitress, and then I might have had to knee you in the groin for being shallow."

He folded her into his arms. "I wish I'd known your mother."

"I wish you had, too. She'd have given you all sorts of shit for being such a pretty boy." She went up on her tiptoes and kissed his lips.

"Pretty boy?"

"You know, so good-looking that you're almost too pretty?"

He tickled her ribs and she shrieked. "I'm kidding!" He grabbed her ribs again, and she doubled over in laughter. "Okay." She laughed. "Okay. You're manly and rugged and kinda ugly." She ran out of the kitchen in her bare feet, and he trapped her against the living room wall.

"Kinda ugly, am I?" He rocked his hips against hers. "I'll show you kinda ugly."

"Well, you do have a huge—"

"Hey!"

"*Heart*, you pig. Although that other thing makes up for your prettiness, too." She kissed the bottom of his chin and rubbed her hand over his shoulder. "And you have a hot tattoo, which by the way, I'd love to hear the story behind."

"Maybe one day I'll tell you. If you can get past my prettiness." He took her in a sensuous kiss, and when he drew away, she was breathless. Just as he'd hoped. "See you tonight, babe." He headed for the door.

"Tonight? I don't live here."

He turned back. "Wow. Am I *that* used to you being around? You're not going to steal my stuff, are you?" He took a step toward the door.

"Wait. You're leaving me here? I don't have my car."

"God, I forgot." He truly had. "Get your sexy little ass in gear."

She wiggled her butt and slipped her feet into her heels.

"Christ, Rebecca. You're like a walking centerfold. The customers are going to love you." He handed Rebecca her purse and slipped his arm around her waist. "I've never been jealous a day in my life, and just the thought of you around those flashy high rollers has my stomach twisting in knots."

"Oh, please. Do I look like I can be wooed any easier than you can?"

Most of the women he'd dated treated him as if they were lucky to be with him. Rebecca never did, and that confidence made her sexier than a pretty face and hot body ever could.

"No, you don't, but will you do me a favor?" He locked the door behind them, and they headed out to the car.

"Maybe."

"Can you make yourself less attractive when you're with the customers?"

She stuck her front teeth out like a beaver. "Is this better?"

"Much."

THE ASTRAL RESORT was known for the casino, but the restaurants were close behind, with stellar reputations and world-renowned chefs. Even at seven thirty in the morning, the kitchen Rebecca was working in smelled heavenly. Rebecca had been paired with Daphne Wrigley for her training period, which she was thrilled about because they'd hit it off right away. Daphne had a mass of fiery red corkscrew curls cropped just below her ears, catlike green and slightly slanty eyes, and flawless olive skin, save for a spray of freckles across the bridge of her upturned nose. She had to be in her fifties, at least, but her snarky attitude made her seem much younger.

"Always look the customers in the eye, and if they get touchy, which they will, just fend them off with smiles, and lots of *darlins* or *if only I wasn't married*." Daphne lifted Rebecca's left hand and looked at her ring finger. "It doesn't matter that you're not really married."

"Flirt well, got it."

"Bigger tips that way." Daphne glanced at Rebecca's butt. "Shake it, wiggle it, shift it around, and your tips will triple."

"Triple?" Pierce would love that. He'd looked so cute when he was jealous. She'd never been with a man who was jealous, and she liked the way he'd handled it with humor instead of in a controlling fashion that would have sent her running for the hills—and running was the last thing she wanted to do.

"Triple." Daphne pointed out where to turn in her orders and showed her around the kitchen so she'd know exactly what she was doing.

She had been trying not to think about the fact that Pierce owned the resort, but it was hard not to as she took in the massive stainless-steel kitchen with twenty or more employees bustling about. How did one person manage to own so many resorts? It seemed overwhelming to her, but Pierce was perfectly at ease. The few times he'd been reading over his documents or on the phone, discussing business, he was completely focused and serious, but as soon as he hung up, he was perfectly relaxed with her again. He'd even gone from a heated discussion with a man named Jeff to the bedroom with Rebecca five minutes later and, good Lord, the man didn't miss a beat. She realized now that she hadn't thought to ask if they should keep their relationship on the down low, but she assumed so, given his position.

"Did you memorize the whole menu?" Daphne

asked.

"Of course. Marlow tested me on it." Marlow was the kitchen manager. She was a serious woman with stern, beady eyes and a forced smile. Luckily, she didn't appear to micromanage, considering that she'd handed Rebecca over to Daphne and then disappeared.

"Great." Daphne pressed her shoulder to Rebecca's and lowered her voice. "If a customer asks you how something's made and you forget, just compliment them on what they're wearing or their hair or something. They always forget and move on." She nodded as if she knew all the tricks, which Rebecca was sure she did.

The breakfast rush kept her on her toes, but orders were simple morning fare. No complications other than gluten-free waffles and egg whites. That she could handle. When it came time for her lunch break, Daphne pulled her aside.

"Whatever you do, make sure you're back on time. Marlow hates tardiness."

"I'm just going to look over the employee board to see if I can find a room to rent."

"You're looking for a room?" Daphne's eyes widened.

"Yeah, if I can find one I can afford."

"I haven't posted it, but Henry and I are looking for someone to rent a room."

"Henry?" They'd been so busy that Rebecca and Daphne hadn't had time to get to know each other on a personal level yet.

"My husband. Been married forever, hon. He's a

good man, my Henry." Daphne's voice softened. "You know what they say: Bad things happen to good people, and my Henry, well, he's a little older than me." She patted her hair. "He's sixty-seven, and I'm...*forty* something." She winked. "We women count backward when we hit fifty. Anyway, he was laid off from his accounting job at the newspaper six months ago, and we were okay for a while, but things are tight. He's a little embarrassed about having to rent a room, but we do what we need to."

"Well, no one knows that better than me." Rebecca felt like she could confide in Daphne. She leaned in close and whispered, "I've had to stay in my car for a few days."

"Oh, Rebecca." Daphne placed her hand on her forearm and squeezed. "Hon, we own a three-bedroom house about ten minutes from here. Let's see if we can help each other. Do you smoke?"

"No."

"Into late-night partying?" Daphne arched a brow.

"No." Rebecca hadn't had a roommate other than her mother for so long that she'd almost forgotten about worries like smoking and partying all night long.

"Drugs?" Daphne asked.

"No. Really, I'm pretty boring."

"Do you have a boyfriend?"

"Yes. Our relationship is still sort of new." It felt really good to say that. *A boyfriend.* She had a boyfriend. *Oh my God, I have a boyfriend.*

"Is he trouble? Because we don't want guys knocking down our door at midnight, or freaking out and causing fights. No loose cannons." Daphne put her hand on her hip and shook her head.

"He's not anything like that. He's..." *Dreamy*. "He's a professional, very nice. He won't cause any trouble." *Dreamy? Holy cow. Dreamy? What kind of word is that, anyway? That's never even been in my vocabulary.*

"I guess given your situation, you're looking for a place ASAP?"

"Now. Today. This second." It dawned on her that she might not be able to afford the room. "How much is the rent?"

"Three hundred, utilities included. Oh, and the room is furnished, so if you have furniture, it may not work." Daphne touched her arm again. "Please tell me you want to see it."

"I do, yes, but honestly, as long as your husband isn't a crazed rapist or serial killer, I don't even care what the room looks like. I'll take it."

Daphne's eyes widened. "For real?"

"For real. Thank you." Rebecca said a silent thank-you to her mother, whom she was sure had found more of those heavenly strings after all.

Rebecca took down the address from Daphne and made arrangements to follow her over after work; then she retrieved her purse and went into the break room to check her texts. She was so excited about a finding a place to live that she was ready to burst. *I'm doing it, Mom. I'm going to be okay.* She realized that it had been so long since she'd had any exciting news to share, other than this job, which she'd shared with Pierce, that she didn't have anyone to tell. She would tell Andy when she went back to the gym, but when she saw that she'd received a text from Pierce at eight o'clock that morning, sadness pressed in around her. She couldn't share this with him. He didn't know she'd been sleeping in her car, and if she could help it, he wouldn't find out until it was part of her past, not her present.

She read his text. *What have you done to me? I can't concentrate on a darn thing but you.* She held her phone against her chest, relishing in the warmth flushing through her body and memories of the look in his eyes when they were making love last night.

She thought of how sincere he'd been when he'd said, *Bec, I don't want any secrets between us,* and the way he looked at her when he'd asked if she was running from something. Maybe she was running after all. Running from a world of pitiful looks and sighs. Running from what she could have been if she weren't as determined as she was. But she couldn't tell him that, either.

No, she couldn't tell him any of it. As painful as it had been when she'd pretended not to know why he'd asked her if she wasn't telling him something, or if she was married, she'd had to do it. Pierce had a big heart, and if he'd heard she was staying in her car, he would have wanted to save her. It wasn't his fault he was chivalrous. He just was, and she loved that about him as much as she disliked it when it came to her circumstances.

No, this was one secret—*the only secret*—she'd ever keep from him, and as soon as they were together long enough, she'd reveal that secret to him carefully. He would have to understand that she held it back only to allow their relationship to grow and flourish, pity-free.

ACQUISITIONS WERE LIKE heroin. The mere thought of them brought a rush of adrenaline, and the craving for the next one never receded. Pierce had always been that way. Even as a kid, if he wanted something that belonged to one of his siblings, he'd strategize and plan, then negotiate until it was his. Pierce loved almost every step of the decision-making process, from deciphering the numbers and quantifying the return on investments to the actual negotiations. The only part of the process that wasn't invigorating was the due diligence process. Pierce didn't like to wait for answers, and he abhorred dishonesty. When he found a snake in the grass, which he had many times in his business dealings, it not only pissed him off, but pushed him from reasonable to ruthless.

This week his team of financial experts were handling the due diligence for the Grand Casino. He wanted the Grand in a bad way. It was an older property that sat on a prime piece of real estate, riddled with promise. He was sure he could make it rise to success, but when he'd met with the owner, he'd gotten a bad vibe. It was all he could do to wait out the process and hope he was wrong. He had a feeling he wasn't. He trusted his gut, and his gut told him something was off. Now it was a waiting game. Mr. In Control had zero control over how things would turn out during the due diligence process, and he hated the feeling of being at anyone's mercy.

Except Rebecca's. He smiled as the memory of her taking control thrummed through him. In the blink of an eye, Rebecca went from lying beneath him, savoring every thrust and every kiss, to pushing him onto his back and driving him out of his mind as she teased and tasted, then rode him hard until they both went a little crazy. Relinquishing control in the bedroom wasn't new to Pierce. He'd give women a little room to play before. Usually that's all it was, playtime. Something a woman might do to keep his interest and add a little zest to a sexual tryst. But Rebecca brought control to a whole new level. The way she touched him, holding his hips firmly against the mattress while she made sweet love to him with her mouth and taking him right up to the edge and then moving away, leaving him throbbing, aching, pleading for more.

Shit. He was getting hard just thinking about it.

It was five o'clock in the afternoon, and between thoughts of Rebecca and the due diligence that was taking place, every minute had felt like there was a fire under his ass, making it impossible for him to sit still. He'd attended several meetings, and finally he'd taken a walk to the security room, where he was able to sneak a peek at Rebecca in the restaurant through the video surveillance monitors. He'd seen her waiting on tables, looking professional and beautiful, and he filled with pride and much, much more.

What is it about you, Bec?

"Something wrong, sir?" Chappie, the security manager, had asked.

"No. Just had a few minutes and wanted" —*to see the woman who is turning me inside out*—"to see how things were going."

139

He'd wanted to head down during lunch to say hello, but since it was her first day of work, he didn't want to create an issue. He knew damn well that the minute anyone found out they were dating, she'd be treated differently, as if she were a direct line to promotions and greatness. It was one reason he'd never dated his employees. He'd been chased by many, some probably not intent only on sleeping their way to a better position, but some, he was sure, had chased him solely for that purpose. There were plenty of cards on the table, and he didn't need to deal from the house deck. He could thank Treat for that advice. It was good advice, too, except now he *was* dating someone who worked for him, even if he'd gone out with her prior to her actually being hired.

And he wasn't about to stop dating Rebecca, or pretend they weren't a couple. But he didn't need to make her first day difficult or confusing, even if staying away from her for more than eight hours was quite possibly the most difficult thing he'd had to do all day.

He collected his files for the evening with the hopes of seeing Rebecca for dinner. They'd made plans to meet after work, and when his phone vibrated, he hoped it was her. A quick glance at the screen told him it was his sister, Emily, and disappointment washed over him.

"Hey, Em. How's it going?"

"Crazy good. I've got a big passive house project for a school in Denver. I'm really excited about it. How are you?" Emily was tall, slender, and as pretty as she was sharp, with dark eyes and brown hair that she wore to the middle of her back.

"Great. We started the due diligence on that casino I told you about a few weeks ago." Emily was five years younger than Pierce, and growing up as the only girl in a family of six kids had made her tougher than most women. But Pierce and Emily were close, and he knew that as sharp-witted as Emily was, she was equally as sensitive. He worried about her.

"Good luck. I hope it goes well. I was talking to Max the other day, and she said she and Treat are having dinner with you this week."

"Yeah, they are. They just confirmed this morning for Thursday night."

"So...are you going to tell me who she is or do I have to ask?"

Pierce had been wondering what had spurred the call from Emily, and now he understood. Emily loved to be in the thick of her brothers' love lives, and earlier that morning he'd told Treat that he wanted to bring Rebecca to dinner with them. The Braden grapevine had obviously picked up speed.

"Seriously? It's been what, a few hours since I told Treat I was bringing Rebecca to dinner?" He pictured Emily's eyes wide, a grin on her face. He was sure the whole family had heard by now, or would hear within ten minutes of their call.

"Rebecca. I like her name."

"Em." He shook his head. "It's dinner, not an engagement."

"I know, but you never bring women to family events, and even though it's Treat and Max, they're family, so..."

"So you assume it's something more than a date?" Which it totally was.

"Yup."

He let her answer hang in the air between them, knowing it would only irritate her. He loved Emily, and he didn't even mind that she pried into his love life on occasion, but she was fun to get a rise out of.

"Pierce! You're not going to tell me anything? How about just how long you've been dating?"

"Em."

"Give me something. Are you bringing her to Luke's engagement party?" Her voice was so hopeful it made Pierce smile.

"Honestly, you're jumping the gun, Emily. I'm not even sure she'll come to dinner with Treat and Max. I just wanted the option there. I haven't asked her yet." After their intimate weekend together, he assumed that they'd be spending much of their free time together. Now he wondered if he was the one jumping the gun.

"Okay, that's got me even *more* excited. You would never tell Treat about a woman unless you really, really liked her." She squealed.

"God, Emily. You need a boyfriend."

"Yeah, tell me about it. My brothers are dropping into Loveland like flies. You guys whore away your merry lives while I'm the one hoping for love, and then these amazing women drop from the sky and fulfill your every dream. Totally unfair, Pierce."

His heart went out to her. It *was* unfair. Emily deserved to be happy, and she deserved to be with a man who would love all the things about her that he and his brothers did—including her stubborn attitude and quick wit. "You're right, Emily. If any of us deserves a great relationship, it's you. Life's weird that way."

"Tell me about it. All the good men are either taken or gay."

He pictured her in her office overlooking the Colorado Mountains, surrounded by drawings of her latest project and daydreaming about finding Mr. Right.

"There's an idea. You could get a sex change, bat for the other team." He laughed.

"You laugh. I might just do that." She sighed. "Well, I just have one question for you, big brother. What is it about Rebecca that flicked your internal switch from *playboy* to *boyfriend*?"

"Boyfriend?" He hadn't aligned himself with that word in years. *Boyfriend*. Hm. He liked that where Rebecca was concerned.

"That's what Max said, that Rebecca was your girlfriend. Isn't she? I mean, you wouldn't bring her to meet Treat and Max if she was just another casino floozy."

"No, I definitely wouldn't. Yeah, I guess I am her boyfriend. It's all very new, Em. And, to be honest, very powerful. Unreal." He leaned back in his leather chair and turned toward the window, remembering how ethereal their first kiss had been, and how things had magnified ever since.

"I want *unreal*. You're lucky, Pierce. I'm happy for you."

"Thanks, Em. When do you leave for Tuscany?"

Emily had been bummed lately, feeling lonely and needing some excitement in her life, so their brother Wes had bought Emily tickets to go see a villa in Tuscany she'd been dying to see. They each had trust funds that had been passed down for generations, but their mother had brought them up to be frugal, and Emily would never have dipped into those funds for what she would call a frivolous trip. The irony was that it wasn't frivolous at all. She'd earned it in so many ways. Emily had always tried to take care of her brothers, even though she was younger than all but Luke. She watched out for them, helped them anytime they asked, and she was their biggest cheerleader in everything they did. Pierce only hoped that Emily felt the same love coming back to her.

"I put it off until after the project I mentioned is done. Then I can go with a clear head. I'm excited. It gives me something to look forward to. Hey, Pierce, do you need me to pick up a gift for Luke and Daisy for you?"

Normally he'd have jumped at the chance to have Emily pick out something nice for his brother and future sister-in-law, but as he gazed out the window, he envisioned picking something out with Rebecca.

"That's okay. I'll pick something up. Thanks, though. Oh, and when you share the Pierce and Rebecca gossip with everyone, do me a favor and make me look good. Tell them I'm playing hard to get, going down kicking and screaming."

"Well, are you?"

He pictured a smirk on her face. "Not even close."

Chapter Ten

REBECCA PULLED UP in front of Daphne's house wearing the smile that had been plastered on her face for the entire day. She'd texted Pierce before leaving to follow Daphne home, and they'd made plans to meet at his place later that evening. She had wondered if three nights in her car would turn into three years and if she were just fooling herself into believing that she'd find a way back to a more livable home. She could hardly believe she'd gotten lucky enough to find a place to live so quickly, and an affordable one at that. It would have taken her forever to afford a place to live while working for ten dollars an hour at the bar. Luckily, she'd saved every penny she'd earned before quitting, and Daphne had wanted only the first month's rent and a security deposit of half of a month's rent, which left Rebecca with a little cash in her pocket, and she'd also be earning enough to pay Mr. Fralin, as promised.

She stepped from the car and surveyed the quaint

brick rambler. The house was fairly benign, with three average-sized windows and a black front door. The front yard was small but neatly manicured, and it would have blended in with the other ramblers on the street if not for the lovely maple tree that stood tall and full just to the left of the driveway.

Daphne flung her arms into the air. "Welcome to our humble abode."

"It's really nice." Daphne had been a big help to her throughout the morning, giving her tips on which regular customers were pickier than others, and when she'd seen Rebecca texting Pierce at the end of their shift, Daphne had thrown her arm over her shoulder as if they'd known each other forever and peeked at the message. *Sexting your boyfriend?* she'd joked. Rebecca had felt her cheeks flush at the comment. She hadn't had a boyfriend in years, and when she was caring for her mother, sex had been the farthest thing from her mind. And before that, sex had been vanilla, whereas making love with Pierce was spicy as a jalapeño pepper, and since they'd come together, she couldn't stop thinking about it. The comment had made her contemplate the idea of sexting, which she quickly dismissed. She could be *all that* behind closed doors, but the idea of putting something so intimate in a text, where anyone could get ahold of it? No way.

The house smelled fresh, as if someone had just cleaned. The front door opened to a narrow foyer with aged hardwood floors.

"Daph, that you?" A deep voice came from down the hall, followed by a gray-haired man with a paunch belly.

Daphne kissed him on the cheek. "Henry, this is Rebecca. Rebecca, this is my Henry."

He had serious dark gray eyes, and at the moment they were darting between Daphne and Rebecca as he wiped his hands on a dish towel that was slung over his shoulder.

"Rebecca Rivera, nice to meet you." She reached a hand out in greeting.

"Yes, Daphne told me you were interested in renting a room." He pressed his lips together.

"Thank you for giving me the opportunity. I really appreciate it."

Henry looked her up and down. "You're welcome, but we won't have any partying or men in and out of the bedroom."

"No, sir. I'm not like that. I'm two classes away from a business degree, and once I save enough money to take the last of my classes, I'll be studying in my free time." She shot a look at Daphne, hoping he wasn't going to change his mind about the room and wondering why he seemed unfriendly when Daphne was one of the friendliest people she knew.

He nodded. "I'll let you and Daph get settled, then. I'll be in the kitchen."

Daphne opened the foyer closet door. "Feel free to hang your coats, keep boots or shoes, whatever you want, in there." As soon as Henry was out of earshot, she leaned in close and whispered, "He's a little embarrassed by this, but he's really an old softie. He'll warm to you quickly. I promise."

I hope so. She let out a relieved sigh. She could relate to his discomfort, especially at his age. It was one thing to lose a job in your twenties, but in your sixties, she didn't imagine that there were many places hiring people of retiring age.

She followed Daphne down the hall. Daphne waved her hand toward a step-down living room to their left. "Living room. Just keep it clean in case you have your sexting boyfriend over." She wiggled her eyebrows.

"*Tsk.* I don't sext. I'm not even sure I'd know how."

"I'm teasing, hon. I wouldn't have offered the room if you'd come across as a loose type of woman. I've been watching you. You're very serious, and you handle the customers with finesse. Cool and confident."

Cool and confident. Rebecca liked that. She followed Daphne through the living room, up one step to a dining room, and through a doorway to a cozy, wood-paneled den. She could see herself curled up on the sofa beneath the reading lamp, studying.

"This is great."

"This room is very soothing. It's Henry's favorite room in the house. Come on. I'll show you the kitchen and your room."

She followed her through the dining room to a comfortable kitchen. Light wood cabinets hung from the walls, and white appliances were tucked efficiently into Formica countertops. There was a table for four in the corner of the room. Daphne opened a pantry on the far wall.

"Food." She swung open another door. "Basement."

Rebecca was glad to see the house was orderly.

She and her mother had always kept a neat house, save for the rogue pair of shoes or magazines that seemed to have minds of their own. They walked down a hall lined with photographs of Daphne and Henry. Rebecca noticed that there were no photographs of children, and she wondered if that was by choice.

She couldn't wait to put out pictures of her mother in her room. She missed seeing her, and the photos helped. She rubbed the ring on her index finger, thinking of how much she and her mother would have loved living in a little house such as this one. They'd always lived in apartments, and it was Rebecca's dream to one day own a small house of her own.

"And this is your room." Daphne opened the door to a moderately sized bedroom. There was a double bed against the far wall, across from a tall, dark wood dresser. Bedside tables graced both sides of the bed, and light spilled in through a double window that faced the backyard. Daphne opened another door. "And your bathroom."

"This is perfect." Rebecca sat on the bed. It was soft and bouncy. She didn't mind that she'd be sharing the house with Daphne and Henry. She didn't care that she might have to share in the yard work, and of course, the housework. She had a new friend and a home to sleep in, and that was enough to make her feel blessed. And, most important, she'd done it on her own.

And I have Pierce. She smiled at the thought.

"Daphne, I can't thank you enough."

"You're helping us as much as we're helping you.

Do you want me to help you bring some stuff in?"

They unpacked Rebecca's car, and she went to work putting her clothes away and making her room feel like home. She took the top off of the last box she had to unpack, the most important box, and withdrew three framed photographs. She held one in her hands and sat on the bed, relishing in the image of her mother at eighteen, holding her when she was just an infant. Her mother had been beautiful before she'd gotten sick. She and Rebecca shared the same big eyes and high cheekbones, and before her illness had sucked the color from her skin and the luster from her hair, her mother's skin had been a shade darker than Rebecca's and her hair had been shiny with fashionable natural curls. Rebecca studied her mother's face in the photo. While Rebecca must have gotten her pointy chin from her father, her mouth was all Rivera.

I miss you, Mom. I think you'd like it here. She ran her finger over the picture and then set it on the dresser and wondered what Pierce would think of her room. Would he think it odd that a twenty-seven-year old woman didn't have her own place, or would he not care at all? He didn't seem to flash his wealth, and she was glad for that. If he had, she probably wouldn't have given him the time of day.

And now she couldn't imagine a day without him.

She set the other two photographs of her and her mother on the dresser beside the first, and then she withdrew a wooden box that she'd painted in second grade and given to her mother as a Mother's Day gift. Hand-painted red flowers with blue leaves that only a mother could love adorned the top and sides of the box. She lifted the lid and smiled at the sight of the photograph, cracked with age and glued to the inside of the lid. Her lips were smushed against her mother's cheek, her eyes closed. Her mother's cheeks held the color of joy—and life. She'd taught Rebecca so much in what now seemed like such a short period of time. To be confident, enjoy life, and that there was nothing she couldn't achieve if she put her mind to it. Her mother had been good at dropping lessons like others dropped names, but perhaps the most important lesson Rebecca learned from her mother was the one that went unsaid.

Life is too short to pretend. Rebecca didn't pretend in any way. She tried not to hide her feelings, or lack thereof, and she tried not to cover her opinions with lies or to put on airs to seem like something she wasn't. No, Rebecca had learned to just be herself and to allow the good, the bad, and the excellent to come as it may.

When she'd met Pierce, she'd pushed away the sparks that had flown between them and tried to ignore the way the air charged and heated and the way his eyes were like a giant vortex of passion and kindness that sucked her right in. In the span of a few days, she'd come to enjoy the heat of his stare as he snuck peeks at her, the way that he laughed a little under his breath and shook his head when they were teasing each other, and the whisper of his breath across her skin. She lay back on the bed, which was now covered with her own sheets and blanket and felt more like her own. She looked up at the ceiling and then closed her eyes. If she tried really hard, she could bring forth his scent and the sound of his voice.

Her phone vibrated and she reluctantly opened her eyes, wanting to stay with thoughts of Pierce a moment longer, but he was the only person who would text her. She retrieved her phone from the dresser and read Pierce's message.

Can't wait to see you. Almost done with your errands?

Errands. The word sent a stab of pain through her chest. She hated not telling him the truth, but she believed that for now, keeping the truth from him was the right thing to do. She thought of Henry and wondered if she'd be better off trying to get to know him instead of running off to spend time with Pierce.

I'm going to be a little longer. Want to skip it and see each other tomorrow instead?

He texted back a minute later. *Not a chance. Want to stay at your place tonight? I can whip over.*

She smiled at his offer, but after meeting Henry, she wasn't sure they should ever stay in her room. She felt as if it would be disrespectful, and there was no need when they could stay at Pierce's house. A new worry entered her mind. Would Henry and Daphne mind if she didn't come home at night? Oh gosh. She probably should have thought this through a little better. She didn't want to seem unappreciative, but she was a grown woman, after all.

She texted him back. *It's okay. I'll be over in a little while. Can't wait to see you!*

Daphne poked her head into Rebecca's room. "Hey, Rebecca. Henry made a wonderful roast. Want to join us?"

She could eat quickly, and this would be the perfect way to get to know Henry a little better. "Sure, thank you."

Daphne handed Rebecca a key. "Great. I'll set another place. I almost forgot to give this to you."

"Daphne, I can't thank you enough. Your house is lovely, and I really appreciate you letting me move in so quickly."

"When you told me you'd been living in your car for the past few days, I knew it was fate." She hugged Rebecca and picked up one of the framed pictures. "Oh, what a beautiful picture."

"Thanks. That's my mom."

"She looks nice."

"She was." Rebecca realized too late that she hadn't told Daphne about her mother's passing.

"Was?" Understanding flashed in Daphne's eyes. "Aw, Rebecca." She gathered Rebecca in her arms. "I'm sorry. I didn't know." She drew back with a wrinkled brow. "If you ever want to talk, I'm a really good listener."

"Thank you." Rebecca was glad that Daphne didn't dwell on the topic.

They followed the warm, spicy aroma to the kitchen, where Henry was cutting the roast.

"Can I do something to help?" Rebecca asked.

Henry ignored the question and continued cutting the meat. Daphne put her arm around her shoulder. "Sure. Why don't you make a salad while I set out the silverware."

Rebecca began cutting lettuce and dicing

tomatoes.

"You don't need to cut them fancy," Henry said, eyes still on the roast.

"Habit, I guess. My mom loved colors in our meals, so we always added red, orange, and green peppers, tomatoes, and things like chick peas, and chopped the colorful veggies up real small so they would add more color. If it bothers you, I could—"

"Henry, Rebecca's mother passed away."

Henry stopped slicing and shifted his eyes to Rebecca. There it was. That look that always seemed to follow the news of her mother's death.

"It's okay." Rebecca pointed to the diced veggies. "See? She's still very much around."

His smile put a fissure in the steel wall he'd erected around himself. He glanced at her several times while she was mixing the salad.

At the dining room table, as he piled salad onto his plate, Henry said, "I think I like the salad better this way."

Daphne smiled and squeezed his arm. Rebecca loved that they sat beside each other instead of across from each other. She'd never understood the idea of formality at dinnertime. Wasn't dinner supposed to be about families coming together?

They ate dinner and talked about Rebecca's first day of work. It was nice to share the day with them. It was nice to feel like she had a home, too, although after spending the weekend with Pierce, she felt at home there even more.

"May I ask how you lost your mother?" Henry asked.

She still hadn't come up with an answer that would not incite pity, and she loathed the question too much to dwell on coming up with one now. "She had cancer, and I'm glad she's someplace better now."

Henry glanced up at Daphne and drew his thick white brows together. "I'm sorry to hear that. Were you young?"

She smiled. "It was almost two months ago."

"Oh, hon. That's very recent. Are you sure you're holding up okay?" Daphne asked.

And there was the pity again. "Yes, thank you. I'm really okay, actually." She needed to change the subject to avoid becoming a charity case. "Do you have any children?"

They exchanged a painful glance of sadness and acceptance blended together.

"No, it's just us," Daphne answered.

The silence that followed was filled with the unanswered question, *By choice?* Rebecca sensed that they hated that question as much as she disliked questions about her mother's death, so she let the silence settle in.

After dinner Rebecca helped clear the table. "Thank you for dinner, Henry. It was delicious."

He nodded. "Did I hear you say you're taking classes?"

"Not right now, but I only have two left before I get my business degree, and I hope to take them when I save enough money."

"I worked in the business office of the newspaper plant. What do you want to do once you graduate?" He crossed his arms and looked at her with what she'd imagine a fatherly gaze would look like.

"I don't know. I'm really good at negotiations and figuring things out, or at least in class I am. Practically? I'm just not sure. The things I want to do aren't in line with just one aspect of business. I guess I hope that at some point I can get an entry-level job in a growing business and gain experience in several different areas and then sort it out. I worry I'll get bored if I'm just crunching numbers, which is why I didn't go into accounting, and I'm not a marketer, but I enjoy the marketing process." She shrugged. "I guess the answer is that I'm not sure."

He nodded again, which she was quickly learning was his standard response.

"And this boyfriend of yours? What does he do?"

Uh-oh. She realized that she needed to talk to Pierce about how to answer those types of questions where his employees were concerned. Was it okay to tell them he owned the resort?

"He's a real estate investor." She began putting away the condiments from dinner, hoping she could shift the conversation away from Pierce.

"Did he know your mother?" Henry asked.

"No. Unfortunately, he didn't."

Henry nodded again before patting Daphne on the shoulder and disappearing into the den.

"Don't mind him. He's still coming to grips with his employment status, but he liked you. I can tell."

Rebecca began washing the dishes. "It's okay. He's very nice."

"He is, when he's not trying to figure out how to handle a roommate after years of only the two of us.

Move over, hon. I can do those. We have a pretty efficient agreement. Henry cooks and I do dishes. Besides, don't you have a boyfriend to sext?" She shoved Rebecca out of the way and took over washing the dishes.

"Daphne, would you be offended if I spent the night at my boyfriend's house sometimes? I don't want to seem ungrateful, or have you and Henry think poorly of me."

"Darlin', you're a beautiful young girl. Live your life. We're providing a roof over your head, but you don't need to report to us."

Even with Daphne's blessing, Rebecca couldn't shake the feeling that at least tonight she should stay there. She'd felt Henry warming to her when they were talking, and she knew how embarrassing it was to have your life situation change dramatically. She thought making an effort toward him might lessen his discomfort of renting to her—and she needed the room.

She went back to her bedroom and called Pierce.

"Hey, babe. Are you on your way?"

He sounded so hopeful that she almost changed her mind. "Actually, would it be okay if I stayed here tonight and we got together tomorrow?"

Her stomach sank with the silence that followed.

"Is something wrong, Bec?"

"No. Not at all. It's one of my roommates. He's having a hard time, and I think talking might help." She looked around the bedroom and knew that after spending three nights together, she was going to have a heck of a time sleeping without him.

"Want me to come there?"

"No. I'm sorry, Pierce. This place is relatively new to me, and I just need a night. Do you mind?"

"Whatever you need, babe. Tomorrow, then."

The disappointment in his voice was palpable. "I'm sorry. I'm going to miss you like crazy." Maybe she could talk with Henry and then go see Pierce. *Ugh.* What message would that send to Henry? Why did she care? Because she did care. That's who she was. Henry was obviously going through a lot, and she was clearly an intruder into his world. Being someone who loved her privacy, she understood that completely. Rebecca wasn't one to ignore someone else's suffering. She and Pierce could go twenty-four hours without seeing each other, couldn't they? She'd gone twenty-seven years without him in her life. Why now did one night alone seem torturous?

They made arrangements to meet tomorrow after work, and by the time they ended the call, Rebecca already missed him.

She grabbed the notebook that she used for her budget and headed into the den.

PIERCE PACED HIS living room, wondering who the guy was who could keep Rebecca from seeing him. He eyed the files from the meetings he'd had earlier today. He needed to review his notes and prepare for tomorrow. Maybe this was a blessing in disguise. He picked up the files and tried to wrap his mind around the issues in two of his West Coast properties. He spread the reports and spreadsheets on the coffee table and sat, elbows on knees, staring at them, but his mind drifted back to seeing Rebecca on the security camera while she was working. It was obvious that the customers loved her. She took a little more time with them than the other waitresses did, and she was attentive to their requests. He remembered what she'd said about her job at the bar. *He didn't like us talking to the customers, and, well, I think people come into bars to unload…*And when he'd asked her about what other jobs she'd held, she'd said, *Caretaker.*

He picked up a report, and a smile eased the tension in his jaw. Damn, was he ever blind to have gone straight down Jealousy Road. If there was a person going through a hard time, he had no doubt that Rebecca would never walk away. When he turned back to his files, it was with a clear head and a warm heart.

Chapter Eleven

THE FIRST THING Rebecca did the next morning was reach for her phone. She was rewarded with a text from Pierce. *Hated waking up without you. Can't wait to see you tonight. P.* She texted back, *I hated it more. Xox.* She hadn't slept well, and until that minute, she'd written it off to being in a strange house, but the house didn't feel strange at all this morning—she did, and she knew it was because she missed Pierce. And now her stomach was doing flips in anticipation of seeing him later that evening.

She dressed for the gym, then into the kitchen and made coffee. Henry hadn't said more than a handful of words to her the night before as he sat at his desk in the den working on something that had him mumbling under his breath while she worked on her budget. She hadn't minded the quiet, and even though she'd missed Pierce when she went to bed, she was glad she'd stayed. When Henry had said good night to her, she could feel him warming to her. She'd stayed up later than Henry, working her budget over and over based on her new salary, and even with paying Mr. Fralin each week and paying off her mother's remaining debts, she should be able to afford classes by the spring. The next item on her list was saving enough money to take her mother's ashes back to Punta Allen, and she hoped she could save enough to do that by the holidays, assuming, of course, that she found an amazing travel deal.

Another day full of hope lay ahead.

She was going over her budget one last time, when Henry sauntered lazily into the kitchen wearing a robe pulled tight across his belly, a pair of striped pajamas beneath. His gray hair was matted in some places, sticking up in others. He had bags beneath his eyes, and Rebecca wondered if he hadn't slept well. Then again, it wasn't yet six. She was heading out to the gym in a few minutes, but she was glad to see him.

"Good morning." Rebecca had always been a morning person. She woke up ready for whatever the day held, which probably was reinforced as her mother's condition worsened, because she needed to be fully awake no matter what time her mother needed her.

"Morning." He poured himself a cup of the coffee that Rebecca had made.

"I hope you don't mind that I made coffee. I'll buy some today to replace it."

He sat down across from her. "It's coffee, Rebecca. We can afford coffee."

Darn it. She hadn't meant it that way. "I'm sorry. I just meant—"

"Don't worry about it."

"I *do* worry about it, Henry. I'm not sure if Daphne told you or not, but..." She paused, feeling funny about revealing what she hadn't even revealed to Pierce, but chances were pretty good that Daphne had already told Henry, and if anything, it might help ease his embarrassment. "I was living in my car for a few days before you rented me a room. I know what it feels like to have stability ripped out from under you and thrown so far away that you think you'll never find your footing again."

He scoffed, rubbed his tired eyes, and looked away.

"I'm sorry. It's just that when you've had as much taken away from you as I have, you learn to recognize and separate the things that are a reflection of who you are and those that are caused by something out of your control. Believe me, for a control freak like me, that's a hard realization." She paused, giving him time to tell her to shut up if he'd like, and when he didn't, she continued. "You were laid off." She shrugged. "Economic times are tough right now, but you're still the same man you were when you went to work every day."

He locked a steely gaze on her, and Rebecca held her breath.

"That's easy for a young gal like yourself to say. There aren't many companies looking to hire an old man." He leaned his elbows on the table. "What are you working on?"

She closed the notebook. "Just looking through my budget, forecasting the next few months."

"Forecasting." He raised his brows.

"I like to know where I stand."

"Rebecca, if you don't mind me asking, how did you end up living in your car? That seems...extreme." He sat back and crossed his arms.

She met his stare. "Taking care of my mom ended up being a full-time job. She'd had a stroke near the end, and I had a hard time keeping a job."

He lowered his chin and looked down his nose at her. "Did she have disability income?"

"Yes. She did. But she was only eighteen when she had me, and she was a single mother, so she never had the chance to make a career for herself. She was only earning thirty-four thousand a year when she went on disability. She took home only sixty percent of that, and since she didn't pay for her own disability insurance premiums, she had to pay taxes on the income." It had been a harsh realization when the IRS notified her mother of back taxes that were due. Her mother hadn't known that if she didn't pay her own disability insurance premiums that she was responsible for paying taxes on the income she received. "Not to mention the never-ending medical bills."

He shook his head. "They screw you every which way but sideways."

"Yeah, well, we found that out the hard way. She didn't realize that was the law until after she didn't pay the taxes the first year. But in all honesty, she needed every penny of the income she earned, so even if she had known, she probably wouldn't have paid the premiums. Disability insurance is one of those things that you don't think about until you need it, and for her, it was too late at that point. It took the IRS about a year, but they came for their money, so I used my paychecks to help her pay off the taxes she owed and to pay for her medical expenses. Anyway, to make a long story short, without a job and with what we owed and everyday expenses, we couldn't afford the apartment we lived in."

His eyes filled with empathy, and Rebecca turned away with the painful memory of the days after her mother's death, when every day felt terminal. Between waking up every day and having to accept that she'd never see her mother again and waiting for Mr. Fralin to turn her out on the streets, she'd been a nervous wreck.

"My landlord was really good to us. He let us stay for the last two months of her life, and then he let me stay for a few weeks to get myself in order." *Through the fog of taking care of my mother's things and learning to function again would be more accurate.* "But it wasn't fair of me to stay in an apartment when he needed the income. I eventually found a job at a bar, and I knew it wouldn't be long before I'd have enough money to find something cheaper, a room in a house like this, or something similar."

"Weren't you worried? A single woman like yourself living in your car?"

"Not in the way you're thinking. I'm pretty good at self-defense. But I was embarrassed about it. I had a gym membership at Fitness Heaven, so I had a place to shower. It's open twenty-four hours. As much as I knew I'd get out of the mess I was in, I was scared to death about people finding out. Let's face it: Living in a car sounds bad. It sounds dirty."

His gaze softened. "And then you got the job with Daph?"

She nodded. "Yeah. It was a miracle."

He smoothed his robe over his chest, and an unexpected smile lifted his lips. "You give me hope, Rebecca."

"I do?"

"Yes. I've tricked myself into believing that this is who I am and that I'll never be the type of man who can take care of Daphne again." He laughed under his breath. "Amazing what a little youth can do for you."

"What do you mean?"

He shrugged. "Well, Rebecca, if you can come out of what you've endured with a smile on your face and hope that practically jumps off of your skin, then what the hell is a wise old bastard like me doing feeling sorry for himself? I'm going to borrow a little of your youthful exuberance and see if I can figure something out, too.

"Tell me something, Rebecca. This boyfriend of yours, is he a good guy? Because this is a racy town, and I'd hate for you to fall into something with a guy who isn't worth his weight in salt."

He's the best guy. "Yeah, he's a good guy."

He smiled as Daphne came into the kitchen. "Morning, Daph."

Daphne kissed his cheek. "Good morning. Are you calling the bank today about the mortgage?"

"I'll take care of it. Can we please not talk about that at the crack of dawn?"

Rebecca shifted her eyes away, uncomfortable with the tone of their conversation. The fact that they'd needed to rent a room had told her that they were having financial difficulties, but she didn't need to be privy to the details. That would surely underscore Henry's discomfort.

Daphne touched the top of his head. "You're right. I'll wait until the crack of lunch." Her hand slid down his shoulder, and Henry reached up and squeezed it.

They spoke to and touched each other like nothing the other person could do could change their love, and it warmed Rebecca's heart to witness such comfort. She was beginning to sense that she and Pierce might be headed in a similar direction, and although it was a little scary that it was all happening so fast, she hoped they were.

"Where are you off to so early, Rebecca?" Daphne asked.

"The gym. It's good for my brain."

"Did you sleep okay?"

Not really. I missed Pierce. "Yeah. The bed's wonderful." *And lonely.*

As Rebecca walked away from the kitchen, she heard Henry say, "She has no one looking after her." She stopped to listen, worried that he thought she couldn't handle things on her own.

"Daph, I want to make sure this boyfriend of hers is good enough for her."

"Oh, Henry. I knew you'd like her."

With a smile on her lips, Rebecca gathered her clothes and gym bag and walked out the front door.

Chapter Twelve

IT WAS FOUR o'clock in the afternoon before Pierce had a second to breathe. He'd worked straight through lunch and had just come from a meeting with a national foundation that was wooing him as a sponsor for an event they were putting on next year. He pulled out his cell phone, intending to text Rebecca so she'd receive it after her shift. He was scrolling through several missed calls from his mother and siblings when Kendra knocked on his door.

He glanced up from his phone. "Hi, Kendra."

"Sorry to bother you, Pierce, but you had a call from Jeff while you were in the meeting. It appears that he's found issues with the Grand. I told him you'd call him back as soon as you were free." She set the message on his desk.

Pierce sighed. "Damn. I was hoping my gut was off on this one."

Kendra pointed her pencil at him. "Your gut is never off, Pierce. I'd think you would know that by now."

"I'll call Jeff." He picked up the message with Jeff's number on it.

"Luke called you, too, and your mom, and Treat wanted to know where to meet you for dinner Thursday night."

As she listed his family members, he realized that he was waiting to hear that Rebecca was trying to reach him as well, which was silly, because she'd call his cell phone, and she was at work. He'd already mentally cataloged her in with the people he loved most.

"I'll call them back. Thank you."

"I had a nice chat with both Luke and your mother." She raised her brows. "Want to tell me who Rebecca is?"

"Christ Almighty!" He shook his head. "My family just gave *Family knows no boundaries* a whole new meaning. I'll have to alert my uncle Hal. It's his catchphrase."

"Catherine and I agreed that for you to mention a woman to Treat, she must be very special."

He pictured the conversation between his mother and Kendra, scheming to pry more information out of him.

"Well, if you two are in agreement, then you don't need my two cents."

She smiled down at him. "Pierce, we're all happy for you. She must be very special, but you don't have to share anything with me. I'm happy just knowing that you might let a woman get to that big heart of yours. You've kept it locked away so tight that I worried you might never step out of your bachelor ways."

He rubbed his temples with his fingers and thumb and settled back in his chair with a sigh. "Her name is Rebecca Rivera." He flashed a teasing smile. He would be happy to tell Kendra all about Rebecca, but he was anxious to talk to Jeff and find out what kind of shit had hit the fan. And he enjoyed teasing Kendra as much as he enjoyed teasing his family members. "That's all you get for now. I need to return these phone calls."

"Rebecca Rivera," she said with a nod. "I know you're dying to call Jeff, but please call Catherine first. She's climbing out of her skin over something Emily's said." Kendra spoke with a motherly tone, and while that probably should have annoyed Pierce, it was one of the things he liked about working with Kendra. She wasn't afraid to share her opinions or put him in his place, and sometimes he needed that. She was trustworthy and loyal, and she treated his entire family like they were her own.

"Will do." He dialed his mother's number.

"You, my son, are the talk of Trusty," his mother said when she answered the phone. He pictured her smiling with the tease, her brown eyes vibrant and full of joy. His mother was always full of joy. It took a lot to drag her down, and everything around her accentuated her positive spirit, despite what she'd gone through with his father before they'd moved to Trusty. Her front yard burst with colorful flowers, and her house was layered with rich textures, light colors, and photos capturing some of their best family moments.

"I'm going to strangle Emily."

"Oh, Pierce. She followed your rules. She told us that you were going down fighting. Just because she added, *Yeah, right*, shouldn't make a difference." His mother laughed.

"And then you told Kendra?"

"Someone has to keep an eye on you there. Besides, Kendra knew something was up. She said you've seemed lighter on your toes lately." Pierce's mother, Catherine, was down-to-earth and close to each of her six children. She could be tough as nails, had instilled lessons of fairness, honesty, and strong work ethics into their heads as far back as Pierce could remember. She was also sensitive and thoughtful, and he was sure that if she'd been in the room with him, she'd have noticed he was lighter on his toes, too.

"Okay, Mom. Her name is Rebecca Rivera, and yes, she's gotten to me like no woman ever has." It felt good to say that out loud. *Really good.*

"I assume you've checked out her background?" she said in a serious tone.

"No."

"Pierce, a man in your position—"

"Trusts his gut."

"Okay. Yes, I can see that. But women are very sneaky," she warned.

Pierce had never let anyone get very close to him, and he knew his mother worried because suddenly he was, and she wanted to protect him from being hurt the way she'd been hurt by his father.

"She's not sneaky, Mom, though I appreciate your

concern." He spun around and looked out the window. "She is one of those women who does everything for herself."

"Oh, one of *those*," she said sarcastically. "The kind that takes care of herself."

"Yes." After a moment of thought, he added, "Like you."

"Hm. She pays for her own stuff, then."

"Exactly."

"Gets mad when you try to do too much."

"Yes. How do you know?"

"Because that's the only type of woman who could hold your interest."

"What exactly does *that* mean? I like to do things for her."

His mother sighed. "Pierce, you don't like *easy*."

He arched a brow. "I might disagree with that."

"Let me rephrase that. You are a man, after all. You're competitive and aggressive. A woman who is too easy might be fine as a...distraction, but she'd bore you in the long run. She wouldn't be your equal, and while you're every bit an alpha male, like your brothers, you're too smart to settle for someone who's not equally as bright or equally as aggressive as you are. A life partner has to understand where you're coming from on all levels. It sounds like maybe you've met your match."

She paused, and Pierce realized that she knew him better than he knew himself.

"Pierce." Her voice softened. "I know that you remember what things were like when your father lived with us."

His chest constricted. "Mom. Please."

"Hear me out. I know you remember what it was like when he left, even if you don't like to talk about it."

"Mom." He clenched his teeth against the painful memories that came with her words.

"No, no more running, Pierce. Just hear me out, honey, please. I don't thrust my opinions on you often, so give me a few minutes. You can forget what I say the minute I hang up if you want, but please hear me while I say it."

He sighed, wishing like hell he could hang up the phone and walk away. His mother didn't force her opinions on him often, so he sucked up his discomfort and paid her the respect she deserved. "Go on."

"Honey, not everyone is like your father. It's okay to trust, and I know you like to control things, but, Pierce, you'll drive a woman away if you try to make her something she's not. Especially a strong woman."

"I'm not trying to make her anything, Mom." The words felt hollow. Wasn't he wishing she'd let him fix things for her? Didn't some small part of him think she'd eventually allow him to wave his money and make her problems go away?

"I'm not saying you are. I'm just saying that if she's really used to handling things herself, well, a guy who likes to make things better for everyone might want to help her with the things she struggles with. I mean that with love, Pierce. When your father left, you took on his role with your brothers and sister as best you could, and there was no dissuading you. I swear you took the entire burden of your father's leaving off their shoulders and carried it on your own. When Ross and

Wes had nightmares, you took them into your room. When they acted out, you set them straight, and when they cried, you put on a stiff upper lip and helped them feel better. You were a little father at age six."

Pierce heard regret in her sigh.

"I tried to dissuade you from trying to take on so much responsibility, but you were a stubborn little thing, and I wasn't exactly at my strongest."

Pierce closed his eyes. He remembered arguing with Ross when he'd taken out his anger on their mother, and later, holding him while he cried about their father leaving. Those months that followed were hard, but Pierce hadn't realized that they could have defined so much of who he was.

"Honey, you're a good, strong, successful man. I'm sure Rebecca knows those things. If she's the way you say, then let her flourish and enjoy the same self-respect you've earned. She'll need it."

He swallowed against the emotions that clogged his throat. "Her mother died a few weeks ago. Should I still let her handle things? Or is it okay to want to help her through? Because everything inside me says she's taken care of others long enough, that now it's her turn."

"Oh, honey. That poor girl." His mother was silent for a minute. "Pierce, this will be hard for you to understand, because you are very much of a fixer, but it's the best advice I can give you. By allowing her to take care of the things she feels she has to, you *are* helping her."

Chapter Thirteen

PIERCE SPENT THE evening stewing over the issues that his due diligence team had uncovered with the Grand. He was meeting with Jeff and the team tomorrow to go over the details, and there was nothing he could do before then. That didn't stop him from wearing a path in front of the windows of his home library while he waited for Rebecca to arrive and tried to convince himself not to dwell on the Grand until he had a handle on how deep the issues ran.

He spotted the headlights of Rebecca's car coming up the driveway, and on his way outside, his mind traveled back to the things his mother had said. As much as he trusted his mother's advice, he wasn't convinced that letting Rebecca handle everything on her own was the right thing to do—or that he was even capable of stepping back and letting it happen.

He took Rebecca in his arms and kissed her. "Mm. That was way too long to go without seeing you." He kissed her again and slid his hand to the curve of her butt.

"It felt like forever, but I'm glad I got a little time with Henry. Thanks for understanding." She reached for the back door of the car to grab her overnight bag, and Pierce retrieved it for her.

Henry. She'd said his name with compassion, and Pierce had to remind himself that she was a compassionate woman in general and to tuck away the jealous feelings that tried to sneak in. "I wouldn't have minded staying at your place. You didn't have to drive all the way out here." They walked inside hand in hand, and Pierce swore the house grew warmer, felt more like home, once Rebecca stepped inside.

"I didn't mind. Besides, I have roommates, so..."

He put her bag in the hallway. "Roommates? Like sexy hot guy roommates?" He was only half teasing.

"Superhot. One's an MMA fighter. You might know him, Big Johnson?"

He swooped her into his arms as she threw her head back and laughed. "Big Johnson, huh?" He kissed her neck, which only made her laugh harder. "I'll give you Big Johnson."

"Yeah, I bet you will." She wrapped her legs around his waist, then settled her lips over his.

He pressed her back against the wall. "Better be careful. You might find yourself in a compromising position." He didn't give her time to respond as he took her in another greedy kiss, getting his fill for all the hours he'd missed her.

"Good Lord, Pierce." She pressed her hands to his cheeks and kissed him softly. "When you kiss me." She drew in a deep breath and blew it out slowly. "I can barely think."

He took a step back, giving her room to shift her legs to the floor. She kept them wrapped around his middle.

"Carry me to the couch," she said with a mischievous grin.

He cupped her ass and kissed her as he crossed the floor and then lowered himself down, with Rebecca straddling him. She ran her hands through the sides of his hair, and he touched his lips to hers again.

"It wasn't my intent to greet you with my carnal desires on display, but you're too incredible for words." He kissed her chin, her lips, the soft pillow of her cheeks. The points of her nipples pressed against her cotton V-neck tee, and she was looking at him like he was the most delicious thing she'd ever seen—or tasted—as she ground her butt into eight inches of rock-hard desire. Her eyes held the hazy mist of lust, and her hair was sexily mussed.

"You push every sexual button I have, Bec. I didn't mean to come on so strong."

"No?" She tilted her head and licked her lips. "Oh, darn."

With a soft laugh he shifted her onto her back, positioning himself above her on the couch. He tangled his hands in her hair and kissed her again, meeting her arching hips with his hard desire. He pulled back with a need for air, and she reached for his neck and drew him into another unyielding kiss. He was straining to keep control. He'd thought about what Emily had said about him and his brothers whoring their way through life, and he wanted Rebecca to know his feelings for her went far deeper than sex, but damn if their kisses weren't pulling him under, into a slow blurring of right and wrong and all things rational. His hand slid to the bend of her hip, and lust coiled deep in his belly as a moan of pleasure slipped from her lips into his lungs. Again, he tried to pull away, make an effort to talk, but when their eyes met, the connection rooted deep within his soul, demanding more of her.

"Becca," he said between heated breaths. "We should...talk."

"I know." She kissed him again. "Later."

She reached for him again, and he sank into the most seductive kiss, slow and impassioned. She met every lap of his tongue with a sweet laving of her own, slaying his good intentions. She reached for his pants, and he gripped her wrist and held it above her head, earning him a gloriously naughty moan that darkened her eyes and made his heart race.

"You like that, huh?" He tugged her shirt down her arm and dragged his teeth along the smooth column of her neck.

"Jesus, Pierce. I'm already wet."

Holy hell. He couldn't stifle a groan. Forget behaving. Forget talking. He captured her next breath in his mouth, kissing her hard and deep, a preview of what was yet to come. He pushed from the couch and carried her in his arms. She shifted as he carried her to the bedroom, opening her mouth wider, taking more of his kiss, his tongue, his lips as he lowered her feet to the floor. Rebecca clutched his shirt—and a fistful of chest hairs—driving him crazier by the second.

"God, I love how you turn me on," he whispered against her neck.

He didn't think of the words he said; he just let his emotions speak for themselves. He didn't care if he said *like* or *love* or *fuck* or *damn*. He could no better rationalize a thought than he could refrain from hooking his thumbs in her jeans and panties and pulling them straight to the ground, then crouching to help her lift each foot from the harsh material and stepping out of his own clothes. He turned her around, pressing his hard length to her sweet, round ass, and took her neck in his mouth, sucking as she ground her backside into him. He clutched her waist and held her tightly, slid one hand flat against her stomach, and lower, until his fingers touched her curls.

She arched her neck. "Touch me, Pierce. Love me. Make me come."

He slid his hand down the curve of her belly to her inner thigh. She gasped a breath and held it as he squeezed his way back up her thigh to her sex and stroked her wetness. She craned her neck, and he took her in another kiss as he plunged his fingers deeper. She turned in his arms, and he touched and teased her into halted breaths. Her lacy red bra scratched his chest as she pressed against him, her body pleading for more. Using his teeth, he dragged each strap down her arm, until the flimsy material balanced at the edge of her taut nipples. He could smell her arousal as he slid his finger in and out of her velvety heat, and— *finally—God, finally—*unhooked her bra, freeing her luscious breasts. He brushed his thumb over her nipple as he dragged his tongue along her lower lip. She gripped his wrist at her center and urged him deeper, holding him there as she rose to the edge and went up on her toes as an orgasm tore through her. He caught her gasps in his mouth, his fingers still working their magic, and as the thrum of her release eased, he took her to bed.

It was his turn.

He wanted to be inside her. Now. Fast and hard and buried so deep she could feel him in her throat. He paused long enough to think about a condom. *Goddamn condom.* For twenty years he'd used them faithfully, and now, with Rebecca, he wanted to feel her, *all* of her, without a latex sheath between them.

He gazed into her loving eyes. "Bec, are you on the pill?"

She shook her head. "It's been years since I've been with anyone."

He closed his eyes as disappointment welled inside him, and then he reached for a condom, tabling the conversation for another time.

She was tight and eager as he slid into her. She wrapped her arms around him, bringing him as close as he could be, hip to hip, his heat buried deep inside her. All of the emotions he'd been battling came rushing forward.

"Rebecca, look at me. Be with me."

Her lids fluttered open. Her gaze was sensual, and he knew he wasn't imagining what he felt between them. He'd been with enough women to know that the look in her eyes ran deeper than desire. Her lips curled up as her eyes focused on his.

"I..." The words were on the tip of his tongue, but they were so big that he began to wonder if they needed more of a stage, a momentous presentation.

"What...?" She ran her fingers along his back, sending shivers of wanting through him.

"I'm falling for you, Becca. I know you're working on your life and you've just lost your mom, but...You've become everything to me."

Her brows drew together, and she pressed her hands to his cheeks in that way he'd come to love—and crave. "I know. I can see it in your eyes."

He touched his forehead to hers.

"And I feel it, too. We're totally in sync, even if we're from different worlds."

He breathed a sigh of relief, and with all of the love that she'd woken within him, he lowered his lips to hers, sealing their words, and their bodies took over.

Chapter Fourteen

MUCH LATER, REBECCA and Pierce lay on the bed, nose to nose, each with a hand on the other's cheeks. Rebecca's mind was still floating in the clouds from their lovemaking. Pierce made love to her as if he cherished every second just as much as she did, like he wanted it to go on forever. He didn't rush her after his own release. He took his time, caressing her cheek, her hip, her arms, pressing soft kisses to her face and remaining inside her until he was too soft to hold his place. She played their lovemaking over in her mind, lingering on his whispers in her ear. She'd heard the desire in his voice when he asked if she was on the pill, and she'd nearly said to make love to her and just pull out, but she had too many things she had yet to accomplish to take a chance like that. Pierce had been with so many women that she had to be smart, too.

"I never imagined feeling like this about anyone," Pierce admitted. "You. Us. It's all so unexpected."

She cuddled in closer. "Completely unexpected.

Relationships haven't been anywhere near my radar screen for years."

He kissed her lips and draped his arm over her waist. "Did you miss intimacy? You're so young to have given up so much for so long."

She shook her head. "When you're in that situation, there's no room for missing or wishing for something else. At least for me there wasn't. I was busy trying to remain employed, which I didn't do a great job of, keeping track of pills and medical appointments, and...I don't want to talk about this, because you're going to fall into pity mode like everyone else and I don't want to ruin what we have." She was frustrated with herself as much as the situation. There was always a look when she spoke of these things, and she knew she overreacted to it, and sometimes she called it pity when she wasn't even sure it was. But whatever it was, it made her feel uncomfortable, and it bothered her enough that she was unable to keep herself from reacting so vehemently to it.

"Babe, talk to me. Let me into your life. I promise I won't pity you. I want to know all of you, not just the sexy, fun parts. I want to understand what you've been through and where you hope to go. It's really okay for people to say they're sorry and to feel sad that you missed out on things; that's not pitying you."

Rebecca sat up and pulled the sheet over her chest. She loved how he wasn't afraid to express himself, even if she might not want to hear what he had to say, and that he cared enough to ask difficult questions. Most guys would stay away from uncomfortable subjects like her mother's death, as if her disease were contagious. He said all the right things and she believed him, but he still didn't understand.

"Don't you see, Pierce? I didn't miss out on anything. I made sure of it. I was there for the only thing that mattered—spending time with, and taking care of, my mom. If you would have given me a million dollars and said, *Here, hire someone to care for her and go live your life*, what do you think I would have done?"

"Aw, Bec."

"No, I'm being serious." She wasn't yelling or even raising her voice, but her tone was serious and she saw in Pierce's eyes that he heard it loud and clear. "Pierce, I loved taking care of my mom as much as I hated it. It was hard, damn hard, but we had time together that, if I were too wrapped up in myself, we never would have had."

Pierce wrapped his arms around her and pressed her head to his chest. *Chivalrous*. It's who he was.

She remained against him for a minute, maybe two, then pushed away gently. "I know you care about me, and I know you want to hear all about what I've gone through, but you can't look at me like that, or I can't open up to you."

"Like what?"

"Like you wish you could fix it." Her heart was in a tug-of-war. She loved that he cared and wanted to fix things for her, and at the same time, she hated the *fixing* part. She never felt like she'd missed out on life, and she didn't want to be seen as someone who had.

"How can I change that, Bec? I know I can't fix it, but I'm human, and I care about you, so you're going to see that I wish I could."

"Then wear sunglasses when we talk." She felt herself smile.

"Wait. Stay right there." He leaned forward and brushed something from her shoulder.

"What was it?"

"It's that chip you carry around." He smiled and it made her smile.

Rebecca knew that she wasn't an easy person for someone to love. She was strong and she had her own beliefs about who she was and how she lived her life, and she could only hope that Pierce might someday understand why those things were hard to change—or even if they ever would.

"Look, I get it. Okay? My father left, and I hate it when people act like I missed out on someone great, because I didn't. I think it's the same feeling as you get when people say they're sorry about your mom. That look is why I don't talk about him, so I really do get it. I just can't help that I care enough to want to fix it for you. I'm afraid that no matter how hard I try, you're going to see that look in my eyes, Bec. Maybe you don't really want to open up to me."

She dropped her eyes and ran her thumb over her mother's ring. "But I do like to talk about my mom with you. I don't talk to anyone else about her. Maybe we can find a middle ground? I'll talk and you look away."

"I like the sunglasses better. That way I can still look at you." He pulled her across his lap and kissed her. "I'll try not to look at you in a way that makes you uncomfortable. Let's talk about something else. Tell me how your first two days of work went. Do you like it so far?"

"Yeah. I love it so far. We're always busy, so time goes quickly, and it's not a mentally taxing job, so when I take my last courses, I'll still have the brainpower to study at night." She shrugged as if that was all there was, but in truth, she was ecstatic to no longer be living in her car.

"When are you going to take classes?" he asked.

"As soon as I have the money. I've only got a couple classes left before I graduate, and I should be able to take them in the spring."

"I can help you pay for them."

"Pierce, stop." She shifted from his lap and gathered the sheet around her.

"Stop what? I'm just offering to help so you can finish the courses."

He looked so baffled, and it didn't surprise Rebecca. He couldn't possibly understand what she was feeling, but he would never be able to if she didn't explain it to him. Rebecca pushed her irritation away and drew upon the patience she'd learned so well during her mother's illness. She took his hand in hers and tried to explain again.

"I love that you want to help, but I'm not a project. I don't need charity. I *want* to do this on my own. I know you care for me, and I know you would be willing to help me out of the goodness of your heart, but you need to understand, and accept, how that would make me feel like you were trying to fix things."

"Guys are fixers. It's a known fact." He pulled her close again.

"Right, which is maybe why I didn't miss dating. I don't need fixing." She took his face in her hands and stared into his eyes. "Hear me, Pierce. If this relationship is going to work, you can't offer to fix things for me. Got it?"

"You know, even women who have everything at their fingertips let their boyfriends offer to do things for them."

She kissed his nose, because he was so damn cute when he was trying to get his way. "Then you should date one of them if you need to fix women. I'm a woman who doesn't need fixing. Take me or leave me."

She inched to the edge of the bed, and he scooped her back with his powerful arms. "You're asking a lot of me. It will go against everything I've ever believed. But for you, I will try to do things your way. You'll have to cut me some slack, though. And as far as taking or leaving you goes..." He dragged his finger from the center of her collarbone to her belly button. "I've taken you, and I'll take you again, and again, but I'll never leave you."

Chapter Fifteen

WEDNESDAY MORNING THEY got up early and went for a three-mile run. Rebecca was competitive by nature, and working out with Pierce was great motivation, even if he taunted her during their run by running behind her and making sexual innuendos, which she also secretly loved. And showering with him? Oh Lord, there was nothing like the feeling of his big hands, lathered with soap, sliding over her wet skin, caressing every inch of her body like it was new to him when he'd spent the evening before loving those very same parts. And she had to admit that touching him, taking him in her mouth while water ran down her back, added a whole other level of erotic sensations to their lovemaking. She loved watching him dress in his business suits, covering all those godly muscles as if they didn't exist. It gave her a thrill knowing just how glorious that hidden body was.

Rebecca grabbed her purse on the way out the door. She was trying to get used to carrying it since she wanted access to her cell phone and there were no pockets in the black skirts she wore for work.

"Is your phone on?" After his brother had given him a hard time for forgetting to turn on his phone, Rebecca had gotten used to reminding him to do so. She loved how he feigned hating the nag, though she could tell by his smile that he liked it.

"Oh, you think you know me, don't you?" Pierce pulled out his phone, turned his back, and she knew he was turning it on. When he turned around and held it up with a big smile, she laughed. "It was on. See?"

She tossed her purse in the car and Pierce folded her into his arms.

"What would I do without you?" He nuzzled against her neck.

"Oh, probably miss a lot of morning phone calls."

"Do I really have to go another long day without you? How about meeting me for lunch?"

"Are you at all worried about people seeing us together? I wanted to ask you about that. How do you think we should handle it so you aren't seen as a letch?" She smiled, and she could tell by the gleam in his eyes that he knew she was joking.

"Seen as a letch? I've never dated women who work for me."

She arched a brow.

"Well, until you, of course. I'm not going to pretend, Bec. My cousin Josh went through that. He and his fiancée, Riley, hid their relationship because she worked for him, and it pretty much sucked. I don't think we have to flaunt it, but if I want to see you, I'm going to see you, and if you want to see me, then I want that door open twenty-four seven."

"Well, one of my roommates works with me. Should I let her know?"

"I think honesty is best. Your coworkers might treat you differently, so maybe you should just be ready for that. You know, the whole dating the boss thing, but I've never dated anyone who works there before, so it's not like they can say that I make a pattern of it, or anything like that."

"But you *were* a player. You told me so yourself." She touched his arm. "I've handled a lot worse things than comments."

"Even the thought of someone saying something to you about my dating habits pisses me off. I've never flaunted women around the casino. I'm a respected businessman with a reputation to uphold. I came and went through a side entrance if I was staying at the hotel, and it's not like I woke up with those women and took them to breakfast." He kissed her softly. "Let's just be us, and we'll deal with whatever comes up."

"Okay." She drew in a deep breath, readying herself to ask what needed to be asked. "I don't mean to be a buzzkill, but you asked if I was on the pill."

"I just want to be closer to you."

"I know, but you've had a..." *Oh God, how on earth can I say this? "Busy* social life."

"You're wondering if I'm clean." His voice was serious.

She was so nervous she could only manage a nod. It wasn't a comfortable thing to have to ask, but things that were important were rarely easy.

"I've always used condoms. I could be the poster boy for Trojan, but if you want me to get tested, I will. Whatever you need to make you comfortable."

She fiddled with the button in the middle of his chest. "I'm sorry. I know how this all must sound. I'm just paranoid."

He lifted her chin and gazed into her eyes with the same look he had last night when they were making love. "Babe, if you're willing to go on the pill, I'm willing to take a simple test. We're worth it. I'll have Daisy, Luke's fiancée, do it when I go home next weekend. I'd rather keep something like this private. She's a doctor, and I trust her."

She nodded, and he folded her into his arms again.

"You can ask anything of me. I'll always tell you the truth."

"I know." Rebecca hadn't ever had anyone that she could really trust besides her mother, and with Pierce, she believed that he really would always tell her the truth.

He opened her car door, then closed it. "Drive to work with me. Why should we take separate cars? I want you to come home with me after work anyway, and it'll give us more time together."

She glanced at her car and her pulse quickened. She hadn't realized that her car had become some type of security blanket. It had been the one stable thing in her life after her mother died. Without it, she'd have had no place to stay after she left her apartment. It's not like she was getting rid of it, but somehow not having it with her—*just in case*—made her nervous.

"What if I need it?"

"You can always use my car." She eyed his Jaguar and had no desire to drive it. It wasn't having a car that was an issue; it was having her car.

"I'm kind of used to having it."

"I think this is one of those control freak issues you were talking about the other day. Okay. Take your car." He kissed her again and opened her car door for her.

She held on to his hand. "I'm sorry. It's kinda weird, isn't it? That I need my car?"

He shrugged. "No more weird than me wanting to fix things for you. We'll just have to adjust."

As she climbed into her car, he must have sensed her discomfort, because he lifted her chin so he could see her eyes and said, "Don't sweat the small stuff, Bec. It's all fine. Lunch?"

"Definitely."

"Great. There's one more thing I keep forgetting to ask you. My cousin Treat and his wife, Max, are coming into town for dinner tomorrow night. Will you have dinner with us? I'd really like you to meet them."

"Are you sure you wouldn't rather spend time alone with them?" Her heart was going crazy at the idea of meeting his family, even though they weren't his immediate family. It was a big deal and confirmed just how much he liked her.

"I'd rather spend time alone with you, but short of that, I'd rather you were with me every second of every day."

Rebecca was glad she was sitting down, because he said everything she felt, and if she were standing, her legs would have surely failed her.

"Okay," she managed.

They made plans for Pierce to come down and meet her at noon, and after a long kiss goodbye, Rebecca drove to work feeling ridiculous for needing her stupid car. *Tomorrow I'll leave the darn thing at home. At Pierce's,* she corrected herself.

Chapter Sixteen

REBECCA HAD BEEN trying to find a quiet moment to talk to Daphne, but the morning had been crazy busy, and now that it was lunchtime, she bit the bullet and pulled Daphne aside.

"Daphne, I need to tell you something."

"Sure, hon. What's up?" Daphne picked up an order from the counter and reviewed the ticket, matching the items to the order.

"You know how I told you that my boyfriend was a businessman?"

"Sure. Oh, Henry wants me to check him out." She winked. "He's such a worrywart. I knew he liked you."

"Well, you'll get a chance to in about five minutes."

Daphne's eyes lit up. "He's coming here?"

Rebecca fidgeted with her order pad. "He sort of owns the place."

"What place?" Daphne cocked her head.

Rebecca lowered her voice. "He owns the resort."

Daphne pulled another waitress over. "Wilma, can

you take this to table six, please? I need to talk to Rebecca."

Oh shit. Daphne sounded so serious that Rebecca didn't know what to expect.

Daphne pulled her over to the break room. "Honey, are you talking about Pierce Braden? Tall, dark, and scrumptiously handsome? The gentleman of all gentlemen, Pierce Braden?"

Scrumptiously delicious, too. "Yes."

"Oh, hon." Daphne hugged her. "Everyone here loves the man. We're talking serious big boss crush by every woman in the place."

"It's not like that, Daphne. I had no idea who he was when we started dating, and I don't care what he has. I care about who he is."

She searched Rebecca's eyes. "Good. Okay, good. That's good."

"I just wanted you to know, because you asked me who I was dating and I didn't want you to think I didn't trust you. It's all kind of new, so I wasn't even really sure how to handle it, but we talked about it and he doesn't want to pretend we're not together, so..."

Daphne hugged her again. "Sweetie, he's such a nice man. Everyone loves him." A flash of worry passed over her face, then faded just as quickly.

"What is it?"

Daphne leaned in close. "It's just that, you know, he is a good man, Rebecca, and we all want him to end up with a good woman, and you're *definitely* a good woman, but...Word around this place is that he's kind of a ladies' man, if you know what I mean."

She'd expected to hear just that, but she hadn't

expected it to hurt the way it did, like a paper cut, quick and sharp. "I know. He told me."

"He did?" Daphne patted her chest like she was trying to calm her racing heart, which, knowing Daphne, she was. "Good. Good, Rebecca. Then—"

"I know all about his past. He was very honest, and I trust him, Daphne. I mean, I really trust him, like I've never trusted anyone before."

Daphne reached for her hand and gave it a thoughtful squeeze. "Trust your heart, Rebecca. That's what I would do. Henry was no saint when I met him, the little dog." She smiled. "Heck, girl. I wasn't very pure either, but we knew from day one that we were meant to be together. The universe has a way of figuring out the things in life that get hung up between our heads and our hearts."

"Thanks, Daphne. I was worried that people around here might treat me differently."

"Oh, they may. You are *dating* not only the best-looking man in Reno, but the big guy on campus, too." She patted Rebecca on the back. "Just ignore any snide looks and keep being who you are, darlin'."

"Pretty easy, since I have no clue how to be anyone else."

They went back to work, and Rebecca felt much better having come clean to Daphne. She hated keeping secrets. It wasn't part of who she was, despite her *Secrets are a girl's best friend* comment she'd tossed out on her first date with Pierce. Not telling him about staying in her car was also weighing heavily on her mind, but that was a secret of a different kind. She had every intention of telling him about that at some point. She just wasn't sure when that point was going to be.

She was finishing up with a customer when Pierce walked into the restaurant. Her heartbeat didn't just quicken; it sprinted. The employees lifted their eyes in his direction, stood taller, and watched as he weaved through the tables, heading directly toward Rebecca with a confident gait and a look in his eyes that shot right to her heart. Everywhere he went, he commanded attention. Even Rebecca's customers glanced his way as she waited off to the side.

Oh God! Her legs had turned to jelly and she wasn't thinking straight. The last few nights came rushing in, swirling inside her and warming her all over. She was dating the boss. Did everyone in the restaurant know who he was? She felt her cheeks flush as she tried to figure out what to do. Should she go right to him? Go back and place the order? She had no idea where her boss was, but it didn't matter, Pierce didn't give her a chance to decide. As she walked away from the table, he came to her side—in a cloud of heat that sizzled and burned. He casually placed a hand on her hip, leaned down, and kissed her cheek.

"Hey, babe."

It was a simple, sweet kiss. She'd made love to him, touched and tasted every inch of him, and that simple kiss blew away her brain cells like fluff in the wind. It was all she could do to smile.

"Almost ready?" he asked.

She cleared her throat and forced herself to answer. "Yeah. Just let me get my purse from the back."

"I'll come with you." He kept a possessive—protective?—hand on her lower back as they walked through the kitchen. The chef looked up and smiled.

"Hey, Mr. B. I've got your order up in two minutes. Robin has your table ready in the courtyard."

"Thanks, Bob."

Bob ran his eyes between the two of them as they headed into the break room. Rebecca tried to act calm, cool, and collected but feared she failed miserably and that everyone could see her insides were doing some sort of shake, rattle, and roll dance. She grabbed her purse from her locker and drew in a few deep breaths before returning to Pierce's side. He was reading the schedule that hung on the wall, with one hand in his pocket, his hair brushed back from his face, and his clean-shaven cheeks calling to her to touch them. She pictured him going gray around the temples, fine wrinkles around his eyes. She could see the two of them together as they got older, Pierce wanting to fix all the things that were difficult for her and her wanting to stand her ground. She could see them making love and waking to the sound of a crying infant, chasing a toddler through the park. Oh Lord, she could picture forever with him and they'd known each other only a few days—and, by golly, it felt real. How could she be so certain? It made no sense and perfect sense all at once. From her head to her toes, and everywhere in between, she was one hundred percent in love with Pierce. She lifted her hand to cover her mouth, as if she could silence her thoughts.

She might be able to quiet her mind for now, but there was no way she could silence her heart.

Chapter Seventeen

PIERCE AWOKE THURSDAY morning with Rebecca's arm draped over his stomach and her cheek pressed against his chest. He pulled her closer, and she snuggled in with a sleepy, contented sigh. She wore a camisole and panties, and looked sexy and adorable at once. In sleep, her face was totally relaxed. The pucker of stress he'd sometimes noticed around the corner of her eyes was gone and her lips were slightly curved upward. He usually sprang out of bed to fit his run in before work and then arrived early at the office so his day stayed on track. That jolt of get-up-and-go wasn't there. His mind was laden with *Don't-move-a-muscle. Hold her. Enjoy her.* And his body was enjoying the feel of her against him entirely too much to move.

His efficient and overachieving business mind tried to sever his lovesick thoughts with reminders of his due diligence team's discovery of liens against the Grand for unpaid payroll taxes, which were not reflected in the books, and according to the books, made no sense. He had his team doing more discovery today, going through the actual books, not just tax return and financial statements. Based solely on what he knew at this point, the Grand was worth several million dollars fewer than what they'd been led to believe. He'd spoken to William Benson, the owner of the property, and Benson was adamant about the asking price. The end of the day would bring answers.

Those powerful thoughts tried to push him out of bed, to get his legs moving so he could work the numbers over in his head a million times during his morning run. Rebecca opened her eyes and spread her hand across his stomach, then lifted her head and looked at him, her eyes reflecting the same love that had held him in place.

"Hi," she whispered.

His stressful thoughts were no match for Rebecca. Nothing was. He brushed a strand of hair from her cheek. "Hi, babe."

"I'm sorry. I have you trapped." She pushed away and he pulled her back.

"I like feeling trapped by you." He kissed her forehead and she smiled. They didn't have to fool around; he just wanted her close.

"Are you okay? You look stressed." She touched his cheek, and he leaned in to her palm.

He thought he'd rid himself of the stress, but she saw right through him. "I'm fine. Just work stuff."

"That acquisition you mentioned?" She leaned up on one elbow.

He tried to play it off as no big deal, even though it was one of the biggest deals he'd considered in a long time. "Yeah, we'll have answers later today." He still didn't want to move away from her. She calmed the nagging business voice in his head that had pushed him into overdrive for so many years. She tempered it, adding a balance to his life that he hadn't realized was missing.

"You said you had to make a decision in twenty-four hours. Why is that?"

Rebecca didn't ask many questions about his work, and he found the questions she did ask curious. "Because they need to sell, and I'm ready to buy."

"Self-imposed deadline, then." Her eyes sharpened.

"Pretty much."

"That makes sense. You like to move fast."

"Yeah, I do." *You have no idea.* It had been only a week and he was ready to move her into his house.

"I like that about you. You're decisive, which is probably why you're so successful. But what if you needed more time to make a decision? What if it didn't feel right?"

He thought about it for a minute. He only made decisions that felt right, and they usually came quickly. "I don't know. I haven't had that happen yet."

"Would you grant yourself time to think about it or force yourself to decide? I'm asking because in one of my business classes, that was a major topic. What drives entrepreneurs, and do their hasty decisions weaken or strengthen their efforts?"

"Your business class, huh? Well, I think if I wasn't sure, I'd take the time until I was sure, but I'm pretty decisive."

She nodded and her eyes grew even more serious. "I think I'm the same way. I wanted to tell you something last night, but I thought it might sound funny. I gave myself time to think about it, but it's been bugging me, so I'm just going to say it. I'm glad you came in to get me at work. I hated feeling like I had to hide our relationship, even for just a couple days."

He'd struggled with that decision. He knew it might backfire and make things more difficult for Rebecca, but Pierce wasn't the kind of man to pretend, much less let the woman he was falling in love with go unclaimed in the public's eye. She was the woman he adored, and he wanted the world to know it.

"When I saw you standing there talking with that elderly couple, I was so proud to be with you. I probably shouldn't have kissed you in the restaurant, even if on the cheek, but I couldn't help myself." He lifted her gently so they were eye to eye.

"Apparently, the women have major crushes on you." She kissed the corner of his mouth. "But they're happy for us."

"Major crushes, huh? Maybe I need to reconsider the dating pool."

She cupped his privates with a wicked grin. "Oh yeah?"

"Kidding. Kidding." He carefully lifted her hand and laughed. He shifted her onto her back and pinned her to the bed with his weight. "Do you know how much you turn me on? Just being with you? Hell, Bec, just thinking about you?"

"Well, I am pretty hot." She flashed a mischievous

smile.

He laughed again. "Yeah, you are, you little vixen."

She giggled and then her eyes grew serious. "I want to tell you something else."

"Uh-oh."

"It's nothing bad. I was thinking that we could drive in together today." She bit her lower lip.

"What about needing to know your car is there?" He rolled to her side, giving her space to think without the added pressure of feeling how aroused he was.

She turned and faced him, so close their noses touched. "I would rather know you're there."

It was a small thing, something that shouldn't make him warm all over, but this was the same woman who'd decked a man and had turned Pierce down for a drink. It was *huge*. He nuzzled against her neck.

"Thank you."

"But I have to go by my old apartment after work and drop something off with the landlord, and if you want me to stay over again, then I need to pick up clothes for tomorrow from my place."

"Baby, I'll do those things with you. Tonight's dinner with Treat and Max, too."

He glanced at her bag on the floor by the closet. "Why don't you bring a week's worth of clothes tonight? A month's, whatever."

"Pierce, I'm not moving in." She touched his cheek.

"Not exactly the reaction I was hoping for," he admitted. He'd thought that Rebecca was in sync with him on how fast they were moving. Now he worried that maybe he was moving too quickly for her comfort.

"I've got my own place, even if I only stay there sometimes. It's a good thing. You could get sick of me."

"Not a chance."

"You might want time alone."

"Wrong again." He kissed her softly, relieved that she was only worried about him not being fully committed and not something bigger, like her own feelings for him. He could assuage her worries because he'd been committed to her since the first night they met.

"You might want to go back to your old playful ways." She traced his arm from shoulder to wrist.

He pulled her beneath him again. "The only person I want to play with is you." He couldn't hold in his feelings any longer, even at the risk of scaring her away. He searched her eyes and took the plunge. "I fell over the edge, Rebecca. I tried to hold it back, but I can't. I love you."

He could feel her heart racing. She opened her mouth to speak, and he kissed her again before she could say a word.

"You *love* me?" She searched his eyes.

"I do." He kissed her again, and when she drew back, she gulped in air. "Are you okay?"

She nodded, her eyes damp with tears. "I fell, too. I was too scared to say anything, but you were right there. You caught me."

Chapter Eighteen

PIERCE STORMED OUT of the meeting with the due diligence team, leaving twelve of his employees to stare after him. He'd known something was off with Benson. Nearly five million dollars in uncollectable accounts receivables had been left on the books instead of written off. The sneaky bastard thought he could play Pierce for a fool. Well, Pierce was nobody's fool.

He kept his head down as he entered the executive reception area, every determined step increasing his anger.

"Treat called when you were in your meeting, and so did William Benson," Kendra said as Pierce stormed past her.

"Thank you," he grumbled. *Benson, the snake.*

She followed him into his office with a notepad in hand and stood across the desk from him with practiced grace while he paced by the windows. He had a tough decision to make about the Grand—the

209

issues with the books didn't change the fact that he wanted that prime piece of real estate, but the deal just became far more complex and risky. He was glad he'd be speaking with Treat. He was a great sounding board. He knew how to handle tricky deals. But Pierce was too angry to think coherently at the moment. And then there was Kendra, standing on the other side of his mahogany desk in her proper suit, pen at the ready. A major deal was about to implode, and if he had been any other person, he might lash out, take it out on everyone in his path, but Pierce wasn't that person. He drew in a deep breath and ran his hand over his face, stifling the anger boiling inside his chest.

"Mr. Benson was returning your call from yesterday requesting a meeting. He's in his LA office and said he's free Monday morning. Does that work? I can book you a flight out on Sunday evening and a room at the property near the airport."

He turned to face Kendra. Her face was a mask of professionalism, her voice steady, businesslike.

"Yes. Monday. That's fine, but I'll stay with Jake. I'm sure he won't mind, and I'd like to see him." It would be nice to have some alone time with his younger brother before he came to visit for Luke and Daisy's party.

"I'll have a car waiting for you at the airport. Pierce, tell me what else you need and I'll get out of your hair." She knew him so well.

He hadn't seen Rebecca at lunch today, and it was thoughts of her that eased the fire in his belly. She'd told him last night that she called her doctor and had an appointment Monday to get on the pill, and he agreed to get tested, as promised, when he went home for Luke and Daisy's engagement party. He smiled to himself, despite the frustration of his earlier meeting. There wasn't another woman on earth he'd do that for.

"Pierce?"

He looked up, feeling calmer now. "Yes. Sorry, Kendra."

"It's okay. Before your meeting, you said to have the legal team on standby. Should I get them on the phone?"

He tried to force his mind back into work mode, but his thoughts drifted back to Rebecca and what she'd said that morning about giving himself time to make decisions. He *should* take a few hours to talk to his accounting and legal teams and hammer out all the options for the Grand. He *should* take the time to decide if it was still a viable option or not. But that wasn't what *he* needed. He needed to see Rebecca. A little time with her always centered him, and for the first time in his professional career, being with a woman was being moved to the top of his to-do list.

"You know what? I'm not ready to do this yet."

"What do you want me to tell them?"

"Tell them I need a day." He went to his desk and glanced over the pictures of his family and realized that Rebecca was missing. He needed a picture of her. Hell, he needed her. Always. He was glad they'd driven in together that morning, because it would make the ride home that much sweeter.

"Can you please do me a favor?"

"Of course."

"I forgot to make dinner reservations for tonight."

Kendra rolled her eyes. "Of course, Pierce. But, you know, you need a wife."

I think I might be working on that. "Believe it or not, Kendra, I do hear you when you say that. At least now I do. Would you mind making reservations at the Château? Four for eight o'clock, and please request a quiet booth."

"Of course. I'll also call Treat and let him know. Is there anything else I can do?" Kendra arched a brow. "You're all jumpy, so you've got something going on in that brilliant mind of yours."

He glanced down at his desk again. "Yeah, I do need something else, but it's something I have to do on my own."

Pierce stopped in the gift shop on his way to meet Rebecca after her shift. He walked into the restaurant with an armful of red roses as she was on her way out with another waitress. They were walking shoulder to shoulder and laughing. Christ, he loved her laugh. Rebecca glanced in his direction and their eyes met. She smiled, and her gaze drifted to the flowers. She grasped the other woman's arm. She was an older redhead with a friendly smile, and when she noticed the flowers, she patted Rebecca's hand.

"Pierce." Rebecca sounded breathless as she came to his side.

"Hi, babe." He kissed her cheek and breathed her in. She smelled like fresh air, with a hint of cooking spices. "These are for you." He laid the flowers in her arms.

She went up on her toes and kissed him. "They're beautiful, but you didn't have to do that."

"It's not about what I have to do. It's about what I want to do, and this is just the tip of the iceberg."

He draped an arm around her and smiled at the redhead. "Hi, I'm Pierce."

"Oh, sorry. This is Daphne. Daphne, this is Pierce." Her eyes filled with love when she said his name, and it made him feel warm all over, like the luckiest guy on earth.

Daphne held a hand out to Pierce. "Mr. Braden, it's a pleasure to meet you."

"Pierce, please. And the pleasure is all mine. Rebecca said you showed her the ropes. Thank you."

Daphne glanced at Rebecca. "She's amazing. The customers love her, and so do Henry and I."

"I rent a room from Daphne and her husband, Henry," Rebecca explained. "Daph, we'll be over in a little while to pick up a few things for the weekend. I'll see you then?"

Pierce had been trying not to worry about who Henry was, and as Rebecca explained, his hidden worries eased.

"Yes, and Henry will be glad to meet Mr. Bra— Pierce." Daphne leaned in close and lowered her voice. "He worries about her like she's his own daughter."

"Then I like him already."

"She seems nice," Pierce said on the way out to the car.

"She is, and so is her husband." She inhaled the beautiful flowers.

"How long have you rented from her?"

"Little while."

Rebecca gave him directions to her old apartment

complex. He parked the car in the parking lot. "Stay right there, please."

"Why?"

He smiled. "I said, *please*." He went around the car and opened her door, then reached in to help her out. "That wasn't so bad, was it?"

"No," she said quietly. "But it makes me feel weird."

"Bad weird, or you can get used to it weird?" He scanned the parking lot, cataloging the group of five guys huddled around a motorcycle at the end of the lot and the run-down cars that filled the space between. He couldn't imagine Rebecca living there. With a protective arm around her waist, he led her across the lot.

"Weird, weird, but to be honest, I kind of like you *wanting* to do things for me. I'm just not good at the accepting part. But you can open my car door if it makes you happy."

"It makes me happy." He opened the door to the rental office. "How long did you live here?"

"My mom lived here forever, but I moved out for a little while and moved back in after she got sick."

An older man with dark hair and bright blue eyes looked up from the desk where he was working. When he saw Rebecca, a smile brightened his eyes. He rose to his feet and came around the desk with one hand extended, palm up.

"Rebecca." He took her hand in his and patted it with his other hand. "So nice to see you."

"Hi, Mr. Fralin. This is Pierce Braden."

Pierce noticed that she didn't introduce him as her

boyfriend and he wondered why.

Mr. Fralin nodded and extended a hand. "Mr. Braden, it's a pleasure."

"Nice to meet you."

"I brought you what I promised." Rebecca handed him an envelope. "I'll be back again next week. Thank you again, Mr. Fralin."

Mr. Fralin's smile faltered. "Rebecca, I've told you that this is unnecessary."

She drew in a deep breath. "Yes. And I told you it was necessary for me. Thank you again, Mr. Fralin."

On their way out of the building, Pierce noticed a rough-looking man wearing filthy clothes eyeing Rebecca. He draped an arm over her shoulder.

"What was that?" he asked.

"What?"

"The envelope." He opened the door for Rebecca and set a dark stare on the man whose eyes were still trained on her.

"Oh, nothing."

Pierce climbed into the car, and as they left the parking lot, he stole a glance at Rebecca, who was fidgeting with the stems of the bouquet. "It didn't feel like nothing."

"I owe him some rent money, and I'm just paying him back a little each week." She looked out the window, and he could tell by the rigidity of her shoulders that she didn't want to talk about it, but he couldn't help himself.

"How much do you owe him?"

"Don't, Pierce." She sighed, still looking out the door. "It's not much, and I can handle it."

"Bec—"

She turned to face him. "This is one of those times when you need to wear sunglasses, okay? He helped me out when my mom was sick and I lost my job. He said I didn't have to pay him back, but I am. Okay?"

He clenched his teeth. Her goddamn pride was thick as lead. "I don't like you going there alone."

"I lived there without a bodyguard for a long time. I think I can handle it."

There was more than one way to skin a cat. "How about if I pay him what you owe and you can pay me back?"

She reached for his hand. "Pierce, you're doing it again. This is my thing, okay? Why do you think I didn't introduce you as my boyfriend?"

"You tell me."

"Because your suit costs more than the entire building."

"So you're embarrassed that I'm successful?"

"No, I don't want him to get the wrong impression. He knows me, Pierce. I mean, he's seen me at my most desperate, and I don't want him thinking that...Damn it. This is so hard to explain. *Boyfriend* implies...Well, it implies our relationship, but I want to pay him on my terms, and I don't want you to feel like you need to help. I don't need you to fix it, and I don't need you to protect me when I go there. I just need you to support my need to do what I feel is right."

He felt like she was cutting off his balls.

But the truth was, he respected the hell out of her for it. As painful as it was—and it was goddamn torturous—he shoved his ego aside. "Okay, but a compromise means two-way street, not bulldozing. I would rather you didn't go there alone." Pierce felt like he was taking a walk down Rebecca Lane, learning more about who she was, what it really meant to care for her mother and live paycheck to paycheck, and how strong and resilient she really was.

She narrowed her eyes. "You're impossible."

"Maybe so, but you've got me so hamstrung that you don't let me be half the man you deserve."

"Fine. It's a deal." She climbed over the console and kissed him. "Trust me, baby. You are every bit of a man in all the ways it counts."

Chapter Nineteen

DAPHNE AND HENRY'S house was a modest brick rambler. It reminded Pierce of many of the smaller homes in Trusty, Colorado. It was built on a quiet street, and inside, the house was clean and smelled of home cooking. It had a calm, pleasant vibe, and as he followed Rebecca down a narrow hall to her bedroom, it brought back memories of his teen years. It had been a very, very long time since he'd followed a woman into a shared living situation.

Her bedroom was small, and it had a distinctly different feel from the rest of the house. This bedroom, with the photographs on her dresser, books beside the bed, and her clothes hanging in the closet, felt very much like Rebecca and smelled like the perfume she was wearing the first time they'd met. The titles on the bedside table caught his eye. *Marketing and Branding. The Hidden Entrepreneur. Understanding Acquisitions and Mergers. The Art of Business.* He wondered where the romance and women's fiction titles were. Didn't all women prefer light reading to business? Rebecca didn't fall into any other typical womanly trends. Why would her literary interests be any different?

He picked up one of the photographs of her mother. There was no question about it being anyone else. She and Rebecca had the same beautiful, expressive eyes and high cheekbones.

"Your mom was beautiful."

Rebecca came out of the closet with an armful of dresses, skirts, and blouses. Pierce wrapped his arm around her and pulled her in close.

"Yeah, she was." She set her clothes on the bed and Pierce took her hand in his.

"And you were about the cutest little girl I've ever seen." He kissed her temple and lifted her left hand, the one with the ring she ran her thumb over every time she spoke of her mother. "Was this ring your mom's?"

"How'd you know?"

"Every time you talk about her, you rub it with your thumb."

"Yeah, she said my father gave it to her. It was too big, so she always wore it on her index finger. After she died, I liked having it on. I can't believe you noticed that."

"I notice a lot." He settled his lips over hers.

"Oh, excuse me."

Pierce turned toward the man's voice.

"Sorry, Henry." Rebecca's cheeks flushed, but when she looked up at Pierce, there was no embarrassment, only love. "This is my boyfriend, Pierce. Pierce, this is Daphne's husband, Henry."

Henry looked like the kind of man who would be right at home with a grandchild on each knee, with short gray hair and a friendly smile. He looked at Rebecca with a caring, fatherly gaze, and it warmed Pierce to know she had another person who seemed to care about her. "It's a pleasure to meet you, Henry." Pierce shook his hand.

"Nice to meet you, too, Pierce, and I'm sorry to interrupt."

"We weren't..." Rebecca stumbled over her words.

"We were just getting a few of Rebecca's things for the weekend," Pierce explained.

"Oh, are you two going away?" he asked.

"No. In fact, I have to work Sunday," Rebecca said. "But I'll be staying at Pierce's."

"Ah, right. Rebecca, I wanted to let you know that after our talk the other night, I got a little creative and put a few more feelers out in a different direction. You never know." He winked.

"I'm so happy to hear that, Henry." Rebecca embraced him. "I know everything will work out for you."

"Well, you kids have fun." With a nod, Henry disappeared down the hall.

"Creative?" Pierce asked.

Rebecca peered out of the bedroom and then whispered, "He was laid off from his accounting job and hasn't been able to find anything for months."

"Maybe I can hook him up. I'll give him my number on the way out."

"Pierce, you don't have to save everyone." She wrapped her arms around his waist. "But it's very nice of you to try to help him. I know they would appreciate any opportunity you can find. Thank you."

"I'll connect him with Chiara and we'll see where it goes. Oh, before I forget, I need to shop for Luke and Daisy's engagement gift. I know you said you have to work Sunday, but would you like to go shopping with me Saturday?"

"Sounds fun."

He picked up one of the pictures of her mother. "Would you like to bring a few pictures over? Maybe put one on the mantel and one in the bedroom?"

"You wouldn't mind? I do love having them near me."

"This room feels like you, babe. Bring as many pictures and as much stuff as you'd like. I want my place to feel like you, too."

Chapter Twenty

THE CHÂTEAU RESTAURANT was another one of the restaurants at the Astral, and it was a world away from any restaurant Rebecca had ever been to. Dimly lit, with waiters donning bow ties and black vests and patrons that smelled of money, it should have been intimidating, but thankfully, Rebecca drew upon her belief that people were people and money was like clothing—strip it away and the wealthy were just like everyone else.

She hadn't been nervous about meeting Pierce's cousin Treat or his wife, Max, until the second she saw them crossing the restaurant lobby. They were a handsome couple, both with thick dark hair, Max's long and wavy, Treat's cropped short and neat. Treat was well over six feet tall and dwarfed Max's petite frame. He had one hand protectively around her shoulder, and his dark eyes locked on Pierce. The family resemblance—and the realization that she was meeting a member of Pierce's family—hit her like a brick.

Gulp.

Pierce looked amazing in his dark suit and light blue dress shirt. He'd told Rebecca a million times how great she looked in her little black dress, and still there was something nerve-racking about meeting his family. She had no family to speak of. Her mother had been an only child, and her grandmother had died when Rebecca was a toddler. Rebecca's mother hadn't seen her own father since she was an infant. Pierce had become, she realized, the closest thing to family she'd ever had besides her mother.

"Pierce." Treat opened his arms and embraced him.

"It's good to see you." Treat turned a sincere smile her way. "And you must be Rebecca. It's a pleasure to meet you."

He kissed Rebecca's cheek while Pierce hugged Max, who was simply stunning. Her dress was similar to Rebecca's, a simple black, above-the-knee number. She was wearing it with heels that weren't low enough to be dowdy and weren't high enough to be slutty. She, like Rebecca, wore very little makeup, which made Rebecca feel at ease.

"Hi, Rebecca. I'm Max." Max leaned in close and hugged her.

"Hi, Max, Treat. It's nice to meet you both."

Pierce slid his arm around Rebecca, and her nerves calmed a little more.

"I hope you brought pictures of Adriana," Pierce said as they followed the hostess to their table.

"Treat has a thousand pictures of her on his

phone." Max laughed.

"There's nothing wrong with being proud of our daughter." Treat pressed a kiss to the back of Max's hand.

That was something Pierce had done so often that Rebecca wondered if all the Braden men were as charming as Pierce, and apparently, Treat.

Once they settled into the intimate corner booth, Rebecca took a moment to drink in the surroundings and remembered what Chiara had said about the owner decorating the restaurants to honor his family members. The restaurant featured enormous scenes from motion pictures, which Rebecca guessed featured the movies that Pierce's brother Jake had been in. It warmed her insides anew, that family was so important to Pierce. And as Treat shared some of his favorite pictures of his daughter, she realized again the magnitude of what it meant for Pierce to introduce her to Treat and Max.

"She does look like your mother, Treat." Pierce leaned close to Rebecca as he scrolled through the pictures. He pointed out Treat's brothers and sister in some of the pictures and told her a little about each of them.

They ordered dinner, and Treat and Pierce caught up on siblings and cousins.

Max leaned across the table. "Are you still nervous?"

"Is it that obvious?"

"Oh, no, not at all. But I've been where you are. I remember how overwhelming it was to meet Treat's family. At least it's just the two of us. We're the easy ones."

"Easy ones?" *Are there hard ones?*

"Well, you know, big families tease a lot, but Pierce and Treat are the oldest siblings, so they're more reserved, I think."

Treat leaned down and kissed Max's cheek. "Is she telling tales about me?"

"I'm telling truths."

The waiter took their order, and Treat filled their wineglasses. "Pierce, tell me about the Grand."

Rebecca's ears perked up. She hadn't wanted to ask about the acquisition, because Pierce seemed like he didn't want to talk about it when she'd brought it up to him before work that morning.

All hints of Pierce's smile disappeared, replaced with hooded eyes and a deep, serious voice. "It's a mess, Treat. They've got liens on the property for unpaid payroll taxes, and it appears that the records we were shown weren't accurate. Based on those books, the company should have a net worth of twenty-seven million, but with the new information my team turned up, it looks more like twenty-two million."

"Are you going to walk away or offer him less?" Treat asked.

"I think it's got potential, but he's not interested in anything less than the original offer, and I'm not going there." The muscle in Pierce's jaw bunched.

"Pierce, there are plenty of other properties, and if you let this one sit, if he really wants to sell, he'll come down. You know how this works." Treat reached into his jacket pocket and took out his phone. "I received notice today about a casino over in Vegas that's having trouble. Maybe it's time to switch gears."

"I want this location. I know I can turn it around, and Jeff—he heads up the due diligence team—thinks that there are several areas where we can achieve higher profits. I just need to wear Benson down."

"Excuse me, Pierce." Rebecca touched his leg.

"Yeah, babe." There was an edge in his voice. He was in work mode. Uptight work mode, in fact.

"I'm sorry. I don't mean to interrupt, and I don't claim to know much about any of this, but wouldn't an earn out be an option in this situation?" She held her breath. She had learned about earn outs in one of her finance courses during a practical application study.

Pierce and Treat shared another look, one Rebecca couldn't read.

"An earn out," Pierce said.

"Yes." Her heart beat faster as she recalled all that she had learned. "For example, the business was worth twenty-seven million dollars with your original estimate, and you believe that based on the net present value of the next five years' projected earnings, the present value is twenty-two million. Couldn't you offer twenty-two million with a two-year earn out? If the property exceeds the projected income on which the offer was based say, in two years, then you commit to pay them a percentage of the income earned over that projected amount. Maybe ten percent? Not to exceed the original offer of twenty-seven million?"

Pierce blinked several times. "Rebecca, how do you know about earn outs?"

"Well, I don't really. We had a practical application project in one of my classes. I love the way business and finance work hand in hand, so I came up with an idea. When I brought it up to my professor, he said that it's called an earn out." She shrugged. "It seems like a great option, but from what he said, most business owners don't like earn outs. They want to sell and be done with it, but with a business that's in debt, well, that owner might be willing to agree to an earn out so he can get the liens paid off with the proceeds of the sale. And now that the liens are out in the open, it's not like they can hide them from the next potential buyer. So really, it's in his best interest to take it."

"Rebecca, would you like a job?" Treat smiled.

"Seriously, woman. What are you doing waiting tables?" Max asked.

"Oh, I love my job." *Treat couldn't be serious. Could he?* He looked serious. *No, he's just being nice instead of telling me that I have no idea what I'm talking about. I should shut up.*

Pierce was strangely quiet.

Rebecca moved her hand from his lap. "I'm sorry. I shouldn't have said anything."

He reached for her hand, and as he spoke, he had the same calculating look in his eye that he'd had when he was reviewing his files.

"Bec, it's a brilliant idea. I was so locked into trying to make the return on investment for the current offering price work for us that I didn't even bother to think outside the box." Pierce shifted his eyes to Treat. "Genius, right? Win-win?"

"Absolutely, if your team's sure you can make the

business sustain itself and turn a profit," Treat answered. "And, of course, if they'll go for it."

"Pierce, did you have any idea that Rebecca knew this much about acquisitions?" Max asked.

"No, but if there's one thing I'm learning about Rebecca, it's that there's a lot more to her than she lets on." He gazed into Rebecca's eyes. "I don't think there's a damn thing she can't do."

No one but her mother had ever had that much confidence in her abilities. She hoped he wasn't just being nice. "It was just an idea. I mean, I know it's not that big of a deal."

"That's where you're wrong, Rebecca." Treat locked eyes with Pierce. "Pierce and I have more than thirty years in the business between us and neither of us came up with that option. It's a very, very big deal."

Chapter Twenty-One

PIERCE LAY IN bed Saturday morning with his eyes closed, thinking about dinner with Treat and Max Thursday night. After dinner that night, while Pierce reviewed the documents for the acquisition again and called Jeff and his attorney, Rebecca had fallen asleep. Pierce crawled into bed behind her and he'd lain awake most of the night thinking about how she'd pulled the earn-out option out of thin air, and he'd thought about it all day Friday, too. Then again, she had been handling her mother's medical bills, her mother's tax issues, and had been going to school for business. Maybe it shouldn't have surprised him, but he'd known plenty of business school graduates, and very few, if any, would have picked up on the rarely accepted earn-out option as a consideration for the Grand.

He felt Rebecca stir beside him, and he kept his eyes closed, unwilling to let go of the peaceful moment and face the day. He could lie there with Rebecca all day.

Her breath whispered across his cheek. "It's Saturday, and neither of us has to work."

He opened his eyes, and she was smiling down at him with heavy lids. "What's our plan for today?"

He rolled her onto her back, slid his thigh over hers and his hand beneath her camisole, brushing the underside of her breast with his thumb.

"We have to buy Luke and Daisy a gift, remember?"

He kissed her softly. "Right. Good thing you remembered. I was thinking about staying in bed all day." He lifted her camisole and as he kissed his way up her belly, he remembered that he was going out of town on Sunday.

"Bec, I have to go to LA to hammer out the deal with the Grand. I'll probably only be gone a few days, leaving Sunday night and coming back Tuesday, if all goes well."

She ran her fingers through his hair and frowned. "See? You've ruined me."

He arched a brow.

"Before you, I never worried about spending my days alone. Now? The first thing that went through my mind was, *Two whole days?* And after my heart went a little crazy, my next thought was, *How will I sleep without you?*"

He grinned. "My evil plan is working. Let me sweeten the deal. After I come back, the next weekend is Luke and Daisy's engagement party—will you come with me and meet my family?"

She drew in a sharp breath. "Pierce, I'd go

anywhere with you, but are you sure? That's more serious than meeting your cousin. Don't feel pressured to—"

"Babe, the only pressure I feel right now is between my legs." He reached down and slipped out of his skivvies, then drew her panties off and moved over her. "Will you come home with me?"

"Of course." She eyed the condoms on the bedside table.

"Don't worry. I would never do something you didn't want."

"Oh, I want, Pierce Braden. I want big-time, but it's just a few more weeks."

"Weeks? I can handle that. I've waited for you my whole life."

LATER THAT AFTERNOON, Pierce and Rebecca walked through the mall trying to decide on a gift for Luke and Daisy. It had been ages since Pierce had stepped foot in a mall. He was used to crowds at his resorts, and of course, in the casinos, but while he loved being with Rebecca, the crowded mall brought his protective instincts to the forefront. He realized that he was sizing up every man who walked by, and while he wasn't usually a judgmental guy, if they looked the least bit shady, he drew her closer.

"Where do people shop for an engagement gift?" He pulled Rebecca closer as three teenagers pushed past them.

"Gosh, how do I know? I've never been to a real engagement party."

He pulled her into a photo booth in the center of

the mall.

"I've never been in one of these," Pierce said as he pulled a five-dollar bill from his wallet.

"I have, with my mom. They're so fun." She waited for Pierce to sit down inside the booth; then she sat on his lap with her arms around her neck, and he tugged the curtain closed.

He pulled her into a kiss just as the first flash went off.

"Ready? Look surprised!" She whispered into his ear, "I want to blow you."

He didn't have to feign his surprise. The flash illuminated the booth and caught him wide-eyed and openmouthed.

"Ha! Gotcha!" Rebecca kidded as he pulled her close for the last picture.

They both smiled, or so he thought. When the pictures developed and dropped from the silver slot, the third picture revealed Rebecca looking at him like he was everything she ever wanted.

"God, I love you," he said as the second copy fell from the machine.

"How could you not? I mean..." She held the pictures up. "Look how cute I am."

They each kept a copy of the filmstrip. Pierce folded his in half and put it in his wallet, and Rebecca put hers into her purse.

"Do you mind if we stop in at Hallmark? I want to get a few things." Rebecca reached for his hand and guided him toward a display of calendars. She picked up one and rifled through the pages, then another, and then a third.

Pierce would never tire of watching her. She wore jeans that hugged her ass and the black boots that she'd been wearing the first night they'd met, with a simple white cotton shirt. The outfit probably cost her next to nothing, but to Pierce, she looked like a million bucks.

"What are you looking for specifically? I can order you a beautiful leather day planner."

She smiled up at him. "This isn't for me. It's for you."

"I won't use one of those. I'd probably lose it, and I'd definitely forget to write in it."

She pressed her hand to his chest. "That's just what I was thinking. So, instead, let's get one of these." She picked up a small desk calendar, the type that were meant to have the pages discarded at the end of each day.

"Why do I need that? Kendra keeps my calendar."

"Yes, I know she does, and thank God for her. I thought we could put it by the bed and each night I could write a little reminder, like, *Turn phone on*, or if you have a meeting coming up, like dinner with Treat, I could write, *Make reservations*."

He rolled his eyes. "Did Kendra ask you to do that?"

"I don't even know her. You've never introduced us." She set it back down. "Never mind. I was just trying to help."

He pulled her against him. "I love the idea, and I love you for thinking of it. Kendra's been trying to get me married off for two years, and her biggest complaint is that I forget those types of things."

"I'd imagine it's your family's biggest complaint, too, since you miss their calls the most."

They paid for the calendar and went to check out the mall directory.

"Rebecca."

Pierce turned at the unfamiliar male voice and tightened his grip on Rebecca's hand as a handsome, muscular man approached.

Rebecca pulled from his grasp and hugged the man. "Andy, hi. This is my boyfriend, Pierce. Pierce, this is Andy. He does personal training at my gym. Chiara in HR is his girlfriend. He's the one who hooked me up with her."

Pierce shook Andy's hand. "Nice to meet you, Andy. I'm glad you sent Rebecca our way."

"Well, all I did was get her in to see my girlfriend." He turned back to Rebecca. "So, I know you got the job, but I haven't seen you for a few days." He lowered his voice. "I guess you found a place to live? No more parking lots?"

Parking lots?

Rebecca's eyes widened. She shot a worried look at Pierce, then turned her attention back to Andy. "What? No. I rent a room in a house, but lately I've been staying with Pierce." Her words fell fast and shaky.

"Good, because I was worried."

"No need to worry. I'm doing great. Hey, we've got to go. I'll catch up with you at the gym." Rebecca walked away without waiting for Pierce.

He forced himself to push past the confusion simmering in his mind. *A place to stay? Parking lots?*

"Nice to meet you, Andy, and thanks again for connecting Rebecca with Chiara."

He caught up to Rebecca. She was walking fast, her lower lip trapped between her teeth, her brow furrowed.

"Let's try Macy's," she suggested.

"Rebecca, what did he mean by *no more parking lots*?" He flashed back to the evening when they went to the parking garage to get her bag and she didn't let him near her trunk.

"Nothing."

"Rebecca, we said no secrets, remember?" They were entering Macy's, and as Rebecca practically dashed toward the back of the store, Pierce reached for her hand. "Bec, slow down. Please?"

She stopped walking, faced him with her brows drawn together, and crossed her arms. Her chest rose and fell with heavy breaths—and in those few seconds, he understood.

"Okay. I stayed in my car for a few nights, okay?" She spoke quietly and held his gaze with a distraught expression.

"Babe." He reached for her hand, and she shrugged him off.

"Don't." She turned away. "Can we please just get the gift and talk about this when we're not in public?"

"Forget the gift. I don't care about the stupid gift." He was trying to wrap his mind around Rebecca sleeping in her car, which was a tough pill to swallow. If he added the fact that she hadn't trusted him enough to tell him that she was living in her car when they met, it burned like hell. "Let's go talk now."

Tension thickened with each passing minute on the silent drive back toward Pierce's house.

"Do you mind if we go someplace other than home to talk?" Rebecca asked in a soft voice.

He reached for her hand. "Sure. The park?"

She shrugged. "Someplace where there aren't a million people maybe?"

Pierce drove to the River Trail and walked down by the river. The sound of running water was soothing but not soothing enough to quell Pierce's simmering emotions. He knew by now that pushing Rebecca wasn't the answer. She'd explain when she was ready, and he respected that, walking silently beside her. He draped his arm over her shoulder and tried to be patient as they walked down the quiet, rocky trail along the riverbank. A breeze rustled the leaves of trees as they passed beneath. A dirt clearing led to the edge of the river, and without a word, Rebecca crossed the clearing and sat on a rock by the water. Pierce sat beside her and leaned his elbows on his knees, trying his best not to let her see his eyes. He knew they'd betray him and she'd see how badly he felt for her. It wasn't pity, but he knew that love and caring could mimic pity in her mind.

"I came here the week after my mom died. I'm glad you chose this place to talk. I feel safe here, like she's nearby for some reason." Rebecca looked out over the water.

Pierce put his arm around her again. "You're safe, Bec. I'm here, too."

She nodded. "I know."

"Bec..."

She turned sad eyes toward him and drew her shoulders back. "You didn't bring your sunglasses." She smiled, but it was forced and it faded quickly.

"I don't pity you, Becca. I love you."

She looked down at her hands and drew in a deep breath. Her hair curtained her face. "I know you do."

Pierce tucked her hair behind her ear and lifted her chin. "Talk to me, please."

She nodded and dropped her eyes again, then looked out at the water. "I told you that Mr. Fralin let me and my mom stay in our apartment. Well, after she died, I stayed for another few weeks. I kept thinking that I'd get a job and raise enough money to afford to live there, and eventually I got the job at King's Bar, but that was only about two weeks before I met you. I felt so trapped. I owed Mr. Fralin two months of rent when she died, plus almost six more weeks for letting me stay afterward while I pulled myself together, and every day I stayed it cost him money in unearned rent. I felt guilty, and even though I had years to prepare for my mom dying, I wasn't prepared." She blinked at the tears that dampened her eyes.

Pierce drew her against him and kissed her temple. "I don't think anyone's ever prepared, no matter how long they have before it happens."

"Yeah," she whispered. She sat silently for a long while, rubbing her hands together and gazing out at the water. When she finally spoke again, some of the strength had returned to her voice.

"When I met you, I was staying in my car. It was only a few nights, and then Andy hooked me up with Chiara, and I got the job and rented a room from

Daphne."

He didn't know which hurt more, knowing she'd had to stay in her car or knowing she'd kept it from him. "Is that why you wouldn't let me near your trunk when we picked up your bag?"

She nodded, still not meeting his gaze.

"Rebecca, you slept over at my house. We were so close. I know we moved quickly, but why didn't you tell me?"

"That would have gone over really well." She crossed her arms, then uncrossed them and pushed from the rock to her feet. "Oh, hey, by the way, I live in my car. Tell me you wouldn't have run the other way." She turned her back to him, and Pierce rose and placed his hands on her shoulders from behind.

"I wouldn't have run the other way."

She scoffed. "Then you would have wanted to fix it for me."

How could he deny the truth? "Becca—"

"I know we said no secrets, but this is a little different, don't you think?" She turned to face him, and the determined look in her eyes was reminiscent of the first night they'd met, when come hell or high water, it was her against the world. But she wasn't alone any longer.

"No, I don't. Honesty isn't pick or choose."

She rolled her eyes. "It is when you're living in your car and you meet a guy who you really, really like—and he looks like his clothes cost more than your car. Pierce, my life is so far out of your realm that you couldn't possibly understand it." She took a step away, and he reached for her hand again.

"Rebecca, my life wasn't always what it is now. This isn't about living in your car. This is about trusting me with the truth. Would you ever have told me?" He didn't know what to think. He felt hurt, but at the same time, he knew that wasn't her intent, and he *wanted* to understand everything about Rebecca, including, and maybe most importantly, this.

"Yes. Later. Much later."

"When? When I asked you to marry me? When we had kids? When would you have trusted me enough, Rebecca?" His voice escalated and he paced, trying to calm himself down.

"I don't know. I just know that this isn't like lying about cheating on someone. I didn't do this to hurt you, Pierce. I did what I felt I had to." Her eyes welled with tears, but her voice was so angry that he couldn't tell if they were tears of anger or sadness.

"And I didn't do it to deceive you. I kept it from you so you could decide if you liked me for me without having to fix me or toss me aside because I was...homeless." Her shoulders dropped as the word fell from her lips.

Homeless. Holy Christ. Homeless. The word stung Pierce as badly as he could see it had stung her. He reached for her hand and she shrugged away. It was agonizing not being able to hold her, feeling like they were on the opposite sides of a fence when really he wanted her inside his fence, always, right there beside him.

"Okay, okay," he managed. "Let's both take a deep breath." He scrubbed his face with his hands. There was so much he wanted to understand. "Why the car,

Rebecca? Why didn't you stay at a shelter?"

"You won't understand." She sat back down on the rock.

"Try me."

She drew in another uneven breath. "Because staying at a shelter is like saying I'd really hit rock bottom."

"It's about being safe."

"I was safe."

"In your car? Do you know what could have happened to you?" Just the thought made his skin crawl.

That sent her to her feet again, pacing the small clearing. "Yes. Okay? Yes. Every time I walked into that cold parking garage, I knew what *could* happen to me. Every time I woke up to the sound of a car door slamming or wheels squealing, I knew." A tear slipped down her cheek. "I did what I had to do, and damn it, Pierce, I made it out the other side without any of those awful things happening to me, and—*oh God*—I showered at the gym every morning after my workout, I kept applying for jobs, so please don't think that I was dirty or any of those awful things that go along with being homeless."

The word stung as badly the second time around.

"I wasn't dirty or...*broken*. I was just broke." She covered her face with her hands, but not before Pierce saw tears stream down her cheeks.

He folded her into his arms and didn't release her when she halfheartedly shrugged him off. "Oh, Becca. I don't care about any of those things. I just wish you would have told me."

"Right." She sniffled, wiped her tears. "So you could *save* me."

"Maybe," he said honestly. "I don't know. I certainly liked you enough to want to save you. But I have a feeling you wouldn't have let me." On the surface she looked vulnerable, fragile, with damp eyes and a trembling lower lip, but behind the tears he saw fierce determination.

"I love you, Rebecca. Whether you lived in your car, on the street, or in a boat on a river makes no difference. My love for you isn't contingent on any of those things. It's unconditional." He pressed his lips to her forehead.

She closed her eyes and he held her close, feeling her heart beating against his. He knew how hard this was for her. She wore her pride like armor, and to have this secret revealed—a secret she thought was so powerful that it might change his love for her— explained the fight he felt in her rigid body.

"I'm sorry I didn't tell you. I was so worried that you would judge me."

"The only judgment I'll make is that you impress the hell out of me, Rebecca. You've overcome so much, and you haven't backed down on your principles, or let it define you. I think I'm the luckiest guy on earth to have you in my life."

When he tried to draw back and look into her eyes, she fisted her hands in his shirt and pressed her cheek to his chest.

"Don't look at me. Just hold me. Please just hold me."

Chapter Twenty-Two

IT HAD BEEN hours since Pierce had found out about Rebecca living in her car. In an effort to move past the reveal of her most intimate secret, they'd gone to a specialty store and bought a set of monogrammed champagne flutes for Daisy and Luke, had a nice dinner out on Pierce's patio, and still Rebecca couldn't shake the feeling of embarrassment. She hated that now when he looked at her he probably saw an image of her sleeping in her car. He'd never say as much—she'd probably scared him into keeping that kind of thought to himself. But she saw something different in his eyes, and she'd been trying to dodge it all evening. It was inescapable. It followed her around the room, stealing pieces of them. He kissed her more softly, more lovingly, instead of heated and impassioned. And what made matters worse was that she wasn't sure if it was intentional or a reflection of how she was acting.

Pierce was busy talking on the phone to someone

about the Grand, and as much as she hated herself for it, she just wanted to be alone. She needed to come to grips with the fact that now he knew. He was acting like he accepted the revealing of her most embarrassing point in her life like it didn't make any difference at all, but she knew it had to. How could it not?

I lived in my car.

How could he just accept it? He had to be connecting her to something unsavory, didn't he? Or was she losing her mind? One minute they were driving down Meet My Family Lane and the next, she could barely look at him without feeling like he pitied her.

She needed to get past this.

Rebecca closed her eyes and rested her head back on the couch, listening to Pierce's voice filter in from his home office. His voice was sharp when he was discussing business; his answers were succinct and confident, unlike when he was talking with her. Everything about Pierce was different with her than with anyone else. She smiled at the thought of how his rich, smooth voice wrapped around her like a velvet drape and warmed her to her core.

Will it still feel that way? Or will I always see and hear pity no matter what he does?

Oh God. She loved him so much it hurt to think about things between them being different. She heard footsteps approaching from his office, felt his presence behind the couch, and a moment later, she felt his lips on her forehead.

She loved his lips on her forehead.

"Sorry that took so long, babe."

Smooth as silk. She opened her eyes and damn it. She was sure it was her imagination, but she saw something different in his eyes. They were softer. Softer? Like he had to handle her with kid gloves? *Ugh.* She couldn't take it. Even if it was in her mind, she needed to figure out how to get past it, and she couldn't do that here with him.

She rose to her feet. "Pierce, would you mind if I stayed at my place tonight?"

"Wha...? Your place?" He came around the couch and reached for her hands. "Why?"

"I just need a little space to think. I..."

He drew her down to the couch beside him. "Babe, talk to me. Please don't shut me out. What's wrong?"

"I can't—" *Look at you without seeing pity.* She looked away. "I just need a little time to think clearly."

"To *think* clearly? How about telling me what's really going on? Are you upset that I said I wished you'd told me about staying in your car?" His tone was compassionate, but she heard an edge to his voice.

"No. No, that's not it. I just...I think I need time to deal with it all coming out in the open." She met his gaze, and everything good about them swirled around her. She was herself with Pierce, and even though she knew it was a struggle for him not to wave his money around and make all her troubles go away, he respected her need to do some things for herself. At the same time, he pushed in the areas that made sense. And she liked those things he pushed for: opening doors for her, pulling out chairs, wanting to protect her when they were out. She'd noticed the way he held

247

her tighter when other men were around and the way he always took an extra second to make sure they were in sync in the bedroom. She loved so much about him that she needed to get ahold of this other stuff that was clouding her vision before she ruined everything.

"I feel funny about all of it. I'm sorry I didn't tell you right away, but I did what I felt I had to. Now that you know, I just feel weird. I think I need a little time to digest it all."

He pulled her closer. "Can't you digest it with me?"

"No, because every time I look at you, I feel it between us." She pulled back. "Not between us like breaking us up, just like it was this big thing that..." She shook her head to try to clear her thoughts. "I don't know how to explain this except to be brutally honest."

"Babe, I'm used to your brutal honesty, so go ahead. Give it to me."

"You're looking at me with probably the same look you always have, but I see something so different. You've been kissing me with all the tenderness and all the love a woman could ask for, and I can't shake the feeling that it's because of everything that's come out. It's stupid, and I realize that, but, Pierce, even if you can get past this, I need to be able to get past it, too."

"I'm past it, Bec. You lived in your car. I get it." He stared into her eyes. "What do you need to get past? You're no longer in that car. You've got two places to live."

He wasn't hiding a damn thing. Not one single emotion. It was all right there on his face—*he loves*

248

me—but *damn it*, she still saw pity.

"Hard times call for drastic measures. You did what you had to do, and keeping it from me was just what you felt was right. I hope that you know now that there's nothing you can't trust me with, but I don't think of you any differently than I did before I knew. What you see in my eyes is love, Rebecca, plain and simple."

"That's just it, Pierce. You can tell me all the right things, but it isn't changing what I see and what I hear. I *know* this is my issue, not yours. I love you so much. God, I never thought—never dared dream—that I'd ever love someone, or be loved by someone, as much as I love you. And yet here we are. My mom's pictures are in your house, my clothes are in your closet, and you? You've taken up residence in my heart and there's no evicting you."

That earned her a smile that made her vision even cloudier.

"What are you really afraid of?" Pierce kissed the back of her hand.

"Nothing." It was a knee-jerk response. She was afraid of plenty of things. Not being able to make her life happen the way she wanted it and being looked at like a charity case fought for the top of the list. Maybe they weren't normal fears for a woman her age, but they were hers, and she couldn't do a damn thing to make them go away. She had other fears, too. Like right now, she was afraid that walking out the door might change things forever with Pierce, but staying there and not working the kinks out in her own mind might do more harm than a night or two apart could ever do.

This was one of those times when she wished she had her mother to talk to. She didn't allow her mind to go down that lonely path often. Rebecca had become an expert at compartmentalizing her feelings, and the only way to keep herself from hurting too much was to keep those wish-my-mom-was-here moments in a compartment called Don't Go There.

She went there.

She couldn't help it.

Pierce was so deeply embedded in her heart—in her every breath. He was nestled up against the memory of her mother. She closed her eyes against fresh tears and felt his arms gather her close again. She breathed him in, feeling safe and loved—and like she needed to clear her stupid head before she ruined everything.

"Babe," he whispered. "It's okay. Stay at your place if you need to. Do you want me to drive you over?"

She shook her head and gripped his shirt so tightly she thought it might rip, but she couldn't let go.

He kissed the top of her head; then he pressed his big, safe hands to her cheeks and wiped her tears with his thumbs.

"Hate me if you must, but I wish I could fix whatever's making you so sad."

She laughed through her tears. He lowered his lips to hers, and her salty tears mixed with their kisses. She tried to kiss her heartache away, but it just made her feel like there was a deep well traveling down the center of her body and boring an ugly hole. She pushed away, breathing hard at the thought.

"You know I love you, right?" she asked.

He nodded.

"Say it. Please. I need to know that you know I'm not walking out that door to break us up. I'm doing it to keep us together." She knew she was overreacting. She had a feeling in her gut that her loathing of pity was a mask for something else, but for the life of her she couldn't figure out what—and she knew she needed to before it ruined everything good in her life.

He wiped her tears again, and the edges of his lips curved, just a little, like his smile was afraid to come forth. "I know you love me, Rebecca. But don't ask me to pretend that I don't want to beg you to stay. I can't do that any more than I can pretend that I don't want to pay off your debt, pay for your classes, and set you up with a job you're worthy of, where you can learn and grow and make all your dreams come true." He pressed a hard kiss to her lips. "All I can do is love you and trust that you know what you need, and hope that one day you'll find what you need right here by my side."

PIERCE PACED HIS driveway long after Rebecca's taillights disappeared. He was trying like hell to be understanding, but damn it, this sucked—and it fucking hurt. What was he supposed to do now? He was a man with the means to do just about anything, except look at the woman he loved in a way that showed her how much he loved her and couldn't be misinterpreted as pity.

He didn't pity her.

Damn it. He was sick of having his hands tied.

Rebecca needed him to love her the way she deserved to be loved. He respected her pride—maybe too damn much—but didn't she have to respect his, too?

There was only one thing he could do, because there was no fucking way he was going to let their relationship hang in the wings while he was in LA.

He went inside and set up the calendar Rebecca had picked out for him, and then he wrote the things he planned for the next few days and set an early alarm on his phone. If he could give his all to his business, he could give more than that to Rebecca—in ways she couldn't help but love.

He hoped.

Damn, did he hope.

Chapter Twenty-Three

REBECCA DRAGGED HERSELF out of bed Sunday morning with puffy bags under her eyes from crying most of the night and an ache in the center of her chest that felt like it had taken up residence. Exercising was the last thing she wanted to do, but she'd been here before—too overwrought to move. She knew that she could go down with the ship or right its course, and if she could make it through losing her mother, she could make it through pulling her head out of her ass and getting around her stubborn force field against feeling pitied. *Pitied.* She couldn't escape the feeling of a demon much bigger than pity gnawing at her insides and clawing to get out—and buried too deep for her to grasp and figure out.

She forced herself to get out of bed, and she went into the kitchen and made coffee. While it brewed, she sat at the table and rested her head on her arms, struggling to try and understand what she was really feeling.

"I thought I heard you come in last night." Henry poured two mugs of coffee and placed one in front of Rebecca. "It's only five thirty. What are you doing up?"

"Going to the gym if I can convince my body to move."

"Mm. Bad night?" Henry sipped his coffee. His hair was disheveled, and he was wearing a blue robe with a white T-shirt and a pair of blue plaid pajama pants beneath.

"Not really a bad night. I think I just have a bad head." She sipped her coffee and grimaced at the pungent taste.

Henry set his mug down on the table. "Nah, you have a fine head. Want to talk about it?"

"No thanks, Henry. My head really isn't fine right now."

"Getting it out of your head might help." He shrugged one shoulder. "Just offering."

Rebecca sighed.

"It's okay, but I'm here if you want to talk."

Henry retrieved the newspaper from the porch and came back into the kitchen. He must have picked up his reading glasses from the living room, because the thin wire frames were now perched on his nose as he sat down and opened the newspaper to the Classifieds section.

"Are you going to call Chiara?" Rebecca asked.

"Already have. I left her a message right after Pierce gave me her number. She called back yesterday." He lowered the newspaper. "I couldn't believe it. On a Saturday. I guess when she heard I was referred by Pierce Braden, it put a jump in her step."

"Maybe." *His name puts a jump in my heart.*

"I have an interview with her tomorrow. She said they don't have anything now, but they're working on an acquisition, and if it comes through and my references pan out, yada yada." He rolled his eyes. "Then they'll need to hire in the accounting department. So I'm going in to get the ball rolling."

"That's great, Henry. I hope that comes through for you." She checked the time. "I better get to the gym."

Henry reached for her hand as she passed his chair on her way to the sink with her mug. "Rebecca, you have a good head on your shoulders. It's when your heart and head begin to war that you have to worry."

She smiled, but it was a halfhearted smile at best. "My heart and head want the same things. I think the problem is that my head is stuck in survival mode, and my heart is ready to kick into first gear."

He squeezed her hand before releasing it. "Sweetheart, healing takes time. You should honor your head and your heart so they don't both rebel."

Rebecca washed her mug, trying to figure out what that meant—or how she could even do such a thing.

She grabbed her gym bag and her clothes for her workday and then headed out to her car. It was barely six o'clock and she felt like she'd slept two hours. She zipped her hoodie, rounded her shoulders against the chilly morning air, and tugged the door shut behind her. She lifted her eyes and her breath caught in her throat. Her legs refused to move.

Pierce.

Dressed in a dark suit and tie and wearing a smile that lifted the corners of his eyes, he stole what little breath she had left in her lungs. He came to her side and took her gym bag and clothes.

"I'm not here to pressure you." He settled a hand on the curve of her back and kissed her softly on the lips.

"Why...? Why are you here?" With the help of his hand urging her forward, she remembered how to walk.

"Because I love you." He hung her clothing on the hook in the back of her car, set her gym bag on the seat, and then opened the car door for her.

"You drove all this way to open my car door?" *God, I love that.*

"No. I drove all this way to see you *and* open your car door." He motioned her toward the car. "Go ahead and get in. I don't want to mess up your morning schedule."

"How did you know what time I'd be leaving?"

"I didn't. I've been here for a while."

Oh God. Oh God.

Rebecca settled into the driver's seat, and he leaned in and kissed her again. He smelled so good. She couldn't help but wrap her arms around him and keep him close.

"I missed you last night," she said against his lips.

"I missed you, too." He crouched beside her and placed his hand on her thigh. "What time do you get off work?"

"Three." The fact that he wasn't even mentioning

how her *thinking* was going made her love him even more.

"My flight leaves at five." He furrowed his brow; then he shook whatever he was thinking away and kissed her again.

He rose to his feet, and Rebecca grabbed his hand.

"Pierce—" The desperation in her voice startled her. She reminded herself he wasn't leaving her by going to LA. He was doing what he needed to do for work. *I'm the one who walked away.*

He flashed his easy smile that made her insides go soft—and she searched his eyes. *Love. And a hint of...Stop. Just stop it.*

"Thank you. I'm going to miss you so much while you're gone." *And hopefully figure out my shit so we can move forward.*

"I already miss you."

AT THREE O'CLOCK Pierce waited at the entrance to the restaurant for Rebecca. She'd looked exhausted this morning. He'd wanted so badly to ask her what was going on in that sharp mind of hers, but he'd promised himself he wouldn't go there. He'd intended to greet her after she went to the gym, too, but she'd been so gracious about him just showing up at her house that he worried she'd think he didn't trust her if he showed up at the gym, as well. He was trying his best to understand all the things that made Rebecca comfortable, and walking that thin line took all of his focus—because his nature was to show up at the gym, wait for her until after she got out, then show up at work and open her door again.

Overkill.

It had been part of who he was for so many years that it took a cognitive effort to restrain those urges. He knew that being too aggressive would push Rebecca away. But Pierce wasn't successful for nothing. Finesse was another one of his skills, and he intended to use it. Rebecca had said that she saw something in his eyes, and he'd just have to keep showing her that what she saw was not pity, but the love he felt for her. He hoped if she saw it enough, she'd recognize it for what it was.

He spotted her as she crossed the restaurant. She smiled as she passed the other waitstaff, but Pierce saw right through the smile to the pain that lay beneath, mixed and muddled with fatigue. Rebecca was nearly on top of him before she saw him.

"Pierce." The smile that spread across her lips this time was as real as the thundering of his heart.

"Hi, babe." He leaned in and kissed her.

"I didn't expect to see you. I thought you had to catch your flight this afternoon."

He draped an arm over her shoulder as they walked out of the building. "I do. I delayed it. I wanted to see you one last time before I went."

"Pierce, you can't rearrange your schedule for me."

"I already did. Besides, you can tell me what I can and can't do when it comes to helping you out in certain ways, but you can't control everything I do where you're concerned."

"Control? Is that what you think I'm trying to do?" She said it with a smile, but he heard a thread of irritation in her voice and felt her tense beneath his arm.

"What would you call it?"

"Doing for myself the things I should. Standing my ground. Keeping hold of a shred of my pride. This is who I am, Pierce. It's who I was before I met you. My mom and I had no one to help us, and damn it, I held us together, and I did it with pride."

Her voice was full of determination, but damn if he didn't hear sadness lacing her words. He knew that saying so would only piss her off.

"I'm not trying to take away from who you are and all that you've done, Bec. You're amazing, and you're more than capable of whatever you set out to do. I know that about you and I'm not trying to demean it in any way."

She was silent as they walked through the rotating doors of the resort. It reminded him of their first date, which brought his mind back to Rebecca sleeping in her car and pulled at his heartstrings.

"Good, because you can't." Her tone softened a little. "No one can."

"Okay, fair enough." He kissed her temple. "You're a smart woman, and I know that you realize that everything you said, no matter what you call it, is all about remaining in control."

"It is not."

He let her stew with that thought while they walked through the parking garage to her car on the fourth floor. He kept his arm around her shoulder as they went in and out of the elevator, and she had yet to relax beneath his touch.

When they reached her car, she turned to face him. Her eyes were no longer sad or angry. They were confused.

"Control?" she asked.

He shrugged. "Why are you taking time to think, Rebecca?" So much for giving her the space she needed. He really did suck at giving up control as much as she did—they were quite a pair.

"Because I need it." She crossed her arms and narrowed her eyes, as if she were assessing her own thoughts.

He closed the gap between them and spoke softly. "Think about it, babe. You're used to doing everything. Controlling every aspect of your life, making sure you are doing the things you need to so you don't end up someplace you don't want to be. And you're good at it."

"You do the same thing."

It was an accusation, and probably true. "Yes, but I admit I'm a control freak, and I've given up a lot of control to you. All I'm saying is that you didn't get to tell me about staying in your car on your terms. Andy spilled the beans, and that left you feeling out of control."

"But Andy didn't make you look at me like you pity me." She held his gaze with a serious stare.

"No, he didn't, and I don't look at you like I pity you, because I don't pity you. Honestly, Bec, I think you're skewing your perception to fit your need to control things." He didn't even realize he felt that way until that second. The pieces were falling into place—at least for him. He'd relinquished control of so many aspects of his life for Rebecca. He'd set aside the desire to do things for her, with her. Things he hadn't wanted to do for any other woman—take her to Tahoe for the weekend. Hell, take her to Paris, for that matter. Take her shopping and lavish her with gifts she'd find over the top and he'd think weren't enough to show how much she meant to him. But he didn't mind giving up those things. They were just that, *things*. He realized that those visible effects of his love weren't what mattered. What mattered was that when she looked into his eyes, she saw into his heart and felt the love he had for her. And now the one thing that meant the most was being blurred—and he wondered if it was driven by another fear he had yet to understand. She'd relinquished control of smaller things—letting him open doors—and big things, like talking about her most intimate feelings, revealing the things she'd gone through when caring for her mother. Now it was all coming to a head, as if revealing that she'd slept in the car had pushed her over the edge, and she was scrambling to regain the control she lost. Or, what had him even more worried was what if he was wrong, and it wasn't as much about control itself? What if she needed to regain control so she didn't lose her footing and accidentally reveal something even more intimate?

Something so frightening she had to see *him* as the bad guy.

"CONTROL THINGS? IS that what you think I'm doing?" She reacted viciously to his suggestion. "This isn't about control." She rooted around in her purse for her keys and turned away from Pierce. *Control. My ass it's about control.* She waited for him to touch her shoulders, or her hips, the way he always did when she was upset.

He didn't.

"Then tell me what it is, please. Because I don't pity you. Jesus, Bec, how could I? You're the smartest, most determined woman I know. There's nothing pitiable about you. Hell, Rebecca, there's nothing you can't do."

"I don't know, okay?" *Don't cry. Oh God, don't cry. Please don't cry.* She found her key and unlocked the door to her car.

She sensed him move in closer. His chest pressed against her back, his scent engulfed her, and his cheek—oh God, that clean-shaven cheek she loved to touch—pressed against hers.

"Then let's figure it out together," he whispered.

I can't. I'm afraid. "H-how? You're leaving, remember?"

"I'll stay."

She closed her eyes against the welling tears. She knew he meant it. He would stay, and she wanted him to stay more than she wanted anything else in the world, but then she'd throw his staying into the pity bin—because she was that fucked up at the moment.

"You can't. You've got the Grand acquisition to solidify."

He turned her around gently. "Rebecca."

If love had a sound, it was in the way he'd said her name, and dear Lord, she heard it loud and clear.

He ran a hand down her cheek and traced the line

of her jaw with his finger. "You are more important than any business deal. You've opened something inside of me that I didn't even know existed. And last night I felt like I'd been cut open, and the very thing that made me feel whole for the first time in my life was gone."

She splayed her hands against his chest. He felt so good, safe, real. *Whole.* He felt whole. Was it only because she was there with him? She pressed her cheek to his chest and listened to the sound of his breathing, and she knew in an instant that he was telling the truth. He wasn't whole. It was a facade. Something for the rest of the world to see.

Only he didn't hide behind that charade for her.

Why couldn't she give him the same truth?

Because I don't know what I'm afraid of.

"Don't stay, Pierce." She swiped at her damp eyes and drew her shoulders back. Crying would only make him stay. He needed her to be strong, or he would give up the very thing he'd been working on for months. "Go make your business deal happen. I have to go to my doctor appointment tomorrow, and I'll be here waiting when you get back. Hopefully with a clearer head."

"Rebecca, what is it? Am I too much? Do I come on too strong? Do I represent something you don't like?"

He searched her eyes, and she knew he wouldn't find the answer he was looking for. How could he when she didn't even know it?

"No, Pierce. You represent everything I strive to be. Successful, strong, confident."

"Maybe it's all too fast for you, and you don't

realize it." He ran his hand through his hair and turned away. "Is that it? You were pretty honest with me at the beginning. You said you weren't looking for a relationship, and I plowed my way into your life."

Her mother's words sailed through her mind and clung to her like a badge of courage. She'd heard her mother say it only once, in the days before she died, and she finally understood them.

"Love doesn't need an invitation, Pierce."

His gaze softened, and when he lowered his forehead to hers, she felt her walls come crumbling down.

"I'm trying to understand," he said quietly. "Is there something more you're not telling me? Because it sure feels like there's more, and I feel like it's control, but if you say it's not, then I trust you. But if this...us...if we're not right for you, you need to tell me, because nothing has ever felt more right in my life."

"We are right." The determination in her voice startled her. "We are. I know that in my heart, Pierce. We are right as rain. But..." She drew in a deep breath and clung to him again. "I'm scared, okay? Petrified, really. But I can't talk about any of it, because I don't understand it. You just have to trust that I can figure this out—that I *will* figure this out."

He took a step back, taking the air from her lungs along with him.

He shifted his eyes away. When he finally met her gaze, the emotion in his eyes cut straight to her core.

"I trust you, Rebecca."

It was exactly what she'd asked for, and it hurt like hell.

Chapter Twenty-Four

PIERCE SAT IN the back of the sedan watching the traffic roll by as the driver made his way through the streets of Los Angeles toward Jake's house. He couldn't stop thinking about how he'd fucked up things with Rebecca. Why couldn't he keep his goddamn mouth shut? He'd known he'd push her away, and still he'd pressed for answers.

He pulled out his cell phone and considered calling her. She might get even more upset. He gazed out the window, aching to clear the air with Rebecca. He owed her an apology, and the longer he delayed it, the more it bored a hole in his gut.

He pressed her speed-dial number.

"Hey there. How's sunny California?"

Her sweet voice brought a smile to his lips. "Hi, babe. Just like sunny Reno only without my favorite person."

"You get brownie points for that one."

He heard the smile in her voice, and it eased the

tension that had tightened the muscles across his shoulders. "I wanted to apologize, Bec. I'm really sorry for pushing you this afternoon."

"It's fine, really."

"No, it's not. My need for a resolution shouldn't come before your need to figure things out on your own timetable. I'm sorry, Bec. I'll try to be more respectful of your feelings." Pierce didn't care that the driver could hear every word he said. He only cared that he said them to Rebecca before it was too late.

"It's okay. I know this is me, Pierce. It's my issue, and it's got to drive you batty. I know how crazy it is for me to tell you that I love you and then tell you that I still love you but need space. It makes me feel a little crazy in my own head."

"You're not crazy. You've been through so much that it's crazy you can function at all." He realized how true those words were. Her mother died almost two months ago. *Two months.* Why didn't he slow down and think about that when he was with her? *I was too busy trying to fix everything.*

"I can handle it, Pierce."

There it was. Determination and misinterpretation wrapped up in one single sentence. How could he make her understand? He rubbed his temples.

"Babe, I didn't mean that like it sounded. I meant that you are amazing."

"Oh."

"We're doing a lot of miscommunicating lately."

"I think that's my fault," she said. "I've been thinking about what you said, and maybe you're right.

Some of this has to do with control."

"I don't know if I'm right. I just know that I want to..." He stopped himself from saying, *fix it.* "I can't wait to see you again."

"Me too. Pierce, I'll figure this all out. I know I will." Her voice softened, and he pictured her fidgeting with a seam on her clothing, or gazing up at her mother's picture, her eyes serious as she tried to work out whatever was going on in her mind.

He recognized the road that led up to Jake's house and knew he had only a few minutes left to talk to Rebecca before seeing his brother. "Are you okay? Do you need anything?"

"Just to rewind time about a million years."

He smiled at that and wondered when she'd go back to. Before they met? When her mother was still alive? Before she got sick? Or did she mean before she was even born so she could *really* start over?

"If I had the power, I'd do it for you. I love you, babe."

"I love you, too. Hey, Pierce?"

"Yeah?"

She was quiet for a long time. Pierce listened to the cadence of her breathing, a sound he'd come to know when she'd fallen asleep in his arms and in the wee hours of the morning before she awoke.

"I know I can handle anything, but I'm glad you're sticking with me through this."

"You don't have to handle anything alone ever again."

"Says the man who can handle anything."

"That's where you're wrong. I always thought that

I could handle anything, but when you walked out the door last night, I realized how wrong I was."

JAKE'S FIVE BEDROOM, Mediterranean-style home sat atop seven sprawling acres in the Hollywood Hills. Pierce was excited to see his brother, but as the driver pulled up in front of the house and parked behind one of Jake's motorcycles, he got a funny feeling in his stomach. His and Jake's good times had usually revolved around women, and he hadn't taken that into account before nixing the idea of staying at one of his properties. Pierce stepped from the car and realized that he'd forgotten to call Jake and tell him he was coming. While the driver put his bags on the front porch, Pierce peered into Jake's four-car garage. Every bay was occupied, and there was music coming from inside the house. At least his brother was home.

He thanked the driver, gave him a hundred-dollar tip, and then rapped on the door. When Jake didn't answer, he let himself in. One thing he could always count on with Jake—if he was home, his door was open. Jake was thirty-four years old, but he lived like he was running a co-ed dormitory. A trail of wet footprints led from the marble foyer across the hardwood floors in the living room and out the French doors.

Pierce set his bags down and followed the footprints to the pool in the backyard. Through the years, he and Jake had had more good times than he could count—usually beginning with meeting Jake's buddies for a beer, or hitting an after-party once filming wrapped for one of Jake's projects, and ending with both of them wondering what the names of the women were who'd accompanied them the evening before. Now it turned Pierce's stomach thinking of how many faceless women he'd made out with. Even after just a couple of weeks with Rebecca, he knew he'd never go back to that lifestyle—hell, he knew after a night with Rebecca that she was the only woman he wanted.

He heard Jake's voice before he spotted him among the harem of bikini bodies standing by the covered bar at the opposite end of the pool. Jake's hair was a shade lighter than Pierce's and their other siblings, but he shared the same dark Braden eyes as the rest of them. He had a perpetual tan and a body built for his stuntman career: solid muscle and ready to take a beating, as proven by the multitude of razor-thin scars that etched their way into his torso, arms, and legs. He'd somehow avoided facial scars, except for one particular scar that rode the boundary of his hairline. That particular scar came from a wrestling match with Pierce when they were teens.

Three blond, buxom women turned as Pierce approached. He had to hand it to Jake. He'd always loved big-breasted women. The blondes had large breasts that were too perfectly perky and round to be natural, small waists, slim hips, and a look in their overly done eyes that practically screamed of sex. They were triplets, Pierce realized. *Hello, Ready, Willing, and Able.*

"Who is this, Jake?" One of them asked as she raked her eyes down Pierce's Armani suit. In his mind, Pierce named this woman *Ready*.

"Pierce. Bro, what are you doing here?" Jake came around the bar and embraced him.

"I had a meeting in town. I should have called."

Ready was the tallest of the blondes. She looped her arm into Pierce's. "So...You're Jake's brother?"

"Mm. I see the family resemblance," said the blonde with the longest hair—whom Pierce aptly named *Willing* because of the way she arched her chest toward him when she spoke.

"Yeah, we're brothers." Pierce peeled Ready's arm from his. "Jake, I was hoping we could catch dinner."

"I've got dinner for you." The third blonde, whom Pierce had named *Able*, wiggled her shoulders at Pierce.

How did I ever find women like this attractive?

"Man, you're just in time. We're going to a party in about thirty minutes." Jake narrowed his eyes. "You want a drink to loosen up that stress? You look like you're carrying the world on your shoulders. Girls, help him out of that jacket, will ya?"

"Our pleasure." Able grabbed his collar and slid his jacket off. "Oh, this is nice. Armani." It rolled off her tongue like spun gold.

Ready loosened his tie. "We'll loosen you up."

"I've got it, thank you." Pierce stepped away from their hungry fingers and loosened his tie.

"So, party, then?" Jake handed him a drink.

A party was the last place he wanted to go. He'd like for the next twenty-four hours to pass as quickly as possible so he could get back to Rebecca.

"Actually, I'm beat. I'll hang out here, if you don't mind. I'll catch you when you get back." Pierce gulped down his drink and set the glass on the bar.

"Bro. Really? We just wrapped filming the last in the Trojan series. Everyone's going to be there." Jake draped an arm around Able and Willing. "And I've got an extra woman for your arm."

Ready giggled and pressed her body against Pierce's side.

Pierce peeled Ready's hands from his chest again. "Nice, Jake, but actually, things on that front have changed."

"Whoa? You've gone gay on me?" Jake laughed.

"Hardly. I've gone monogamous." He watched his brother's smile fade and his eyes narrow.

"Monogamous. What the hell is happening back there in Trusty? You guys are dropping like flies. I'm not sure I should come home next weekend for Luke's party."

Willing ran her finger along the waistband of Jake's low-riding jeans. "Monogamy is no fun. Right, girls?"

The other girls *Mm-hm*ed in agreement.

"I wasn't in Trusty. I was in Reno." Pierce grabbed his jacket from where Able had set it on the bar.

"Girls, give us a minute, will you?" Jake watched them walk to the far end of the pool before joining Pierce at the bar. "What's up?"

"Nothing. I thought I'd see if we could catch dinner."

"Not that. What's up with the monogamy shit?" Jake glanced back at the girls and shook his head. "Pierce, look at them. How can you turn *that* down?"

"Jake, you do realize that you're only a few years

away from forty, right? Don't you ever want to have a real life? A family?" Pierce laughed at the words coming from his mouth. "Listen to me. Shit, give me that drink." He took Jake's drink from his hand and gulped it down.

"No shit. A real life? Man, I have more women than I could ever want. What more is there?" Jake glanced back again. Able blew him a kiss.

Pierce slapped his brother on the back. "I never thought I'd be the one saying it, but, Jake, there's a hell of a lot more than tits and ass out there waiting for you."

Jake squinted at him, moved in close and searched his eyes, then drew back. "Well, you're not high. What the fuck? Am I being punked?" He made a show of looking from side to side.

Pierce shrugged, unable to repress his smile as he thought about Rebecca. "I met a woman and she changed everything. Rebecca Rivera." *Rebecca.* He shifted his eyes to the blondes. Rebecca was ten times as pretty as they were, and he didn't need to interview the blondes to know she was ten times as smart as all three of them combined.

"I bet a night with the triplets could change that." Jake raised his brows with a mischievous grin.

"No, thanks." He turned his back to the girls. "I know what you're thinking. The same thing I was thinking when Wes and Luke each said they were in love. *Not me. Never me.*"

"Shit. It's not even a consideration. You can do what you please, but life is too sweet right now to change a damn thing." Jake shook his head. "But I will skip the party so we can hang out."

"No. You don't need to do that. Go. Have fun. I'll be here when you get back. We can catch up then."

Jake pushed from the bar. "No chance in hell. Family first. Just give me a minute."

Two hours later, they were eating dinner at the Palm, an exclusive restaurant that catered to the stars. Jake loved nothing more than flashy lights and starstruck women. While Pierce enjoyed fine meals and used to enjoy the company of racy women, he didn't need the fanfare.

"Jake." Brad Parlor, an A-list actor recently named Sexiest Man Alive by *The Stars* magazine, opened his arms as Jake rose to greet him. "How's it going, man? I heard you were wrapping up Trojan. That's gonna be a blockbuster."

"Thanks, Brad. I'm slated to work on your movie next month." Jake touched Pierce's shoulder. "You know my brother, Pierce. He's in for the night."

Pierce rose and shook Brad's hand. "Good to see you again."

"I was down in Texas last week, hit your casino and lost a few grand." Brad flashed the smile that won women over worldwide.

"Sorry, man, but hey, thanks." Pierce sat back down while Jake talked to Brad and then greeted two brunettes with hugs and promises to call.

Until tonight, Jake's lifestyle hadn't seemed like it was lacking a damn thing. Pierce watched his handsome and charming brother in action while he longed to be with Rebecca, and that longing made him realize all that Jake was missing out on. Sex before

Rebecca was fun, a great stress reliever at the end of a grueling week. Making love with Rebecca filled his soul with emotions that carried through their intimacy, making it more meaningful, and in doing so, more intense and passionate.

God, he missed her.

Jake was busy with a blonde now, making small talk about the party he'd skipped. Pierce pulled out his cell to text Rebecca. He must have forgotten to turn the ringer on after he got off the airplane, because there was a missed call from her. He turned his ringer on, thinking of how she'd have reminded him to do it if she'd been traveling with him, then dialed her number.

The call went to voicemail, and he left her a quick message. "Hi, babe. Just missed you. Hope your night is going well. I'll talk to you later."

Jake settled back into his seat. "Sorry 'bout that. You sure you don't want to hit the party later?"

"Yeah, I'm sure. But you can go, Jake. I'm a big boy."

Jake waved to another blonde across the room, and that small act rubbed Pierce the wrong way. Just because Pierce had become a one-woman man didn't mean he had to thrust his behavior on Jake. He was too damn edgy with all the stuff going on between him and Rebecca. He'd only annoy Jake. He needed to go back to Jake's, look over the documents for tomorrow's meeting, and hopefully sleep the hours away so he could get back to Rebecca quicker.

It turned out that convincing Jake to go to the party was easy. *Dude, what would you rather do, sit around with your boring older brother or hook up with some gorgeous chick?* If he couldn't change Jake's mind about women, he might as well use it to his advantage. He also knew his brother well enough to understand that he wouldn't come home before three in the morning—long after Pierce had gone to sleep. Pierce didn't mind. He was too preoccupied to visit anyway. He took a cab back to Jake's house and used the key his brother had given him to let himself inside.

Every floor in Jake's house, with the exception of the bedrooms, was either hardwood or marble. The ceilings were all nine feet or higher, and Jake's high-end taste in furniture gave his house a model home feel, so different from the feel of Pierce's. Granted, like Pierce, Jake owned several homes. Real estate was a solid investment, and all of the Bradens were careful with their investments. But Pierce knew Jake preferred this particular residence. It suited his lifestyle perfectly—posh location, entertainment at his fingertips with a billiards room, the pool, and a large media room. It had all of the amenities that used to make Pierce feel at home and comfortable. Now it made him long to be back home with Rebecca.

He grabbed his bags and headed up to the guest room. He was toweling off from a shower when Rebecca called.

"Hey, babe."

"Hi. I hope I'm not interrupting you and Jake. I went out to the store with Daphne and forgot my phone."

It was so damn good to hear her voice. "You're not interrupting. Jake's at a party. I came back to prepare for tomorrow."

"You skipped going to a party with Jake? I hope he didn't mind."

"I love how you worry about everyone else. He's fine. He loves parties and I..." He sat down on the bed. He didn't want small talk, and he didn't want to minimize what he was feeling. "I used to love them, but, Rebecca, I can't pretend that everything is fine. The whole scene up here is so far from where my head is now that we're together that I just want to be with you. I miss you."

Pierce grabbed his wallet from the dresser and took out the picture from the photo booth.

"I miss you, too." Her voice softened, and he pictured her eyes warming and her cheeks lifting with her smile. "I've been thinking about things, and I think I need to bite the bullet and instead of taking my last classes in the fall, I'll use that money to go to Punta Allen and spread my mom's ashes. I think part of my trouble is that I haven't had any closure with my mom's death. Having that might help me move forward and see things more clearly."

"God, I wish I was with you right now. I'll support whatever you want. Whatever you need." He set the picture on the nightstand by the bed, fighting the urge to tell her that he'd buy the tickets tonight and that she didn't need to finish her last two classes or work another damn day in her life if she didn't want to. Whatever she wanted, he would make happen. He had enough money for two lifetimes—for both of them. But if there was one thing he understood now more than ever, it was that until Rebecca believed—one hundred percent trusted—that what she saw in his eyes was love, all the gestures in the world wouldn't change a damn thing.

Chapter Twenty-Five

JAKE ARRIVED HOME from a hard night of partying as Pierce was heading out Monday morning. Jake had called just after midnight to see if Pierce wanted him to head home, but Pierce had already crashed for the night and missed his call, retrieving the message only an hour ago. Now, as his brother sauntered through the living room with a sated grin on his face, Pierce shook his head. He knew he had no right to judge Jake. He'd joined his brother in carousing too many times to count.

Pierce dropped his bags and embraced Jake. "It was good to see you, Jake."

"You, too. Call me next time; let me know you're coming. We'll make plans." Jake rubbed the stubble that peppered his square jaw. "And despite me giving you shit, I'm happy about you and Rebecca."

"Thanks. I know it's gonna sound crazy coming from me, but I hope that one day you'll allow yourself to settle down and be loved the way you deserve. Not everyone's like Buddy." Pierce saw Jake's body stiffen and the muscle in his jaw bunch. Their father had done a number on all of them, and whether it was buried deep in their subconscious, as Pierce thought was the case with Jake, or they wore it on their sleeves, like Luke had, the scars ran deep. Pierce didn't think for a second that he was above being counted among Buddy's casualties. No, he'd been aware for more years than he'd care to admit that his need to control his environment and his need to earn enough money to be able to buy his family anything they could ever need both stemmed from Buddy's abandonment. As the thought rose to the surface, he realized that while he'd never shared those thoughts with anyone, it was time he shared them with Rebecca.

An hour later, Pierce sat across from William Benson in Benson's corporate office. Between worrying about today's meeting and thinking about how much he wanted to help Rebecca accomplish all of the things she wanted to but feeling hamstrung by her pride, he hadn't gotten much sleep. Running on just a few hours of sleep had been a way of life for Pierce for so long that whether or not he was rested, he remained a shrewd businessman. It was the ability to push past what most people stumbled through that gave him his edge.

"Are we going to cut to the chase, or shall we piddle around the issue?" William Benson was an elderly man with stark white hair, bushy eyebrows, and midnight-blue eyes. He wore eyeglasses with thick black frames and lenses too large for his narrow face and sat behind his large mahogany desk with his legs crossed and his hands folded in a relaxed fashion.

Pierce was an up-front guy, and he'd like nothing more than to nail the old bastard to the wall for misleading him about the value of the Grand. Maybe a team of lesser-skilled accountants would have overlooked the millions in accounts receivables that, for various reasons, should have been written off— renegotiations after the fact, businesses closed, delivery of goods and services deemed unacceptable. Pierce's expert staff uncovered those misappropriated, uncollectible funds, as well as other issues.

"I'm not a piddler, William. Despite the inappropriate books you provided, I'm going to make you an offer, and then I'm going to get up and walk out that door. You'll have twenty-four hours to make your decision. After twenty-four hours, the offer will be null and void." Pierce leveled a narrow-eyed, serious stare on the old man. "I want to be very clear about the terms of the offer. They are written in stone. I will not negotiate, and I will not return with another offer should you turn it down."

He pushed a file containing the offer across the wide desk. "Asking price, twenty-two million. Two-year earn out. You'll find all of the details within the written offer." He rose to his feet and extended a hand. Normally he'd say something akin to, *It's been a pleasure*, but Pierce was still busy repressing the urge to tell the snake that he looked forward to taking over the business and leaving William Benson's measly twenty-two million in the dust when he turned the Grand around and tripled the profits.

With a firm handshake and a silent nod, Pierce

headed out the door—and back home to Rebecca a day early.

REBECCA RAN FASTER, lifted heavier weights, and did more sit-ups than she'd done in months. Working out usually cleared her mind, but today her mind seemed to be filled with quicksand. It held on to uncomfortable thoughts and wouldn't let them go. How could she even think she saw pity in Pierce's eyes? She knew it wasn't real, but at the same time, it felt as real as the floor beneath her.

"Chin up, Rebecca." Andy crouched beside her. "You know you'll get better results if you go a little slower and use better form. What's going on? You're racing through your routine like a bat outta hell."

She continued doing crunches. Even if they were too fast and too sloppy to do much good, the exertion felt great.

"Working out the kinks in my head." She panted as she pushed her body through too many searing, painful crunches. She wasn't scheduled to work today, and after working out, then going to her doctor appointment, she planned on stopping by Mr. Fralin's to pick up her mother's urn. She'd left it there under the premise that the urn was more secure in his wall safe than it would be in her car until she was settled. She had a feeling that leaving her mother's ashes there was one of the niggling kinks in her head. She wouldn't always be the woman whose mother recently died, and the faster she got her own head out of that position, the quicker she'd heal. She needed to put her mother in her final resting place. The sooner the better.

"You didn't tell me that you were dating Pierce Braden. Chiara mentioned it the other day, but until I saw you at the mall, I thought it was just a rumor." He pointed to the client he'd just finished working with. "Greg. Great job." He gave the guy a thumbs-up.

"No rumor. It's real."

"He seemed like a good guy. Chiara raves about how he treats all of his employees. Talk about luck, going from your car to dating the richest guy in Reno."

"It's not like that." She stopped doing crunches and sat up, sweat beading every inch of her skin. "In fact." She inhaled deeply, trying to calm her breathing from the difficult workout. "He didn't know about me living in my car until you mentioned it."

"Oh, shit. Really?" He pushed a hand through his short hair. "I'm sorry. Geez, I should have recognized the way you ran off without him when I mentioned the car, but I was only thinking about getting my new phone. I hope I didn't screw things up for you."

"Only in my head." She wiped the sweat from her brow with her forearm.

"What does that mean? Were you dating him when you were still staying in your car?" Andy's eyes widened, and when she didn't answer right away, his voice grew more serious. "Rebecca?"

They walked to the water fountain, and Rebecca drank mouthfuls of cold water.

"Yeah. I was."

"And you didn't tell him? Was he pissed?" Andy gave her a hand towel and a bath towel.

Rebecca wiped her face. "No."

"I'd have been," he admitted.

"Why? What business would it have even been of yours where I was staying?" She knew she should have told Pierce, but hearing it from Andy just drove that regret deeper and pissed her off.

Andy leaned against the doorframe. "Are you really asking me that? Aren't relationships all about trust? Rebecca, you of all people know this crap." He lowered his voice. "Remember when that girl I used to date came in every day for a week and tried to get me to start seeing her again? You told me to tell Chiara even though I wasn't doing anything wrong."

She rolled her eyes. "That's different. She could have misunderstood and thought you were cheating or leading her on if she found out from someone else."

"Now that I've been with Chiara for so long, there's no difference in my eyes. I think, if anything, he'd have a right to feel like you didn't trust him, and you know what that does?"

Oh God, really? Why did I open my mouth? "Go ahead; burst my bubble."

"Hey, you know my motto. Anything worth having is worth the pain it takes to get it." He nodded as if doing so validated his creed. "I know you, Rebecca. You're a good egg. You're honest to a fault—usually, anyway—but you're also overly sensitive."

She rolled her eyes. She hated being called overly sensitive, but Andy had pulled that card before, and he knew her well enough that denying it wouldn't work.

"You know that keeping something from him is the same as lying, which tells me that you didn't tell him because of the whole sensitivity thing that you hide behind."

"Hide behind?" She glared at him.

He paused while a woman walked past and then lowered his voice. "Rebecca, don't you see? This is way bigger than you being worried about how people see you. It was just you and your mom for so long. Rebecca and Magda Rivera against the world. It was hard. It was all-consuming. And you and I both know that even though you wanted to be the one caring for your mom, it was torturous." His eyes filled with empathy and understanding that only a true friend could possess. He wasn't making fun of her, and as he touched her arm, she felt that it hurt him as much to bring the truth out in the open as it did for her to hear it.

A sharp pain shot through her heart. He knew her too damn well, and it pissed her off, but part of her thought he might be right. When she opened her mouth to reply, nothing came out.

"Look, I know it's hard for you to let anyone into your world, but guys like Pierce Braden are one in a million, and I saw the way he looked at you. Chances are, he knows you're sensitive, too, and he'll overlook this, but if I were you—" He shook his head. "I'd worry about what else this makes him question. Trust is trust."

She swallowed past the thickening lump in her throat. "Great. So you're saying that when I see pity in his eyes, which is what I feel like I see, I'm reading it wrong? He's really questioning my trustworthiness?" *Holy shit. What else can go wrong in my life?*

"No. I don't know the guy. He might not question your trustworthiness at all; that's just what it would make me think. But if you think you see pity, you might be misreading it. I don't mean this judgmentally, but pity is like a recurring theme in your life. When anyone tries to help, you immediately go down the pity trail. And don't think I didn't see it flash in your eyes when I told you to call Chiara."

He had her there. She had felt it when he suggested that she call Chiara. *A recurring theme? Could he be right?*

"Why don't you just talk to him?"

"I did." She banged her forehead on the wall.

"Hey, don't get sweat on my wall," he said with a teasing smile. "What did he say?"

"That it's..." She could hardly believe she was saying this out loud. It would be the first time she'd said she loved a man to anyone other than Pierce. She did love him. *I do. I really do.*

"He says it's love that I see, not pity."

His eyes widened. "Damn, girl. Is that where you're at? That explains a lot." They walked back to the registration desk.

"It explains nothing except that now I'm also worried that he doesn't trust me."

"I said I could be wrong about that, but if you're worried, fix it." He went behind the desk and pulled out a chart, scribbled something, and lifted his eyes to her when she didn't respond. "Rebecca, trust is a two-way street. If he says he loves you, you have to trust that as much as he has to trust that you'll tell him things. You should know this. Do you love him?"

"Yes. I really do."

"Seems easy, then. You're not a shy girl, Rebecca,

so why are you not in his face telling him whatever's on your mind?"

She sighed, thinking about what Pierce had said about her trying to regain control of her life. "I do trust that Pierce loves me. There's no doubt in my mind. So, what does that mean? Am I projecting my fears onto him?"

Andy shrugged. "Now you're out of my league. Trust, I get. Projecting fears?" Andy held his hands up in surrender. "That's way out of my realm of understanding."

She leaned across the desk and grabbed him by the shirt, tugging him down so they were eye to eye. "You are a great friend even if it's your fault I'm in this mess."

He laughed. "Hey, that's all on you. I was just an unknowing messenger who spilled the beans."

"Right again. Jerk. I wish I could hate you." She released his shirt. "But I need someone to knock sense into me, I guess. It might as well be you." She couldn't shake the feeling of something poisonous slithering inside of her and trying to get out, but taking it out on Andy wouldn't do any good.

She headed into the locker room thinking about projection. Did she *expect* to see pity and become blind to everything else?

It could be.

Oh God. I will not be one of those loser girls who becomes a self-fulfilled prophecy.

Chapter Twenty-Six

REBECCA DROVE BY the park to try to climb out of her own head after going to see her doctor and picking up her new birth control pills. She returned home and ran a load of laundry. She was procrastinating, but every time she thought about holding her mother's urn in her hands, she felt empty inside. She had a feeling that if there was any truth to what she'd felt since her mother passed away—that her mother was always nearby—then it could also be true that the reason she hadn't felt her mother around for the last day or two was because her mother was giving her a sign. *My stubborn mother.* She imagined her mother's strong, determined voice before disease stole that piece of her, too. *Mi dulce niña, what are you doing? Don't let the past determine your future. Open your eyes, niña. Stop knotting up these darn strings. I'm pulling as hard as I can.*

She set a basket of laundry on the bed and glanced at the package of birth control pills she'd begun taking only an hour earlier. It was freeing, knowing that she wouldn't have to rely on Pierce to be responsible for both of them. She wanted to have children one day, and she'd let her mind drift a few times to the possibility of having children with Pierce. She still believed, truly believed with all her heart, that a future with Pierce was possible—and right—even with the hard time they were going through. But having children was a decision she wanted to make *with* him, not have it made accidentally for them.

She folded the last of her laundry and sat down on the edge of her bed, wishing Pierce was there with her. She lay back on the bed and looked up at the ceiling, reflecting on her wish. She didn't feel like the same woman who had kneed a guy in the groin and then punched him in the jaw. She lifted her hand and held it in front of her face, fisting and unfisting her fingers. She'd felt so strong for so long. She'd needed to, with her mother unable to care for herself and Rebecca feeling like she might fall apart at any second but knowing that falling apart wasn't an option. She'd built walls around her heart, her mind, and even her body, in an effort to keep her emotions from herself, as much as everyone else. It would have been so easy to spiral down into self-doubt and self-pity—but she had remained strong. Looking back at what their lives were like toward the end, when her mother couldn't get up out of bed, her body bloated and sedated, she couldn't fathom how she'd made it through each day, much less the last few months, but she had. She goddamn had, and she felt proud to have been there by her mother's side.

As she lowered her hand and wrapped her arms around her middle, she realized she'd not only walled off those emotions, but she'd masked them with strength. It was more than a need; it was her best survival technique.

She closed her eyes and whispered, "Being strong is hard. So damn hard." Tears slipped down her temples as she waited for her mother's voice to rescue her. She held her breath, waiting, hoping, praying to hear her mother's voice, and when it didn't come, she rolled onto her side and cried. Her body shook as sobs she'd kept hidden deep inside burned and bubbled through her chest and lungs, leaving her lips on the wings of ragged, painful breaths.

Rebecca had cried many times after her mother died, but the tears that pooled on her bedspread and in her hair weren't solely for the mother she'd give anything to have back. They were for herself. For the woman she had become out of a dire situation, for the woman she left behind and might never be again—and for the woman she desperately wanted to be but was afraid to accept. She curled into a fetal position and rocked forward and back, trying to rid herself of the tentacles of fear that gripped her. Was it wrong to let some of the strength she'd worn like armor go? To let herself be loved without looking for an ulterior motive behind every glance? What if she let Pierce in—*really let him in*—and he didn't like the weaker Rebecca? The Rebecca who loved when he opened doors and told her she was beautiful? The Rebecca who loved that he was constantly aware of other people, pulling her closer when he felt protective and stealing glances at her when he thought she wasn't looking. What if she said she didn't want to handle everything by herself? Could she afford to love with her whole being and risk being abandoned again? *Mom didn't abandon me! It wasn't a choice!*

Stop it. Just stop the bullshit questions and say what you really mean.

She opened her eyes with the determination of the voice in her head. It wasn't her mother's voice admonishing her. It was Rebecca's own voice calling her out on her deepest fear.

She pulled her knees up tighter against her chest, as if they could shield her from the truth. She gritted her teeth and held her breath as the thought that she hadn't allowed herself to acknowledge broke free and forced its way into her mind, as sharp and as painful as shards of glass.

What if I let all that strength go...and he dies?

She heard the wailing a second before she registered that it was coming from her own lungs.

Oh God. Oh God. Oh God.

Nonononono.

She buried her face in her pillow even though she was home alone and dug her fingers into the comforter so hard her knuckles hurt. She didn't want to hear the torturous sounds of the truth as it tore from her lungs. She didn't want to feel the ice-cold piercing of her heart, but she knew she had to feel those things—*accept those things*—if she was ever going to move forward.

Open your eyes.

No.

Open your goddamn eyes. You're not a quitter.
No! I can't.

She could always make herself get through anything. *Anything.* All it took was determination and the voice in her head that never doubted her. The voice she'd concocted when her mother was no longer strong enough to cheer her on and she needed to dig deeper to find the strength not to cry at the sight of her mother moving closer to death with every hour. Her mother's voice had taken over for her own voice after her mother died. It happened seamlessly, during the weeks when Rebecca was trying to piece her new motherless life together and convince herself that getting out of bed every day was a good idea and the best choice. The *only* choice. It had been her mother's voice that convinced her that she would get through the pain and emptiness of being orphaned, while her own voice had been swallowed by grief. She was still, after all, a grieving daughter.

Now that voice she relied upon had silenced. She was alone in her mind, the quiet of the room split only by the sound of her sobs.

Alone.

But I was always alone.

The thought brought harsher sobs. She'd always known she was alone in her caretaking, and somehow egging herself on in third person had made her feel safer, less alone, stronger. And afterward, when she was alone in their apartment and she'd used up all of her emotional reserves in caring for her mother, her mother's voice had taken over. Her mother pulled her through when she was simply surviving, finding a job, dragging her tormented, devastated ass out of bed instead of being swallowed by sadness.

Desperate times. Desperate measures, she reminded herself.

Shut. The. Fuck. Up.

She pushed herself up to a sitting position and wiped her eyes. Her body shook with each sob she tried to swallow.

"This isn't a desperate time," she said aloud. "And I am *not* alone."

She swiped angrily at her tears with her forearm, sucking in hampered breaths as she struggled to regain control of her emotions.

"This is anything *but* a desperate time. It's a hopeful time."

She looked up at the ceiling, with her breathing under control. "I'm cutting the strings, Mom. I'm tired of getting tangled up in them." A single tear slipped down her cheek. "I love you. I will always love you, but it's time for me to stop worrying about what Pierce thinks of me, or of what I had to do. It's time for me to let him love me."

Chapter Twenty-Seven

REBECCA PULLED INTO the parking lot of her old apartment complex and parked by the office. She stepped from her car and remembered that even though she felt safe, she'd told Pierce she wouldn't go there without him. She'd fought him on his request, and a big part of her still felt like it was overprotective of him, even if it was a loving gesture. She'd lived there for years and hadn't needed an escort, and she didn't need one now. But as she stepped from the car with a strange heaviness in her chest, she wished he were there with her. And when the part of her that was used to being in control of everything tried to push that wish aside, she gathered it back around her heart and allowed herself to feel and accept it. She loved him, missed him, and she was about to pick up her mother's urn. If ever there was a time when she could use support, it was now. She had no idea if she might fall apart when she saw Mr. Fralin, or when she held her mother's urn in her hands for the first time since she'd handed it over to him. Now she needed Pierce's strength, and she didn't care what she saw in his eyes.

With a deep breath, she crossed the parking lot and headed inside.

"Rebecca." Mr. Fralin reached for her hand as she came through the door and drew her in close. "Would you like to sit down?"

Her heart was beating so fast she couldn't sit still. She'd give anything to have Pierce's reassuring hand on the small of her back, his whisper in her ear, telling her things would be okay and that he was there for her.

"No, thank you," she managed. "I'm a little too nervous to sit." Rebecca looked around the rental office, suddenly remembering when she'd been forced to request a smaller apartment because they couldn't afford the rent for the two-bedroom. Mr. Fralin had never made her feel bad, and as he stood before her now, with her hand in his, it struck her that she'd never even looked for an excuse to believe there was any pity in his eyes—and yet she had with Pierce.

I'm an idiot.

She wasn't afraid of Mr. Fralin being taken away. She appreciated him, and she loved him for what he had done for her and for her mother, but she wasn't in love with him like she was with Pierce. Losing Mr. Fralin would be heartbreaking. Losing Pierce would be devastating.

She had been pushing Pierce away so she didn't get too attached. The realization nearly knocked her to her knees.

"Rebecca? Rebecca, are you okay?" Mr. Fralin

looked at her with an assessing gaze, and she realized she had zoned out and hadn't heard him talking to her.

"I'm sorry. I...I was just thinking about something."

He nodded as if everyone zoned out, thinking about losing the man they loved.

"Shall we retrieve your urn?"

Her legs moved robotically as she followed him into the back office, her mind still reeling with her stupidity. How could she have allowed herself to ruin things with a man she'd give her own life for? She'd spent so much energy trying to find a reason to back away the last time she saw him that she'd almost lost sight of how real his love was. *Oh God.* What if she'd already ruined things?

She waited while Mr. Fralin went into a smaller room with the wall safe. Her heartbeat was frantic with worry about her relationship with Pierce and anticipation over receiving her mother's urn. When Mr. Fralin appeared with the urn in his hands, she froze, expecting to fall apart. He set it in her hands, and she didn't crumple to the floor. Her legs didn't wobble, and she didn't stop breathing. She gripped the urn tightly against her body and felt the prickling of her nerves begin to ease.

"Thank you, Mr. Fralin." Her voice was quiet, but at least it hadn't failed her. She gazed up at the man who had made her mother's last days easier, and gratitude swelled inside her. Her words came easier now. "You've been so generous. I appreciate everything that you've done for us. For me." And then she remembered that she'd brought him his money, and somehow her brain was functioning normally again as she reached into her pocket and withdrew a twenty-dollar bill. "I'll be out of town this weekend, so I brought this week's money with me."

"Rebecca, please." He lowered his voice. "Please keep your money."

She really wanted to change where Pierce was concerned and to allow him to do more for her and not only accept it, but enjoy it, but even though she could use the eighty dollars a month she'd agreed to pay Mr. Fralin, this was something she felt too strongly about to let go.

"Mr. Fralin, I don't expect you to understand this, but I lost my mother. All I have left is my pride. I would appreciate it if you would allow me to pay you back."

His thin lips didn't quite smile, but he nodded, and she saw understanding in his dark eyes. "As you wish."

Rebecca handed him the twenty-dollar bill. "Thank you for everything." She left his office with her arms wrapped around her mother's urn, holding it close to her body. In the hallway, she took a deep breath, her heart still beating rapidly. Even though she had honed her ability to get through hard times on her own, she still wished Pierce were there with her. She leaned against the wall, and the next deep inhalation brought strength.

Baby steps.

She used her butt to push open the door, careful not to jostle the urn too much. Outside, she squinted against the blazing sun as she headed toward the parking lot—and stopped cold at the sight of Pierce's car parked next to hers. She lost her breath at the sight of him stepping from the car in his business suit, wearing a pair of dark sunglasses. He crossed the lot with the confident gait that struck her as perfectly Pierce: in control, determined, and making a beeline straight for her. He smiled, and—*finally*—her brain sent the signal to her legs to move. She nearly sprinted the distance between them and fell into his arms, clutching the urn between them.

She gazed up at her reflection in his sunglasses. She was smiling, with fresh tears streaming down her cheeks, and she didn't care. "What are you doing here?"

"When you didn't answer your phone, I went to your work, and they said you were off today, so I went to your house. Henry said they came home as you were leaving to come here." He leaned down and kissed her. "You got your mother's urn."

She knew he expected to find her overwhelmed with sadness, just as she'd expected to feel, and she might never understand why instead of feeling devastated, she was beginning to feel renewed.

"I did."

"And? How are you feeling?" He gently rubbed her arms. "Are you okay?"

"You're here. I can't believe you're here." Her brain spewed her thoughts out like lava. He was right there with her, holding her as she needed to be held. He'd never failed her, not once. Not even when she'd tried to push him away.

"I'll always be here," he said easily.

She finally let go of the fear that had been buried

too deep for her to understand. She knew in her heart that Pierce would always be there for her, but hearing it helped to clear her thoughts a little more, so she could tell him what else she had to say. "I needed to bring her home, and eventually, I need to set her free." She felt stronger by the second now that he was by her side. She had a million things to say to him—and she didn't want to wait another second.

She needed to see his eyes. "Can you take off your sunglasses?"

He smiled down at her. "I can't, because my girlfriend said that when we talked about certain things, I needed to wear them. When Henry said you came here, I put them on."

She bit her lower lip to keep from laughing. "You really are the best boyfriend ever. But I don't need you to wear them while we talk anymore. I think I understand it all now."

He slipped off the sunglasses, and the love in his eyes was so intense that Rebecca struggled to find her voice again.

"I've...I've done a lot of thinking, Pierce, and for the first time in my adult life, I can breathe a little easier." She leaned against him, soaking up his strength, not wanting to let go of the urn, or him, or delay the conversation. "I feel like I can make decisions separate from what's best, or what I need, and make them based on what I want." She loved the way he waited patiently for her to finish, even though she could tell by the way his mouth twitched that he had something to say.

"I want to be with you, Pierce. I don't want time to

think. I mean, I needed time to think, and it helped tremendously, but I know you don't pity me. I really know that, in my heart, where I had to believe it. I think I've always known that."

"I don't pity you. I respect the hell out of you."

She smiled. "I know that, too. I was looking for *my* fears in your eyes. I worried I'd be pitied, and I was looking for it, maybe even waiting for it. I was scared that I'd let you in and then you'd leave, and...I feel so stupid. I realized that I was so busy looking for pity that I looked right past the love and twisted and turned it into something dark and dirty, because I was scared."

"Rebecca—"

"Wait, please. Let me finish. All this stuff hit me all at once and I kind of went to pieces. It was cathartic, an eye opener, and I'm so sorry that I didn't tell you about staying in my car. But if none of that had happened, I never would have figured all this other stuff out."

"Babe, you don't have to explain."

"Yes. Yes, I do, because I want you to know where I was coming from, so you can understand where I am now. I was scared shitless, from the moment my mom told me she was sick until after she was gone, but I didn't want to admit I was scared. More importantly, I couldn't admit I was scared. I probably would have fallen apart."

"Survival mode," he said softly.

"Yes. I know it well. I think I could write a handbook on survival. But I don't want to be afraid anymore. I want to be a normal couple, Pierce. I want it to be okay for me to feel scared, or sad, or elated, and with you, I feel safe enough to do that. I don't want to live the rest of my life standing my ground and proving who I am."

"I love who you are."

She smiled at the truth in his eyes. "Then you know that I'll probably always stand my ground to some extent, regardless of my conviction right now."

He cupped her cheek. "Yes, my beautiful, controlling girlfriend, I do know that."

She let herself relish in his touch before finishing her thoughts. "There's another side of me that wants to come back out. It's a softer side, the one I shoved behind a brick wall when Mom got sick, and you may not like it as—"

He lowered his mouth to hers and kissed her. Oh, how she needed that kiss! She didn't understand how one kiss could make her feel so completely loved, but when Pierce kissed her, his love consumed her. There was no other way to describe the feeling of how her worries disappeared and a net of safety surrounded her. She felt his hand grip her mother's urn, which was a good thing because her knees were turning to wet noodles and she didn't have much hope for her other muscles holding up.

Pierce ran his thumb over her lips. "I know and love your softer side, Rebecca. I'm so happy that you realized all of those things. I've never felt anything but respect for you and what you've done in your life. I love you, and nothing can ever change that."

She pressed her cheek to his chest. "I see that clearly now."

Pierce lifted her chin so their eyes met again. "Is it my turn now? I have to come clean, too."

"Of course. I'm sorry. I'm talking and talking. It just feels so good to get through all this baggage."

"It turns out that my bags are pretty full, too. While I was away, I realized that I can't give up who I am even to soothe your need to handle things on your own. Part of loving someone is helping them through things."

Oh God, no, no, no. "What—"

He pressed his lips to hers again, easing her worries.

"Shh. Let me finish. I'll pick my battles, and you'll win sometimes. I promise. But you need closure, and *we* need you to have that closure. But before we can get that closure, you need to know what's going on in my mind. I've been thinking a lot, too, and I realized that part of the reason I can't give up who I am is because when my father left, he took part of me with him. He took the part that believed in true love, the part that allowed a person to completely give themselves over to another person."

He gazed into her eyes, and she wasn't sure she was even breathing anymore.

He touched his forehead to hers, and the familiar intimacy allowed her to release the breath she'd been holding.

"I never knew that piece of me was missing, Rebecca, until you came into my life and I realized that my father no longer owned that piece of me. I was afraid. I've never even admitted it to myself, but I was afraid of everything that went along with being abandoned by a parent." He drew back, his face a mask of seriousness.

"I lost my father, and even though it was his choice, and even though I tell everyone that he didn't matter because he was a selfish asshole, it was—is—a very big deal. He broke me, Bec. He made me afraid to love. And you…" He tucked her hair behind her ear and kissed her forehead. "Rebecca, your strength and your conviction in who you are and how you're treated, your love, and your empathy for others, God, everything about you—your touch, your feminine side that I adore—all those pieces of you helped me to heal."

"Pierce." She clung to his waist.

"You don't have to say a word. I know exactly what you're feeling, because I feel it, too. With you, I'm whole again. Now it's my turn to help you heal." He reached into his jacket pocket and handed her an envelope. "Tickets to Punta Allen."

Her eyes filled with tears. She opened her mouth to object, and he pressed his lips to them again.

"Before you tell me you can't accept them, please hear me out. These tickets are for six weeks from now. It was the only time you had three days in a row off work, and I knew you wouldn't want me to pull any strings with your boss. That's called a *compromise*, and if we're going to make this work, we both need to work on learning about compromising." He smiled, and tears spilled down her cheeks.

"Pierce, I…" She swallowed against her gut reaction to turn the tickets away and inched her body even closer to his, bringing them thigh to thigh, the urn pressed between their stomachs. Rebecca pressed one hand flat over his heart and closed her eyes, sensing the pure, honest love behind the gift. When she opened her eyes, he was still smiling, and she felt her lips curve up in return before saying the two words that came so easily in most situations—though she was only just beginning to get used to thinking them, much less saying them, with regard to accepting his help.

"Thank you."

Chapter Twenty-Eight

PIERCE PRACTICALLY HEARD the pieces of his life clicking into place after feeling out of sorts for the last two days. He'd bought the tickets to Punta Allen at the risk of upsetting Rebecca, but what he'd told her about not giving up all of the things he wanted to do for her was true. Rebecca wasn't the type of woman who wanted to be lavished with jewels or clothing, and Pierce realized that he wasn't the type of man who was looking to do those things. Maybe on special occasions, but Rebecca had forced him to learn what love was really about—and while material items had their place, they weren't the things that filled a person's soul. Those were the things he wanted to do for Rebecca. He wanted her to fall asleep in his arms knowing she was safe, and though he was sure he could afford whatever she wanted, most importantly, he'd be there for her through the most difficult times and, hopefully, the most enjoyable.

He took off his suit coat and wrapped it around

her mother's urn.

"Your jacket." Rebecca touched his hand.

"It's fine. That's why they make dry cleaners." He brought her hand to his lips and kissed it, then nestled the bundled urn on the floor of her car so it didn't slide around while she drove. "Where to?"

She furrowed her brow in that adorable way that told Pierce she was debating something; then she ran her finger down the center of his chest. She could do that every day for the rest of his life and he'd never tire of it.

"Would you mind if we kept the urn at your house until we go to Punta Allen?" Rebecca asked. "I'd feel better if it was with us."

Us. "I love the way you think."

They drove separately to Pierce's house, and it felt like a very big moment as they carried the urn across the threshold. Pierce watched Rebecca walk into the living room and assess where to set the urn. He didn't say anything, didn't want to influence her decision. He knew she'd find the perfect spot. She was wearing the same jeans she'd had on the night they'd first met, and at least twice since they'd been together. Even though the fit hadn't changed, showing off the luscious curves of her hips and her strikingly small waist, she moved easier in them. She'd always been confident, but her confidence had been bound by thorns when they'd first met, and now she moved gracefully around the couch to the mantel. She tilted her head to the right and then to the left in a thoughtful pose. A moment later she went to the table by the window and ran her finger along the streak of sunlight that spread across the center of the cherry wood.

"Do you think it should be in this room?" she asked.

"I think it should be wherever you want it to be."

She crossed the room toward the library. "This is really my favorite room in your house. It feels warm and inviting." She sat on the curved couch with the urn in her lap and glanced over the bookshelves. "Did you know that I love to read?"

He sat down beside her. "I did see some light reading by your bed. Business and marketing books." He raised his brow with the tease.

She leaned against his shoulder. "I am a little obsessive about information. I love learning about all the things that go into a successful business, but I also love fiction. As we were driving here, I was thinking of where we could put the urn, and this room kept coming to mind. I haven't had time to read for pleasure in forever. I was so focused on Mom and school that the luxuries of life went out the door."

The idea of books being luxuries made Pierce realize how much he took for granted. He'd had more downtime in the last two weeks than he'd had in the last year, and now that he'd had a taste of it, he wanted more. With Rebecca.

"I have a feeling you're going to love my brother Wes's girlfriend, Callie. She's a librarian." He smiled thinking of his rugged, dude-ranch-owning brother and sweet, innocent Callie Barnes. He never would have paired Wes with someone so sweet, but they were perfectly suited for each other, just like he and Rebecca. Callie brought out the softer side of Wes, and

Rebecca brought forth emotions in Pierce that he only realized this second he'd always *wanted* to feel.

"We're going to Trusty this weekend, right? For the engagement party? I can't wait to meet your family."

"I can't wait for you to meet them, but you should know that they'll be surprised about you and me." After Jake's reaction, he thought it better to warn her ahead of time, because if there was one thing the Bradens loved, it was giving one another a hard time—always in jest, but always with a touch of truth, too.

"Really?" She arched a brow and flashed a mischievous grin. "Surprised that Good Time Pierce is now a one-woman man? I can't imagine why they'd be surprised."

He shook his head and laughed.

She rose to her feet and walked to the window, then turned and faced him with a wide smile. "Don't worry. I think I can handle it." She set the urn on the mantel and then lowered herself to Pierce's lap. "But I know that if I can't, you can."

"And I always will." He brushed Rebecca's hair away from her face so he could see her more clearly. "Bec, other than the things you want career wise, what are you looking for in life?"

She fiddled with the buttons on his shirt. "What I want now and what I wanted before my mom got sick are very different." She unbuttoned two buttons. "When I was younger, I thought I'd travel and see the world. My mom always talked about visiting Punta Allen, so that was on my list. The Greek islands was another dream, and of course, those places would be wrapped around some magnificent business that I ran, though I had no idea what I would do in that regard."

"And now?"

She slid her hand inside his open shirt and caressed his chest. "Now?"

She kissed his chest, and she was so close that he couldn't resist slipping her shirt from her shoulder and kissing the exposed skin.

"How can I think with you doing that?" She arched her neck back, opening up to him.

"You started it." He kissed the curve of her breast, trailing kisses along the depth of her cleavage. "I missed you, but I can wait. Tell me what you want now."

She finished unbuttoning his shirt and pushed it from his shoulders, then brought her lips to them, kissing his muscular pecs and then laving them with her tongue.

"Right now? This very second?" she whispered.

He lifted his hips, pressing his arousal against her hips. "No. I know exactly what you want this very second." He pulled her shirt off, and with one quick flick, he unhooked and tossed aside her lacy bra and then filled his palms with her full breasts.

Rebecca sucked in air as he brushed her nipples with his thumbs, bringing them to taut peaks that he had to taste, inciting a sexy, wanting moan from Rebecca. The desire in her eyes mirrored the lust coursing through him.

"Tell me what you want in life, Bec." He kissed the tops of her breasts, knowing he was stealing her thoughts second by second and loving it as her eyes fluttered closed and she tangled her hands in his hair.

"To be..." She panted. "Happy. To be..."

He ran his hands along her ribs, sliding his thumbs along the waist of her jeans, then leaned her back and took her belly with openmouthed kisses from hip to hip.

"To be?" he whispered. Her heated skin and heavy breaths were driving him crazy. He brought her back to sitting, and she clutched his shoulders, her eyes closed, her lips slightly parted. Oh, how he wanted to be inside her glorious mouth. He took ahold of the button of her jeans.

"To be?" he urged, desperately wanting to know what she really wanted—wanting to know if *he* was what she wanted. Needing to hear it from her lips. She had opened up to him so much, he felt closer to her by the second and wanted more.

"To love and be loved," she said in one long breath.

With one yank, the button came free. "Anything else?" He unzipped her jeans and ran one finger along the edge of her panties, then gripped both thighs, squeezing as he followed them from her knees to the curve near her sex.

"No. I just..." She unbuttoned his pants. "I just want you, Pierce. I don't care what we have or where we go. I want you. With me. Inside me. By my side. I want you in every way."

He took her in a hard kiss, swiping her mouth as if he were tasting her for the first time—claiming her and marking her. She clawed at his shoulders, meeting each swipe of his tongue with a fierce stroke of her own.

"Rebecca." Her name came fast as he kissed her jaw, her collarbone, her shoulders, every bit of flesh he could reach. He took her breasts in his mouth again, loving them, sucking them, as she ground her ass into his lap. He lifted her from his lap, holding her steady as he ripped every stitch of clothing from her body and then tore off his own.

She cupped his balls, and as the shock of pleasure shot through him, she took him in her mouth—deep. Sucking and stroking, loving him until he thought he might explode. In one swift move, he lifted her into his arms, and she slid down, taking the tip of his arousal into her wet center with a moan as she settled her teeth over his neck and sucked—sending a bolt of lightning to his loins. Holy Christ, she felt amazing. They were both lost in a frenzy of need and want. She dug her fingernails into his arms, sparking his brain to function and take a step back. He wanted her to have everything she ever wanted—including peace of mind. It took all of his willpower to lift her higher, off of his thick length before he lost all control and pushed deeper inside her.

"Condom," he grunted.

"Mm-hm." She continued sucking the life out of his neck as he carried her into the bedroom. Her legs straddled his waist and her bare breasts pressed against his chest; her heart pounded frantically against his.

"Hold on tight," he commanded.

She tightened her arms around his neck, her legs

around his middle as he adeptly slid on the protective sheath. He clutched her waist and eased her down onto his throbbing heat. She squeezed her thighs around him as he thrust into her over and over again. He backed her up against the wall so he could penetrate deeper; then, buried to the hilt, his balls wet with her juices, he stilled, chest to chest, eye to eye.

"I love you, Rebecca, but I've got to fuck you." There was a time in every man's life when he had to say those words, and he knew Rebecca was feeling the same consuming obsession of their love.

Her eyes narrowed. "What took you so long?"

With one arm, he swiped everything from the dresser, sending his colognes and other paraphernalia to the floor, and set her down on the top of the dresser, gripped her below the knees, spreading her legs wider, lifting them higher, opening her to him so she felt every deep thrust. She clutched his biceps for balance.

"Deeper," she urged.

"Holy fuck, Bec." He drove harder, deeper, then lifted her with one strong arm and spun them around to the bed. She pushed away and turned onto her hands and knees, then cast a hungry stare over her shoulder, sending her hair seductively over one eye. Her glorious ass was there for the taking. No fucking way was he going there right now. He might want to fuck her, but fuck as in love her hard, not break new boundaries.

"I read in *Cosmo* that you can go deeper like this."

Jesus, she was too hot. *Cosmo?*

She arched her back and lowered her shoulders as

he entered her again. The first thrust was sheer heaven, pulling a groan from his lungs. He reached beneath her and caressed her breasts, lifting her so they were as close as two bodies could be.

She gasped a breath and he stilled.

"Are you okay?"

"You just feel so good." She moved up and down, driving him out of his mind.

He squeezed one nipple and slid his other hand lower, teasing her sensitive bundles of nerves. She breathed fast, halted breaths, tightening her thighs, squeezing him inside her as she climbed to the peak and arched against him. Her hand flew up, and she grabbed hold of his hair—exquisite pain heightened his pleasure. She cried out his name as the orgasm sent her hips bucking, her body pulsing around him. He sank his teeth into the back of her neck, wanting to share the mix of pain and pleasure.

"Oh God...Oh God...I'm gonna..." She cried out as she came again.

Need gripped every nerve in Pierce's body as he worked her over the final wave of her orgasm. Then he flipped her onto her back, lifting her knees to his sides. When their eyes connected, all that urgency came to a screeching halt. He was overcome with the love he felt for her. He kissed her tenderly, a whisper of his lips against hers.

All their talk from earlier in the afternoon came rushing back to him. Their honesty, their fears, their love. He felt like the breath was being sucked from his lungs with the intensity of it all. He lowered his forehead to hers, panting. "I didn't know it was possible to love as wholly as I love you."

She shook her head and stroked his cheek. Pierce closed his eyes and pressed his hand to hers, savoring the feel of her palm on his face.

"You asked me what I wanted." Her voice was thick with emotion.

When he opened his eyes, she smiled.

"You, Pierce. Holding your hand, sitting beside you, talking to you. Making love to you. I want you, Pierce. Just you."

He settled his lips over hers, kissing her tenderly. He touched her gently, savoring the feel of her beneath him, and brought her right up to the edge again. Holding her there, drawing out her pleasure as much as his own, and then finally—blissfully—they gave into the passion and spiraled over the edge together.

Chapter Twenty-Nine

THE REST OF the week passed in a blur with one shining night. They'd celebrated Pierce's ratification of the deal on the Grand with a romantic candlelit dinner and a walk in the park. He credited the deal to Rebecca's suggestion of proposing an earn out, and when she'd tried to dispute it, he'd stuck to his guns and forced her to accept the accolade. She was still trying to get used to compliments and recognition for her efforts, but she had to admit that it felt damn good to have come up with a winning solution for something so meaningful in Pierce's life after how much he continued to do for her.

Pierce reached across the console of the rental car as they drove from the Denver airport toward his mother's house in Trusty. He squeezed her hand.

"I'm glad you came with me."

"Me too. I'm kind of getting used to doing everything with you." They'd been driving into work together, and when Rebecca worked an evening shift last night and Pierce had a late meeting, he made arrangements for a security guard to walk her to her car. She didn't complain, and it had been a big step for both of them. He worried about her in ways she sometimes felt were unwarranted, but then again, who was she to judge what gave him peace of mind? She'd struggled with gaining her own peace of mind, and he'd been supportive. They were working on that aspect of their relationship—the art of compromising, which was difficult for two people who liked to control, but Rebecca knew that they'd come out on top of that, too.

He pressed her hand to his lips. "Good, because I'm already used to it."

SHE STAYED AT Pierce's house each night, and there was no better feeling than waking up beside the man she loved, except maybe falling asleep in his arms.

"Thank you for not wearing the skintight minidress." Pierce flashed a teasing smile. When they'd woken up this morning, he'd grabbed the calendar by the bed and reviewed the things he'd written the night before. Then he'd handed the calendar to Rebecca with a coy smile. She read his notes—*Turn on phone. Remind Rebecca to wear something homely so my snake brothers don't hit on her. Fly home*—and she'd baited him by saying she'd wear a skintight minidress and four-inch heels.

"I figured I should check out your brothers in person before I go flashing all my hotness around like that." She knew that he wasn't worried, and she loved that they could tease each other without worrying about offending each other. There wasn't a man alive who could take her away from Pierce, but his heart was in the right place.

He rolled his eyes.

Now, as they drove up the long tree-lined driveway toward his mother's house, her stomach knotted. She smoothed the skirt of her summer dress. It was one of her favorites, and the fact that it was a gift from her mother before she'd gotten sick made it all the more special. She hadn't had many occasions to wear it. They'd moved most of her clothes to Pierce's house, and when she'd seen it in his closet, she'd known this was the perfect occasion. The dress was easy to wear, with an empire waist and an A-line skirt. The intricate designs in browns, grays, and beige made it the perfect mix of dressy and casual for an afternoon engagement party. Her favorite part of the dress was the elegant detailing, with contrasting striped piping all over, rose-button placket, and straight neckline. She felt pretty and feminine in the sleeveless dress. Pierce was holding her hand across the console of the rental car, and as always, he read her body like a blind man reads braille.

"Relax, Bec. They'll love you as much as I do."

"I'm not nervous about that. I'm nervous about how *much* I love you."

She stole a glance at Pierce, in his faded Levi's and black polo shirt. He looked so damn hot that she had been looking at him all morning. Things in the keeping-her-attraction-to-him-to-herself department were easier before they came clean about everything—their feelings, their pasts, their secrets.

Those things had given her something else to focus on, even if only subconsciously. With them pushed out of the way, when she looked at Pierce, emotions flooded every inch of her body, and she knew his family would see that.

"Don't worry. I know people see it written all over my face when I'm around you, too. Kendra said that since we've been dating, I'm lighter on my toes, whatever the hell that means."

"It means—"

Pierce slammed on the brakes, and they both flew forward as a body flipped across the front of the rental car.

"Oh my God." Rebecca clutched her heart and bolted from the car. She raced around to the front of the car and crouched by the man lying facedown on the pavement, while Pierce moved like he was walking in slow motion with a pinched look on his face. She wanted to smack him. Didn't he see the man lying on the ground?

Pierce stood with his hands on his hips and an angry look in his eyes.

"Call nine-one-one. Pierce! Oh my God." She touched the man's head with a shaky hand. "Are you okay?"

"Get up, you jackass." Pierce kicked the man's black leather boot. "This is such bullshit."

"Pierce!" She couldn't believe he would treat anyone like that. With her heart in her throat, she lowered her ear to the man's mouth to see if he was breathing. She couldn't see his face very clearly, as it was smushed against the pavement. She held her breath and listened for breathing sounds.

"Pretend I'm not breathing," the man whispered.

Rebecca stumbled backward and fell on her ass. She shot a look at Pierce, realizing finally that she'd been had.

"Rebecca," Pierce said flatly. "Meet my jackass stuntman brother, Jake."

Brother? She didn't understand. Her heart was racing from the shock of seeing him hit.

Jake jumped to his feet with a shit-ass grin on his face and a sparkle in his eyes. He opened his arms. "Rebecca, what a pleasure to meet you."

She was still so shaken she was panting. She pushed to her feet. Her eyes darted between them, and in the space of a breath that fear turned to anger.

"Brother?" She smacked Jake's rock-hard abs, then pushed Pierce's chest. "How could you do that? I was scared shitless. That's not funny. That's...that's..."

"Hey, it was him, not me." Pierce reached for her and she pushed him away.

"I'm sorry. I didn't mean to scare you." Jake laughed, and Pierce silenced him with a dark stare.

"You're an ass, Jake. You really scared her." He looked at Rebecca as she paced, trying to calm her racing heart; then he shot Jake another heated look. "Jackass."

Rebecca wrapped her arms around herself, and after a few deep breaths, she realized she'd just hit Pierce's brother. *Shit.* She hadn't even met him yet. *Shit. Shit. Shit.*

Pierce placed his hands on her arms from behind. "I'm sorry, babe. I should have warned you that he does that stuff. I wasn't thinking."

She pulled from his arms and forced herself to turn and face Jake. Great, *now* she saw the family resemblance.

"I'm sorry I swatted you." She hated that she couldn't keep the annoyance from her voice, but damn it—she was annoyed, and still a little frightened.

"You know what? I'm not sorry. That sucked. Jesus, Jake. I'm sure you're a great guy, but you nearly gave me a heart attack, and you had me thinking that Pierce had lost his flippin' mind because he stood there calling a dying man a jackass."

Jake's brow furrowed, his smile faltered, and he dropped his eyes for a beat. "I really am sorry, Rebecca. Pierce, man, I didn't mean to freak her out."

"She should have leveled you." Pierce draped an arm around Rebecca's shoulder and kissed her temple.

"Yeah," Jake admitted. "You'd have had every right to level me. I am sorry, Rebecca. I didn't mean to frighten you. This is kind of what I do with my family, but I guess you wouldn't know that." He stepped forward, and he looked so apologetic that Rebecca's anger faded as quickly as it had appeared. "Forgive a stupid man?"

"Of course. I probably overreacted."

"Like hell," Pierce said.

Jake opened his arms, and Rebecca smiled up at him and mumbled, *Jackass*, as she met his embrace with her own.

Jake turned to Pierce with open arms. "Bro?"

Pierce faked a punch to his gut, and the two of

them feigned punches and laughed. Rebecca couldn't help but laugh with them. She'd never seen this side of Pierce, and she loved the way their playful taunts enlivened him. A car pulling down the driveway parked behind their rental car. Both men turned as a gorgeous pixie of a woman with long brown hair and dark, unmistakably Braden eyes, dressed in jeans and a glittery gold tank top climbed from the car in black heeled boots and sprinted to them as if she were wearing sneakers. She launched herself into Pierce's arms, sending him stumbling backward with a laugh.

"I missed you, too, Emily."

His sister wore a wide smile as she hung on to Pierce for all she was worth.

"You're here!" She dropped to the ground and fell into Jake's arms. "I missed you, too, you big lug." Emily flashed her smile toward Rebecca. "Rebecca?"

"Hi." Rebecca had the urge to get in on the family fun and hug her. It had been so long since she'd had a family of her own, and Emily's energy was contagious.

"I love your dress." Emily embraced her.

"Thank you. I love your top." Rebecca relished how comfortable she felt with Emily already, and how easy the three of them were with one another. She'd always wondered what it might be like to have siblings. It didn't take more than a minute for her to see how much they enriched one another's lives, even with Jake's prank. The love they had for one another was evident.

Emily looped her arm in Rebecca's. "Come on. We'll talk on the way to the house and leave the boys to play in the dirt." She tossed her keys to Jake.

"Sounds good to me." She glanced at Pierce. "Do you mind?"

"Yes, but I know better than to argue with Emily. Go. Have fun. I'll be in in a sec."

PIERCE WATCHED REBECCA walk away. He was sure that by the time they reached the house, she and Emily would be as close as sisters, and it brought him comfort. Emily would probably share embarrassing stories about Pierce, and he imagined Rebecca would think they were *cute*. When she was safely out of earshot, he pushed those warm, loving feelings aside and turned on Jake.

"You're an idiot." He closed the gap between them so they were eye to eye. "Her mother died two months ago."

"I'm sorry, man." Jake held his hands up.

Pierce wanted to grab him by his goddamn collar and knock some sense into him, but Jake hadn't known about Rebecca's mother, and Jake was just being Jake. He clenched his jaw and fisted his hands, squeezing the fury out of his muscles.

"Grow up, Jake. Christ Almighty." He spun around and stepped away to walk off the lingering anger. "I love ya, man, but you've got to climb out of your own head and grow up."

"*Tsk*. Hey, whatever." Jake waved a hand in the air. "I apologized, and I *am* sorry, but let it go already." He arched a brow.

Pierce turned on him again. Even though he knew Jake had been kidding around, he couldn't help it. When it came to Rebecca, his claws came out. "Let it go? I love her, Jake. Did you see how scared she was? If you weren't my brother, I'd have kicked your ass and left your ragged body on the side of the road."

"Damn, Pierce. It was a joke." His voice softened.

"Yeah, I get it, okay? But when it hurts Rebecca, it goes from joke to serious pretty damn quick. You hurt her, I hurt you. Got it?" Pierce sucked in a breath to calm his anger.

"Yeah. Got it." Jake shook his head. "Man, I really had no idea."

"No shit, you had no idea. You've been clueless ever since Fiona fucked you over in high school. Get over it already. Grow up and think of someone else for once." Jake and Fiona had dated for more than two years in high school, and though they'd planned on going to the same college, after their high school graduation, Fiona had dumped Jake out of the blue. He'd never let anyone get close to him since.

"Shit. My life has *nothing* to do with her."

The anger in his eyes told Pierce otherwise. Jake would never get over Fiona, and now that Pierce had Rebecca in his life and understood what it was like to love someone so completely, he felt bad for Jake. Pierce shook his head and exhaled loudly before slinging an arm over Jake's shoulder and muscling his forearm against his neck.

"Come on, asshole. Let's get inside before Emily messes with Rebecca's head."

Jake laughed. "Too late. You know Emily works fast."

Pierce wasn't worried. Emily adored each of her brothers, and there wasn't anything she could say that would upset Rebecca. Rebecca already knew that the Braden men weren't exactly a monogamous crew— that is, until they fell in love and handed their hearts over to the women they loved.

Chapter Thirty

EMILY AND REBECCA crossed the wide hardwood foyer into a large great room with thick throw rugs over more hardwood. There were bottles of champagne on the tables, finger foods, and napkins that read *Daisy and Luke* and today's date. The house wasn't overly decorated, and although it was large, it wasn't ostentatiously furnished. Two oversized white sofas faced a stone fireplace that climbed the two-story wall to the cathedral ceiling. The mantel was littered with framed photographs of Pierce and his siblings at various ages. Rebecca lingered on them for a minute, instantly picking out Pierce from the others. His eyes were serious, and in most of the photos, he had an arm or a hand on a sibling.

"Mom," Emily called into the kitchen, which was off to their left. "Come meet Rebecca, Pierce's girlfriend."

Catherine was a few inches taller than Rebecca and shared the same high cheekbones and wide smile as Pierce. She had almond-shaped eyes with thick lashes, and seeing her and Emily together, Rebecca realized that Emily had those traits, too. Catherine looked comfortable in jeans and a blue blouse, and when she opened her arms, Rebecca understood why Pierce and his siblings had such easy natures.

"Rebecca, it's such a pleasure to meet you." Catherine hugged her and kept her hands on her arms when she drew back. "Pierce has told me so much about you."

"Uh-oh, should I worry?" She was only half teasing.

"Not unless it's a crime to rave about a woman," Catherine answered. "Did you meet Jake? He said he was going to greet you and Pierce."

Rebecca relayed the story of Jake's prank to Catherine and Emily.

"He really is a great guy," Emily insisted. She moved in closer to Rebecca and said, "But his pranks can be a pain."

Rebecca could see how much Emily loved him, and in the short amount of time she'd known her, she felt like they'd already become friends.

"I'm sorry, Rebecca. I can't even make up an excuse for him." Catherine smiled, and as with Emily, her love for Jake was evident.

"I see you met my mom," Pierce said as he came through the front door and joined them.

Jake closed the door behind them. Catherine pressed her lips together and dropped her shoulders.

"Jake Braden, didn't I tell you not to pull any pranks?" Catherine touched Rebecca's hand. "I'm sorry if he frightened you. He's forever pulling stunts around here."

"Don't worry," Pierce said. "She gave him shit for it already."

Catherine raised her brows toward Rebecca. "You did?"

Gulp. Rebecca shrugged and smiled. "I kind of couldn't help myself. I was really scared."

"A woman after my own heart. You've got to give it right back to these boys." Catherine reached for Jake's hand. "They play hard, but they love hard, too."

Jake stepped from his mother's grasp and held up his hands. "I don't want any part of this discussion. Just because my brothers bit the monogamous bullet doesn't mean I'm going to."

Emily rolled her eyes. "With my luck, even *you* will find love before me."

"No way in hell," Jake said.

"Hey, maybe you'll find a guy in Tuscany," a deep, masculine voice boomed from the stairwell.

"I wondered where they were," Pierce said.

A young bloodhound bounded up the stairs and into the room with her tail wagging, anxiously rubbing against everyone's legs.

"Oh my gosh, she's so cute." Rebecca stooped to pet the dog, and the pup climbed up her legs and licked her face.

"Sweets!" The deep voice stilled the excited pup into sitting by Rebecca's feet. Two more of Pierce's handsome brothers entered the room, followed by two gorgeous women, whose eyes lit up when they saw Pierce and Rebecca.

"Sorry about that," the petite brunette said. She smiled as she crouched to pet the dog. "Sweets gets a little excited. I'm Callie, by the way, and this is Wes." She touched Wes's leg, and he reached for her hand and drew her up beside him.

"Hi, Rebecca. Sweets is ours. She's still learning her manners." Wes opened his arms and hugged Rebecca. "We've heard a lot about you."

Callie leaned in for a hug next. "All good things," she whispered in Rebecca's ear.

Rebecca had to stifle the urge to say, *Really? Yay!*

"And I'm Daisy, Luke's fiancée." Daisy had white-blond hair and vibrant blue eyes. Rebecca knew from Pierce that she was a doctor, and he'd shared with her the struggles that Daisy had encountered growing up model gorgeous. He'd said that she'd had a hard time being taken seriously, and she'd dyed her hair after she'd gone away to college in an effort to escape the stereotypical Barbie taunts. She'd eventually come back to Trusty and made amends with the people who used to harass her. He told her that she and Luke falling in love had helped them both to accept parts of themselves that they'd previously had trouble accepting.

"Daisy, congratulations on your engagement." Rebecca hugged Daisy, realizing that she wasn't carrying any more baggage than anyone else was. Rebecca's baggage was just different. She looked over Daisy's shoulder at Pierce, who had one arm over Luke's shoulder. He glanced up, and their eyes connected and held just long enough for her pulse to quicken.

"Thanks," Daisy said. "We're excited. Of course, no one around Trusty can believe that one of the Braden boys is actually going to tie the knot. Luke, come say hello to Rebecca." Daisy leaned in close to Rebecca and whispered, "When they fall in love, they fall hard. Luke had to convince *me* to get married." She reached for Luke's hand. "I can't wait to get to know you better, Rebecca. We'll catch up when the boys are busy talking. I swear when Luke gets together with his brothers, they could chat for hours."

"A relative hen party—oops, cock party," Emily said as she crouched to love up Sweets. The pup rolled onto her back, and Emily scratched her belly.

"Emily." Catherine shook her head. "Daisy's right, though. They're worse than a pack of teenage girls."

"My masculinity takes offense to that statement, Mom." Luke was the youngest of Pierce's siblings. Rebecca could imagine him as a badass troublemaker with at least three days' scruff on his strong jaw and the barbed-wire tattoo on his biceps, but when he stole a kiss from Daisy before opening his arms to Rebecca, all that toughness rolled away.

Rebecca glanced around the room. To the right of the fireplace was a leather love seat with two colorful blankets draped over the back. A deep burgundy armchair and a leather recliner, separated by what had to be a hand-carved cherrywood table, were situated on the far side of the fireplace. Just beyond the living room was a large dining room with a wooden farmhouse-style table that was longer than any table Rebecca had ever seen. French doors led from the dining room to an enormous deck, with a spectacular view of Trusty and the mountains. The house felt warm and homey. It might have been the enormous men flopping on the couches, or Emily cozying up with her legs tucked beneath her in the leather chair, or it could have been Pierce's arm around her shoulders. Catherine's house overflowed with the feel of a big, close-knit family. Rebecca half expected to feel sad, as she had no family to speak of, but she had Pierce, and she could see herself embracing his family as if it were her own.

"I hear you have a hell of a punch," Luke teased.

"Luke!" Daisy smacked his arm.

Luke's comment brought Rebecca back to the conversation. She waited for her cheeks to flush and embarrassment to send her sprinting from the room, and when those things didn't happen, it shocked her as much as she could tell it surprised Pierce, who was watching her from a few feet away.

"I guess Pierce told you how we met?" She eyed Pierce as he came to her side.

"Sorry, babe, but I was proud of you." Pierce kissed her cheek.

His family was so openly affectionate that she couldn't help but slip her arm around his waist and snuggle in close.

"It's okay," Rebecca said. "I'm kind of proud of it, too."

"You go, girlfriend. I would never have the guts to do that," Daisy said. "But I can't even count the number of times that it would have been amazing to knock some jerk to the floor."

"Well, I admire the hell out of you for it. I heard

you also turned Pierce down the first time he asked you out." Luke stared at Pierce, and a coy smile formed on his lips. "Daisy never turned me down."

"You're a liar." Daisy poked him in the side. "Don't mind him. I swear they're so competitive it's crazy."

"The only girls who never turn you down are the ones in your pasture, and they only hang around you because you feed them," Pierce said.

"Hey, don't knock my girls." Luke turned at the sound of the front door opening.

Pierce nuzzled against Rebecca's neck. "His girls are his gypsy horses. I told you about them, right?"

"Yeah." She hoped to see the beautiful horses one day.

"Those horses really do adore him. I'm just giving him hell," Pierce said. "You should probably get used to it."

"I love how you guys bait each other."

Pierce touched his forehead to hers. "And I love that you're here with me." He lifted his head as Ross arrived and joined them in the living room.

Ross looked just like his pictures, with serious eyes and dark hair worn longer on top and cut close on the sides. She knew Ross was the Trusty town veterinarian, and he was the brother that was closest in age to Pierce, but while she'd seen a similarity to Luke in the pictures in Pierce's house, in person, Ross and Luke looked even more alike.

Sweets scampered across the hardwood and pawed at Ross's legs. Ross crouched beside her, scratching her head behind her floppy ears.

"How's the best girl in town?" Ross kissed

Sweets's snout.

"Hey!" Emily snapped. "I currently hold that title, thank you very much." Then, more softly, she added, "Only no one knows it yet."

Catherine sat beside Emily on the couch and draped her arm over her shoulder. "Oh, honey, your time will come. You can't force love. It comes when it's damn good and ready."

"Sis, you know any man you think you love will have to pass our judgment first," Pierce said with a serious tone. He and Ross exchanged a nod full of brotherly goading.

"Oh, please." Emily rolled her eyes.

"Speaking of judgment." Ross arched a brow. "You must be Rebecca. It's nice to meet you. I'm Ross." He leaned in for a hug. It wasn't a hug full of brawn and bravado like Wes and Luke had given her. It was a warm embrace, as if he'd known her forever.

Pierce pulled her out of his arms. "He's a smooth one, Bec. You've got to watch him."

Ross shook his head. He was more reserved than Pierce's other brothers, as if he were taking in his surroundings rather than taking them over.

"Yeah, I'm the one to watch, all right. Me and all my women." Ross crossed the floor and kissed his mom on the cheek, then sank into the couch on Emily's other side and draped an arm around her shoulders. Sweets curled up at his feet. "Were you complaining about meeting a man when I came in?"

"Maybe." She flashed a cheesy grin.

"You're leaving for Italy soon. Romance capital of the world." Ross's eyes widened. "I'm sure you can hook up with someone there."

Jake was sitting on the other couch. He kicked his boots onto the coffee table and crossed his arms. "Hey, don't encourage Emily to *hook up.*"

"Says the man who bed *Ready, Willing,* and *Able* the other night." Pierce shifted his eyes to Jake, who shrugged.

"I don't want to know this about you." Emily covered her ears.

Jake grinned at Pierce. "Hey, jealousy will get you nowhere."

Pierce didn't have any visible reaction to what Jake said. Rebecca didn't worry if he missed his bachelor lifestyle. It was apparent in every glance, every touch, every kiss, every word he spoke and the look in his eyes that he adored her—but she did wonder if he'd even respond to Jake. He was casually filling the champagne glasses; then he handed them out, slowing by Jake and holding the glass just out of his brother's reach.

After a minute of an alpha stare down, he handed the glass to Jake and sat down beside Rebecca on the couch.

"Jealous?" Pierce settled his hand on Rebecca's thigh and spoke in a smooth, even tone. "I've got news for you, Jake. There's nothing and nobody in the world who would be worth missing a single night with Rebecca."

As Pierce rose to his feet with a champagne glass in one hand and her hand in the other, she knew that she didn't have to worry about his family seeing how in love with Pierce she was. She had a feeling that in this family, it would be more of a problem if her love wasn't evident.

"Okay, now that we've all had our fun, I'd like to make a toast to Daisy and Luke. This is their engagement party, after all." Pierce lifted his glass. "Daisy, I still have no idea how you tamed my baby brother."

"*Pfft.*" Luke shook his head and looked away.

Pierce lowered his chin and stared at Luke until Luke met his gaze. "But I'm damn happy you did, because I've never seen Luke so centered or so happy. I never realized that he was missing something in his life."

He looked across the room at Callie and Wes, snuggled so close they could have climbed under each other's skin, and then his eyes shifted to Rebecca. Her pulse quickened with the look of love in his eyes that blazed a path straight through her.

"I never knew I was missing something—or someone—either." He held Rebecca's stare for a beat, then shifted his attention back to Luke and Daisy. "Daisy, Luke, you opened my eyes just enough for me to slow down and take notice when Rebecca came into my life. So while I'm toasting the two of you with great hopes that your life together will always be more than you could ever hope for, I'm also saying thank you. Because now my life is just that." He leaned down and hugged Daisy, then kissed her on the cheek and whispered, "You're the best thing that ever happened to him."

Daisy's eyes dampened.

Pierce pulled Luke up to his feet and wrapped his

arms around him. They patted each other's backs, and Rebecca couldn't hear what Pierce said to Luke, but whatever it was, Luke's hand stilled on Pierce's back, then pressed harder, pulling him closer.

Each of Luke's siblings stood and said something sweet about Daisy and Luke, and when their mother rose, the room grew quiet. All eyes were on Catherine, but it was the look in her children's eyes that nearly stopped Rebecca's heart. Their love for their mother stirred her longing for her own mother. Pierce, who was sitting beside her again, wrapped his strong arm around the back of her neck, his large palm pressed flat against her cheek, and drew her to his chest. He kissed the top of her head, and as his mother spoke about Luke and Daisy and said things Pierce should be listening to, he wrapped his other hand around Rebecca and touched his forehead to hers.

He held her so tightly she could barely breathe. How did he always know exactly what she needed? She needed to feel Pierce's protective, loving arms, his heart beating strong and sure, as her chest ached with sadness for the mother she'd never hold again. And from his embrace, his love filled every empty crevice that it could claim with the promise of the future she and Pierce were destined to have.

"I'm sorry, babe," he whispered. "I know you miss your mom. I can't bring her back, but I'm here, I love you, and I'm not going anywhere."

Rebecca felt a tap on her shoulder and she turned, her eyes damp, too. Pierce's mother held her arms open and motioned for Rebecca to come to her. *Don't cry. Don't cry.* She felt Pierce's grip ease, his hands slide from her back as she rose to her feet, and then Catherine's arms were around her and her soft cheek was pressed to Rebecca's.

"It's okay, sweetie. Let those tears fall. Pierce loves you, so we all love you. That's how families work."

Sweetie. Sweet girl. Mi dulce niña. Family.

She felt a wall of muscle press against her back. *Pierce.* She heard Daisy and Callie whispering, then felt Callie's arm squeeze between her and Pierce. Daisy did the same on the other side.

"Aw. I want to hug her, too." Emily pushed herself into the fold.

Rebecca heard Jake, Luke, and Wes talking. She couldn't make out what they were saying, but it didn't matter. She could only imagine how ridiculous they looked, all huddled together around *poor Pierce's girlfriend who'd lost her mother.*

She couldn't hold the thought long, because she didn't believe it. This family would no sooner pity her than they'd turn away from helping one another.

"See? I told you they were the best family ever," Daisy said.

"It's like I have three sisters now," Emily said. "Rebecca, you can share my mom anytime you want."

"That's right, honey. Whether you need a hug or someone to go watch a chick flick with, I always have room for one more person in my heart," Catherine said as she drew apart, and the others followed suit.

Except Pierce.

He pulled her in closer and pressed his cheek to hers. "I was just thinking of the night I first saw you storming across the bar. You were so beautiful. I think

I knew I loved you right then." He paused, and as his words took hold, he asked, "That night you told me that your mom had warned you about men like me," Pierce whispered. "Was she right?"

Rebecca looked into his smoldering dark eyes and swallowed against the emotions threatening to steal her voice. While the others talked and poured more champagne, Rebecca wasn't embarrassed over missing her mother, or the group hug, and she wasn't worried about anyone else hearing what she was about to say.

"I was confused," she began. "You weren't the guy she warned me about. You were the guy she hoped I'd meet—the one who loves me as much as she did."

Chapter Thirty-One

Five weeks later...

PIERCE AND REBECCA arrived at Punta Allen just before sunset and settled into their beachfront cabana. Punta Allen was a small Mayan fishing village at the end of the Boca Paila peninsula. With fewer than five hundred residents and only one way in or out, the village didn't need much to maintain its population. Punta Allen was on the opposite end of the luxury spectrum from the resorts Pierce owned and was used to, but even though the village was run by two generators that ran for three hours only in the morning and seven hours in the evening, from the moment they stepped onto the white sandy beach, he felt as though they'd found the most romantic spot on earth.

The cabana was made of concrete, with two columns out front supporting a roof over a small patio area—minus the patio. An inviting white hammock hung from the columns, and although the cabana was built on the beach, there were pockets of verdant foliage with long spiky leaves and full spiny bushes. Tall palm trees made the simple, one-room cabana feel like it was on an island by itself.

Rebecca's hair was piled on her head in the messy bun he loved so much. Quintessential Rebecca style—thrown up in a hurry with a few tendrils falling in gentle waves around her face. She looked sexy as hell. While she unpacked, he went into the small bathroom with a suitcase that contained her mother's urn and the items he needed to open it. When Rebecca was ready to spread the ashes, he wanted it to be easy for her. Removing the lid was no easy feat—or so he'd been told—and he didn't want her to become upset if she had trouble. They'd talked about it ahead of time, and Rebecca had been relieved that he offered.

He set the urn on the sink and dipped a Q-tip into fingernail polish remover; then he ran the wet end along the lid to remove the gluing. It took several minutes to clear enough glue away to allow the next step. He used a butter knife to gently pry open the space between the lid and the urn, then repeated the acetone process until the lid finally came off. He closed his eyes for a moment, thinking of Rebecca. On the trip over, she'd said that she had a surprise for him, and as he held her mother's urn, he couldn't fathom that she was thinking of him at all during such an emotional time. He thought of their first date, when she'd told him that her boss at the bar hated how she talked to the customers. He remembered the way she'd unbuttoned the top two buttons of her blouse and let her hair down as she'd said, *I think people come into bars to unload, you know? Talking seemed to help them...*

He smiled. That was Rebecca, always thinking of others. She had a heart the size of the moon, a spirit as bright as the sun, and he wanted—*God, he wanted*—to give her the happy world she deserved.

He found her standing by the screen door, looking out over the beach.

"Are you ready, babe?"

Rebecca had opened up to him so much over the last few weeks, and she'd been sure of her need and readiness to say goodbye to her mother, but Pierce was still worried. Rebecca had insisted that she was ready, and now, as she glanced at her mother's urn, and her eyes warmed, he saw relief pass over her face. She really was ready.

"Yeah," she said just above a whisper. "I am."

She held his hand tightly, rubbing her thumb over his as they carried the urn onto the beach. Her feathery thumb stroking was one of her nervous mannerisms he'd picked up on over the last few weeks, as they'd come to know each other so well that sometimes words weren't necessary to convey their thoughts. They'd become perfectly in tune to each other with every aspect of their lives, from their work ethics to how they spent their downtime. Pierce had taken to discussing his business ventures with Rebecca. She was like a sponge, listening intently, scribbling notes, and pulling out the information from some secret compartment in her brain weeks later after hashing it over in her mind day after day. She always came back with a unique perspective. Rebecca had a knack for thinking outside the box and conveying her thoughts succinctly. She also had the ability to drive him out of his mind. In the midst of an in-depth conversation, she'd climb onto his lap with a playful smile and lavish him with sensual kisses, while he rattled on about whatever issues they were discussing. She'd kiss his cheeks, his lips, his forehead, nibble his ear, and whisper all the things she wanted to do to him until all his blood rushed south and he couldn't think past loving her.

The sand was warm beneath their feet as they made their way across the beach toward the dock.

"I can almost see her here, as a little girl, running across the beach toward the dock with her hair hanging in a thick, tangled mass." Rebecca smiled. She'd been much more relaxed lately, and he assumed some of that came with the settling of her life, but he'd seen other changes that could only be attributed to her believing, really knowing in her heart, that he loved her unconditionally and letting go of all of the lingering worry that she never voiced but he knew she felt—that at any time, her stable, happy life could spiral out of control and she'd lose everything as she'd lost her mother and too many jobs to count. She talked more about her childhood and, thankfully, her mother. Pierce felt as though he knew Magda Rivera, and he desperately wished he could have met the woman who'd raised such a remarkable, loving daughter.

"When was the last time your mother was here?" he asked as they stepped onto the weathered wooden dock that eased over the lagoon like a lonely, forgotten moment.

"I think she was seven. I like it here, Pierce. It feels *right* being here with you. Thank you." She wrapped her hand around his biceps and snuggled in close as they neared the end of the dock where the small boat he'd arranged for was waiting.

"I was just thinking the same thing. And wondering if we should buy the entire village." He flashed a joking smile, and she bumped him teasingly with her shoulder.

"I'm going to stop telling you when I like things if you're going to offer to buy them all."

When they were on the plane he'd chartered, she'd said how nice it was, and he'd offered to buy one. He was only half kidding. He'd do anything for Rebecca.

"Don't ever stop telling me. I'll try to stop offering, but it's hard. I want you to be happy." They sat beneath the *palapa* roof at the end of the dock with their legs hanging over the turquoise water as it lapped at the pilings. Pierce had always thought that his brothers were his best friends, but in Rebecca he'd found a different type of best friend. He didn't have to hide or pretend with her. If he was angry, sad, elated, or horny, her love for him was as strong as his was for her—and she called him on his shit and didn't let him brood over issues that he couldn't control. He knew without a doubt that whatever they faced, they'd get through it together.

Rebecca rested her head against his shoulder. "All I need to be happy is time with you. Nothing else matters. We could live under a tree in the woods and I'd be happy."

He knew it was true because he felt the same way. "I'd build you a tree house."

"Would you wear work boots, cutoff shorts, and no shirt? Because *that* I could get into." She placed her hand on his thigh.

Pierce laughed. "You know I would, but then you'd have to wear a little Tarzan and Jane type of getup. Fair's fair." He knew she'd do that, too. Rebecca was his every sexual fantasy come true. She was a sensual, passionate woman who knew what she liked and wasn't afraid to ask for it. From the bedroom to the boardroom, they were perfectly matched.

Rebecca rose to her feet and pulled Pierce up. "Let's go, Tarzan, before it gets dark and we get lost at sea."

Pierce helped her into the rowboat and then handed her the urn before climbing in himself. He'd wanted to arrange for a bigger boat, but Rebecca had insisted that her mother was a simple woman and would want a simple sendoff. She didn't want the noise of a motor or the distraction of luxury.

He rowed them away from the dock. Rebecca sat facing him, with her mother's urn on her lap, her arms wrapped protectively around it and her bare feet between his.

"Isn't it weird that we lived in Reno my whole life, but Mom talked about this place so much that it felt like I'd been here? I feel like I've come back to a place I loved. In elementary school, kids used to draw pictures of the places they'd gone on vacation. Disney World, camping, their grandparents' houses. I used to draw pictures of this beach that were based solely on what she'd told me."

"I think it's nice that you were close enough to your mom to become so entrenched in someplace she loved. I'm sure she's smiling down on you now, proud of the woman you are."

Rebecca dropped her eyes to the urn, and the edges of her lips lifted into a smile. "This is far enough out."

They were a couple hundred feet from shore. Pierce settled the oars in the boat and placed his hands on Rebecca's knees. This was one of those times when words weren't necessary. Emotions sifted over Rebecca's face. Her soft gaze narrowed, her brow furrowed just a little, and the edges of her mouth pinched tight. In the next breath, all that tension disappeared, and her lips parted. Her eyes remained on the urn, but she placed one delicate hand over Pierce's and slid her fingertips into his palm.

He pressed a kiss to the back of her hand.

"This is it," she whispered.

She lifted damp eyes to him, causing his to well with tears, too. His chest tightened, as he knew hers was, with a feeling of finality. He wanted to take her in his arms and hold her until the pain went away—and he would, when she was ready. Her hands trembled as she picked up the urn.

He searched her eyes for an indication that she was really ready.

A single nod. A hard swallowing of emotions as she blinked against her tears.

Pierce cupped her cheek just to let her know he was there for her; then he placed his hands on top of hers and settled the urn onto his lap. He turned sideways, straddling the bench, and took Rebecca's hand as she moved carefully between his legs, her back to his chest. He placed the urn between her legs and pressed his face to hers from behind. Warm tears slipped between their cheeks.

"I love you, sweetheart," he whispered.

Rebecca reached up and placed her hand on his cheek. "I know. I've always known."

He reached around her waist with both arms and opened the lid. Her neck bowed. The night was silent, save for the sounds of the water swishing against the sides of the boat, gently rocking the small vessel. He felt her body trembling against his chest, and he embraced her from behind. *I'm here, babe.*

She lifted her head, and he felt her hand stroke his; then she inched closer to the edge of the boat, holding tightly to his arms as he inched forward with her.

When she lifted the urn, he covered her hands with his, stabilizing it, and pressed his cheek to hers so she could feel his presence. She held the urn in front of her, still over the boat, and he wondered what she was thinking and if she was going to say anything to her mother. Each of his family members had wanted to come along, to be here for her. She'd become very close to his mother, Emily, Daisy, and Callie, who had brought her into what Pierce called their Private Girl Club, because they passed secrets by text and phone calls that made Rebecca giggle like a schoolgirl. He had asked her if she wanted to hold a ceremony, but Rebecca said her life with her mother had been private, and it wouldn't feel right. She wanted to do this alone, with just the two of them.

He felt her shoulders rise as she drew in a deep breath and exhaled ratchety and slow.

"This isn't the end, Mom," she said just above a whisper. "This is me setting you free." She lifted the urn with Pierce's hands still holding hers, and she shook her mother's ashes into the water. They floated on the surface, slowly darkening as they soaked up the sea. Rebecca brought the urn to her chest and pressed her back to Pierce's chest again.

"This is me setting us free, too, Pierce. This is our beginning." Tears streamed down Rebecca's cheeks as she curled sideways against his chest and melted within his arms.

He didn't know how long he held her as they drifted toward shore and the moon rose in the dark sky. He didn't know when the sounds of the sea were replaced with the sounds of Rebecca's heart beating against his, or how he managed to tie the rowboat to the dock. His mind was absorbed with helping Rebecca feel safe as he carried her back down the dock, across the sandy beach, and into the dark cabana. Sometime between *This is our beginning* and the moment he set her on the bed, he knew that tonight was the night he'd been waiting for.

He took a step away, and Rebecca reached for his hand.

"I'll be right back, babe. I just want to go to the bathroom." He hated lying to her, but there was no other way he could do this.

When he returned, she was lying beneath the

sheet, her hair spread across the pillow, her bare shoulders calling out to him. He set his wallet on the nightstand, took off his clothes, and climbed in beside her. Her body was familiar and warm. She felt so damn good. She always felt so damn good.

"God, I love you, Becca." The words were like a mantra in his mind—one he knew he'd never tire of.

He settled his lips over hers, kissing her tenderly, lovingly stroking her back to the curve of her rear, letting her guide their pace. She pressed her hips to his arousal and rolled onto her back. He was careful tonight. With all she'd been through, he didn't want to force himself on her, or love her too roughly. He wanted her to feel loved, cared for. Cherished. She spread her legs, making room for him as he kissed her neck, her shoulders, and the tops of her beautiful, lean arms. He would never get enough of her. She tasted sweet and smelled of coconut lotion she'd bought at the airport. He wanted to satiate her every need. His hands traveled down her sides, gripping her waist as he lowered his mouth to her breasts and stroked her nipples to hard points, then settled his mouth around one and sucked the way she liked. He was rewarded with her writhing beneath him. Her breaths quickened, and she pushed his hand between her legs.

"Touch me."

She was hot, wet. Ready. Every stroke drew a gasp from her lungs, every flick of his tongue on her breasts brought a rocking of her hips. He throbbed with the need to be inside her. She pushed at his hips, urging him forward. He reached for his wallet to retrieve a condom and she grabbed his wrist. He looked into her eyes, and her lips curved into a smile. Love and desire heated inside of him. Daisy had tested both of them when they were home, because Rebecca insisted that she couldn't ask Pierce to do that for her unless she was willing to do it for him, even though her sexual experiences paled in comparison to his. They were both clean, and they'd been waiting for her birth control pills to take effect before making love without protection.

She drew his hand back to her hip and whispered, "It's our beginning."

He lowered his forehead to hers as he slid deep inside her. Feeling the full intensity of their love for the first time, they both stilled. Buried deep, his heart so full he couldn't wait a second longer, he laced the fingers of his left hand with hers and brought it to his lips. His lips brushed against her mother's ring, which she still wore every day, another thing he loved about her. Rebecca was the most loyal person he knew. She gazed up with love in her eyes, and he felt himself falling deeper in love with her with every breath—and knew he would just keep falling.

"I don't want just a beginning. You're my yesterday, my today, and I want you to be my tomorrow every day of my life. I can't imagine a single day without you by my side." He'd thought of a million ways to say what he wanted to say, and now it all fell away. His emotions were laid bare, and it was all he could do to form the words that came.

"I can't imagine a day without you, either," Rebecca said.

"Then let's not. I love everything about you, Bec.

The way you look at me, your touch in the morning. The sigh you make right before you fall asleep in my arms. I love the way you watch babies when we're in the grocery store, or walking through town, and the way you helped that old man across the street when we first met. I even love that you can deck a guy. God, Bec, I love you so much it literally hurts sometimes. You've become the very air I breathe."

He felt her heart beating as fast as his. Her eyes filled with fresh tears, and when she smiled, they dripped down her cheeks.

"Marry me, Rebecca. Let's make this the beginning of our forever."

"Pierce." His name left her lips like a secret.

He touched his forehead to hers, shifted his hips, moving deeper inside her again. "Will you be my wife, Rebecca, because I want to be your husband more than anything in this world? I want to love, honor, and protect you. I want to offer to buy you things you don't need and have you laugh at me and tell me no. I want to walk through the park and kiss you under the streetlights. I want to have a family of our own, so you can love our babies the way that your mother loved you, and I want to bring them here, every year if you want, so they feel connected to your mom, too."

She reached up and touched his cheek, now openly crying tears of joy.

"I'll never tire of your touch," he said. "And even when we're old and gray and our bones creak, I can promise you, I'll never tire of touching you. Marry me, Becca."

She nodded.

"Yes?"

"Yes. Yes, I'll marry you. There's no other man on earth I could ever love."

Pierce lowered his mouth to hers and could barely contain his excitement at finally being able to give her something to signify his love for her. He reached into his wallet and pulled out the ring he'd designed for her. He'd struggled between his desire to give her more than she could ever want and her love of simplicity, and he'd finally come up with a design that he hoped she'd love. He held her left hand and slid the ring onto her finger. Two carats of inlaid canary yellow and white diamonds—so as not to be too flashy or to overpower her mother's ring—wrapped in an intricate setting of two bands crossing over each other. The colors set off her mother's ring just as he had hoped.

"Pierce," she whispered as she admired the beautiful ring. When she opened her mouth again, no words came out. He wiped her tears with the pad of her thumb, and when their lips met, all of the emotions of the past few weeks coalesced, guiding their love and sealing their promises of forever.

The End

Please enjoy a preview of the next
Love in Bloom novel

Flirting with Love

The Bradens

Love in Bloom Series

Melissa Foster

NEW YORK TIMES BESTSELLING AUTHOR

MELISSA FOSTER

Flirting with

Love

The Bradens

Love in Bloom: The Bradens
Contemporary Romance

Chapter One

ROSS BRADEN HANDED Flossie, a frail fifteen-year-old tabby with thinning fur and soulful eyes, to Alice Shalmer. Alice had recently retired from the Trusty, Colorado, library, where she'd been the head librarian for thirty-plus years. She lived on the outskirts of town and had seven cats, but Flossie was her favorite.

Alice clutched the cat against her thin chest and buried her angular nose and pointy chin in her side. "Think I'll get another year out of my old girl?"

No, he didn't, but Alice knew this already. They'd been playing the I-hope-so game for several months already. No need to drive the sadness home.

"I sure hope so." And Ross truly did.

Alice pushed her black frames back up her nose and smiled. With Flossie safely snuggled against her, she left his office, closing the door behind her. It was Friday morning, and as the Trusty town veterinarian, Ross had a long day ahead of him. He didn't mind, as Fridays were reserved for well checks, giving him a

357

less stressful workday than the rest of the week. And Friday night was just a few hours away. He was already thinking about his options—call one of his brothers and have a beer in town, or drive down to one of the neighboring towns and connect with one of the handful of women he'd dated over the past few months, getting lost in her for a few hours. Ross didn't date women in his hometown, where gossip was as plentiful as the grass was green. He preferred to keep his private life to himself, and driving half an hour in either direction offered him the comfort and privacy that he desired.

"Ross?" Kelsey Trowell poked her head into the exam room where Ross was washing his hands. Her long dark hair was pulled back in a casual ponytail. Kelsey was in her midtwenties and rarely wore makeup. In the standard Trusty attire of jeans, cowgirl boots, and a T-shirt, she looked about eighteen years old. She was smart, efficient, and sweet as molasses. More importantly, she was one of the few women around who wasn't trying to rope a husband, or more specifically, wouldn't try to reel in Ross, one of the last Braden bachelors, making her ideal for her position.

"Yes?"

Knight, one of Ross's three Labradors, walked into the exam room behind Kelsey. She reached down and stroked Knight's thick black fur as he passed.

"I told your two o'clock she could come in at ten. She had a hair appointment that she forgot about and couldn't reschedule."

Ross arched a brow and reached for a chart. "We wouldn't want Mrs. Mace to miss her hair appointment, now, would we? That's fine."

Kelsey moved to the side as Sarge, Ross's three-year-old golden Lab, joined Knight, now lounging at Ross's feet. Ross's *boys* were always on his heels.

"Want me to take the boys out of the office so you can bring Tracie Smith back with their new silky terrier? Her daughter, Maddy, is so cute. She hasn't put their new puppy down since they got here. Oh, and your next two appointments are here. Everyone seems to be early today. Should I get them set up in the other exam rooms?"

Ross looked up from the chart he was studying. It was eight forty and Tracie's appointment was at eight forty-five. "No. I need to run upstairs for a second. When I come down, I'll get Tracie and Maddy." He closed the file. "Justin Bieber? Tracie named her puppy Justin Bieber?" Tracie had grown up in Trusty, and she was a few years younger than Ross. Justin Bieber was her family's first puppy.

"Maddy named him." Kelsey lowered her voice. "Leave it to an eight-year-old girl."

Ross took the back stairs two at a time with Sarge and Knight on his heels. His house and the veterinary clinic were connected by a front and back staircase, as well as a door that led directly to his kitchen. The property spanned thirty acres, with an expansive view of the Colorado Mountains. He snagged his cell phone from the bedside table and slanted his eyes at Ranger, the two-year-old golden Lab feigning sleep on his bed.

"Off."

Ranger opened one eye and yawned, then crawled to the edge of the bed and slithered off. For the past six years, Ross had been the veterinarian and trainer for Pup Partners, a service-dog training program run through Denton Prison. Denton, Colorado, was forty miles west of Trusty. He had a hard time letting go of the dogs that didn't make the cut, hence his three boys.

Ranger climbed atop his doggy bed and closed his eyes. Ross headed down the front stairs to the reception area of the clinic with Sarge and Knight in tow. They'd wait for him outside each of the clinic rooms while he met with families throughout the day, but when Ross was in the lobby or his office, his boys remained by his side.

Maddy Smith jumped to her feet and held up her silky terrier with a smile that radiated from her green eyes. "Dr. Braden, look at our puppy! His name is Justin Bieber. I named him. Isn't he so cute?"

Tracie settled a hand on her excited daughter's shoulder and shrugged. "She loved the name." Tracie freed Maddy's fiery red hair from where it was tangled in Justin Bieber's leash.

"It's a great name," Ross said as he petted the adorable puppy, while Mack, a Burnese mountain dog and Ross's nine-o'clock patient, sniffed his legs.

"How's it going, Dr. B.?" Mack's owner, David, nodded.

"It's a fine day so far, David. I'll be ready for Mack in a few minutes. Thanks for waiting."

Kelsey was talking with Janice Treelong by the registration desk. Janice held her cat in one hand and clutched her young son Michael's hand with the other. Ross was unfazed by the three patients. Fridays were his easy days.

A woman burst through the door with a squealing piglet in her arms. Her shoulders rounded forward as she turned from side to side, struggling to restrain the wiggling animal.

"Can someone please help me? I'm so sorry; something's wrong. I don't know what to do." She leaned over the registration desk, her long blond hair curtaining her face as the piglet slipped from her arms and ran across the desk squealing loudly. Janice's son shrieked, sending her cat into full panic mode. The cat jumped from Janice's arms, then bolted down the hall. Knight turned in the direction of the cat while Sarge tried to climb the desk to get to the piglet, which Kelsey was trying to capture. Ross was drawn to the blonde, but he forced himself to focus on the ensuing mayhem.

"Leave it," Ross said in a calm, deep voice as he took a squirming Justin Bieber from Maddy to keep from having one more loose animal to contend with. Sarge and Knight sank onto their butts, tails wagging with a whimper. As trained service dogs, Sarge and Knight immediately responded to Ross's commands. He was used to animals sparking one another into a frenzy, and he'd long ago honed his calm demeanor, which helped keep the animals from getting too riled.

"Stay." Ross eyed the dogs—then the blonde.

David struggled to keep ahold of Mack's leash as he also tried to go after the cat.

Janice pointed down the hallway where her cat had disappeared and Ross nodded. "Go ahead."

"Kelsey, piglet," Ross instructed.

"Trying." Kelsey lunged toward the squealing

piglet.

With Justin Bieber tucked under one arm, Ross stood between Mack and the registration desk. "David, can you please take Mack into room two?" *Two down, one to go.*

"Can do." David pulled a reluctant Mack down the hall.

Ross handed Justin Bieber to Tracie. "Room three, okay? I'll be in in one minute."

"Sure. Sure." Tracie grabbed Justin Bieber and Maddy's hand, then disappeared down the hall.

"I'm so sorry. I didn't know what to do, and I didn't see a crate to carry him in, and—"

Ross turned to address the woman who had wreaked havoc in his clinic. Correction. The incredibly gorgeous woman with hair so silky it reflected light in at least seven shades of blond and green eyes as bright as springtime buds. Holy Christ, she was beautiful, and *definitely* not from Trusty. There were beautiful women in Trusty, Colorado, but none with skin so flawless and with such luscious curves they looked like they'd stepped out a fashion magazine.

"Got it! Room four." Kelsey had the piglet wrapped in the hoodie she kept on the back of her chair. She carried it down the hall to the last open exam room.

"I'm so sorry. I didn't mean to cause so much trouble. He won't eat, and I've tried everything. I couldn't find a carrier or anything, and—"

"It's okay. We'll take care of him. Relax. Take a deep breath." His day had just gotten a whole hell of a lot better. He drew in a deep breath, too, to curb his rising interest.

She nodded, breathed deeply, then closed her eyes and drew in another few deep breaths. Ross took advantage of those few seconds and slid his eyes down her body. She wasn't wearing anything tight or revealing: a simple white peasant blouse with lacy sleeves and jeans tucked into flat-bottomed, brown boots. She was only a few inches shorter than Ross, five nine or ten, he guessed, and when she opened her eyes and smiled, it sent a jolt of electricity straight to the center of his chest.

"Better," she breathed. "I'm really sorry."

"It's okay. I take it this isn't *your* piglet?"

"No, it's mine. I mean, it is now. I just took over my aunt Cora's farmette, and the pig was hers, so I guess it is mine now." She glanced around the empty waiting room, and even with her thin brows pushed together, she still looked like she was happy. She placed her hand softly on Ross's forearm.

Ross had always kept a professional distance between his clients and his personal life. It had been easy to maintain that aura of professionalism, as he only dated women from outside his hometown. He looked down at her hand on his arm and the side of his mouth quirked up, despite his best efforts to remain unaffected. Suddenly, his easy day just got complicated.

"Cora Aslin, as in Cora from Trusty Pies?" Cora owned a farmette on the other side of Ross's property, and she'd run a pie-making business from her home before passing away unexpectedly a few weeks earlier. She lived on the property adjacent to Ross's. The two properties were separated by a willowy forest. Ross knew her well, and she'd spoken of her niece often. There were no secrets in Trusty, where gossip spread faster than the wind could pick up a whisper. Word around town was that Cora's sister had raised her niece to be a stuck-up California girl. Well, she certainly looked like a Cali girl.

"I'm sorry for your loss," he said. "Cora was a lovely person."

"Yes. I loved her very much, and I miss her." She looked around the waiting room. "I've cleared you out. I'm sorry. I'll just go wait in..." She pointed her thumb down the hallway. "Room four?"

"Yes, four." He held out a hand. "Ross Braden, by the way."

"Elisabeth Nash, sorry." She placed her hand in his and squeezed lightly. It was the same way Cora used to greet him, and he felt a jolt of sadness at the reminder.

"Elizabeth," he repeated.

"E—*liss*—abeth."

Ross arched a brow. "Right. Sorry. E*lis*abeth." Maybe the rumors had her pegged correctly after all.

ELISABETH WAS SITTING on the floor of the exam room singing to the piglet, who had finally calmed down, when Dr. Braden came in. *Dr. Hot and Sexy Ross Braden, able to handle chaos without so much as a flinch.* He looked down at her with inquisitive raven-dark eyes and ran his hand through his thick dark hair, giving her a quick glance at the sexy widow's peak on his forehead before his hair tumbled back down over his forehead. He crouched beside her, and the room got about fifty degrees hotter.

"Singing to a piglet, that's a new tactic. Usually people hum to them. That's what mother pigs do to calm their babies."

"I wondered why he liked it so much," she whispered. "He fell asleep." She reached for the end of her hair and twisted it, then caught herself and dropped her hand. Growing up with a mother who relied on her looks for everything, Elisabeth had worked hard never to follow that same awful path, but sometimes the nervous habit returned.

For a minute, Ross simply stared at her; then his eyes traveled down her legs to the piglet by her feet. She felt naked beneath his slow gaze.

"Exhausted himself. When was he born?" he asked. His deep voice brushed over her skin like a caress, regardless of the matter-of-fact way he'd asked.

She was surprised at the way her body was reacting to him, warming to his voice, his gaze. She was used to handsome men. In Los Angeles even the garbagemen looked like models, but Ross was effortlessly handsome, with his thick dark brows that angled slightly inward, eyelashes so thick and long they gave his eyes a seductive quality, and scruff. *Why the hell did he have to have scruff?* Scruff amped up a man's sexy quotient by about a zillion degrees. In Elisabeth's experience, the guys who didn't have to work at looking good were the most egotistical, least caring men of all—and the hardest to resist. Not that she had a lot of experience. Much to her mother's chagrin—*You're too picky*—her social calendar had been full of more dogs and cats than men.

"Two weeks ago, maybe two and a half. I'm sorry. Is there a pig doctor around that I should have taken him to? I looked through Aunt Cora's phone book, and under vet there was just your first name and address: *Ross, 15 Staynor Way.* You're practically right next door, so I jumped in my car and brought him over."

"How did you get him to stay still long enough to bring him over?" Ross pushed his hand gently beneath the sleeping piglet and captured it in one strong hand, then rose with it pressed against his body. It awoke and squealed and squirmed. Ross tucked it beneath his arm like a football and moved to the counter.

"I sat in the backseat for about fifteen minutes in your parking lot, just kind of talking to him, until he calmed down enough to grab him and race inside."

"Is he eating?" Ross didn't look at Elisabeth. He was focused on the piglet, feeling its body, its legs, while it squirmed and fought his every touch.

"Not much, and he's so much smaller than the other piglets. I just got scared when he wouldn't stop screaming, or squealing, or whatever you call it." She wasn't sure if it was the seriousness of Ross's gaze on the piglet, or the perfect bow of his lips, or maybe the way his dress shirt hugged his biceps, but something was making her babble like an idiot, and what made it worse was that she couldn't take her eyes off of him. *I'm a staring, babbling idiot.*

A knock at the door startled her out of her Ross-induced trance.

"Come in, Kelsey," he said without looking at the door.

The receptionist came into the room and closed the door behind her. "I thought you could use some help."

Elisabeth watched the two move in tandem, like they'd been working together forever as Ross took the piglet's temperature and weighed it, which was a feat in and of itself. Elisabeth wondered if they were dating, although Kelsey looked very young and Ross looked to be in his midthirties, which would also not be out of the question by LA standards. Then again, nothing was out of the question by LA standards, which was one of the reasons she'd been overjoyed to come back to Trusty, a town she'd visited only as a child. Trusty had left such a strong impression of wholesomeness and peaceful living in her young mind that she'd built her hopes and dreams around one day returning.

Kelsey slipped out the back door of the exam room and returned a few minutes later with a baby bottle. She handed it to Ross and smiled at Elisabeth.

"I'll get your paperwork together so you can complete it at home. You can drop it by this week sometime." Kelsey turned back to Ross. "Mrs. Mace called and canceled. Something about her husband not feeling well."

Ross nodded as he secured his hand beneath the piglet, with his palm against the squirming baby's chest, and plugged its mouth with the bottle. The side of his mouth quirked up, softening his serious demeanor.

"Thanks, Kelsey. I hope he's okay."

Alone in the exam room again, Ross leaned his

butt against the counter and finally looked at Elisabeth. He didn't say anything at first, just lifted the side of his mouth again in a semi grin that made her insides warm.

"He's the runt, I take it?" The piglet snarfed and grunted as it sucked the bottle. Ross's sleeves were folded up just above his elbow. The muscles in his forearm flexed against the piglet's efforts. He was somehow gentle yet firm with the piglet, and it drew Elisabeth to her feet and closer to him.

"Yes. He's much littler. His name is Kennedy."

That earned her a genuine, full-on smile. "Kennedy?"

"Yeah. I think he's strong even though he's little, kind of like Jackie O, but he's a boy, so I can't call him Jackie. I mean, I guess I could, but…" She shrugged and smiled. "I guess I just liked Kennedy."

"It's a fine name. Well, *Kennedy* needs nourishment. He's squealing because he's not getting enough. This"—he nodded at the bottle—"is goat's milk. Piglets have trouble digesting cow's milk. They need the immunity protection from the mother's milk, but when they can't get enough, supplement with goat's milk or a goat replacement formula."

Goat replacement formula? There is such a thing? "Okay. Where do I get it?"

"They sell it at the feed store right in town, or if you want it straight from the farm, Wynchel's, on the other side of town, sells it." He looked up and their eyes caught.

Elisabeth's pulse quickened, and as if Ross could sense the change, he smiled.

"How's the rest of the litter?"

"Good, I think." She pulled her phone from her pocket. "I can bring them in for you to give them a once-over." She texted a note to herself to buy goat's milk.

He took the bottle from the piglet's mouth and set it down. "You don't have to bring them in. I'll come by and check them out. Is there a day or time that works for you?"

Elisabeth wondered if he made house calls for everyone, or if he felt the air heat up every time their eyes connected, too, and would make a special trip just to see her.

"A house call?"

"Sure. With farm animals, it's easier for everyone and less stressful for the animals."

So much for him feeling the heat.

"Um, anytime is good, I guess. I'm still getting settled and trying to figure out Aunt Cora's business and the whole farm thing."

He ran his eyes down her body, deliberately this time. *Okay, maybe he does feel the heat after all.* She felt her insides melt. Oh, yes, Ross Braden definitely had a sexual edgy side that probably landed any woman he wanted beneath him.

"You don't have much experience with animals, do you?" His lips curved up in a sexy smile.

She was still hung up on that seductive stroll of his eyes down her body. His remark startled and mildly offended her.

"I have a lot of experience with dogs and cats. I ran a pet bakery and pet spa in Los Angeles, thank you very much." She pocketed her phone.

"Pet bakery and...Never mind. I meant farm animals." He reached for the door and shook his head. "I'll be right back."

She let out a frustrated breath. *No experience with animals. Please. I love animals.*

He returned with the piglet safe and secure in a cat carrier. "I'll carry him out for you. This is safer than letting him run around your car while you drive, but don't leave him in this once you're back home. It's too small."

Still disgruntled at the way he'd dismissed her business, she snapped, "I would never leave him in there."

If he noticed her attitude, he didn't show it as she followed him out of the exam room. Two Labradors, one black and one tan, were waiting by the exam room door. She pet them as they followed Ross out to the car. She hadn't had any contact with dogs and cats since leaving LA, and she missed them. Petting them helped calm her agitation.

Ross opened the back door and set the crate on the seat, then opened the driver's side door for her.

Surprised by the gesture, she settled into the car. "Thank you for all your help." *Mr. Tall Dark and Confusing.*

Ross rested one arm on the roof of the car and leaned down so they were eye to eye. He wore a pair of tan slacks with a black Trusty Veterinary Clinic polo shirt. She tried not to notice the impressive bulge in his pants just below his leather belt.

"Take my number in case you have any more

emergencies." A dog sat on either side of him.

She pulled out her phone and tried to act nonchalant as he rattled off his phone number and she put it into her contact list. She didn't ask if it was his office number or personal number. She couldn't. His eyes were boring a hole right through her. It was a wonder she could process anything at all. Surely he was just being nice, anyway. She was new in town, and he...*Oh God.* He made the smell of animals and antiseptic soap sexy. Elisabeth imagined women probably followed him around just like his dogs. The thought gave her pause and intrigued her at the same time.

Down, girl.

She set her phone on the passenger seat and turned to thank him again. His face was so close she could see every whisker on his square jaw and three sweet lines in his lower lip that she wanted to run her finger over. He smiled, and her mind turned to mush again.

Jesus, what am I? A dog in heat? These types of thoughts surprised her. She wasn't looking for sex, and even if she had been actively searching for a man, she wanted a relationship, not just sex. Anyone could have sex, but it took two people who were really in love to have a meaningful, lasting relationship, and that's what she dreamed of.

"Ross," Kelsey called from the porch of the clinic. "Luke's on the phone for you."

Ross held Elisabeth's gaze for a minute longer. "Welcome to Trusty, Elisabeth. I'll swing by when I'm free."

It took her a minute to breathe—and to remember why he was stopping by. *To check out the piglets.* She needed to get a grip. Maybe he could give her a shot of *Ross repellant*, because she had a life to build and a business to maintain, and a man like Ross would probably chew her up and spit her out.

But, oh, would the chewing up be delicious.

(End of Sneak Peek)

To continue reading, be sure to pick up the next
LOVE IN BLOOM release:

FLIRTING WITH LOVE, *The Bradens*
Love in Bloom series

Please enjoy a preview of the next
Love in Bloom novel

seaside
Hearts

Seaside Summers, Book Two

Love in Bloom Series

Melissa Foster

Melissa Foster

NEW YORK TIMES BESTSELLING AUTHOR

MELISSA FOSTER

seaside
Hearts

Love in Bloom: Seaside Summers
Contemporary Romance

Chapter One

THERE SHOULD BE an unwritten rule about drooling over construction workers, but Jenna Ward was damn glad there wasn't. She sat on the porch of the Bookstore Restaurant, soaking up the deliciousness of the three bronzed males clad in nothing more than jeans and glistening muscles that flexed and bulged like an offering to the gods as they forced thick, sticky tar into submission. Their jeans hung low on strong hips, gripping their powerful thighs like second skins and ending in scuffed and tarred work boots. What red-blooded woman didn't get worked up over a gorgeous shirtless man in work boots?

God help her, because she needed this distraction to take away her desire for Peter Lacroux, which went hand in hand with summers on the Cape and consumed her in the nine months they were apart. She zeroed in on one particularly handsome blond construction worker. His hair was nearly white, his jaw square and manly. She wanted to march right out to the middle of the road that split the earth between the restaurant and the beach and be manhandled into submission. Right there on the tar. Wrestled and groped until all thoughts of Pete evaporated.

"Wipe the drool from your chin, *chica.*" Amy Maples handed Jenna a margarita and, pointedly, a fresh napkin, as she settled into the chair across from her. "Good Lord, woman. What's up with you this summer? I swear you're in heat. I can practically smell your pheromones from over here."

Jenna gulped her drink and righted her red bikini top, which was trying its damnedest to relieve itself of her enormous breasts. Even her bikini top was ready for a man. A *real* man. A man who craved her as much as she craved him.

Jenna reluctantly turned away from Testosterone Road and faced her best friends. The women she had spent her summers with here in Wellfleet, Massachusetts, for as long as she could remember and the women she hoped would help her through her most important summer *ever.*

Okay, she'd self-defined it as such, and it was probably a poor excuse for *most important*, but that's how it felt. Huge. Momentous. Gargantuan. *Great.* Now she was thinking about other huge things...

"You've been here for a week, and you still haven't told us why you're all claws and hormones. Want to clue us in, or are we supposed to guess?" Bella Abbascia was a brazen blonde—and she, like Leanna Bray, the disorganized brunette of their bestie clan— had already found her true love. A feat Jenna only dreamed of. Ached for might be more accurate, and

Bella was right; it was time to come clean.

Jenna downed the last of her drink and slapped her palms on the table.

"I don't care what it takes; this is *my* summer. I'm done pussyfooting around. I want a man. A *real* man." She slid her eyes to the construction workers again. *Yum!* She tried to convince herself to feel something more for the construction worker, but the only person her mind found yummy was Pete—and it didn't seem to want to make room for others.

She wasn't above faking it to pull herself through the charade. Maybe if she tried hard enough, she could talk herself into believing it.

"So, you're going after Pete?" Leanna sipped her margarita and arched a brow. "How is that any different than every single one of the last five summers?"

"Oh no. Peter Lacroux can kiss my big, sexy ass."

"Jenna!" Amy's eyes widened. The sweetest of the group, she was perfectly petite, with kindness that sailed from her green eyes like a summer breeze.

"You do have a mighty fine ass, Jen," Bella said. "But you've had a wicked crush on that man forever. If you're going to focus your attention on someone—" Bella bit her lower lip and shook her head as one of the construction workers wiped sweat from his brow, pecs in full, drool-inciting view. Bella raked her eyes down his sculpted abs. "Um...Okay, yeah. They're pretty damn hot. But why throw Pete away?"

Jenna had been over this in her mind a hundred times. She locked her eyes on her glass and exhaled. "Because I'm not going to spend another summer chasing a man who doesn't want me. And this is a tough summer for me. I have to break up with my mother, and that's enough heartache for a few short weeks."

"Break up with your mom? Can a person do that?" Amy glanced around the table.

"I gather she's not taking your dad getting remarried well?" Leanna asked. "I had such high hopes when she didn't fall apart during the divorce."

Jenna rolled her eyes. "So did I. You'd think that two years after her divorce, she'd be able to sort of compartmentalize it all, but, girls, you have no idea." Jenna shook her head and held up her glass, indicating to the bartender that she needed another drink. She could have gotten up and retrieved the drink herself, but Jenna wanted the diversion of the sexy waiter who would deliver it to their table. She'd take as many diversions as she could get to keep from thinking of Pete.

"She's gone...hmm...how do I say this respectfully? She's not gone cougar, but she's definitely acting different. She's dressing way too young for a fifty-seven-year-old woman, and I swear she thinks she's my new best friend. She wants to talk about guys and sex, and what's worse is that she suddenly wants to go dancing and to bars. I love my mom, but I don't need to go to bars with her, and talking about sex with her? *Please.*"

"I was wondering what was going on when she texted you a hundred times last night." Bella pulled her hair back and secured it with an elastic band. "She's going through a hard time, Jenna. Give her a break. She was married for thirty-four years. That's a long time. I'm not even married to Caden yet, and if we broke up and he married a younger chick, I'd be devastated." Bella and Caden met last year when Bella had been busy rearranging her own life. She'd started a work-study program for the local school district, fallen in love with Caden Grant, a cop on the Cape, and now she was as close as a mother to his almost sixteen-year-old son, Evan. The Cape was a narrow stretch of land between the bay and the ocean. Bella and Caden lived on the bay side in a house that Caden had owned when they'd met, and they would be staying at Bella's Seaside cottage on and off this summer.

"I get it, okay? I just...God, it's just so hard to see her struggling with her looks, and honestly, you know I adore her, but she's sort of making a fool of herself. It's been two years since the divorce. She just needs to get over it and move on. I do feel bad because I had to take a firm stand and tell her that I wasn't going to come home until *after* the summer."

"Why do you feel bad? That's what you do every summer." Amy eyed one of the construction workers, a water bottle held above his mouth, a stream of wetness disappearing down his throat. "Holy hotness." She fanned herself with her napkin.

Jenna watched the guy wipe his mouth with his heavily muscled forearm. "Yeah, but she wanted me to come home to *hang out* with her a few times." The sexy waiter brought Jenna her drink.

"Thank you, doll." She watched his fine ass as he walked away.

"Doll?" Amy giggled.

"See?" Jenna bonked her forehead on the table. "That's *her* word. Doll? Who says that? You have to help me. She'll ruin me, and I swear if I spend one more summer lusting after Pete, then I'll be empty on all accounts. My mother will hate me, my hoo-ha will be lonely, and I'll use words like *doll*. Jesus, do us all a favor and shoot me now."

"Yeah, well, about that whole Pete thing?" Leanna nodded toward the crosswalk, where Pete Lacroux was crossing the road carrying the cutest damn puppy.

Holy mother of God, he is fine. I want to be that puppy. Those construction workers couldn't hold a candle to Pete, and Jenna's body was proof as her pulse quickened and her mouth went dry. His shoulders were twice as broad as those of the boys on the pavement, his waist was trim and—*holy hell*—he shifted the pup to the side, giving Jenna a clear view of the pronounced muscles that blazed a path south from his abs and disappeared into his snug jeans. Those damn muscles turned her mind to mush. Yup. She'd gone as dumb as a doorknob.

"Breathe, Jenna," Amy whispered. "You are so not over him."

Jenna couldn't tear her eyes from him. Years of lust and anticipation brewed deep in her belly. *Just one more summer? One more try?*

No. No. I can't do this anymore. "The man's one big tease. I'm moving on." She forced herself to tear her eyes away from him and guzzle her drink.

And then it happened.

She felt his presence behind her before he ever said a word. Jenna, the woman who could talk to anyone, anytime, had spent years fumbling for words and making atrocious attempts at flirting with the six-foot-two, dark-haired, mysterious specimen that was Peter Lacroux, but despite catching a few heated glances from him, she remained in the friend zone.

Regardless of how her body reacted to him, she didn't need to beg for a man she could barely talk to, or follow after him like that adorable puppy snuggled against his powerful chest.

She was totally, utterly, done with him.

Maybe.

PETE EYED THE women from the Seaside cottage community, or the Seaside girls, as he'd come to refer to them, on his way across the street. They hadn't spotted him watching them as they ogled the young construction workers from the patio of the Bookstore Restaurant. Pete had done the community and pool maintenance for the cottages at Seaside for about six years. He was a boat restorer by trade, but when he'd begun working at Seaside, his career hadn't yet taken off. By the time word got around that he was an exceptional craftsman, he was too loyal of a man to stop doing the maintenance work. Besides, the girls were fun, and he'd become friends with the guys in the community, Tony Black, a professional surfer and motivational speaker, and Jamie Reed, who'd developed OneClick, a search engine second only to Google. And then there was Jenna Ward, the buxom brunette with the killer ass, a cackle of a laugh, and the most intense, alluring blue eyes he'd ever seen.

Fucking Jenna.

He watched her eyes shift to him as he neared the restaurant. Other than his craftsman skills, reading women was Pete's next best finely honed ability—or so he thought. He could tell when a woman was into him, or when she was toying with the idea of being into him, but Jenna Ward? Jenna confused the hell out of him. She was confident and funny, smart, and too fucking cute for her own good when she was around her friends. Just watching Jenna sent fire through his veins, but when it came to Pete, Jenna lost all that gumption, and she turned into a...Hell, he didn't know what happened to her. She grew quiet and tentative when she was near him. Pete liked confident women. *A lily to look at and a tigress in the bedroom.* His mouth quirked up at the thought. He wasn't a Neanderthal. He respected women, but he also knew what he liked. He wanted to devour and be devoured—and with Jenna, who swallowed her confidence around him, he feared his sexual appetite would scare her off. Besides, with his alcoholic father to care for, he didn't have time for a relationship.

Jenna turned away as he stepped behind her. Her hair was longer this summer, framing her face in rich chocolate waves that fell past her shoulders. Pete preferred long hair. There was nothing like the feeling of burying his hands in a woman's hair and giving it a gentle tug when she was just about to come apart beneath him.

He held Joey, the female golden retriever he'd rescued a few weeks earlier, in one arm, placed his other hand on the back of Jenna's chair, and inhaled deeply. Jenna smelled like no other woman he'd ever known, a tantalizing combination of sweet and spicy. Her scent, and the view of her cleavage from above, pushed all of his sexual buttons, despite her tentative nature around him. But he had no endgame with Jenna Ward. No matter how much he wanted to explore the white-hot attraction he felt toward her, he respected Jenna and treasured her friendship too much to take her for a test ride.

"Hello, ladies."

"Aww. Can I hold her?" Amy jumped to her feet and took the puppy from his hands. Joey covered her face with kisses.

"She's a little shy," Pete teased. He'd found the pup in a duffel bag by a Dumpster behind Mac's Seafood, down at the Wellfleet Pier. The poor thing was hungry and scared, but other than that, she wasn't too bad off. The first night Pete had her, the pup had slept curled up against Pete's chest, and they'd been constant companions ever since.

"Yeah, real shy. How's she doing?" Leanna asked.

"She's great. She sticks to me like glue." He shrugged. "I was just coming over to get her a bowl of fresh water, maybe a hamburger."

"Hamburger?" Leanna wrinkled her thinly manicured brow. "How about puppy food?"

"Puppies love burgers." Chicks were so weird with their rules about proper foods. He glanced down at Jenna, whose eyes were locked on the table. She usually went ape shit over puppies, and he wondered what was up with her cool demeanor.

"Want to join us for a drink?" Bella slid a slanty-eyed look in Jenna's direction.

He felt Jenna bristle at the offer. He should probably walk away and give her some breathing room. She obviously wasn't herself today. He was just about to leave when Amy grabbed his arm and pulled him down to the chair beside Jenna. *Great.* Now Jenna had a death stare locked on Amy. Pete was beginning to take her standoffishness personally.

"Sit for a while. I want to play with Joey anyway." When Amy met Jenna's heated stare, she rolled her eyes and kissed Joey's head.

"How's the boat coming along?" Leanna Bray was a quirky woman, too. Her cottage had always been a mess before she met her fiancé, Kurt Remington. Every time Pete had gone by to fix a broken cabinet or a faucet, she'd had laundry piles everywhere, and sticky goo from her jam making seemed to cover every surface, including herself. Almost all of her clothing had conspicuous stains in various shades of red, purple, and orange. Kurt was as neat and organized as Jenna. He'd taken over the laundry and didn't seem to mind picking up after Leanna. In any case, her place was much more organized these days.

"She's coming along." Pete had been refinishing a custom-built 1966 thirty-four-foot gaff-rigged wooden schooner for the past two summers. Working with his hands was not only his passion, but it was also cathartic. He'd spent the last two years pouring the guilt over his father's drinking into refitting the boat.

"What will you do with it when you're done?" Amy Maples looked like the girl next door, with her sandy blond hair and big green eyes, and acted like a mother hen, always worrying about her friends.

Pete shrugged. "Oh, I don't know. Maybe I'll sail someplace far, far away." He'd never leave his father, or the Cape, but there were days…

That brought Jenna's eyes to him. Jesus, she had the most gorgeous eyes. They weren't sea blue or sky blue or even midnight blue. They were more of a cerulean frost, and at the moment, pointedly icy. *What the hell did I do?* He racked his brain, going over the last two weeks, but he hadn't seen Jenna for more than a minute or two. He couldn't imagine what he'd done to warrant her attitude.

Jenna raised her eyebrows in Amy's direction. "Time for *me* to go away." She rose to her feet, bringing her red-string-bikini-clad body into full view. The tiny triangles barely covered her nipples and the bottom rode high on her hips, exposing every luscious curve.

Pete shot a look around the patio—every male eye was locked on Jenna. Jenna wasn't even five feet tall, but she had a better body than any long-legged model. *How the hell can a woman have a body like that and not be one hundred percent confident at all times?* He stifled the urge to stand between her and the ogling men.

"Where are you going?" Bella's eyes bounced between Pete and Jenna.

"I'm going to do what I came here to do. There's a construction guy with my name on him over there." Jenna lifted her chin toward the sky, and her pigeon-toed feet carried her fine ass off the patio, across the grass, and directly toward one of the young construction workers.

"What's she doing?" Pete narrowed his eyes as Jenna approached a ripped construction worker. He expected Jenna to put her hands behind her back and sway from side to side like she did when she spoke to him—reminiscent of an excited girl rather than a sensual woman—adorable and confusing as hell.

"Oh. My. God." Bella rose to her feet, her eyes wide.

"Nothing, Pete. She's...Oh God." Amy put Joey in Pete's lap. "Take her. I um...Darn it." Amy reached for Bella's hand as they gawked, mesmerized by Jenna's bold move.

Her shoulders were drawn back, her beautiful breasts on display—proudly on display! *What the hell?* She put one hand on her hip, and holy hell, Pete didn't need to see her face to feel the slow drag of her eyes down that bastard's body in a way similar to how she usually looked at *him* when she thought he wasn't looking. But then she'd go all nervous when he'd approach.

What the fuck?

"Holy shit. She's going for it." Bella sat back down, as Jenna put her finger in the waistband of the guy's jeans and shrugged. "She's something this summer, isn't she?"

Jealousy clutched Pete's gut.

"Yes, and this summer's rock fixation? What's up with pitch-black rocks? She's never collected them before." Amy's voice trailed off as she watched Jenna in action.

Pete made a mental note of the rocks Jenna was collecting this summer. He'd spent five years taking mental notes about Jenna. Every summer she collected different types of rocks—egg shaped, all white, gray, and oval. There was never any rhyme or reason that Pete could see for her rock selection, but she knew what she liked, and the ones she liked ended up all over her cottage and deck.

Jenna's eyes were fixated on the guy. *That* was the Jenna Pete had hoped would talk to *him*, and now...Now he was getting pretty damn pissed off.

"Those aren't local guys; they're contractors," he warned. "They probably have women in every town around here. Want me to intervene?" Jenna wasn't his to protect. They'd never even gone out on a single date, but somewhere in his mind, despite his confusion, she *was* his. Summers to Pete meant six to eight weeks of seeing Jenna, and over the last two years, while his father buried his troubles in alcohol, seeing Jenna meant even more to him. But until this very second, he never realized how much he wanted her, or how much she meant to him. Joey turned her tongue on Pete's chin. Frustrated, Pete lifted his face out of reach.

Leanna shook her head. "God. Look at her go."

Look at her go? You think this is okay?

"Pete, have you heard something bad about them? Should we worry?" Amy's voice was laden with concern. "Bella, maybe we should..."

Pete watched Jenna take her phone from her pocket and type something. A second later the blond guy took his phone from his back pocket and nodded.

"She gave him her number. I can't believe it," Leanna said.

"She wasn't shitting us," Bella said. "Damn, our girl's getting her groove on." She settled back in her seat and petted Joey. "Oh, Pete...*tsk, tsk, tsk.*"

"What's that supposed to mean?" He clenched his teeth so tight he thought they might crack.

"Nothing." Leanna smacked Bella's arm.

Bella set her eyes on him. "A woman like Jenna only comes around once in a lifetime."

He was just beginning to realize how true those words were.

"Bella, don't," Amy warned.

Bella shrugged. "Just sayin'."

He didn't know what to make of the woman who was a wallflower around him and a sex kitten around a random dipshit in the street. Jenna sashayed back toward the table with a grin on her face. That was Pete's cue to get the hell out of there before he was stuck listening to Jenna going on and on about that dipshit. He rose to his feet with Joey in his arms.

"Wait. Don't leave," Amy pleaded. "You didn't get Joey her water."

"I've got to get going." With Joey in his arms, he headed off the patio. Jenna brushed past him without so much as a word, and it pissed him off even more. He couldn't escape fast enough.

"Guess who's going to the Beachcomber tonight? Oh my God. He's even hotter up close." Jenna's voice echoed in his mind as he crossed the street to get Joey a bowl of water from Mac's.

Holy Christ. Like I needed to hear that shit.

(End of Sneak Peek)
To continue reading, be sure to pick up the next
LOVE IN BLOOM release:

SEASIDE HEARTS, *Seaside Summers*
Love in Bloom series

Full LOVE IN BLOOM SERIES order

Love in Bloom books may be read as stand alones. For more enjoyment, read them in series order. Characters from each series carry forward to the next.

SNOW SISTERS

Sisters in Love (Book 1)
Sisters in Bloom (Book 2)
Sisters in White (Book 3)

THE BRADENS

Lovers at Heart (Book 4)
Destined for Love (Book 5)
Friendship on Fire (Book 6)
Sea of Love (Book 7)
Bursting with Love (Book 8)
Hearts at Play (Book 9)

THE REMINGTONS

Game of Love (Book 10)
Stroke of Love (Book 11)
Flames of Love (Book 12)
Slope of Love (Book 13)
Read, Write, Love (Book 14)

THE BRADENS

Taken by Love (Book 15)
Fated for Love (Book 16)
Romancing My Love (Book 17)
Flirting with Love (Book 18)

Romancing My Love

Dreaming of Love (Book 19)
Crashing into Love (Book 20)

SEASIDE SUMMERS

Seaside Dreams
Seaside Hearts
Seaside Sunsets
Seaside Secrets

THE RYDERS (coming soon)

Seized by Love
Claimed by Love
Swept into Love
Chased by Love
Rescued by Love

Acknowledgments

Writing about the Bradens is one of my greatest pleasures, and while that probably stems from coming from a large family, it's bolstered by the support and encouragement of my readers. Thank you for insisting that I continue to bring more loyal, sexy characters into the fray. I look forward to eventually bringing you Hal and Adriana's story, as well as Catherine's, and catching up on all of the Braden clan.

I'd like to thank all of my supportive friends and family for their endless patience and encouragement. You're an inspiration to me on a daily basis, and I appreciate your efforts.

It takes a village to bring a book to publication, and I'm so very thankful for the skills and efforts of my editorial and publication team. My editorial team and proofreaders make my work shine with their superb skills. Thank you: Kristen Weber, Penina Lopez, Jenna Bagnini, Juliette Hill, Marlene Engel, and Lynn Mullan. My cover designer, Natasha Brown, deserves accolades beyond anything I can imagine, as she has yet to bonk me over the head with a hammer for my never-ending tweaks and changes. Natasha, you're a treasure, both in your design skills and your friendship. The technical process behind each publication is something that takes precision and meticulous care, and I am indebted to Clare Ayala for both her friendship and her mad formatting skills. If I had gold stickers, each of these women would be covered in them.

Last but never least, thank you to my husband,

Les, and my youngest children, Jess and Jake, for allowing me the time to create my fictional worlds and being interested enough in what I do to talk with me about it on a daily basis. I love you to the moon and back. Twice.

Melissa Foster is a *New York Times* and *USA Today* bestselling and award-winning author. Her books have been recommended by *USA Today's* book blog, *Hagerstown* magazine, *The Patriot*, and several other print venues. She is the founder of the World Literary Café, and when she's not writing, Melissa helps authors navigate the publishing industry through her author training programs on Fostering Success. Melissa also hosts Aspiring Authors contests for children and has painted and donated several murals to the Hospital for Sick Children in Washington, DC.

Visit Melissa on her website or chat with her on social media. Melissa enjoys discussing her books with book clubs and reader groups and welcomes an invitation to your event.

Melissa's books are available through most online retailers in paperback and digital formats.

Made in the USA
Lexington, KY
27 May 2018